☞ P9-DNM-825

A lifetime spent in rural Pennsylvania and her Pennsylvania Dutch heritage led **Marta Perry** to write about the Plain People who add so much richness to her home state. Marta has seen nearly sixty of her books published, with over six million books in print. She and her husband live in a centuries-old farmhouse in a central Pennsylvania valley. When she's not writing, she's reading, traveling, baking or enjoying her six beautiful grandchildren.

Jo Ann Brown has always loved stories with happily-ever-after endings. A former military officer, she is thrilled to have the chance to write stories about people falling in love. She is also a photographer and travels with her husband of more than thirty years to places where she can snap pictures. They have three children and live in Florida. Drop her a note at joannbrownbooks.com.

Rebecca Kertz was first introduced to the Amish when her husband took a job with an Amish construction crew. She enjoyed watching the Amish foreman's children at play and swapping recipes with his wife. Rebecca resides in Delaware with her husband and dog. She has a strong faith in God and feels blessed to have family nearby. Besides writing, she enjoys reading, doing crafts and visiting Lancaster County.

Amish Christmas Blessings

Marta Perry
Jo Ann Brown

&

Her Amish Christmas Sweetheart

Rebecca Kertz

HARLEQUIN® LOVE INSPIRED®

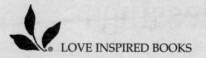 LOVE INSPIRED BOOKS

Recycling programs for this product may not exist in your area.

ISBN-13: 978-1-335-94823-6

Amish Christmas Blessings and Her Amish Christmas Sweetheart

Copyright © 2018 by Harlequin Books S.A.

The publisher acknowledges the copyright holders of the individual works as follows:

The Midwife's Christmas Surprise
Copyright © 2016 by Martha Johnson

A Christmas to Remember
Copyright © 2016 by Jo Ann Ferguson

Her Amish Christmas Sweetheart
Copyright © 2017 by Rebecca Kertz

Printed in U.S.A.

CONTENTS

AMISH CHRISTMAS BLESSINGS

* * *

THE MIDWIFE'S CHRISTMAS SURPRISE
Marta Perry

&

A CHRISTMAS TO REMEMBER
Jo Ann Brown

THE MIDWIFE'S CHRISTMAS SURPRISE

Marta Perry

This story is dedicated to my husband, Brian,
with much love.

If anyone has caused grief, he has not so much
grieved me as he has grieved all of you…
—*2 Corinthians* 2:5

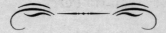

Chapter One

If the door to the exam room at the birthing center hadn't been ajar, Anna Zook would never have heard the hurtful comment.

"...so long as you're the one to catch the baby, and not the Zook girl. She's too young and inexperienced to be birthing my first grandchild."

The door closed abruptly, cutting off anything else that might be said, but Anna recognized the speaker—Etta Beachy, mother-in-law of one of her partner Elizabeth's clients. Despite the fact that Anna had been a full partner in the midwife practice for over a year, many in Lost Creek's Amish community still saw her as the quiet, shy girl she'd been when she began her apprenticeship with Elizabeth.

The December chill outside seemed to seep into her heart. Would the people of Lost Creek ever accept her as midwife, or would she always be walking in Elizabeth's shadow?

Anna tried to concentrate on the patient record she was reviewing, but the doubts kept slipping between her and the page. It was natural enough that folks turned to

Elizabeth, she told herself firmly. Elizabeth Miller had been the only midwife in the isolated northern Pennsylvania Amish settlement for over twenty years. It would just take time and patience for them to accept her, wouldn't it?

The door opened, and a little parade came out—Etta Beachy, looking as if she'd just bit into a sour pickle, her daughter-in-law, Dora, who looked barely old enough for marriage, let alone motherhood, and Elizabeth, whose round, cheerful face was as serene as always.

Small wonder folks trusted Elizabeth—she radiated a sense of calm and assurance that was instantly soothing. Much as Anna tried to model herself on Elizabeth, she never quite succeeded in doing that.

A blast of cold air came into the outer office as the front door opened, and Anna spotted young James leap down from the buggy seat, clutching a blanket to wrap around his wife.

Elizabeth closed the door behind them and turned to Anna, rubbing her arms briskly. "Brr. It's cold enough to snow, but Asa says not yet."

Anna nodded, knowing Elizabeth, so confident in her own field, trusted her husband implicitly when it came to anything involving the farm. Maybe that was the secret of their strong marriage—the confidence each had in the other.

"You heard what Etta said, ain't so?" Elizabeth's keen gaze probed for any sign that Anna was upset.

"Ach, it's nothing I haven't heard before." Anna managed to smile. "Naturally Etta feels that way. She's known you all her life."

"Then she ought to trust my judgment in training you." Elizabeth sounded as tart as she ever did. "I think

Dora might be happier with you, being closer to her age and all, but she's too shy to venture an opinion different from Etta's."

"It will all be forgotten when they see the baby. When are you thinking it will be?"

"Most likely not until well after Christmas." As if the words had unleashed something, Elizabeth's blue eyes seemed to darken with pain. She glanced out the side window toward the farmhouse, making Anna wonder what she saw there other than the comfortable old farmhouse that had sheltered generations of the Miller family.

"Elizabeth?" Anna stood, moving quickly to put her arm around her friend's waist. "What is it?"

"Ach, nothing. Just foolishness." Elizabeth shook her head, but she couldn't disguise the tears in her eyes.

"Tell me," Anna said gently, longing to help.

The older woman brushed a tear away impatiently. "Nothing." She bit her lip. "It's just…this will be the third Christmas without Benjamin."

The name struck Anna like a blow to the heart. She forced herself to concentrate on Elizabeth's pain, not allowing herself to recognize her own. "I know," she murmured. "Perhaps…" Anna tried to think of something reassuring to say, but what was there?

Benjamin, Elizabeth and Asa's third son, had walked away from the Amish faith and his family three years ago. And her. He'd walked away from her, as well.

"I'm sorry," she said finally, knowing how inadequate it was. Elizabeth didn't know there'd ever been anything between her son and her young apprentice, and that was probably for the best, given how things had turned out.

Elizabeth sucked in a breath and straightened. "Asa doesn't want to talk about Ben's leaving. I try not to burden him with my sorrow. But oh, if only our boy would come home to us."

"Maybe he will." Did she wish that? For Elizabeth's happiness, for sure. But for herself—how would she manage if Benjamin did come back?

"I keep praying. That's all I can do." Elizabeth pressed her cheek against Anna's for a moment. "Ach, I must get back to the house and start some supper. Are you coming now?"

Anna shook her head. "I'll finish cleaning up here first."

She'd lived with the Miller family since she'd come from Lancaster County as apprentice to Elizabeth. Each time she'd suggested she might find a place of her own, it had led to such an outcry that she'd given up, knowing Asa and Elizabeth meant it. They treated her as the daughter they'd given up on having after their four boys. How could she walk away from that?

Once Elizabeth had gone, Anna moved slowly around the four-room center, built by Asa and his sons so that Elizabeth would have a place close to home for meeting patients. Still, many of their mothers preferred having babies at home, so the two of them spent hours each week traveling from one Amish home to another.

When she found herself rearranging the stack of towels in the cabinet for the third time, Anna forced herself to recognize the truth. She was avoiding the thing she didn't want to think about—the beautiful, painful truth of her relationship with Benjamin.

Anna stood at the window, but she wasn't seeing the frigid winter landscape. Instead she looked up into the branches of the apple tree in the side yard, feeling the soft breeze of a summer evening brush her skin.

She and Benjamin had come home from a family picnic at the home of Ben's grandparents, and they'd loitered outside for a few minutes, watching the fireflies rise from the hay field and dance along the stream.

Ben had been telling her a story of climbing to the very top of the apple tree in response to a dare from one of his brothers. He'd fallen when a branch broke and broken his arm, but he didn't seem to regret it, laughing at the memory. That was Ben, always up for a dare.

She'd shifted her gaze from the branches to his laughing face, meaning to chide him for such foolishness, but her gaze became entangled with his, and her breath caught, the words dying.

Ben's eyes, blue as a summer sky, seemed to darken as he studied her face. His gaze had lingered on her lips. And then his lips had found hers, and a totally unexpected joy exploded inside her.

She'd never known how long they'd stood there, exchanging kisses, laughing that it had taken them so long to recognize the feelings between them, talking about a wedding. When she'd finally slipped into the house and up to her room, she'd held the warm assurance of his love close against her.

And the next day he'd been gone, leaving only a note for his parents saying he was going to see something of the world.

Anna tried to shake off the memories. She seldom let herself relive them, because the aftermath had seemed so painful. No one knew about her and Ben, so she'd had to pretend that her pain was only for Ben's family, not for herself.

After three years, it should have become easier. One night—that was all she had to block from her memories.

A final check around the center, and she was ready to go. She was just slipping on her coat when she heard a car pull up by the front door.

Anna frowned. One of their Englisch clients? No one was scheduled to come in today. She could only hope it wasn't an emergency.

Footsteps sounded on the porch, and she hurried to the door. She flung it open almost as soon as the knock sounded and stumbled back a step, the familiar room spinning around her.

The man standing on the porch wore boots, jeans and a black leather jacket zipped up against the cold, but he wasn't an Englischer. He was Benjamin Miller.

Of all the ways Ben had thought about his homecoming, the one he hadn't pictured was coming face to face with Anna Zook. She'd changed—that was his first automatic thought. He'd left behind a tender girl whose face had glowed with the impact of first love. Now he faced a woman who wore her maturity like a cloak around her.

"Anna." He said her name heavily, embarrassment and sorrow mixing in his tone. He didn't doubt he'd hurt her when he'd left. She had plenty of reasons not to welcome his return. "It's been a long time."

The words seemed to jolt her out of a daze. "Three years," she said tartly. "None of us have forgotten."

She seemed already armed against his return. Maybe that would make things easier. Whatever else happened here in Lost Creek, he couldn't hurt Anna again.

"I guess not." He gestured toward the door. "Mind if I come in?"

For an instant he thought she would slam it in his face. Then she nodded and stepped back, standing silent as he entered.

He looked around with appreciation. "The birthing center wasn't finished yet when I left. It looks good."

"Your father and brothers did fine work on building it just as your *mamm* wanted."

Was that a reminder that he hadn't been here to help? Probably so. He turned slowly to face her, letting his gaze drift over her. The honey-brown hair seemed to have lost its glints of gold, but maybe that was because it was December, not August. He'd always picture her under the apple tree on a summer night, her heart-shaped face tilted toward his, her green eyes lit with love.

"You've changed." It was inadequate, but it was the only thing he could think to say.

"People do in three years." She glanced at his leather jacket and jeans. "You have."

She couldn't know how much. If Anna's face showed her added maturity and assurance, his must be a map of disappointment and betrayal.

Time to leave behind this fruitless conversation and move on to the family. "Is Mamm at the house?"

Anna nodded, warily it seemed. "She went over a few minutes ago. We've finished with the patients for today, unless there's an emergency."

"I guess I'd best go and face the music, ain't so?" The familiar Pennsylvania Dutch phrase fell easily from his lips after training himself not to use it. He half turned toward the door and found that his feet didn't want to move. *Coward*, he told himself.

Still, his gaze sought Anna's face again. "My family—is everyone well?"

"So far as I know." She bit her lower lip, as if she'd like to say something else but restrained herself.

"If you're ready to go, I'll walk over with you."

She hesitated, and Ben recognized her reluctance. He opened the door, waiting, and Anna walked out with him.

The farm he'd grown up on spread out before him, the grass turning brown with winter's cold, the fruit trees bare. Resting, Daad would have said. Everything rested in winter, building up strength for the spring.

Funny. He'd never expected to cherish the most common of sights—the spring wagon parked beside the red barn, the windmill spinning in the strong breeze, the chickens pecking at the earth inside their pen, hunting for a forgotten bit of grain.

He'd left because he'd thought he didn't belong here. He'd learned the hard way he didn't belong in the outside world, either.

Could he come home again? They'd reached the back door that led into the kitchen. He was about to find out.

Anna hesitated on the step. "Maybe I should wait. Give you time with the family..."

"Mamm always said you were part of the family. There's no reason I can see to back off now." He may as well face all the people he'd disappointed at the same time. He seized the doorknob, turned it and stepped inside.

Daad and Joshua were sitting at the table. Mamm stood at the stove. All three of them turned to stare, seeming immobilized with shock. He waited, all the words he'd rehearsed deserting him.

Daad recovered first. He set down his coffee mug with a thud, his keen blue eyes fastened on Ben's face. Daad looked much the same—lean and wiry, his skin weathered from working outside. His beard was a little longer, a little grayer, that was all.

"So," he said. "You've come back."

It wasn't exactly the welcome given to the prodigal son, but he guessed it would have to do. "Ya," he said. "If you'll have me."

Daad's face was impassive. "It's your home."

As if he'd been waiting for Daad's reaction, Joshua scrambled to his feet, grinning. "It's *gut* to see you, Ben."

"Can this be my little *bruder*?" Ben grabbed his shoulder. "You're near as big as I am."

"What do you mean, near as big? I am as tall, ain't so?" Joshua, the youngest, had always been eager to catch up with his brothers.

"Maybe so." He was already looking beyond Josh to where his *mamm* stood, her hands twisting her apron.

The pain in her eyes shook him, and his heart wrenched. His throat grew tight. "Forgive me, Mammi," he murmured.

Tears filled her eyes, but to his relief they were tears of joy, not sorrow. She held her arms wide. "My Benjamin. You've *komm* home to us."

Ben stepped into her embrace, his heart overflowing with mingled grief and happiness. Grief for the pain he'd caused her—happiness at feeling her forgiveness wash over him in a healing flow.

If he could truly mend anywhere, it would be here.

Mamm, at least, welcomed him with all her heart, despite the pain he'd caused.

Still holding her, he looked over her shoulder at the others. Josh, too young and too openhearted to hold a grudge, was still grinning. Daad—well, Daad was going to be more difficult. He was reserving his opinion, Ben thought. Not quite ready to go back to normal with the son who'd disappointed him so badly.

Anna stood with her back to the door. Anna had plenty of reason not to trust him. And right now she looked as if she thought welcoming him home was the worst idea in the world.

Chapter Two

It seemed to Anna that Elizabeth hadn't stopped smiling in the past twenty-four hours. She'd always known how much Elizabeth missed Benjamin and longed for his return, but she hadn't even realized how much that was reflected in her face. Elizabeth looked as if she'd shed ten years in a single day.

Anna led the buggy horse to the gate and then turned him into the field. Buck seemed to shrug all over, as if delighted to be rid of the harness. He sniffed the icy grass and then broke into a gallop, racing to where the other horses stood at the far end of the field.

Smiling at his antics, Anna headed for the house. She'd volunteered to take the home visits today, so that Elizabeth could be free to enjoy Benjamin's return.

But Anna couldn't deny that she'd had another motive, too. She'd been just as eager to get herself well away from Benjamin's disturbing presence.

Her steps slowed. She'd thought having time alone during the drive would give her a chance to come to terms with Benjamin's return. Unfortunately her thoughts just kept spinning around and around like the windmill blades in a strong wind.

Enough, she told herself. Was she reluctant to accept his return because she worried that he'd hurt his family again? Or was her concern more selfish?

When Anna put it to herself that way, she couldn't help but see the answer. Christians were called to forgiveness. They could only be forgiven as they forgave. If the rest of Benjamin's family could forgive him and welcome him back, then she must, too.

Holding on to the resolution firmly, she marched into the house. As always at this time of day, Elizabeth was in the kitchen. She was bent over the propane oven, her face flushed as she pulled out two apple pies, their crusts golden brown and the apple juices bubbling up through the vents.

"That wouldn't be Benjamin's favorite pie, would it?" Anna forced warmth into her voice as she stowed her medical bag on its shelf by the door.

"Ach, you caught me." Elizabeth transferred the pies to the wire cooling rack and turned, smiling.

Anna's heart gave a little thump. Elizabeth was so happy. How could Anna be skeptical of anything that made her feel that way?

"He'll appreciate those, I know." Surely nothing he'd found in the outside world could match his own *mamm*'s cooking. "Can I do anything?"

Elizabeth surveyed the pots on the stove top. "I don't think so." She glanced toward the clock. "Ben went out to cut some greens for me. I felt like getting ready for Christmas today. Maybe you'd go out and help him bring them to the porch. It'll soon be time for supper."

Well, she'd offered to help. Elizabeth wasn't to know

that helping Ben…seeing Ben…was the last thing she wanted at the moment. All Anna could do was smile.

"Right away. Do you know where he went?" The woods began across the field behind the barn and stretched up to the ridge that sheltered the valley.

"That stand of hemlocks, I think. He knows I like the little cones on the greens to put on the windowsills."

Nodding, Anna buttoned her coat again and went back out into the cold. The brittle grass crackled under her shoes as she walked, and she scanned the skies for signs of snow. But the only clouds were light, wispy ones moving lazily across the blue.

It might be silly for a grown woman to be longing for that first snow of the winter, but she couldn't seem to help it. She loved running outside to feel the flakes melting on her face. She and her sisters used to vie to see who'd be first to catch a snowflake on her tongue.

A glimpse of black jacket among the hemlocks told her where Benjamin was, and she veered in his direction. Maybe it would be natural to wave or call out, but nothing felt natural when it came to Ben. Just the slightest glance from his deep blue eyes seemed to turn her back into the girl who'd thought she'd soon be a bride.

He had his back turned to her. The wheelbarrow next to him was full of green branches, and the clippers he'd been using lay atop them. Maybe he'd spotted a deer or a pheasant and was watching it, standing so still.

The clothes he wore were Amish, the black jacket a bit snug over his broad shoulders. Had he grown since he'd been gone? He certainly seemed taller and broader to her. The black pants and heavy shoes made her wonder what had become of the jeans and leather jacket. He wouldn't need them if he meant to be home for good.

Well, of course he'd come home to stay. He wouldn't be so unkind as to let his family believe that if it weren't so, would he?

His voice startled her. For a moment she thought he'd spoken to her, and then she realized he stood immobile because he was talking on a cell phone. Not so surprising, but still...

Don't judge. She had a cell phone herself, as well as the phone in the center. It was difficult to be a midwife to a widespread practice without one. She didn't use the phone casually, marking off for herself the line between what was accepted and what was bending the rules.

Ben might have a difficult time adjusting to living under the *Ordnung* again after his time out in the world. They'd all have to make allowances for him.

"That's not true." Ben's voice, raised in what might have been anger, came clearly to her ears. "Whatever happened between us is over."

Anna froze. She shouldn't be overhearing this. But she'd already heard. Should she make her presence known or attempt to creep silently backward?

"All right." Ben snapped the words. "I'll see you again, but not until I'm ready."

Anna took a step back, and a branch snapped beneath her foot, loud in the still air. Ben spun. His glare nailed her to the spot. She'd seen his eyes merry and laughing and teasing. And tender, filled with longing. But she'd never seen them freeze over with anger.

He clicked the phone off. "Eavesdropping, Anna?" The words were edged with ice.

Heat rushed to her cheeks. "Your mother sent me out to help you. I didn't realize what you were doing until..."

Her defense withered under his cold stare. When had he gotten those lines around his eyes, that tenseness in his jaw? That was new. Was that what the outside world had done to him?

"It didn't occur to you to let me know you were here, *ja*?" He bent to pick up the wheelbarrow handles. "You've done your duty. I'm coming. Why don't you run back and tell my *daad* that I was out here talking on my cell phone?"

A wave of anger came to her rescue. "I'm not a child, and I don't tattle on people."

"No." His gaze drifted over her. "I can see you're not a child, Anna. You're all grown up now."

Her anger edged up a notch at the way he'd looked at her. "Your clothes don't make you Amish, Benjamin. If you're not ready to leave the Englisch world, maybe you shouldn't have *komm*."

If anything, his face got tighter, until he didn't look remotely like the boy she'd loved. "Mamm may say you're like a daughter to her, but you're not family. It's not your business, so leave it alone."

Shoving the wheelbarrow, he strode off toward the house.

Anna stood where she was, fists clenched. So much for her resolutions. Maybe she could forgive Benjamin for what he'd done in the past. But what about what he planned to do in the future? How could she ever trust him again?

Ben walked into the kitchen after supper, intent on a last cup of coffee. The quick cadences of Pennsylvania Dutch came from the living room, where everyone was settled for the evening, Daad reading aloud something from the latest issue of the Amish newspaper, Mamm sewing and Josh whittling a tiny boat destined for their brother Daniel's oldest for Christmas. He hadn't realized how much he'd missed the sound of his native tongue, and it soothed his soul.

But he was leaving out someone. Anna was there as well, her lap filled with the baby shawl she was crocheting for Daniel and Barbie's youngest. When he'd said she wasn't part of the family, he'd wanted only to hurt her. Not only had that been unkind, it hadn't been true. Maybe she was more a member of the family than he was.

Standing at the counter, he stirred sugar into the coffee, his spoon clinking against the thick white mug. Mamm had already lined the kitchen windowsill with the greens he'd brought in. Amish might not have the Christmas trees that were everywhere in the outside world, but that didn't mean they didn't celebrate the season of Christ's birth in their own way.

A light step sounded behind him, and Ben knew without turning that it was Anna. Funny, how his view of her had changed. He'd thought her a quiet little mouse of a girl when she'd first come to stay with them. But he'd learned she had considerable spirit behind that quiet exterior. Today she'd turned it against him in reminding him that clothes didn't make him Amish, and he didn't like it.

"Ben." Her voice was soft. "May I speak with you for a moment?"

He turned. If she intended to reiterate her opinion of him…

Anna's heart-shaped face was serious, and a couple of lines had formed between her eyebrows. "I want to apologize." She seemed to have trouble getting the words out. "I had no right to speak to you the way I did. I'm sorry."

She'd disarmed him, taking away all the things he'd stored up to say.

"It's okay. I know you're just concerned about Mamm."

Some emotion he couldn't identify crossed her face, darkening her eyes. "She's not my mother, but I do care about her."

"I know." His voice roughened despite his effort at control. "Believe me, I don't want to hurt her."

He already had, hadn't he? Ben backed away from that thought.

"Gut." Anna hesitated. "I hope you're home to stay. It would mean so much to your family."

Would it mean anything to you, Anna? He shoved that thought away, not sure where it had come from.

"A lot has changed since I've been gone. I can't believe how Josh has grown. And think of Daniel and Barbie, having two *kinder* already. And I suppose Joseph will be next."

That brought a smile to her face, warming her eyes and showing him the beauty other people didn't seem to see. "I've never seen your *mamm* so nervous as when Barbie's little ones were born. She said I had to catch them because she couldn't, but believe me, she watched every move."

Ben leaned against the counter, cradling the mug in his hands as he studied her face. "So you're a partner now, not an apprentice. That's great."

Anna wrinkled her nose. "Now if we could just convince our clients of that…"

"Not willing to admit you're all grown up, are they? Folks are slow to move forward here, ain't so?"

She nodded, and again he saw that flicker of some emotion saddening her eyes. Did it worry her that people might still favor Mamm to deliver their babies?

They'd be wrong to discount Anna. There was a lot more to her than most folks thought, he'd guess. For an instant he saw her face turned up to his in the moonlight, alive with joy. Did no one else see that in her?

"Why aren't you married yet, Anna?" The question was out before he realized that it would be better not spoken. Talk about butting in where he didn't belong. "Sorry, I shouldn't..."

Daad came into the kitchen, interrupting the difficult moment. He glanced from Anna to him and then moved toward the coats hanging by the back door.

"I'm going out to check the stock. *Komm* with me, Ben?"

"Sure." Daad was getting him out of a difficult moment—that was certain sure.

Grabbing the black wool jacket that Mamm had put away in mothballs for his return, he followed Daad out the back door.

The air was crisp and cold, making his skin tingle. And the dark—he'd forgotten how dark it was on the farm after living for three years with constant electric lights everywhere. The yellow glow from the windows faded as they walked toward the barn. Daad switched on the flashlight he carried, sending a circle of light ahead of them.

Ben tilted his head back. The stars were so bright it seemed he could reach out and touch them. "How bright the stars are here," he said, his breath misting in front of his face.

Daad grunted. "No other lights to dim God's handiwork."

Daad had never lost an opportunity to point out God's presence in their lives. He'd always said that it was a blessing to be a farmer, because it was as close as one could get to Heaven.

But right now, Daad wasn't doing much talking. If they were going to communicate, it was probably up to him.

"You extended the chicken coop, I see."

Daad flickered his flashlight in that direction. "The roof was getting bad, so we decided to replace the whole thing. Just took a day with everyone helping."

Everyone but him, he supposed Daad meant. He couldn't deny that. "I can't believe how Josh has grown. He's a man already."

A grunt of agreement was Daad's only answer. This was going to be an uphill battle. He hurried to shove back the heavy door before Daad reached it.

Their entrance was greeted by soft whickers from the stalls. Daad lit the propane lantern, and the interior of the barn emerged from the gloom.

A wave of emotion hit Ben, startling him by its strength. Why would he be so moved by the barn? Maybe it was the assurance of Daad's routine. Nothing really needed to be done with the stock at this hour, but still, Daad never went to bed without a last check, just as Mamm had to check each of her *kinder*. Ben had been proud the first time Daad considered him old enough to come along on the evening round.

He stepped to the nearest stall, reaching up to run

a hand along the neck of the buggy horse that nosed him curiously. "You're a handsome fellow." He stroked strong shoulders. "The gelding's a good-looking animal. He's new, ain't so?"

"Went all the way down to Lancaster County for the livestock auction last spring to get him."

Daad sounded as proud as an Amish person was likely to, pride being a sin. Funny, how the Englisch world seemed to consider it right and proper.

"Looks like you got a *gut* deal."

He moved to the next stall, to be greeted with a nuzzle that nearly knocked his hat off. Dolly, the black-and-white pony they'd all learned to drive with. Her muzzle was a little gray now, but she looked fine and healthy.

He patted her, letting the memories flood back… driving the pony cart up the road to the neighbor's farm, the day he'd thrown himself on Dolly's back and urged her to gallop, the feel of the ground coming at him when she'd stopped suddenly, objecting to being ridden.

"Suppose I should have sold Dolly to someone with young *kinder.*" Daad stood next to him, his gaze on the pony. "But she's *gut* with Daniel's young one when he comes over."

Besides the fact that Daad wouldn't have wanted to part with her. Ben understood that—he wouldn't, either.

"There's something I need to say to you, Benjamin." Daad's voice was weighted with meaning. "Your *mamm* and me…well, we'd always thought that the farm would go to you when we were ready to take it a bit easier. I guess you knew that."

He had, yes. It had been an accepted thing. Amish farms typically went to one of the younger sons, because they came of age when fathers were ready to take it a bit easier. And Ben had been the one who'd loved the farm more than Josh, whose mind was taken up by all things mechanical.

Maybe that had been in his mind that last night, when he'd seen himself settling down, marrying Anna, taking over the farm when it was time, building the next generation. It had closed in on him, reminding him of all the things he hadn't seen, hadn't done.

"Still, when you stayed away so long, we had to face the fact that you might not be back. So we decided the farm would go to Joshua. He's young yet, not settled, but I'm good for a few more years." Daad flickered a glance at him, then focused on Dolly. "Only fair to tell you. I don't think it right to change our minds again. This is still your home, but it'll go to Joshua, not you."

It shouldn't have hit him like a hammer. He should have expected it. After all, it was only right. He'd made his choice when he left.

He forced himself to nod, to smile. "Joshua will do a fine job, I know."

It was only now, when it was out of his reach, that Ben realized how much this place meant to him.

Chapter Three

Anna had no need to cluck to Buck when they came in sight of the Schmidt farm on the way back from home visits a few days later. Buck knew that his own barn would soon be appearing and knew, too, that there'd be a treat for him once he was unhitched.

"Easy, boy." Anna said it with indulgence in her voice. Given the leaden skies and cold temperatures, she'd be glad to get into the warm farmhouse kitchen, rich with the scents of whatever Elizabeth had decided to treat her menfolk with today.

The fencepost that marked the beginning of the Miller fields came in to view, with someone in the usual black coat and black felt hat bending over the post. He looked up and waved, and she saw that it was Ben. She pulled the mare to a halt at his upraised hand.

Ben smiled up at her, lines crinkling around his blue eyes. "A ride home, please?" he asked.

"For sure." She gestured toward the seat next to her. If he could act as if things were normal between them, so could she.

He climbed up, settling on the seat, and Buck flicked an ear back in recognition of the extra weight.

"*Komm*, Buck, you remember me, ain't so?"

Anna had to smile at his teasing. "He's not used to having another person along on home visit days." Anna snapped the lines, and Buck moved on.

"You've been doing most of them, seems like." Ben shot a glance at her face. "Mamm's all right, isn't she?"

"Ach, ya, she's fine. I think she feels having me take over more of the home visits might push folks into accepting me."

Elizabeth hadn't actually said so, but Anna could read her pretty well. After all, it had always been the understanding between them that Anna would take over more of the practice as Elizabeth wanted to slow down.

"How's that working out?" Ben had a trick of lifting one eyebrow when he asked a question that always seemed to cause a little flutter in her heart.

Anna forced herself to concentrate. "Pretty well, I think. Etta Beachy even let me check out her daughter-in-law today. Reluctantly."

He chuckled. "Sounds like Etta hasn't changed much. Always has to have everything her way, ain't so?"

Anna shrugged. "She wants the best for her first grandbaby." And she didn't think Anna was the best. She didn't say that aloud, of course. And she certain sure didn't confide the thing that was weighing on her.

Elizabeth seemed sure Dora's baby wouldn't arrive until the New Year, and she'd had plenty more experience than Anna had. But based on her examination today, Anna would have guessed a good week or two earlier.

She'd reminded Dora that babies could easily arrive

two weeks early or two weeks late, just to have Etta pooh-pooh the notion that her grandson would show up any earlier than the date she'd determined, January 6, Old Christmas, which was her husband's birthday.

Anna hadn't felt up to taking on an argument about the baby's sex, either. She sent Dora a meaningful glance, relieved to see a smile and a shrug in return. Maybe Dora wasn't as cowed by her formidable mother-in-law as she'd thought.

Ben put his hands over hers on the lines, startling her, and she realized they'd nearly run right into the barn, buggy and all.

"Ach, sorry. I was woolgathering." She looped the lines and scrambled down before Ben could offer to help her.

"Problems?" he said lightly, coming around to start the unharnessing.

"No, nothing at all." She kept her head down, focusing on the job at hand.

"I see." He patted the mare's neck. "If you decide to talk to somebody, I know how to keep a secret. And I owe you."

For an instant she was struck dumb. Was he talking about her not saying anything about his phone call? Or was that by way of being an apology to saying he loved her and then vanishing?

If she didn't know, it was surely best to say nothing. She managed to glance at him with a smile. "Only a midwife's menfolk would find it possible to talk about the birth of a *boppli* in mixed company."

Ben grinned. "The rest of them pretend they don't even notice a babe is coming until it is safe in its cradle."

As Anna reached up to pull off the headstall, Ben

grabbed it first. "You go in and warm up," he said. "I've got this."

"But you don't know about Buck's treat when he is unharnessed," she said lightly. "You might make a mistake and try to give him a carrot."

"He's a fussy one, is he?" Ben pulled the harness free. "What is it? A sugar cube?"

"That's right." Anna held it on her palm, feeling Buck's soft lips brushing her skin as he took the sugar.

"Spoiled thing," Ben teased.

"A midwife's buggy horse has to be ready for a lot of unexpected trips," she said. "He works for his sugar."

Anna led the gelding toward the paddock while Ben carried the harness to its rack. It was easy, it seemed, to get back to the kind of teasing conversation she'd once had with Ben. Too easy? She couldn't risk falling for him all over again.

Opening the gate, she released the horse. Buck trotted a few steps and then stopped, lifting his head and sniffing the air.

Snow! Anna saw the first few flakes nearly as soon as the horse did. She tilted her head back, scanning the sky for more.

"What are you doing?" Ben had reached the gate without her noticing.

"Snow," she said, unable to keep the glee from her voice.

Ben chuckled. "I'd near forgot that you're like a kid when it snows." A sudden breeze sent a cluster of snowflakes dancing across the paddock. Buck whinnied, pranced in place for a moment and then trotted around in a circle, head tossing.

Ben laughed. "Or maybe like the horse. Sure you don't want to run around in a circle, too?"

"Nothing wrong with getting excited about the first snow." She could hear the defensiveness in her voice.

Ben clasped her by the wrists, and she looked up at his face. "Nothing at all wrong," he said gently. "I'm glad of it, Anna. Makes me feel like I could shed a few burdens and trot around, too."

Still holding her wrists, he swung her around, his face lit with laughter. "We'll both celebrate, ain't so?"

Laughing, Anna swung around with him, face tilted back to feel the flakes on her skin, until she was breathless.

"Stop, stop." She grabbed his forearms, feeling solid muscle under the layers of fabric. "What if someone saw us?"

"They'd think we were a bit *ferhoodled*." He stopped, so suddenly she might have fallen if not for his strong hands holding hers.

For an instant they stood staring at each other, and she felt her heart turn over. Then he was stepping away. "We'd best get inside and get warmed up. Josh will be wanting to get the sleigh out if this keeps up."

He sounded perfectly normal, as if he'd felt nothing at all in that moment when her heart had twisted.

Anna took a deep breath of cold air, knowing her cheeks were burning. So. She'd told herself she could get back to the way they'd been before the night she'd known she loved him. She'd been wrong. Their relationship was a lot more complicated than that.

"I'm telling you, Ben, this is going to be a great winter for snow. Grossdaadi says the woolly bear caterpillars predicted a real snowy winter. We have to get the sleigh ready."

Grinning, Ben followed his younger brother up the ladder to the upper loft in the barn. In some ways Josh, despite his size, was still the little kid brother he'd always been.

"Okay, okay, I said I'd help you get the sleigh ready and I will. Just don't blame me if it sits high and dry for half the winter."

"It won't," Josh said confidently, scrambling the rest of the way into the loft and reaching back a gloved hand to tug Ben up beside him.

"There she is," Josh said proudly. "Let's get it uncovered and down to the barn floor."

"Easier said than done." Ben gave a mock grumble, but truth to tell, he'd have done something a lot harder to have this time to get reacquainted with his little brother.

Together they rigged up the sleigh to the hook used to move bales and lowered it to the floor. Josh was so eager to get at it that he would have tumbled down the ladder if not for Ben's steadying hand.

"Take it easy. The sleigh's not going anywhere."

"I know." Josh grinned. "Boy, it's *gut* to have you home again." He sobered, as if wondering whether that was the right thing to say.

Ben gripped his shoulder for a moment. "Me, too." Regret swept over him. He'd let Josh down when he'd left, not even thinking of him. Dan and Joseph were enough older that Josh would never have confided in them. There seemed no end to the lives affected by his leaving.

Josh chattered as they worked on the sleigh, wiping away the dust that had accumulated over the summer and removing every speck of rust from the runners. "And besides, Anna loves to take the sleigh out. She'll be surprised when she sees it's ready. Anna does so much for everyone, I want to do something nice for her. She really is like a big sister to me." He sent a side-long glance at Ben, as if to see how he was taking that.

Ben figured the safest thing he could do was nod. Obviously everyone in the family would have been happy if he and Anna had married. He couldn't marry to make other people happy, but given how strong an attraction she still had for him, maybe…

No maybes, he told himself. Whatever he did or didn't do here, he couldn't hurt Anna again.

"Anna says…" Josh paused, polishing vigorously at an already shining runner.

When he didn't go on, Ben elbowed him. "Go ahead. What does Anna say?"

Josh rubbed even harder. "She says I should just tell you what I feel."

What now? "Go ahead." He braced himself.

"I guess Daad told you about his plans for the farm?"

"Ya, and it's fine." He hastened to assure him, hoping he sounded convincing. "You deserve it. I'm happy for you."

"But that's just it." The words burst out of Josh. "I'm not happy. I don't want it." He clamped his lips shut and glanced around as if afraid someone had heard.

Ben felt a frown knotting his forehead. "But how can you not want a farm like this?"

"You say that because it's your dream," Josh said. "Just like it's Daad's. Nobody understands that I might want something different."

Josh's voice had risen, and Ben put his hand on the boy's arm.

"Hey, it's okay. Just tell me what you want."

"What I always wanted. You know I always liked working with machines better than anything. I'm the one who fixed the generator when it stopped, remember? And I rebuilt that baler when everyone else gave up on it, too."

He couldn't help but be moved by the passion in Josh's voice. "If you feel that way about it, won't Daad understand?"

"I tried. He just doesn't see. He thinks it's fair that I have the farm, and he won't change his mind." Josh turned his face away, obviously not wanting anyone to see his emotion.

Here was something else to be laid to his account, it seemed. But what could he do? A look at his brother forced a decision. He had to make this right for Josh, somehow.

He grasped his brother by the shoulders and shook him gently. "Listen, we'll work it out somehow. Let me think on it, okay? There must be a way."

"*Denke*, Ben." Josh's expression lightened. "Anna said I should talk to you, and she was right. She always seems to understand."

In other words, Anna had been trying to fill the gap he'd left in his little brother's life. He wanted to resent it, but he couldn't. Anna had paid him a compliment, in a way. She'd trusted he'd find a way to make this right for Josh. He just hoped her faith wasn't mistaken.

Chapter Four

Anna sliced through the dough on the cutting board, turning out the homemade noodle squares that Elizabeth would drop into her chicken potpie. They'd been able to come home early today, with few people venturing out into the snow.

Trying to keep her mind on Elizabeth's voice wasn't easy when her thoughts were completely absorbed by those moments with Ben out by the paddock the previous day. His laughing face as he'd spun her around had even intruded into her dreams. There, she'd been spinning faster and faster until she flew against him and his arms closed around her.

She had to stop this, now. Benjamin had been so frightened at the thought of marrying her that he'd left his whole world behind. It was hardly likely his feelings had changed now.

"I said, it's a *gut* thing no one is due today or tomorrow," Elizabeth said…or rather, repeated, since it was apparent that Anna hadn't heard her before.

Focus, Anna ordered herself. "That's certain sure.

We don't need any women in labor bouncing around trying to get here through the snow."

Once the snow had decided to start, it hadn't let up, and there was four inches at least on the ground. They'd have a quiet time of it until the roads were clear, and it always took some time for the township plows to arrive.

Anna rubbed her forehead with the back of her hand, trying not to touch anything with her floury fingers. Unless she wanted to go around in a constant state of confusion, she'd have to find a way to show Ben that she didn't harbor any lingering feelings for him. Then they could be comfortable together, couldn't they?

"*Komm*, Anna, tell me what has your forehead so tight? That's the third time you've rubbed it in the past half hour." Elizabeth stirred down the chicken broth that had come to a boil. "I know when you're worried."

But she'd never guess the cause of Anna's worry, and Anna didn't dare tell her. "Ach, it's nothing. I was just thinking about Dora Beachy. I'm concerned that *boppli* might be arriving sooner than anyone expects."

"Ya?" Elizabeth turned to her instantly. "Did you say anything to her?"

"I didn't like to, since she's really your patient. I did remind them that babies can arrive two weeks early or two weeks late and still be normal."

Elizabeth nodded approval. "That was the smart thing to say. Of course, a first baby is more likely to be late than early."

"I know." But still, she was troubled. What if they didn't send for help in time?

"Tell you what," Elizabeth said, seeming to read her thoughts. "I'll stop over next week and check on Dora. That will make everyone feel better, ain't so?"

Anna let out a breath of relief. "I'd be so glad. Maybe I'm…"

Before she could finish the thought, they were interrupted by the soft sound of hooves on snow and the jingle of harness bells. Together they rushed to the back porch to find Josh and Benjamin grinning at them from the high seat of the sleigh. Ben held the lines, while Josh jiggled a strap of tiny bells.

"So that's what you two boys have been up to all afternoon." Elizabeth smiled fondly at her sons. "I should have known."

"Get your coats on, you two. We're going to take you for a ride." Josh jumped down to hustle them along. "Hurry up. You first, Mamm."

"Ach, I'm too old for such foolishness," Elizabeth protested, but halfheartedly.

"Never," Anna exclaimed, rushing to retrieve their coats and mittens.

Since the sleigh was a two-seater, Josh took his mother up beside him to the accompaniment of a string of warnings from his *daad*, who came out of the barn to join the fun. They went sliding off down the snow-covered lane, the snow muffling the sound of the horse's hooves.

"Don't worry, Daad." Ben stamped snow from his feet. "He'll be careful with Mamm."

"When you boys start playing around with the sleigh, you forget all about being careful," Asa said, but he was smiling as he watched. "Mind you don't go speeding when you take Anna."

It hadn't occurred to Anna that logically Ben would take her for a ride since Josh had done the first trip. She was still trying to find a way to get out of it when the sleigh came sweeping back, Elizabeth laughing like a girl. Before Anna knew what was happening, she'd been bundled up onto the seat beside Ben.

He shot her a mischievous grin. "We'll show them how it's done, ain't so?"

"You heard your *daad*," she began, then gave it up as Ben guided the sleigh in a broad circle and she had to grasp the side rail to keep from sliding right off the seat.

Ben sent the gelding off toward the woods at a brisk pace, and she held tightly.

"We're not racing, are we?" She tried to sound stern, but the question came out on a giggle. She couldn't help it—it was so exhilarating to fly noiselessly over the snow, the breeze sending flakes to dust her coat and melt against her skin.

"Fun, ain't so?" Ben smiled at her again, and her heart seemed to flip in her chest.

"You might say you did this for Joshua's sake, but we all know better. You wanted to play in the snow as much as he did."

"You're just the same. Remember how excited you got yesterday at the first flakes?" His voice was low and teasing, and Anna had to struggle not to meet his eyes.

"I confess. We're all kids about something, ain't so?"

Ben nodded, but for some reason the words seemed to set up a more serious line of thought for him. They'd nearly reached the woods, where the farm lane ended, and he drew the buggy to a stop.

With the snow muffling every sound, Anna felt as if they were alone in the world. She had to say something.

"The…the hemlocks are beautiful in the snow. Look how it's bending the branches down. It's as if they're…"

"Anna." His voice was low, but it halted her foolish

chatter in an instant. "There's something I must say to you. I've owed you an apology for three years, and I haven't been able to find the words to tell you how sorry I am."

"Don't, Ben. Don't." She put out her hand to stop him and then realized it was much safer not to touch him. But she saw, quite suddenly, what she must say to ease the tension between them.

"It worked out for the best, ain't so? I don't mean you going away, but the fact that we didn't get together." Anna took a breath of cold air and forced herself to go on. "Moonlight and kisses don't make a solid basis for marriage. We're such completely different people now."

Her throat was getting so tight that she didn't think she could say anything more, but maybe that was enough. She risked a glance at Ben's face, but his somber expression didn't tell her anything.

Finally he nodded. "If you feel you can forgive me, that's all that counts. I hope we can be friends again."

Anna forced herself to smile. "Friends." That was all she could manage, but it seemed to be enough.

Ben clucked to the horse and they turned back toward the farmhouse.

Ben did his best not to fidget as the three-hour Sunday morning service drew near the end. He'd been trying to efface himself, in the hope he could fade into the mass of black-coated men. What a wimp he'd turned into while he was away—after all, he'd grown up sitting on the backless benches for worship, and he didn't even remember thinking it was that hard.

Hard was definitely the word for this bench. He shifted his weight slightly and earned a frown from his eldest brother, Daniel. Dan had always felt responsible for the younger ones, and that didn't seem to have changed. His greeting had been restrained, and he'd glanced at Daad as if taking his cue from him. Joseph, so close in age to Daniel that they might as well have been twins, had followed his lead, but as they'd lined up to enter the basement when worship was being held, Joe had given him a quick smile and a wink that warmed his heart.

You didn't expect this to be easy, he reminded himself. It seemed he was saying that a lot lately.

The final prayer, the final hymn, and the long service was over. Bishop John King, passing close as he moved through the congregation, inclined his head gravely. Ben nodded back, guessing what the bishop was thinking—that if Ben intended to stay, he'd have to make his confession before the church. It was an intimidating thought, but the forgiveness granted to the sinner afterward was sincere and complete. The wrong was wiped out as if it had never been.

Daad put a hand on his shoulder. "Not until you're ready," he said softly. "Meantime, help the boys set up the tables for lunch, *ja*?"

Ben's throat tightened. Daad, for all his strictness with his boys, had always seemed to understand. If he ever had a family, would he have that gift? *If*.

"Here, Ben, give us a hand." Joe and Dan were making short work of converting the benches to the tables that would seat them for the after-church meal. "Or have you forgot how?"

Ben grinned at the familiar joshing and grabbed the end of the table Josh was struggling with. "Josh and I will get more done than you two. Come on, Josh." To-

gether they raised the wooden planks easily, fitting them
into the brackets that turned them into tables. Typical
Amish ingenuity, he thought. The benches and tables
had to be hauled from one home to the next for services,
so why not make the best use of them?

Already some of the women were carrying bowls
and platters down the stairs from the Fisher family's
kitchen. Each family took a turn to host worship, but
it only made sense to do winter worship at a home that
had a warm, dry basement instead of a barn.

They were finishing the last table when Ben spotted Anna coming down, her arms around a huge coffee
urn. Anna had made it easy for him to forgive himself
for the hurt he'd offered her. At least he didn't have to
worry about that. So why didn't her rational acceptance
make him feel more content?

"Let me take that." He discovered he'd moved to help
Anna before he'd consciously decided on it. He grabbed
the urn. "It's heavy."

For an instant she resisted, but then she let go and
smiled. "Over here on the end of the table," she said,
gesturing to the long table that was already becoming covered with the fixings of the after-church lunch.

He set it down in the spot she indicated. "I see…"
Ben lost his train of thought when he heard his mother's name, coming from a small knot of women a few
yards away.

"…saying that it's not fair for Elizabeth Miller to just
stop doing her home visits. She's our midwife, and she
shouldn't be pushing us off on someone second-best,
like Anna Zook."

Ben recognized Etta Beachy's strident voice even
though her back was to them. Obviously some things

didn't change. Etta was known as the biggest *blabber-maul* in the church district.

He didn't realize he'd taken a step toward the woman until he felt Anna's hand on his arm. She shook her head.

"Don't say anything," she murmured. "Your *mamm* wouldn't like it, and I don't need defending." Her smile flickered. "Your *mamm* would say that the irritating people in the church are sent to teach the rest of us patience."

Ben gave a reluctant nod. Anna was right, and that sounded exactly like his mother. But still, he didn't like to hear the woman talking that way about Mamm. And what made her so sure that Anna was second-best?

It seemed he'd lost some of his patience while he was living Englisch. He put his hand over hers and squeezed it lightly. "If so, Etta fills the role to perfection, ain't so?"

Anna tried to suppress a giggle and didn't quite succeed. Her eyes danced even as she shook her head at him.

How could he have ever thought her plain? When her face lit with laughter, she had an elusive beauty that intrigued him.

Whoa, don't go there. He eased his hand away from hers. "*Denke.* For keeping me out of trouble."

She glanced away, and a slight flush rose in her cheeks.

"And imagine that Ben Miller, sitting in worship like he belonged there." Etta apparently wasn't finished with his family yet. "He ought to be in the penitent seat. Why hasn't he confessed?"

Interestingly, two of the women had drifted away,

maybe not wanting to be associated with Etta's views. The one who was left tried in vain to shush her with an agonized glance in their direction.

To Ben's surprise, he felt Anna stiffen at his side. Was she really angrier at the slight to him than at the reflection on herself? Of course, knowing Anna, he suspected she wouldn't admit to being angry at all. But she couldn't deny the way her eyes snapped or the flush on her cheekbones.

Oddly enough, that amused him. "Relax," he whispered. "I'll show you how to deal with the Ettas of the world."

Not looking back, he strode over to Etta and her embarrassed companion, hearing a small gasp from behind him.

"Etta Beachy. It's nice to see you after all this time." He produced a smile. "And this must be Sally Fisher, ain't so?"

Sally nodded, her color high. "*Gut* to see you home again, Benjamin. *Wilkom* back."

Etta, obviously not sure what he might have overheard, pressed her lips together into a thin line. For a moment he thought she wouldn't say anything, but then she gave a short nod. "Your *mamm* must be pleased to see you after all this time."

"Three years," he said, determined not to let her ruffle him. "I see you haven't changed a bit." *Still as big a* blabbermaul *as ever*, he thought.

Something that might have been a chuckle escaped Sally. He nodded to each of them before heading for the table where Daad and his brothers were waiting. But on the way he couldn't resist a glance back at Anna.

She shook her head at him, but her eyes twinkled.

Maybe he'd taken the sting out of Etta's comments for her.

Another thought struck him as he took his place at the table and he thought again of her reaction to the criticism of him. Perhaps Anna wasn't quite as indifferent to him as she wanted him to believe.

Chapter Five

The snow was gone from the roads by the time Elizabeth and Anna set out for the Beachy home on Monday afternoon. A brisk wind ripped snow from the trees and sent it swirling in front of the buggy horse who plodded patiently on. Anna was glad of the blanket over their knees, and she tucked it in more snugly.

"Are you sure you want me to be with you on this visit?" she asked, hoping she wasn't repeating herself. "I mean, Etta and Dora might feel freer to talk if I'm not there."

"I've never noticed anything keeping Etta from talking," Elizabeth said. She took her gaze from the road long enough to study Anna's face. "Are you worried that I won't agree with you?"

"Not worried, exactly." But Etta's comment referring to her as second-best seemed lodged in her mind, despite Ben's efforts. "I'll be glad to have your opinion. Maybe I'm wrong, and if so…"

Elizabeth startled her by reaching over to grasp her hand. "None of that, now. Whether we are right or wrong in a particular situation, we must always take the course that's safest for the *mammi* and the *boppli*."

"Even if it makes me look foolish?"

"Even so." Elizabeth smiled. "And not just you. I mind one time when I was so sure I'd heard a second heartbeat. I told the parents, and they rushed around borrowing an extra cradle and getting more blankets and diapers."

"And?" She suspected how this story was going to play out by the way Elizabeth's eyes twinkled.

"Nobody was more surprised than me when I delivered one big, healthy boy. I never have figured out what it was I heard that day." She chuckled. "I was a long time living that down, believe me."

Anna squeezed her hand before letting go. "You're just trying to make me feel better."

"Is it working?" Elizabeth asked innocently.

They were both still laughing when they drove up the lane to the farmhouse.

Etta must have been watching for them. One of the boys ran out to take the horse and offer a hand to help Elizabeth down. Anna jumped down herself, her sturdy shoes landing on the hard-packed snow of the lane. She picked up the medical bag and followed Elizabeth to the back door.

"*Komm* in, *komm* in." Etta was there to greet them. She gave Anna a sidelong glance and addressed Elizabeth. "We didn't know you were both coming."

Elizabeth's smile didn't falter. "I think it best if both of us see every patient a few times. We're partners, after all. If one of us should be busy with another *mammi* when someone goes into labor, we should both be familiar with the case, ain't so?"

Etta didn't look convinced, but she didn't argue, to Anna's relief. Was she feeling a bit guilty after being caught gossiping? Or wondering if Elizabeth had heard about her criticism of Ben? It was certain sure Elizabeth hadn't heard it from either her or Ben, but very often she seemed to know what was happening without being told.

The two of them shed their outer garments, hanging coats and bonnets on the pegs near the back door. Rubbing her palms together, Elizabeth moved to the gas heater in the corner.

"Dora won't want us touching her with cold hands, ain't so?" She smiled at Dora, sitting near the heater in a padded rocker. "How are you feeling?"

"Fine, fine." Dora glanced at her mother-in-law. "Mamm Etta is taking *gut* care of me."

Etta beamed. "Ach, we're all wonderful happy about the baby coming."

There was a little more chitchat, restrained on Etta's part and careful on Anna's, but Elizabeth chattered normally, drawing Dora out on the progress of her pregnancy. It was fascinating to see Dora relax and gain assurance under the influence of her warmth.

That was a place where she needed to improve, Anna decided. Conquering her natural shyness was a day-by-day battle, but she had to keep at it if she was going to be the midwife Elizabeth was.

They all adjourned to the bedroom, where Elizabeth gave Dora a swift, deft exam. Anna, holding the girl's hand, saw the apprehension in her eyes. "It's all right," she said, patting her shoulder. "Everything is fine."

Catching the words, Elizabeth looked up and smiled.

"That's certain sure. It won't be long until you're holding this little *boppli* in your arms."

"How soon?" Etta chimed in.

Elizabeth chuckled. "*Komm*, Etta, you know better than to ask me to pinpoint the birth date. All yours were a bit late, as I recall."

"For sure. I thought James was never going to get here." Etta shot a glance at Anna, as if to say, *you see?*

"'Course Dora isn't going to take after you. Could be anytime from two weeks early to two weeks late and still be normal." She patted Dora's belly. "Just let us know if you start having any contractions or even feeling not quite right. That's what we're here for, and one of us will always come."

Dora nodded, her small face relaxing, and she smoothed her hand over her belly protectively. "James and I pray for a healthy baby, whenever it arrives."

"*Gut.* That's the best way to think." Elizabeth nodded to Anna. "We'd best be on our way. It's turning colder, I think."

Naturally Etta didn't want to let them go without giving them coffee and cake, and they finally compromised by taking a thermos of coffee with them.

"It'll be most *wilkom* on the way home," Elizabeth said, and pushed Anna gently out the door.

The wind caught them as they left the shelter of the porch, and they scurried to the buggy that James had ready and waiting for them. In another moment they were on the road home.

"Brr." Elizabeth tucked the blanket more firmly over them. "It's turning colder. The snow will stay to make it a white Christmas, I think."

"That sounds lovely to me." Anna glanced at her.

"But tell me the truth. You don't agree with me about Dora's baby coming earlier, do you?"

"You heard what I told Dora. Besides, babies have a mind of their own when it comes to that. Still, I can see why you think it." Elizabeth gave a little nod. "Dora is carrying low and in front, just like her *mamm* did. Makes her look as if the little one is about to pop out. But hers usually arrived right about their due date."

Anna nodded, a little relieved though still wondering. "It's a shame Dora's family moved out to Ohio when they did. She'd like having her *mamm* here."

"I'm sure that's so. Although Etta was a bit less opinionated today than she usually is. I almost asked her if she were sick."

Anna was surprised into a laugh. "Ach, I shouldn't laugh at her, but…" She stopped, thinking it might be best not to bring up the subject of Ben's encounter with Etta.

"Something happened after worship Sunday, ain't so?"

"How…" Anna stared at her.

"How do I know?" Elizabeth finished for her. "Because I have eyes in my head." She sighed, staring straight ahead toward the horse's ears. "I was keeping watch on Benjamin, of course. Couldn't help it—I wanted so much for him to feel as if he fits in again."

Anna's mind stumbled over how to respond. "I don't think he would be upset by anything Etta might say. He knows what she's like."

"Ach, sometimes I have thoughts that aren't very Christian about that woman." Elizabeth clutched the lines so tightly that the mare turned her head to look back, as if asking why.

"I know. But Ben took it in stride. He even had me laughing about it."

"I'm wonderful glad you were with him. You always seemed to understand Ben so well." Elizabeth reached out to clasp her hand. "Please, just keep being a friend to him. Encourage him. He needs that right now. Will you?"

Be a friend. Encourage him. And how was she to protect her heart while she was doing that?

But she didn't really have a choice. She squeezed Elizabeth's hand. "Of course I will."

"Slide in there." Ben's brother Daniel gave him a nudge that sent him along the bench at the back of the schoolroom a few nights later. Dan and his wife, holding their two young kids, came in after him, pushing him farther as the rest of the family piled in behind them.

It was the night of the Amish school Christmas program, and even though the family no longer had *kinder* in the school, they wouldn't think of missing it. In fact, there was about as good a turnout for the program as there was for Sunday worship.

Dan pressed him a bit more as he made room, and Ben found himself crunched up against Anna. Not that he minded, but he wasn't sure how Anna would take it. However, she just smiled and slid her coat under the bench to make a bit more space.

"Close quarters," he murmured. "Looks like the whole church is here."

"For sure. No one would want to miss seeing the scholars say their Christmas pieces." She reached out as Dan's two-year-old, Reuben, wiggled his way over adult knees to reach her. "Want to sit on my lap?"

He nodded, one finger in his mouth, and gave Ben a sidelong look as if not sure what to make of this new *onkel* of his. When Anna lifted him, he snuggled against her, still staring at Ben.

Anna ruffled the boy's corn silk hair and whispered to him. "That's Onkel Ben, remember? Can you give him a smile?"

Reuben pulled the finger out of his mouth just long enough to produce a smile, dimples appearing in his rosy cheeks. Then, apparently stricken by shyness, he buried his face in the front of Anna's dress.

Ben wasn't sure whether to find it funny or not. "Guess he's not ready to accept me just yet."

"He's a little shy, like most two-year-olds," Anna said. "Give him time." She stroked Reuben's head lightly. "Besides, it's already past his bedtime."

"I won't push."

That had to be his motto for everything about his return. Relationships might be easy to break but they could be hard to rebuild. Maybe it would be easier with Reuben and his baby sister, since they weren't old enough to have been disappointed by him.

"I thought I heard your voice." The guy ahead of him turned around, a grin splitting his face. "Ben. *Wilkom* back!" Gus Schmidt, once one of his closest friends, pounded him on the shoulder. "Sure is *gut* to see you."

"I'm wonderful glad to be here. You've changed." Ben nodded toward the bristly beard that adorned Gus's chin.

"I'm an old married man by now. Nancy finally put me out of my misery."

Nancy Fisher and Gus had been sweethearts already when Ben left, so he wasn't surprised. But it did startle him to see the *boppli* Gus held on his knee. The little girl babbled, reaching past him toward Reuben.

"This here's Mary Grace." He bounced the tot on his knee and she grinned, showing her few teeth.

Ben shook his head. "Imagine you, responsible enough to be a *daadi*. I never thought I'd see the day."

"Beat you to it, anyway." Gus looked as if he couldn't stop smiling.

The familiar give and take between buddies was a balm to his heart. Here was one person, at least, who hadn't changed in his regard.

"If Nancy knew half the things you got up to, she'd never trust you with a *boppli*. Where is Nancy, anyway?"

"She's been helping out with the props for the program. She'd want to talk to you later, but mind you don't say anything about the mischief you led me into. I had enough sense not to…"

Gus let that trail off, and the tips of his ears reddened. "I mean…"

"It's okay." Ben punched his arm lightly. If he was going to stay, he'd have to get used to folks stumbling over what to say about his jumping the fence. "I always did have to learn everything the hard way, ain't so?"

The teacher walked to the front of the audience just then, and everyone got quiet, sparing Gus the embarrassment of answering. "We'll get together later, ain't so?" he murmured, and turned to face front.

Ben settled back onto the bench and realized that Anna was watching his face, maybe measuring how much he was affected by that conversation. He gave her a reassuring smile and watched her flush a little in return.

Teacher Lydia proved to be Nancy's younger sister. She had more poise than he'd have expected as she welcomed everyone and introduced the program. As usual, the evening began with the youngest scholars, probably because they were too excited to wait.

He might have expected to be bored by the program, given some of the entertainment he'd seen in the outside world. In fact, he was completely rapt. The scholars' innocent faces, intent expressions and sometimes wobbly voices were enchanting. He glanced at Anna. She was watching just as closely, a reminiscent smile curving her lips.

Of course it would be familiar to her. Even though she hadn't grown up in Lost Creek, her school would have had a program that was probably very like this one. No doubt she'd stood up in front of the audience, quaking a bit, to say her lines.

As if Anna felt his gaze, she met his eyes.

"Do you miss it?" he whispered under cover of the song the younger *kinder* were singing. "Being with your own folks at Christmastime?"

She shook her head. "I was there visiting at Thanksgiving. But Lost Creek is home now. And I get out of the *rumspringa* gang Christmas parties."

That comment startled him. Why wouldn't she want to get together with the girls she'd gone through *rumspringa* with? Those were usually the people who became your friends for life.

Then he really looked at her, seeing what he hadn't before. She cradled the sleeping Reuben against her heart, and when she looked down at him, her face was suffused with tenderness. Of course. All those girls would have families by now, except for Anna. And she wanted a family—that shone so clearly in her face.

Ben's breath seemed to catch in his throat. She was so loving and so very lovely as she watched his nephew. He saw her as he'd seen her that night so long ago, when he'd realized without warning that he loved her.

And then he'd panicked at the thought of what that meant—giving up the travels he dreamed of, settling down to the same life as his father and his brothers, with all hope of adventure gone. He'd panicked. And he'd run.

Anna glanced up and caught him looking at her. Her eyes widened, and a tiny pulse beat at her temple. He couldn't look away. Their gazes were entangled. He couldn't see anything but her face, hear anything but the breath she took. It was as if they were alone in the room.

Maybe it was *gut* that they weren't alone, or he'd never be able to stop himself from drawing her into his arms, kissing her sweet lips, holding her tight—

The cell phone he'd put in his jacket began to vibrate. He could switch it off. Ignore it. That's what he'd been trying to do since he came home, but it wasn't working.

He'd left unfinished business behind in the outside world, and it wasn't going to leave him alone. The truth hit him like a blow. He'd never be able to commit fully to the church, to his family or to Anna until he'd made things right with Mickey.

Chapter Six

Breakfast at the Miller house was never a quiet affair, since Josh always had something to talk about. Today his *mamm* was busy teasing him about his efforts to help Teacher Lydia at the program the previous night. Given the way the tips of his ears had turned red, there had been more to his helpfulness than just pitching in.

Anna sent a cautious glance at Ben. Although he was smiling at his brother's plight, he seemed a bit preoccupied. Was he thinking of those moments at the Christmas program when it seemed their hearts had touched? Or was that just her imagination? And how many times did she have to remind herself that Ben had broken her heart once already? It would be foolish to give him an opportunity to do it again.

"How many appointments are scheduled for the birthing center today, Anna?" Elizabeth settled at the foot of the table, nursing a second cup of coffee and leafing through her box of handwritten recipes.

Anna had to scramble to get her thoughts back to business. "I have two, and I think you might have three."

"Is that what you'd call a baby boom, Mamm?" Ben looked up from his plate of fried scrapple.

"No, just the Amish doing what comes naturally," Elizabeth replied, smiling at him.

Anna found herself smiling, as well. Most Amish males didn't mention a baby until it was safely in its cradle for all to see, but the family of a midwife didn't have such scruples.

Elizabeth pulled a card from the box. "There's my *pfeffernuesse* recipe. I wondered where it got to." She set it on the table with a decided air. "You can take all the appointments today, Anna, ain't so?"

Blinking with surprise, Anna nodded. "I guess so. Aren't you feeling well?"

"I'm feeling like playing hooky and baking Christmas cookies today." Her eyes twinkled. "After all, that's why I have a partner."

Anna did a mental run-through of today's appointments. "Some of your mothers might not like seeing me instead of you," she ventured.

"Well, that's too bad, but they'd best start getting used to it. Sooner or later you'll be taking over completely, ain't so? It's time they started seeing you as the midwife. And maybe time you were convinced of it, too."

She thought she had been. Anna tried not to feel hurt and planted a smile on her face. "I'll take care of it. *Denke*, Elizabeth."

By the time the routine had actually started at the birthing center, Anna had convinced herself that Elizabeth was only trying to bolster her confidence. She did need to show a little more conviction in her abilities, she supposed, but it was comforting to know that Elizabeth was there if she ran into difficulties.

It had wondered her sometimes if giving birth herself would make her more qualified to help others. But since that was unlikely to happen, she'd just have to push through with what she knew and had experienced in the past five years of working with Elizabeth.

The day wore on with no unpleasant surprises. She'd just waved goodbye to one of her Englisch clients when she spotted Ben heading toward the birthing center. She waited on the tiny porch, wrapping a shawl around her against the cold, crisp air. As Ben neared, she could hear the snow crunching under his boots.

"What brings you this way?" she asked, half expecting he'd walk on past to the field beyond.

Instead he mounted the steps, brandishing a toolbox in one hand. "Mamm sent me over to mend the drawer in your desk. She says if you pull on it too hard, it flies out into your lap."

"True enough, but if you have something else to do…"

"Not a thing," he said cheerfully, grabbing the door and holding it for her before following her inside. "Besides, if I hang around the scent of Mamm's baking any longer, I'll be sneaking even more cookies than Joshua is."

"That might be hard." She replaced the shawl on the wall hook where it belonged. "That boy has a sweet tooth, that's certain sure."

Ben gestured to the desk. "Okay if I start work, or do you need to get something out?"

"Just let me grab these files." She picked them up.

"I'll work at your mother's desk until the next patient comes."

The next patient, she reminded herself, was Martha Esch, all of whose eight kinder had been delivered by Elizabeth. Somehow she didn't think Martha was going to be eager to change.

"Problem, is she?" Ben seemed to be reading her mind.

She shrugged. "She's one of your *mamm*'s clients. She may not be too happy about seeing me instead." That didn't sound self-pitying, did it? That was the last thing she wanted.

Ben slid the drawer out, emptying the contents on the desk. "Sounds as if Mamm might be right to push the baby bird out of the nest."

Anna's rare temper flared. "I am not a baby bird."

Ben gave her the teasing grin that melted hearts. "I'm the bird that flew the nest too soon. Which is worse?"

Fortunately for Anna, she heard the sound of a buggy pulling up outside. Chin held high, she went to the door to greet Martha Esch.

Martha came in stamping snow from her shoes. "Nippy out today, ain't so, Anna?" She nodded to Ben. "Wonderful *gut* that you're home, Ben. And making yourself useful, I see."

Anna took her coat and hung it from a hook as Martha removed her bonnet and glanced around. "Where is Elizabeth? I have the time right, don't I?"

"Sure you do." Anna took a breath, wishing Ben were not there listening. "She's taking the day off, and she wants me to see her patients. If you'll *komm* to the other room…"

Martha frowned. "Is she sick?"

"No, nothing like that. She deserves a day off now and then, ain't so?"

"I suppose so." She frowned. "Maybe I'll make my appointment for another day, when she's back. After all, she's been the one to catch all my babies. What about tomorrow?" Martha reached for her coat.

Anna very nearly picked up the appointment calendar. She'd tried, hadn't she? Her hand stilled. She was aware of Martha waiting and of Ben, listening despite his pretense of being absorbed in his work.

What did they see when they looked at her? More importantly, what did she see when she looked in the mirror? How could she expect other people to take her seriously if she didn't take herself that way?

She picked up the patient file and turned to Martha with a smile that was as confident as she could manage. "Elizabeth wants me to check you today. I'll make sure that she sees all the notes from the visit. Shall we go in?" She held the door to the exam room.

Martha stared at her for a moment. Then she shrugged, smiling. "Ach, I'm being foolish, ain't so?" And she walked into the exam room.

Trying not to look surprised, Anna somehow couldn't keep herself from glancing at Ben. His eyes crinkled, and he gave her a thumbs-up sign.

Feeling ridiculously triumphant, Anna went to do her job.

Ben stepped carefully from one plank to another in the attic after supper, well aware that he could go through to the bedroom ceiling if he didn't stay on the boards. Josh, with his usual exuberance, was already under the eaves, shifting boxes.

"I thought Mamm said the crèche set was in a small box," Ben said, knowing that he'd have to restack whatever Josh moved.

"Guess so." Josh shifted the battery lantern he was carrying to illuminate another section of attic. Days were too short now to get much light coming through the small windows.

Ben paused, reaching overhead to rest his hand against the rough-hewn timber that made up the rafters. The first of the Miller family to settle here had built the farmhouse from trees he felled when he cleared land for crops. Ben had always figured that made the old farmhouse as much a part of the land as the huge oak tree behind the barn.

"Not here," Josh said, swinging around. "Better try the other side."

"And you'd best be careful where you step," Ben warned. "I'm not taking the blame if you put your big foot through the bedroom ceiling."

"Remember when Dan did that?" Josh grinned. "I was just a kid, but I can still hear Daad yelling."

"And a bit later it was Dan yelling," Ben said. It had been a long time since he'd reminisced with his brother. It felt good.

"Here it is," Josh said, swinging the lantern over a stack of boxes. He picked up the small box and handed it to Ben.

"Sure enough." The box was labeled in Mamm's meticulous hand. "How did it get way back there anyway? I'd think Mamm would have put it away close to the ladder last year."

Josh didn't answer for a moment. "Mamm hasn't decorated for Christmas much the past few years." He wasn't looking at Ben as he made his way toward the ladder.

It took a moment to sink in, and then Ben's heart sank. Yet another thing to chalk up to his account, it seemed. "Sorry." His voice roughened. "Guess I caused even more trouble than I thought. I hope you and I are okay."

"Sure thing." Once again Josh hesitated. "Have you thought about talking to Daad about the farm and what I want to do? I figured maybe we'd have it settled by now."

He'd thought about it plenty. He just didn't have any answers. "I haven't been back long. Maybe it's best to wait."

"I can't wait." The edge in Josh's voice startled him. "Zeb King is going to take on another apprentice at his machine shop in January, and he gave me first chance at it."

Ben studied his brother's face. "Are you sure that's what you want?" Zeb King had one of the largest Amish-owned businesses in Lost Creek, doing all kinds of machine work for Englisch companies.

"Not for good. I wouldn't want to spend my life working for someone else. But Zeb says he'll make sure I learn enough to be able to start my own shop, doing small engine repairs. That's what I really want. I thought it was impossible, but now you're back. You should take on the responsibility for the farm. You said you would."

"Look, I said I'd talk to Daad about it, but I'm not ready yet." He'd hardly been home long enough for Daad to have any confidence in him. Maybe he never would.

But Josh didn't seem to be considering that. "When will you be ready?" Josh snapped the question. Obviously he'd expected Ben's homecoming to solve all his problems.

Ben tried to remind himself that Josh was too young to know problems didn't get solved that easily. The weight of expectations on him was starting to feel heavy.

The last time he'd felt that way, he'd run. He wouldn't do that again.

He met his brother's gaze, trying to see past the anger and disappointment there. "After Christmas," he said firmly. "Mamm deserves a happy Christmas without any family quarrels. If you want to bring it up sooner, you'll have to do it yourself."

Josh's face tightened. "You're the one who got me into this. It's up to you to solve it."

Ben's jaw clenched in response. He'd thought Josh was the one person whose acceptance he didn't have to worry about. Looked as if he'd been wrong.

"You boys coming down soon?" Anna called from the bottom of the ladder. "Your *mamm* is saying she should have gone herself instead of sending the two of you to find something."

"We have it," Ben said, leaning over the opening to see Anna's face tilted up to him. "On our way down."

He turned to his brother. "After the holidays," he said firmly. Without waiting for a response, he climbed down the ladder to where Anna waited.

Chapter Seven

Anna collected the broom and dustpan and hurried out of the kitchen before Elizabeth could think of something else she should do. With only two days until Christmas, Elizabeth had launched into a storm of cooking, baking, and cleaning, sweeping Anna along with her. All of their expectant *mammis* were probably doing the same, so they hadn't had any appointments. Anna's thoughts slipped to Dora. She hoped all was going well there, and that the babe would put off its arrival for another week.

Anna scurried into the living room, intent on her current chore, and was surprised to find Ben there, warming himself in front of the propane heater.

"Ach, you surprised me. I didn't hear you *komm* in."

"Shh." Ben's smile flashed. "I slipped in while you and Mamm were occupied."

"Afraid she has a job for you?" she teased.

"Anna, you know me too well. I don't remember Mamm getting in such a tizzy for Christmas in years. You'd think we were getting ready to host the church for worship."

"She's cleaning everything that stands still, that's

for sure." She gestured with the dustpan. "It's a special Christmas, ain't so?"

He didn't pretend not to understand. "I'd hate to think I was the reason for all this extra cleaning. What are you up to? This room is so clean you could eat off the floor already."

"I'm supposed to brush up any needles fallen from the greens on the windowsills." Anna moved to the nearest window and knelt, realizing a short-handled brush would have done the job better.

"It'll just have to be done again on Christmas morning before the rest of the family arrives," he grumbled, but squatted down next to her to help.

"A little extra cleaning is a small price to pay for seeing her so happy." Anna found she was watching his strong, square hand picking up an elusive hemlock needle. "She's so wonderful glad you're home."

His fingers brushed hers. "What about you, Anna?" His voice was low. "Are you glad I'm home?"

She dared to look into his eyes then, her barriers crumbling away like a snowman in the sun. "You know that I am."

Ben clasped her hand, and his was warm and strong. That warmth seemed to flow into her, radiating up her arm and right to her heart. "Anna." He said her name on a breath that caressed her cheek. His fingers tightened. "I…"

"So there you are!" Asa stamped into the room, with Joshua behind him, trying to get a word out.

"Daad, don't." Josh's tone was anguished.

Ben rose to his full height, and Anna scrambled to her feet, still holding the dust pan. "I'm here, ya. What's wrong, Daad?"

"What's wrong is you putting *ferhoodled* ideas in your brother's head."

"Daad, I keep telling you, it's what I want." Josh sent an appealing look to his brother. "It's only Ben returning made it seem possible."

Elizabeth, drawn by all the noise, came in from the kitchen, wiping her hands on her apron. "What is going on here?" she demanded.

"What's going on is Ben encouraging Joshua to turn away from all my plans for him." He glared at Ben. "He's talking about going as an apprentice at the machine shop, of all things."

Elizabeth put a hand on his arm. "Asa, *stoppe*. You know Joshua always used to talk about doing that. If it's what he wants…"

"It's a boy's foolishness." Asa's voice was harsh. "Joshua will have the farm. That's what we decided. That's what's right."

"But I don't want it," Josh burst out. "Ben does."

Anna realized that Ben's hands were clenched into fists so tight that the skin stretched over the knuckles. She longed to reach out and touch him to ease the tension, but she didn't dare.

"You let the other boys choose what they wanted." Ben seemed to make an effort to speak calmly. "Why not Joshua?" His gaze challenged his father, and Anna felt as if the two of them didn't even notice the others in the room.

A flush mottled Asa's cheeks above his beard. "I am offering Joshua a *gut* life running a thriving farm. That's the best any Amish son could have. And the land has needs, too. It needs someone who won't run away from it."

A gasp sounded from Elizabeth. She was on the verge of tears, seeing two that she loved so at odds. Anna's heart hurt for all of them.

Ben was perfectly still. Only the pulse pounding visibly at his temple and the white line around his lips showed his pain.

He took one step toward his father. "Don't make Joshua pay for your disappointment with me, Daad." He spun and stalked out of the house.

Anna imagined she could hear Asa's teeth grinding together. Then he stamped out in the opposite direction. Elizabeth stood there, hands twisted in her apron, seeing her planned Christmas crumbling around her.

Anna shook off her paralysis and hurried to Elizabeth, putting her arms around her.

"I'm so sorry. So sorry," she murmured.

"It's my fault." Josh looked on the edge of tears. "Ben told me to wait until after the holidays. He said he'd go with me to talk to Daad. But I wanted it settled, and Daad was in such a *gut* mood, and I thought... I thought..." He rubbed his face with both hands, not attempting to finish the sentence.

Anna reached out to pat his shoulder. "I'm sorry, too. I wish I could make it right."

"No one can do that," Elizabeth said, straightening. "Asa and Ben must find their own way to each other."

Anna nodded. But in her heart the question echoed. What if they couldn't? Would Ben go away again?

Anna found herself thinking that supper that night was the most miserable meal she'd ever had in this house. Asa ate stolidly, not looking at anything or anyone but his food. Maybe it was best he didn't try to talk. What was there to say that wouldn't lead to an argument?

Joshua, who normally ate everything in sight, picked at his food, pushing it around his plate. Elizabeth barely made a pretense of eating, her gaze drawn again and again to Ben's empty place.

Anna understood, having difficulty keeping her own eyes averted. It seemed impossible to get any food past the lump in her throat, but she was unaccountably thirsty, gulping down her water and pouring another glass.

Finally the meal was over. Asa and Josh left the kitchen without looking at each other. Anna had a sudden desire to shake them. Though even if she did, it probably wouldn't help.

Suppressing a sigh at the stubbornness of men, Anna carried a stack of dishes to the sink and began running hot water. "Let me do the dishes tonight," she said quickly when Elizabeth gestured her away. "You go and rest."

"Resting won't help." Elizabeth's voice was thick with tears. "I must stay busy."

Nodding, Anna moved over and picked up the drying towel. Truthfully, she was the same way. Doing something was the only antidote to being crushed by sorrow. She tried to think of something helpful to say.

"They'll cool off," she finally said. "Give them time."

Elizabeth stared down at the plate she held, but Anna suspected she didn't see it. "What if we don't have time? What if Benjamin is so hurt he leaves again?" She let the plate slide back into the soapy water and turned to grasp Anna's hands. "Talk to him. Please."

Fear swept over Anna at the thought. "But I don't

know where he is. Besides, he certain sure won't listen to me."

"Ach, Anna, do you think I don't have eyes in my head?" Elizabeth managed a tiny smile. "You are the one person he might listen to. As for where he is—he'd be where he always went when he was in trouble, with the animals."

When Anna hesitated, Elizabeth squeezed her hands. "Please, Anna."

What could she say? "I'll try. But…"

"That's right. Try." Elizabeth released her. "Go now. Don't let him leave us again."

Even if Ben did talk to her, keeping him from leaving might be beyond her abilities. But she had to try. Getting her coat from the peg, Anna pulled it on and stepped outside, glancing toward the barn.

Darkness was drawing in quickly now that they were in the shortest days of the year. Anna shrugged her coat more closely around her and headed for the barn, not sure whether she hoped Elizabeth was right or not.

But as she slipped into the barn, she saw that Elizabeth did know her son. A battery lantern provided a soft glow, and Ben leaned over the stall gate, patting the pony who was nearly as old as he was.

"Visiting with an old friend?" She tried for a normal tone and feared she didn't quite make it.

Ben acknowledged her presence with a short nod. Not very encouraging, but she moved next to him, reaching over to pat Dolly. The pony whickered and lipped at her hand, searching for a carrot.

"Greedy girl," she murmured. "I don't have anything for you just now."

"There's no point in talking." Ben was abrupt, not looking at her. "Nothing left to say."

"You're wrong there. Joshua has plenty he wants to say. He's so sorry he didn't take your advice he's nearly in tears. He feels he ruined everything."

Ben made a small dismissive gesture. "Probably would have turned out the same either way. It's not Josh's fault. Not Daad's either, for that matter. A couple of weeks at home can't make up for three years away."

The misery in his voice twisted her heart. "Give it time, Ben. Please."

His broad shoulders moved as if to shrug off the idea. "Maybe I never should have come back."

Again she felt the urge to shake someone. "Stop it," she snapped. "Did you think it would be easy? You can't give up at the first little obstacle." Ignoring her own pain, she glared at him.

For an instant Ben glared back, but then his expression eased. "Did I once think you were a quiet little mouse? I was wrong. You're more of a lion."

"Only about some things, like seeing the people I love hurt." She ventured to put her hand on his arm. "Please, Ben. Don't make your family go through that again."

He put his hand over hers, imprisoning her close to him. "What a big heart you have, Anna. You can forgive anyone. Even me."

The warmth of his hand against hers was making it difficult to think. "You didn't do it deliberately. If you found you'd made a mistake about me…"

"Is that what you've been thinking all this time?" He swung around so that their bodies were nearly touching, taking her breath away.

"Isn't that what happened?" Anna found the strength to meet his gaze steadily, even though her heart seemed to be pounding in her ears.

"No." His grip tightened painfully. "Anna, you have to believe me. It wasn't that."

"What was it, then?" If she'd had the breath, she'd have shouted the question. What else could she have thought, finding him gone hours after he'd said he loved her and wanted her to be his wife?

"I was just… I panicked. That's the truth. I thought about what it meant. How we'd get married, have kids, have the same life my parents did. The familiar path. But I'd give up my dreams of seeing the world. I'd never know what it was like out there." He jerked a nod to indicate the Englisch world.

She tried to absorb the idea. Didn't it amount to the same thing? He'd weighed marriage with her against the outside world, and she'd come up the loser.

"Anna," he said her name softly. "I'm sorry. I was an idiot."

"The world out there…was it worth it?"

His jaw tightened. "You know the answer to that, don't you? I came back. This is the life I want. But if it's too late…"

Impulsively she reached up to still the words with her fingers over his lips. "Don't. It's never too late unless you give up."

Something flared in his eyes. He took her hand in his. His lips moved, kissing her fingers, then moving to her palm. Then, his gaze holding hers, he moved his lips to the pulse that beat in her wrist.

Warmth swept her, welling up from deep inside. She

couldn't breathe, but she wanted the moment to last forever.

It didn't, of course. But then he stroked her cheek, and followed the trail left by his fingertips with his lips. She swayed toward him even as his arm slid around her and his mouth found hers.

This was no boy's fumbling kiss. It was the kiss of a man who longed for love. All her fears slid away, and she kissed him back with a fire she hadn't known she was capable of.

It might have been a moment or an hour before Ben drew back. She touched her lips, trembling with the joy of being together again.

Ben studied her face as if memorizing it. Finally he spoke. "Three years ago I wasn't mature enough to know what I had here. Now I am."

Her heart swelled, waiting for him to say the words. To say he loved her, he wanted to marry her.

But he didn't, and the moment passed. Instead he sighed and glanced in the direction of the farmhouse. "Guess I'd better go in and try to make peace. Go with me?"

She nodded, chiding herself for her foolishness. She was as greedy as the mare was, wanting everything at once. She must just be happy to know that his feelings for her hadn't changed. Suppressing the vague edge of disappointment, she focused on her happiness. They would be all right.

Chapter Eight

Making peace wasn't as straightforward as Ben had hoped. Mamm just wanted assurance that he wouldn't leave because of the dispute with his father, and he readily gave it, remembering Anna's tart scolding. Josh was suffering from guilt, angry with himself for precipitating the crisis.

"I didn't mean any harm." He met Ben's gaze with the penitent look he'd worn so often as the mischievous little brother when they were growing up. "I was impatient, and now I've spoiled everything for both of us."

Ben clasped his shoulder with a firm hand, giving him a slight shake. "Quit it. Things work out for the best, ain't so? Now at least Daad knows what you want. Give him time to cool off. I'll talk to him again—try to show him how important this is to you. He doesn't want you to be unhappy."

Josh leaned against the kitchen table and studied his face. "What about you? If I messed it up for you…"

"Don't be *ferhoodled*." Ben managed a smile he didn't feel. "I messed up my own life, and I can't expect it to be easy to fix." Again he thought of Anna, her cheeks flushed, her eyes snapping. "Whatever happens with me, it will be no more than I deserve. But Daad's always fair. He won't take it out on you once he calms down."

He hoped. Now to attempt to apologize to his father.

But Daad was elusive, busying himself silently with one chore after another. Ben finally got the message. He wasn't talking, not now. Maybe tomorrow. A night's sleep might put this business into better perspective.

When he walked into the dimly lit hallway, he surprised Anna, just starting up the stairs. She stopped, leaning over the banister, concern in every line of her body.

"Did you speak to your *daad*?" she asked, voice soft.

He shook his head, moving closer—close enough to reach out and touch her hand where it rested on the railing. "He's wonderful determined not to talk to me tonight. I'll try again tomorrow." He grimaced. "Christmas Eve. Maybe that will help."

Her fingers closed over his in a gesture of support. "He'll calm down. I know. Your *mamm* will help him see sense."

"Ach, Anna, are you sure you know what you're doing, getting involved with the likes of me?"

"I'm sure." She touched his cheek tentatively, and his heart seemed to leap. He covered her hand with his, pressing her palm against his skin.

Longing swept over him. All he had to do now was speak, and he knew what Anna's answer would be. They could name the date and put this painful waiting to an end.

No. It wasn't fair. How could he when his future was

so unsettled? To say nothing of his past. Until he had something to offer her, he had to wait.

"Good night, sweet Anna." He dropped a kiss on her palm. "Sweet dreams."

A flush rose in her cheeks. "I know what I'll dream of."

Then, as if startled by her own daring, she fled up the stairs.

By the time he rose in the predawn chill, Ben was hoping that Anna's night had been more restful than his. Pulling on his clothes and carrying his boots, he slipped out into the hallway in time to meet Josh emerging from his room, rumpling his hair and yawning.

"Go back to bed," Ben whispered. "I'll do the milking with Daad. It will give us a chance to talk."

Josh nodded. *"Da Herr sei mit du."*

God be with you, Ben repeated silently. That was what he'd been praying throughout the long night…for God to give him another chance to make things right.

When he got downstairs, Ben found that his father had already headed for the barn. Shrugging on his coat, he picked up one of the flashlights that hung next to the door and followed.

It was crisp and cold outside, with the feel of snow in the air. He crunched his way to the barn, his eyes quickly growing accustomed to the darkness.

Daad was already at work milking one of the black-and-white Holsteins. He'd talked sometimes about getting a larger dairy herd, but that would mean putting in milking machines and a cooler so he could sell to a dairy, and he'd never made the move.

"Sleep in, did you, Josh?" His voice was muffled by the cow he leaned against.

"It's not Josh. I told him to sleep in this morning." Grabbing a stool and a bucket, he moved to the next cow. Daad was silent for a moment.

"Think you remember how to do this?" he said finally.

"Worked on a farm out in Illinois for a time. That got me back into the way of it." His stint in Illinois had been when he'd been working his way homeward, even though he hadn't been sure of his intent himself at the time.

He blew on his hands to warm them and began the rhythmic pumping, enjoying the sound of the milk frothing into the pail. Three of the barn cats began circling him, purring loudly, so he squirted milk into a basin for them, smiling at their instant response as they gathered around, lapping it up.

Daad had lapsed into silence…a silence that lasted until they'd nearly finished. If they were going to talk about what had happened the previous day, it was obviously up to Ben to start.

"I wanted to say I'm sorry for arguing with you." He couldn't say he was sorry about his hopes to intercede in Josh's behalf, since that was just what he intended to do.

Daad didn't answer. Because he'd given up on Ben? Or because he was so firmly wedded to his plan for Josh that he wouldn't even discuss it?

"The farm is yours. You'll do whatever you want with it." Ben pressed down an edge of irritation at his father's silence. "I gave up any claim I might have had when I left, and I'm not asking you to change your mind about me. But I am asking you to give Josh a chance to do what he wants with his life."

"Farming is the best life for an Amish boy," Daad said, repeating the words he'd said so many times before.

"It might be the best life for you and for Daniel and for me, but not for Josh. Like Joseph and his carpentry business, Josh has other plans."

"Someone has to take over the farm. Daniel already has his own place."

"And Joseph has his business. You didn't stop them from doing what they loved." He fought to keep his voice even. It might be too late for him to have what he wanted, but surely not for Josh. "You can give the farm to Daniel's boy, if you want. I'll work it for him until he's old enough to take over. Just give Josh his chance, Daad. Please."

Ben held his breath. There wasn't anything else to say. If it hadn't been enough…

Daad got up, straightening, patting the Holstein absently. "Ach, maybe I was a bit hasty with the boy. I don't want to push him into something that doesn't suit him." He cleared his throat, not looking at Ben. "I'll think on it."

He'd have to be content with that, he supposed, but it was the best he could expect. Daad was deliberate, but he was fair.

"Let's get this milk to the house." Daad picked up two buckets. "If I know your *mamm*, she'll be in a tizzy to get everything ready to go to Daniel's place."

"Right." Holding on to the glimmer of hope, Ben picked up his two pails of milk.

They stepped outside to see the sky growing light

in the east. Over the western ridge, clouds gathered thickly. "Looks like snow coming." Ben slid the door shut.

"Wouldn't be surprised." Daad strode along smoothly, not spilling a drop as he went.

They were nearly to the house when Daad spoke again. "So, are you home to stay, Benjamin?"

"Ya, Daad." Home to stay—to go back to the church, make his confession and his vows, commit to live Amish the rest of his life.

But if he was truly to be right with God, he had to deal with his past, and that meant Mickey. Mickey wanted to see him, so the sooner the better. They could meet in town and have this over with once and for all.

From what Anna had been able to observe at the breakfast table, both Ben and his brother looked a bit less stressed. That surely meant that Ben's talk with his *daad* had given them hope.

Any chance of a private word with Ben slid away as Elizabeth sprang up from the table, intent on getting everything ready to head to Daniel's as early as possible. Anna privately thought that Daniel's wife might appreciate a quiet time this morning before the influx of family, but she was swept away inexorably on the wave of Elizabeth's determination.

Ben, stepping out of his mother's path, gave Anna the suggestion of a wink. *Later*, he mouthed silently, and she nodded, reassured.

Later proved to be midmorning, when Elizabeth had hurried upstairs to check over the stack of wrapped gifts in the corner of her bedroom. A peek out the back door showed Anna that Ben was approaching the house.

Grabbing her jacket from the peg, she stepped out to wait for him.

Ben increased speed when he saw her, taking the two steps to the porch in one long stride. After a quick glance around to be sure no one was watching, he clasped her hands in his. "How did you get away from Mamm?"

"Shh. She'll be back in a moment." She smiled up at him, convinced the news was good. "Well? Did you talk to your *daad*?"

Ben nodded. "Nothing's sure yet, but I think he's ready to consider Josh's plan. Now, if we can keep Josh from rushing into anything again, it will probably work out for him."

"And you? Will it work out for Benjamin, too?" She clasped his cold hands tighter.

A tiny line formed between his brows. "That's not… well, let's say we'll have to wait and see." He glanced down at their clasped hands. "Funny, that I never realized how much this place meant to me until I came back. Now…well, now I don't know what Daad will decide. I can't blame him for being slow to trust again, can I?"

There was a note of sorrow, maybe even of bitterness, in his words that she didn't miss. But before she could find a response, she heard Elizabeth calling from the kitchen.

Ben released her hands with his teasing grin. "Foiled again. We'd best go in."

Hoping Elizabeth would think her cheeks were red from the cold air, Anna hurried inside, intensely aware of Ben right behind her.

"There you are." Elizabeth looked upset. "I can't believe I did such a foolish thing. How could I?"

"What's wrong?" Anna hurried to her, alarmed.

"Ach, I told Barbie I'd bring the pickles and olives and vegetables for the relish tray, and I went and forgot to pick up the jars of olives when I was at the store."

Anna exchanged glances with Ben, trying to suppress a smile.

"That's a crisis for sure, Mamm." He came to hug her. "Christmas Eve will be ruined if we don't have olives, that's certain sure."

Elizabeth swatted at him. "Don't you go making fun of me, Benjamin. I promised I'd take care of it. Well, we'll have to go to town before we go to Daniel's, I suppose. But that will make us late, and I want to be there to help."

Ben planted a kiss on her cheek. "I'll take care of it. I told Daad I'd do the afternoon milking so he can go early with you. I can easily run into town and get them. How many do you want—two of each?"

Elizabeth reached up to pat his cheek. "Ach, you're a *gut* boy. Better make it three, ain't so?"

Anna could tell by his expression that he thought that was far more than needed, but he was wise enough not to argue. "Right. I'll take care of it and see you at Daniel's later." He hugged her. "And calm down. It's just family, after all."

"Family is the most important after faith," Elizabeth said firmly. "And don't you forget it."

Only the faintest flicker of an eyelash showed that he might have been hurt by the words. "I'll get going," he said. With a quick smile for Anna, he went out the back door.

"He is a *gut* boy," Elizabeth said softly, almost to herself. "Pray Asa sees it."

Anna nodded, not sure Elizabeth even noticed that she was still there.

Elizabeth seemed to shake herself. "Now we'll get everything packed up and...ach, what now?"

Anna hurried to take her cell phone from the shelf. A jumble of words assaulted her ear, so fast she could hardly make it out.

"Slow down, James. I can't understand you. Is Dora all right?"

Apparently Dora wrested the phone from her excited husband. "I... Can I see you, please, Anna? I've had some contractions, and Mamm Beachy says that's natural, but I..."

"I understand," she said quickly, raising her eyebrows at Elizabeth. "I'll *komm* right over. Is anyone else there besides you and James?"

"They already left for Onkel Amos's house. What?" This last was addressed to her husband, apparently. Then she came back on the line. "James says we'll *komm* to the center. That way if everything is all right, we can go on to his *onkel's* from there." Her voice seemed to tremble. "Please, Anna. I don't know..."

"It's no trouble at all," Anna said reassuringly. "I'll see you at the center."

She clicked off and turned to Elizabeth. "Did you get that? It's probably nothing, but I'll stay and check Dora. You go on to Daniel's."

"I don't want you driving alone when it looks like snow." Distressed, Elizabeth glanced toward the window. "Ach, what am I thinking. Ben will be coming later. Run and catch him before he leaves for town and tell him to pick you up at the center. Hurry, before he leaves." Elizabeth shooed her with both hands.

Knowing it would only stress Elizabeth more if she disputed her plans, Anna picked up her jacket again and dashed out the door.

She spotted Ben by the barn, standing next to the two-seat buggy. There was no need to hurry—he hadn't even brought out the gelding yet. Still, her eagerness for a private word had her feet scurrying across the frozen path to the barn.

It was only when she was within a few feet of him that she realized she was once more catching him unaware, as he talked on his cell phone. Determined not to make the same mistake again, she opened her mouth to given him warning of her presence. But the words froze in her throat when she heard what he was saying.

"...has to be now. I'll meet you in town in about half an hour." The other party must have spoken then because Ben was silent for a moment.

Now she should speak, but she couldn't find the words.

"Mickey, I can't take it any longer. I can't. It has to be today. Meet me. Don't let me down now."

She gasped then, unable to stop herself. It was as if something had smacked her right in the stomach, knocking the breath out of her entirely.

Ben pivoted, clicking off the call. His face tightened until it resembled something formed from the icicles that hung from the barn eaves. "Well, Anna?"

She had to speak, even though she felt her heart splintering. "I was supposed to tell you to pick me up at the birthing center later. But that won't happen, will it? Because you won't be here. You'll be off someplace with that Mickey you were talking to."

A muscle twitched in his jaw, as if out of his control.

He started to speak but she swept on, the blood pounding so loudly in her ears she could hardly hear.

"Who is she? Your Englisch girlfriend? How long were you going to pretend that you'd given all that up? How could you pretend about...about us?" She would not cry. Not yet. Not where he could see.

Ben's gaze flashed like lightning. "Made up your mind, haven't you? What happened to trust?"

She forced herself to look full in his face. "Trust is earned, Benjamin. I learned three years ago I couldn't trust you. I shouldn't have forgotten that so easily." Unable to hang on to her composure for another instant, she spun and hurried toward the house.

It had happened again. She had given Ben her heart, and he had broken it. The first flakes of snow, drifting down from a sullen sky, felt like tears on her cheeks.

Chapter Nine

Somehow Anna managed to control herself until after she'd seen Elizabeth, Asa and Josh off to Daniel's house. By then the need to weep or rage had passed, leaving her with a dry throat and stinging eyes.

She got her bag, checking to make sure she had everything she needed. Maybe she wouldn't make it to Daniel's at all for Christmas Eve. If so, that might be just as well. She didn't think she could bear to see joy turn to ashes when they realized Ben had left again.

A very faint flicker of hope touched her. He hadn't actually said he was leaving today. But he'd also said he couldn't stand it any longer. Meaning what? This life? Or her? It would have been better if she'd never seen Benjamin at all.

Pulling on her black gloves, she opened the back door and paused. The snow was falling thicker and faster than she'd realized. It must have accumulated an inch in the past half hour. If this kept up, plenty of people wouldn't get where they'd planned to be for Christmas Eve.

Trudging through the snow toward the birthing center, she felt none of the exhilaration that a fresh snowfall usually brought. Now she could only see it as a hazard.

When she reached the small building, Anna stamped the snow off her sturdy shoes and hurried to turn the heat up. The gas furnace came on with a reassuring murmur. Grateful for the blast of warmth, she stripped off her gloves and hung her outer garments up to dry. At least she didn't have to worry about the heat or light going off if the power lines went down, the way some of their Englisch neighbors would.

Anna bustled around, getting the room ready, checking the supply of sheets and towels for no reason at all except to keep her mind occupied.

It didn't help. She was still mentally following Ben on his way to the village of Lost Creek, the gelding clopping along through the snow.

Or would he have taken the car, which had been tucked away out of sight in one of the outbuildings since he'd returned? If he didn't intend to come back…

But no, surely she'd have noticed the sound of a car. She glanced at the businesslike watch every midwife needed. Would he be meeting his friend yet?

Friend. Girlfriend? Or more?

No point in torturing herself this way. Besides, that was the sound of a buggy drawing up to the hitching rail in front of the clinic.

Swinging her black shawl around her shoulders, she stepped out to greet them and frowned. The snow had been coming down fast a few minutes ago. Now it turned the ridge completely invisible, and when she looked down the valley she could no longer see the lights from the distant Englisch farms and houses.

Planting a smile on her face, Anna went to help

James bring Dora up the steps. Reassurance was the first task of the midwife, especially in a situation like this one. "I'm wonderful glad you got here with the snow getting so bad."

James cast a worried look back up the lane toward the road. "Nasty out, that's certain sure."

"Let's get Dora inside where it's warm and see what's happening." She smiled at Dora, seeing the fright in the girl's face. "Here we go."

Together they took her through the waiting room and into the exam room. James, after one nervous glance around, backed out to the waiting room instead.

"There now, if James isn't a typical first-time *daadi*." She assisted Dora to remove her outer clothes and get onto the bed that they used in preference to a more formal exam table.

"I'm *sehr* glad to see you." Dora clasped her hand. "Mamm Etta kept saying these feelings are just practice for the big day, but I can't help being worried. If the baby comes this early—"

"Now, Dora, this wouldn't be early at all. Remember what we told you. Two weeks either way is all right. Now just let me take a look, and we'll soon know."

It didn't take more than a few minutes to know what she was dealing with. Dora was indeed in labor, with the contractions stronger and closer together than she liked to see given the situation. Still, babies arrived when they were ready, snow or no snow.

"James," she called. "Will you *komm*, please?"

James's face was nearly as white as the sheet on the bed, but he came to take Dora's hand. "What…what?" He seemed to run out of words.

Anna focused on their faces, trying to make them

feel her assurance. "Dora's right. It looks as if you're going to have your baby for Christmas."

"But…but…it can't be," James protested. "Mamm says the baby won't be born for another week or more."

Anna pushed down a wave of exasperation, but before she could say anything, Dora did.

"This is our baby," she snapped. "Not your *mamm*'s. The baby is coming. I know."

For a moment he looked taken aback. Then he straightened and gave a crisp nod. "Ya. So what do we do?"

"Since the weather is so bad," she spoke carefully, not wanting to alarm them, "it may be best if we call the emergency squad. They should be able to get through. Otherwise, you may be stuck here until the roads are cleared. All right?"

Dora's face crumpled. "But I don't want to go clear to the hospital. I want to have my baby right here, close to home."

"I know," Anna soothed. "That's what we want for you, too." As tears threatened to overcome Dora, she added, "Let's just call and see what they say about getting here, all right? Then we can decide."

Dora hesitated, then nodded.

Anna stepped away from the bed to retrieve her cell phone. Dora was fine and healthy, and normally there'd be no question of calling anyone to help. But she and Elizabeth were in agreement that they'd call for assistance if any problems arose. She just feared that if she waited, help might not get here in time.

But a glance at the phone took the decision out of her hands. She held up the cell phone to show James. "No service. The weather must be interfering."

James's face tightened. "I'll go myself. The land lines might still be working at one of the farms down the valley."

"No! What if something happened to you? What would I do?" Dora sat up, grabbing his hand, and almost as quickly gasped at the onset of another contraction.

James held her hand in both of his, and Anna seemed to see him turning from an uncertain boy into a man in that moment.

"Hush, now. Nothing will happen to me. It's my job to take care of you and the *boppli*, ain't so? You just listen to Anna, and I'll be back with help before you know it."

Anna nodded. "Take care, now. And be sure to tell the emergency people that it's a first baby and I requested assistance because we might be cut off by the snow." She walked to the door with him as he bundled up against the cold. "God be with you."

James's young face was resolute. "I'll get help. Just… just take care of my Dora." Not waiting for a response, he plunged out into the snow.

Anna let out a long breath. The decision was made. She could only pray that it was the right one and that God would guide her every action this night.

As Anna might have predicted, James's departure sent Dora into a fit of anxiety. She moved restlessly, unable to be still.

"Something will happen to James. I know it will. Or the baby. What if something goes wrong with the baby?" she wailed.

Anna clasped both her hands, forcing her to listen. "*Stoppe*. You are tiring yourself out, and that won't help you or the baby. When the time comes, you have to be strong enough to push. The best thing now is for you to rest a bit between contractions."

"I can't." Dora tried to pull away.

"Ya, you can," she said firmly. Ordinarily she'd encourage walking at this stage, but calming Dora took priority at the moment. "Lean back against the pillow now, and just listen."

Somewhat to her surprise, Dora obeyed, her anxious gaze fixed on Anna's face. With another silent prayer for guidance, Anna began to talk. She kept her voice low and soothing, focusing all her love and attention on the frightened girl. She talked about the baby, about the joy he or she would bring into their lives. She encouraged Dora to tell her about James's courtship. Slowly, by tiny degrees, the tension drained out of Dora. Relaxing, she stopped fighting her body, resting and letting Anna coach her through the contractions.

Eventually Dora fell into a light doze. Anna stood, stretching. She tiptoed to the window and peered out, but she couldn't see a thing. Except that the snow was still falling, steadily cushioning the world, enveloping it in stillness.

Not so still, she realized suddenly. Someone was moving on the porch. Could James have gotten back already? She hurried to the door.

It opened before she reached it to admit a snow-covered figure. Stamping and brushing off snow, he turned.

"Ben! What are you doing here?"

Heedless of her question, he shed his gloves and grasped her hands. "Are you all right? When I heard you were out here by yourself…"

Irrational joy swept over Anna. Ben was here. Whatever he might intend to do in the future, he'd come back now out of concern for her.

"I'm fine." She glanced toward the other room. "Dora Beachy is here. The baby's coming, and James went to try and get through to the rescue squad. Is that how you knew?"

Ben shook his head. "When I saw how bad it was getting, I checked with Daniel to see if everyone had gotten there. They had—everyone but you. So I came."

He said it so simply, as if there had been no question of any other choice.

"But how? It's so bad out." She helped him shed the heavy, soaked jacket.

"Made it as far as Thompson's place with the horse and buggy, but the drifts were getting too bad. I left the horse there. They'd have brought me on the snowmobile, but Frank Thompson had already taken it to get James to someplace where he could call the rescue squad."

"James is all right, then. Thank the *gut* Lord. But how could you walk in this snow?" Her heart shuddered at the thought of him trudging through the blinding snow and darkness. "You could have been lost..." Her throat closed on a sob.

"Not a chance. Once I saw your light I just kept walking toward it." He took her hands again, holding them securely in his. "Toward you."

Anna's heart seemed to swell. He had come to her. Their foolish quarrel hadn't been the end. She didn't even need an explanation for that phone call. She just needed to know that he'd put her first.

"Anna, I have to tell you..." He broke off at a voice from the other room.

"Anna? Is that James? Is he safe?"

With an effort, Anna drew her hands from his clasp and hurried to Dora. "It's not James, it's Ben. But he says James is fine. One of the Thompson boys took him on their snowmobile to get help."

Dora's face brightened. "I knew he'd get through. My James can do anything he sets his mind to."

"That's right." Anna checked her deftly and listened to the baby's heartbeat. "Nice and strong," she said in answer to Dora's anxious gaze.

Dora's eyes widened as a new contraction began. For an instant she lost focus, and Anna recalled her gently, coaching her through it.

"The baby is getting serious," Anna said, smoothing Dora's hair back from her face. "We have some work ahead of us, ain't so?"

Dora managed a smile for the first time since she'd arrived. "Guess so."

"Anna?" Ben ventured far enough to lean in the open doorway. "Anything I can do to help?" He sounded as if he hoped she would say no.

"Start some water heating in the kettle," she instructed. "I may want to brew some herbal tea. And then you can put a blanket to warm in front of the heater." She gave him a reassuring smile. "Don't worry. I won't ask you to catch the baby. That's my job."

Even Dora chuckled at his expression, but then she took on that listening expression Anna had seen so often before in expectant *mammis*. It was as if what was happening inside their bodies was miles more important than anything outside.

A pang of envy went through her with the longing to experience it herself, but this time it was mixed with just a little hope. Maybe, one day…

* * *

Ben had more than one opportunity in the next hour to think that he might be better off out in the snow. But then he'd look at Anna and know how foolish that was. He was here, with her. And if he could help her in any way, he'd happily fetch and carry and try to keep his mind off what she was doing.

Ben tried telling himself that this was like watching a calf or a lamb or any other creature coming into the world. It didn't seem to help much.

Focus on helping Anna, he ordered himself. *That's all you can do now.*

Time ran into itself. Was the night lasting forever, or was it moving at incredible speed? Dora's small face was beaded with sweat, and he wiped it with a towel without being asked. She shot him a thankful look before returning to that fierce concentration that seemed to shut out everything else.

"We're getting close," Anna said, her tone still invincibly cheerful. "Dora, I want you to hold on to Ben's hands. Pull against them as hard as you can when you feel the urge. Don't worry. You won't hurt him."

Dora nodded and grabbed him, fingers clenching so that he felt them bite into his palms. He hung on and looked to Anna for reassurance.

"She won't mind my being here?" he asked quietly.

Anna smiled, shaking her head. "She's too busy to notice who's here, as long as she has someone to hang on to."

She seemed to be right. Dora accepted him almost without seeing him as she put all her strength into a push.

"Great, Dora. Just great. Here's the baby's head."

Anna was focused, her hands deft and strong. "One more push now."

Somehow, Ben wasn't sure how, Dora mustered the strength for another push.

"Easy, breathe now, the way I showed you. Don't push for a moment." Anna sounded calm, but somehow he sensed something was happening.

Dora did, as well. "What's wrong? Is something wrong with my baby?"

"Nothing at all," Anna soothed. "I'm just turning him or her a tiny bit to make it easier, that's all."

He kept his gaze on his Anna's face as he sent up a silent prayer. *Please, God...*

"All right. Just one more push now."

One more, and he couldn't keep himself from looking just in time to see the baby slide out into Anna's hands. For a long moment there was silence, and then an outraged cry sounded lustily. Dora was crying, too, and smiling as well, and it was all he could do to blink back tears himself.

Anna brought the squalling little being to Dora, putting it gently on her chest. "It's a girl. You have a fine, strong baby girl."

Dora's arms circled her child, her face transformed.

His eyes met Anna's across the width of the bed and her face was transformed as well. "We did it," she murmured. "*Denke*, Ben."

He shook his head. "Not me. You did it all."

Funny. He'd grown up knowing that his mother was a midwife, but he'd never really appreciated it until now.

Chapter Ten

It was nearly an hour before Anna had both *mammi* and baby settled. She slipped quietly into the adjoining room, leaving the door open to hear the slightest sound. Ben was leaning back in a desk chair, feet propped on a pulled-out drawer, his eyes closed. She moved a little nearer, a wave of tenderness sweeping over her. He must be exhausted after battling his way through the storm and then helping her deliver a baby. She should let him sleep.

Before she could move away, Ben reached out and caught her wrist, his eyes opening. "*Komm*, sit," he said. "I've been keeping the kettle hot for you." He rose and pushed her gently into a chair. "I'll bring you some tea."

She would argue, but the chair seemed to welcome her, making her realize how tired she was. When Ben brought the tea, she wrapped her hands around the mug thankfully.

"How are they?" He nodded toward the bed.

"Just fine. Both sleeping." Anna stretched her back and then took a thirsty gulp from her mug. "Is it still snowing outside?"

"Slacking off a bit at the moment, but I'd guess this snowfall will go in the record books," he said, settling into the chair he pulled up next to hers. "No signal on the cell phone yet."

"It's a shame we can't let James know everything's all right. He'll be worried." She pushed back a strand of hair that had come free, wondering how disheveled she looked after the long hours.

"Worried," Ben echoed. He captured her hand in his. "Like I was."

Anna's cheeks flushed. "You shouldn't have risked so much to get here."

"I had to." He moved his fingers on the back of her hand, sending warmth through her. "I had to tell you I was sorry for the way I spoke."

"Ach, no." How could he think that? "I'm the one to be sorry. I didn't trust you. I didn't let you explain." Her voice grew husky on the words as her throat tightened. In response, Ben lifted her hand and kissed her wrist just where her pulse beat heavily.

"Not your fault. Mine. I was the one who was too proud to explain." He shook his head. "Stupid. I should have known I could tell you anything."

"You can," she said, feeling her way, "but you don't have to." She realized quite suddenly that she could say the important words without doubt. "I trust you."

He sent her a questioning glance, seeming relieved at what he read in her face. "It's not surprising that you didn't feel you could, after the way I ran out on you."

"Hush." She put her fingers over his mouth. "You told me about it. I understand."

"I told you why I left. I didn't tell you what happened out there." A nod of his head indicated the out-side world. "I didn't tell you who Mickey is."

"You don't have to…" she began.

"I want to." Ben actually looked surprised at himself. "I never thought to tell a soul, but I want you to know."

She had to clear her throat before she could get the words out. "Tell me, then." She wouldn't judge him. Whatever it was, she would understand.

"Mickey was an Englisch kid I got to know when I was a teenager. His family lived in that fancy development over on the other side of Lost Creek."

"He?" Anna said involuntarily.

"Ya, a guy," he said, smiling a little at her relief. "We always talked about hitching our way across the country together, seeing the world. Nothing ever came of it, though. And then that summer three years ago he was back in town, and we got together. Seemed his father wanted him to go on to graduate school, become a lawyer like his *daad* was. Mickey felt like life was getting away from him, and he hadn't done all the things he'd planned. As if his future was all planned out for him."

"The way you felt that last night," Anna said softly, pushing away her own pain at the memory.

He nodded, and she could read the shame in his face. "So you can guess the rest. We took off, making our way west, just bumming around and seeing what we wanted. Mickey had a car and money, and it seemed like we were free."

He stopped, as if not sure how to go on, and Anna knew he had come to the difficult thing—the thing he'd been hiding all along.

"Then something went wrong," she said. "What was it?"

He gripped her hand as tightly as Dora had gripped his when the baby was coming. "It was stupid, I guess. Mickey thought a guy at a store where we stopped had ripped him off. He was steamed about it. He told me to wait in the car for him, and he went back. He said he was just going to tell the guy off. Instead he took the money he figured was owed him."

Anna couldn't suppress a gasp. "He stole?"

"He didn't see it that way," Ben said grimly. "But the police did. Both of us ended up in jail."

"Ach, Ben, I'm so sorry." Her fingers caressed his cheek, hoping she could smooth away the tension. "But *you* didn't do anything wrong."

"No. But…" His face showed the pain that had him in its hold. "We were supposed to go before the judge, and Mickey panicked. All he could think was what his father would do when he found out. If he was convicted that would destroy his chances of ever being a lawyer, and all of a sudden, when he thought he couldn't have it, he knew how much it meant to him." He pressed her hand against his cheek. "Like me, when I came back and realized the farm would never belong to me."

"He wanted you to take the blame." Anna figured it out without his saying it, and her heart ached for him.

He nodded. "Stupid, I guess. But at the time…well, it seemed like I was losing everything anyway, so what difference did it make? Mickey was convinced it would just mean a fine. He'd pay that, and we could walk away."

"It didn't happen like that?" Her heart seemed to be breaking for him.

"The judge sentenced me to seven months in the county jail." He said the words flatly. "Mickey paid the costs. He wanted to give me money, too, but I didn't want it."

"No, you wouldn't." She sought for the words he needed to hear. "It must have been so terrible for you. How could you stand it, being locked up for something you didn't do?"

Ben's mouth twisted. "It was no picnic. Some days I thought I'd go crazy with wanting to walk through a field instead of a concrete exercise yard. But I made it. I had to."

"Why, Ben? Why didn't you come home after you got out of jail?" The words burst out of her.

He shrugged. "Too stubborn. Too proud. I didn't want to admit what a fool I'd been. I thought I wouldn't be welcome. It took me all this time to swallow my pride and admit what I really wanted was to be home again."

For the first time she truly realized why the church considered pride such a sin. It separated you from those who loved you, including God.

"You are home now. That's what counts." She held his hands in both of hers, longing to make him believe her words. "This fuss with your *daad* will settle down. I'm sure of it."

She hesitated, but there was one more thing he probably needed to say. "About those calls from Mickey..."

Ben grimaced. "Maybe he's grown up a bit, like I have. He feels like he owes me something. He wanted to ask my forgiveness." For a moment he was quiet, and she longed to know what he was thinking. "I finally saw that if I was going to come back to my life here, I needed to see Mickey. I couldn't go back to the church without settling my anger with him." He looked into Anna's eyes. "I couldn't ask you to marry me until I'd settled the unfinished business of the past. I had to tell him I forgave him."

Relief swept through her. "And have you?"

"I have." Her heart seemed to heal again at his expression. "Anna Zook, I asked you once to marry me. Now I'm asking you again. Will you marry me?"

A smile teased at her lips. "I only needed once, Benjamin. Ya, I will marry you."

Ben stood, drawing Anna up with him, and pulled her into his arms, and she felt that she, too, had come home.

Several very satisfying kisses later he pulled back just enough to see her face. "I wish I knew what I had to offer you, my Anna. If I'm not to have the farm, I'll have to look for something else."

"It doesn't matter." She was strong in the confidence of his love. "Whatever the future brings, we will handle it. We'll build a life together whether it's here or somewhere else."

He grinned. "Just promise me I won't have to see any more babies being born."

"Only our own," she said, her cheeks flushing. "You won't mind that, will you?"

He drew her close against him, and she longed for the day they would be truly one. "No, I won't mind," he said.

They were still standing close together when the first rays of the rising sun crept over the ridge and brightened the eastern sky. A moment later they heard the roar of a snowplow.

With his hand clasping hers, Ben peered out the front window. "A snowplow, an EMT truck and a police car. It looks like help has arrived in force." He squeezed her hand. "You'll have to tell them that you did fine without their help."

Heart lifting, Anna smiled. "I *had* help." *Thank You, Lord.*

The day after Christmas was known in the Amish world as Second Christmas, a day for visiting with friends and relatives and rejoicing together. As far as Anna could tell, everyone seemed to know already about her and Ben. No one actually said anything, but the knowing glances and frequent smiles gave the secret away.

A steady stream of people had been braving the snowy roads to stop at the house, and Elizabeth was in her element, pressing food and drink on all of them.

As she headed for the kitchen yet again, Anna intercepted her. "You've been on your feet all day. Let me put more coffee on or set out cookies or whatever it was you intended to do."

Elizabeth surprised her with a hug. "I'm so wonderful happy today that I could go on forever, I think." She glanced around to be sure that no one could hear them. "Asa wants to tell Ben himself, but I can't keep it from you, not now. Asa says that with you taking over more of the midwife practice and Ben here to take over the farm, come spring we'll get started on building a *daadi haus* next to this one."

The first thing that registered with Anna was what she'd said about Ben. "You mean it? The farm will go to Ben?"

Elizabeth gave the quick nod that was so typical of her when she was pleased. "Asa sees that Josh is so determined that there's no dissuading him from the job he wants. And he says he's not so *ferhoodled* that he can't see Ben is here to stay now." She squeezed Anna again. "It is just what I always hoped would happen. No one could have given me a happier Christmas. Now you go and visit with folks. I don't need any help just now."

What she wanted to do was to give Ben the good news, but mindful that Asa wanted to do it himself, she contained herself. Still, she maybe should stay clear of Ben for a bit or she'd let the secret out for sure.

A bustle at the door announced the arrival of more visitors, coming in on a tide of cold air and cheerful chatter. Anna blinked at the sight of Etta Beachy and her husband. They were not usual Second Christmas visitors, being neither neighbors nor relatives.

Anna took a step backward. She hadn't seen Etta since the birth of Dora's baby, and she wasn't sure she wanted to encounter her now. Another stealthy step, and she backed right into Ben's strong figure. He steadied her with a hand on her elbow and leaned close to whisper in her ear.

"You're not looking for a place to hide, are you?" he murmured. "After all, this is your home. Our home, in fact."

She spun to meet his gaze. "Your *daad* told you?"

His eyes danced. "Ya. And I see Mamm couldn't resist telling you, ain't so? Have you seen how happy Josh is looking?"

"He'll be as happy as we are." The joy that bubbled up in her just had to be shared.

Ben shook his head. "He couldn't possibly be as happy as I am right now. And you…"

He was interrupted by a rush of movement behind her. The next instant Anna was enveloped in an enormous hug. "Ach, Anna Zook, you are just the person I wanted to see. Our little granddaughter is doing fine, thanks to you, and she's the prettiest newborn I ever saw in my life." Etta's ruddy face beamed with pleasure. "I always said you are a wonderful fine midwife."

Anna heard a chuckle behind her and felt sure that Ben was on the verge of saying something she'd rather he didn't. She gave him a quick nudge with her elbow, not daring to meet his eyes.

"I'm glad they're doing so well. Will they be home soon?"

"Tomorrow, the doctor at the hospital says. Not that we needed him, but with the weather so bad, it was best to be on the safe side, ain't so?"

It was hard to keep a straight face when Ben was standing so close and barely containing himself, but she managed. "Tell Dora we'll stop by to see her in a few days."

"Gut, gut." Etta sent a sly glance from her to Ben. "I hear tell we'll be celebrating with the two of you before long, too. You're just what Benjamin needs, ain't so?" Before either of them could say a word, she'd whisked off to greet someone else.

Anna turned to Ben. "Don't you dare laugh at her," she said. "I like her much better this way."

"I wouldn't dream of laughing." He drew her out of the flow of traffic. "I agree with her. You're just what I need." His intent gaze brought a flush to her face. "And the sooner the better."

For an instant she was afraid he'd kiss her right there in front of everyone, but he didn't. "Happy Christmas, Anna," he murmured softly.

"Happy Christmas, Ben." Joy lent wings to her

words. This truly was the happiest Christmas she'd ever had, and with God's blessing, she and Ben would have many more to share together.

* * * * *

A CHRISTMAS TO REMEMBER

Jo Ann Brown

For my family
Thanks for keeping the Christmas traditions
we share alive

Can two walk together, except they be agreed?
—*Amos* 3:3

Chapter One

From where he stood in the darkened store, Amos Stoltzfus watched a small hand rising over the edge of the shelf. Tiny fingers inched around one of the loaves of bread on display at the front of Amos's grocery store. They vanished, both the fingers and the bread, and soft footfalls rushed toward the front door.

Pushing away from the counter where he'd been arranging bottles of the honey Hannah Lambright had brought in from her hives earlier, Amos cut down the other aisle. He reached the door as the tiny thief came around the corner by the milk cooler.

The little girl didn't look more than four or five. The top of her head wouldn't reach Amos's waist. Her blond hair was neatly braided, and the *kind*'s clothing appeared to be new. There were no holes visible where her blue dress hung below her wool coat. The toes of her black sneakers were scuffed, but the wear was slight.

Someone took *gut* care of the little girl. So why was she trying to steal a loaf of bread? Occasionally one of the local teens would try on a dare to take something from the store without paying for it, but Amos had learned to recognize the warning signs. The nervous way the kid refused to meet his eyes or how the would-be thief wandered around the store waiting for an opportunity to snatch and flee.

Had someone put this *kind* up to a prank while Amos was closing the store? What a low thing to do!

He glanced out the window, but the parking lot was lost in shadow. Darkness fell early as the first day of winter approached. He couldn't determine if someone was waiting there for the girl.

"Hello, young lady," Amos said.

The *kind* stared at him with big blue eyes as she held the bread behind her back. "Hewwo," the child said with a definite lisp that suggested she was younger than she looked.

"Can I help you?"

"No." She shook her head, sending strands of fine golden hair into her eyes. As she raised a hand to wipe it away, she gasped and stared at the loaf she held.

"Wouldn't you like a bag for the bread?" Amos asked. "It may seem not heavy now, but it'll get heavier each step you take beyond the door."

The girl looked from Amos to the bread. Stuffing it onto the nearest shelf, she ran toward the door.

"Wait," Amos said.

The *kind* halted, a sure sign she was reared in a *gut* home. When she looked at Amos, tears glistened on her cheeks.

His heart threatened to break at the terror on the little girl's face. No *kind* should ever have to display such dismay and fear. "Don't you want some peanut butter to go with your bread?" He smiled at the little girl. "Bread is pretty boring without something on it."

She sniffed and rubbed her knuckles against her nose before wiping away tears.

Collecting the bread and taking a jar of peanut butter off a nearby rack, Amos put them in one of the cloth bags his customers preferred. He held it out to the little girl. "Pay me when you can. If you can't, do something nice for someone else. Our Lord teaches us: *give, and it shall be given unto you.*"

The *kind* regarded him, confused, and Amos knew the little girl was thinking only of getting away.

"Take it," he urged. He must look like a giant to her. Though he wasn't the tallest of the seven Stoltzfus brothers, he towered over the little girl.

"Danki," the *kind* whispered. *"Danki,* mister."

"Amos. My name is Amos." He smiled. "If you want, I've got some silverware. You can make a sandwich for yourself before you leave. You won't be delaying me. I need to finish sweeping up."

The girl shook her head and grabbed the doorknob. Turning it, she threw the door open and fled, the bag slapping her short legs.

Amos was surprised when the little girl sped in front of the doors opening into the rest of the businesses at the Stoltzfus Family Shops, the buggy shop and the woodworking and carpentry shops his brothers ran. He'd expected her to race along the road.

His eyes widened when he saw someone move as the little girl skidded to a stop. In the faint light from his brother Joshua's buggy shop, a silhouette of a slender woman emerged from the darkness near the hitching rail used by their plain customers. She put her hand on the girl's shoulder.

What was going on?

Amos paused long enough to grab a flashlight from a nearby display. He strode toward the woman and the little girl. He saw the *kind* whirl and point at him, but neither the woman nor the girl spoke. He struggled to tamp down the outrage rising through him at the thought of a grown woman sending a *kind* to do her dirty work.

He aimed the light at the woman. She was dressed plainly. Like the *kind*, she had a dark coat on. Beneath it, she wore a dark cranberry dress. A black bonnet revealed her hair was as blond as her brows. Her eyes were paler than the *kind*'s, but navy ringed the irises.

Pretty. The unbidden thought formed before he could halt it. However, he took it as a warning. His head had been turned by a lovely woman once, turned round and round until he was too dizzy to think straight. He'd offered her his heart, and she'd spurned him. That had been five years ago, but he'd learned his lesson. Only a fool would be taken in by beautiful eyes and the curve of enticing cheekbones.

"Did you send her into my store to steal?" he asked, anger lacing through his question.

"Who are you?" The woman stared at him with candid curiosity.

"Amos Stoltzfus, and that's my store where your young friend was trying to sneak out with a loaf of bread." He spoke more sharply than he should have, and the woman recoiled.

"No! That's wrong!" She looked at the *kind*. "Were you in the store?"

Before the little girl could answer, Amos demanded, "Why are you letting such a little *kind* out of your sight? It's dark, and *Englischers* often drive their vehicles into the parking lot really fast. She could have been hit!"

"I know." She put a hand to her forehead and rubbed it, then winced. "But I don't know."

"What are you talking about?"

The little girl tugged on the woman's coat and lisped, "Winda."

Or that was what Amos thought the *kind* said until the woman met his gaze. "She means Linda. She tells me my name is Linda and hers is Polly."

"Tells you? I don't understand."

"I've got to assume she's right about our names because I don't remember anything before a half hour ago."

Linda struggled to focus her eyes, which blurred each time she blinked. She saw shock on Amos Stoltzfus's shadowed face. That incredulity was something she needed to get used to, because he wouldn't be the only one horrified she couldn't remember her name or the *kind*'s name when she'd come to herself less than an hour ago. Everything before that was lost in a thick fog.

Her memories must exist. She wasn't a newborn *boppli*. She had no idea what had happened and why she couldn't remember. Was Polly her daughter or her sister or someone else's *kind*? They must have known each other for a while because the little girl acted comfortable around her.

It might be easier to think if her head didn't ache. The pain centered near her right ear, but swelled across her forehead. Her headache made her eyes lose focus and set everything spinning.

"What happened to you?" Amos asked.

"I wish I could tell you." Every word was a struggle, but some sense she couldn't identify warned she needed to stay awake. She must not allow the pain to suck her down. "I remember walking here and deciding to take a break by the hitching rail. That's it until Polly came with you chasing after her."

She wondered if he understood she hadn't realized the little girl had entered the store. It seemed that one minute, the *kind* had been beside her; then she wasn't. Then she returned with Amos. How long had Polly been gone?

He held out a cloth bag. "Here's some bread and peanut butter. I offered to let her eat in the store while I finish cleaning for the day. You're both welcome to come inside."

"Danki." She glanced toward the road and winced as the motion set off a new tidal wave of pain. She tried to ignore it as she reached for the bag. Her fingers closed inches from it. A groan burst from her lips.

Amos put a strong, steady hand under her elbow as Polly cried out her name. Linda realized she was swaying. She closed her eyes and concentrated on keeping her balance.

What's wrong with me? Lord, help me.

"Are you okay?" she heard Amos ask.

"I will be." She stepped away, taking care not to tumble over her feet. Looking into his brown eyes, she murmured, *"Danki* for the food."

He frowned. "It's going to snow. You can't stay here. Do you have somewhere to go?"

She pondered his question and looked at Polly who was watching with dismay. "I must, but I don't know where."

"We're going to see *Grossmammi* and *Grossdawdi,"* Polly said.

Amos hunkered down beside the little girl, and Linda noticed his hair, in the glow from the flashlight, was brown with ruddy streaks. "That sounds like a lot of fun."

"Ja." The little girl nodded so hard Linda had to look away before her eyes unfocused completely.

"You know Linda's name. Do you know the names of your grandparents?"

"Ja." She sounded disgusted that he'd asked such a question.

"Gut for you," Amos said with a smile. "I should have known a big girl like you would know. Will you tell me their names?"

"Ja. Grossmammi and *Grossdawdi."* She grinned with pride.

As he stood, Amos's expression didn't change. He kept smiling, and she guessed he didn't want to upset Polly. He must be a nice man. Or was he? She didn't know if she was a good judge of character or not.

Why have I lost everything, Lord? The anguish came from her heart.

"I assume you don't know their names either, Linda," he said.

"No." It was easier to admit than she'd expected. Or maybe she was too tired and achy and lost to pretend.

"You can't stay here overnight. Once the snow starts—"

When he looked past her, she shifted to see snow-flakes drifting in an aimless pattern. They melted as soon as they touched the asphalt parking lot, but more followed.

Polly gave an excited yell and whirled about, trying to catch them on her tongue. Joy flowed in her laughter.

Linda smiled faintly. Every change of expression sent pain along her face, but it was impossible not to be captivated by the little girl's happiness.

"That settles it," Amos said as he turned off his flashlight, leaving them in the thick gray twilight. "You two will have to go home with me."

"What?" All inclination to smile vanished. What sort of woman did Amos Stoltzfus think she was? Why would he assume that she'd agree to such an arrangement with a stranger? A sob caught in her throat. She was a stranger to *herself*, too.

He held up his hands as if to keep her dismay at bay. "Before I offered the invitation, I should have told you that I live with my *mamm* and some of my brothers." He pointed to the doors of the other shops. "My brothers own these businesses. Our farm is outside the village. There are empty bedrooms since a few of my brothers and sisters have married. You're welcome to stay until…"

She understood what he didn't want to say. *You're welcome to stay until you remember everything.* What if she never did? She'd lost more than her memories. She'd lost herself, everything she was and everything she hoped to be.

"It's snowing, Winda! Isn't it *wunderbaar*?" Polly grasped her hands and nearly jarred Linda off her feet.

Amos's hand on her elbow kept her standing. In not much more than a whisper, because she guessed he didn't want Polly to hear, he said, "She needs to get out of the cold."

"Ja." Linda edged away from Amos's fingers which sent a sensation through her that was *not* cold. How could she be drawn to him now?

"*Komm* in while I finish. After that, we'll head to my family's house."

What choice did she have? Even if she could remember where she and the *kind* were bound, she didn't know how they'd get there on a snowy night.

Calling to Polly to join them, Linda looked at the tall man whose face she couldn't see clearly. "Can I ask you a question, Amos?"

"*Ja.* Ask as many as you wish."

"Where are we?"

His voice was gentle as he replied, "Paradise Springs in Lancaster County in Pennsylvania. That's near—"

"I know where Lancaster County is."

"You do?"

She gave him a weak smile. "Somehow I know things like that, but don't know anything about myself. Strange, isn't it?" She hesitated, then asked, "What day is it?"

"Thursday."

"No, I mean what's the date?"

"December 14th."

"Oh." She wasn't sure what else to say. Curiosity had spurred her questions, but she didn't know what to do with the answers.

"Go now?" Polly asked. "I'm cowd."

Linda shivered. She was cold, too.

"And you're hungry, too, Polly, ain't so?" Amos grinned.

"*Ja!*" The little girl jumped up and down in excitement.

"What do you say to some sandwiches to tide us over until supper, Linda?" he asked.

She opened her mouth to answer, but no words

emerged. Everything and everyone in front of her rippled like a puddle in the rain. The edges of her vision darkened. She thought she heard someone call her name as firm arms kept her from collapsing, but the sound, the arms and the rest of the world vanished into blackness.

Chapter Two

Linda opened her eyes and stared at a white ceiling. No rafters or water stains broke the painted expanse. A propane lamp hung from the center, its flame turned low. She started to move her head, but pain exploded like a sky filled with fireworks behind her eyes. She squeezed them shut and rode the wave of pain until it eased.

Fireworks…

She remembered fireworks. Maybe from the Fourth of July. Standing by a fence and watching them detonate in the distance. Waiting for the bang to follow almost a minute later. The heat of a humid summer day and the smell of freshly cut grass and a charcoal fire. Hamburgers? *Ja*, but when she tried to recreate more of the scene to see where she stood and who else was there, the fragments of memory vanished as if they'd never existed.

Tears filled her eyes. She refused to let them slip past her lashes to fall down her face. Why was she crying? What filled her mind could have been something she read or someone else had described to her. The tantalizing bits of memory might not be her own. *Focus on the here and now*, she told herself. *Guide me, Lord, until I find my way.*

When she opened her eyes a second time, she looked around. She was in a living room if she were to guess by the furniture. A braided rag rug was on the floor in front of a fireplace. A gas fireplace, she realized when she noted how the fire came from behind the logs rather than within them.

A clock ticked steadily. She hoped it wouldn't chime. That would be agony.

Closer she saw a low table. On top was a bowl filled with water. A cloth hung over its edge, and she realized another damp cloth was draped across her forehead. For a moment, she savored its gentle warmth, letting it sink into her.

"How are you doing, Linda?" asked a woman.

Her eyes struggled to bring the woman sitting beside her into focus. Concern was vivid on the woman's face as she wrung the cloth from the bowl and used it to replace the one on Linda's forehead.

"I don't know," Linda replied as she examined the woman's features, desperate to know her.

Someone else spoke. "Don't try to recognize where you are." The deep voice, though the words were soft, resonated through her. She knew that voice! "You've never been here before, and you've never met my *mamm*, Wanda Stoltzfus, before."

She turned her head on the pillow and fought not to wince. Amos Stoltzfus leaned one shoulder against a staircase. His arms were crossed over his chest, and his face was drawn. She couldn't keep from smiling. Not only was he familiar, but his words were the kindest ones she could imagine.

She *had* been struggling to place this room and the woman. Despite knowing her memories were lost, she'd longed to see something she knew.

Some*one*.

And Amos understood. She appreciated his words more than she could have guessed. He walked toward her, and she was amazed such a tall man was able to walk lightly in work boots.

Tears welled into her eyes at his unspoken kindness, surprising her. Was she usually sentimental, or was weakness causing her eyes to fill? Another question she couldn't answer.

He knelt by the sofa. "My name is—"

"I remember your name." The tears bubbled to the edge of her eyelashes at the words she'd feared she'd never use again. They tasted as sweet as the year's first strawberries. "Amos Stoltzfus. You work at a store."

He smiled. "That's right."

"I was there. With Polly!" She tried to push herself up. "Where's Polly?"

"She's fine." Wanda put a gentle hand on her shoulder. "Amos brought you and Polly here." Wanda smiled, and Linda saw the resemblance between *mamm* and son. Something around the eyes and the way their lips tilted when they grinned. Amusement laced through her voice as she added, "He figured one of us women here would know what to do. My daughter-in-law, Leah, is in the kitchen feeding the *kinder*. Your Polly and her Mandy. Are you hungry?"

She was, but many questions demanded an answer before she ate. She pushed herself to sit up. Amos slid his arm behind her shoulders to assist her. She stiffened as the aroma of his shampoo and soap enveloped her.

"Am I hurting you?" he asked, turning to look at her.

Their faces were so close a *kind*'s hand couldn't have fit between them. She stared at his strong jaw and his expressive mouth that was drawn in a straight line. His dark brown eyes, volatile in the parking lot, were now shadowed with worry.

For her.

Silly tears flooded her eyes at the thought of someone caring about her. She'd been alone, save for Polly, not knowing if anyone wondered where they were. Temptation teased her to rest her head on his shoulder and let his strong arms surround her to hold the world at bay.

But she couldn't. For many reasons, but the primary one was the little girl sliding off a chair in the kitchen and watching her with a troubled expression. Another girl, who looked about ten-years-old and must be Mandy, stared, too.

God, help me find the strength.

Linda drew away from Amos. She murmured her gratitude but settled herself against the back of the sofa. Her head felt too heavy, and she let it drop.

"Ouch!" she gasped, sitting straighter. She was horrified to see strands of hair tumbling forward. It must have fallen out of her bun. Glancing at Amos, she groped for her hair. Where was her *kapp*? No man but her husband should see her hair loose and without a cover.

Her fingers froze. Did she have a husband? She had no idea.

"There's a big lump above your right ear." Wanda tucked Linda's loose hair between her shoulder and the sofa, then grimaced. "I'll get you one of my *kapps*, but I wanted to make sure you don't need stitches."

"Where is my *kapp*?" Its shape could be a clue to where she'd come from or where she was going.

"You weren't wearing one," Amos said.

"But why would—"

The cry of Linda's name in an adorable lisp cut through her words. Polly rushed toward her. Linda tried not to groan when the little girl threw herself against her, saying Linda's name over and over. Wrapping her arms around Polly, Linda held on for dear life. This *kind* needed her. Something horrible had happened to them, and she wasn't going to allow it to happen again. It was a vow she intended to keep…somehow.

Amos watched raw emotions racing across Linda's face, and he realized no matter what had happened to her, she cared for the little girl who clung to her. He'd been heartsick when Linda opened her eyes and looked around like a starving soul seeking God's love. His first thought had been to let her know she was safe.

He'd been shocked when Linda fainted in the parking lot. He'd caught her as he tried to soothe Polly's terror, hoping his reassurances would prove to be true. When he'd put Linda in his buggy and assisted Polly in before locking up the store, he'd prayed Linda would awaken. His prayers hadn't halted during the short drive to the farm where he'd been born and lived his whole life nor had they eased when he carried her into the house, shocking his *mamm* and Leah, his older brother Ezra's wife.

When he'd placed Linda on the couch, he'd followed his *mamm*'s instructions and then stayed out of the way while *Mamm* removed Linda's bonnet and coat. Leah had steered Polly into the kitchen when the unmistakable color of blood was revealed on Linda's bonnet.

What had happened to her? Had her injury stolen her memories? A quick search of her coat had revealed nothing to identify her. Polly had said they were traveling, so he assumed Linda had been carrying a purse. Where was it? He guessed she didn't know. Otherwise, she would have seen her name on the ID insert in her wallet. If she'd filled it out. He had no idea if she was organized or not. As his siblings often reminded him, not everyone was as conscientious as he was. He ignored them, because not being careful had led to being made a fool of by Arlene Barkman five years ago.

Polly rubbed tears off her chubby cheeks as she leaned her head against Linda's shoulder. He watched them and was surprised when Leah spoke close to him. He hadn't noticed her coming to stand beside him.

Her voice was a whisper. "Polly loves Linda. I wonder how they're related."

"That should be easy to answer," he answered before he raised his voice to ask, "Polly, is Linda your *mamm*?"

The little girl looked at him as if he'd grown a second head. "No!" In the lisp, he found easier to decipher each time the *kind* spoke, Polly went on, "She's Linda. My Linda. Not my *mamm*."

"Linda is her name. What's your *mamm*'s name?"

She gave him the same incredulous look she had in the parking lot. "*Mamm*'s name is *Mamm*."

"Ask a silly question," murmured his own *mamm*, and his sister-in-law struggled to hide a smile.

Linda gave him a sympathetic glance, which he appreciated. He was spared from trying to devise some-

thing to say when he heard a knock. He went to the door
and opened it, knowing who was there.

"*Komm* in, Dr. Montgomery," he said, stepping aside
to let the tall, slender redhead enter. The *Englisch doktorfraa* was dressed in a navy coat, a skirt of the same
color and an unadorned white blouse.

"Thank you, Amos," she said with a calm smile. "I
assume my patient is in the front room."

"*Ja. Mamm* is watching over her."

"Then she's in good hands."

"The best."

The *doktorfraa* slipped off her coat after setting her
black bag on the stairs. Picking up the bag, she walked
past him.

Amos went into the kitchen when, after introducing
herself to Linda, Dr. Montgomery suggested she'd like
privacy to examine her patient. When his *mamm* joined
him in the kitchen while Leah returned to washing the
dishes, Polly came with her. The littler girl had question after question until *Mamm* distracted both *kinder*
with cookies.

His own curiosity couldn't be deflected so easily.
He glanced into the other room. As he watched, Linda
touched her right forefinger, then her left one to her
nose. Following the *doktorfraa*'s orders, she reached
to do the same to Dr. Montgomery. She paused and
looked past the *doktorfraa* when a giggle came from
the kitchen and Polly asked if she could play, too.

When Linda caught him staring, he expected her to
look away. He expected *himself* to look away. Neither
of them did as, for a breathless moment, his gaze en-
twined with hers. For that second, he sensed the frustration and panic boiling inside her. An urge to put his

arm around her and hold her close until the fear sub-
sided shocked him. He didn't know her or anything
about her, yet he couldn't deny the unexpected longing
crashing over him.

Stop it! he told himself. He'd been fooled by one
pretty woman when he discovered he hadn't known
enough about her. He wouldn't do that again.

Dr. Montgomery closed her bag and sighed, breaking
the connection between him and Linda. "All I can tell
you is that you were struck above your ear, and you've
suffered a concussion which is the most likely cause
of your amnesia."

"There isn't anything you can do to help?" Amos
asked, walking into the front room.

"Other than prescribing two acetaminophen tablets
every six hours for pain, there's nothing I can do but
order some neurological tests and scans. I'll contact
Dr. Vandross, the chief neurologist at the hospital, and
get his advice to see if we need to arrange some tests
and scans."

Linda started to shake her head, then holding it in
her hands said, "I don't have any money, and I can't
ask this district to pay for a stranger's medical bills."

Mamm sat beside Linda on the sofa. "Don't fret about
such things. It'll take a while before the tests can be
scheduled." She raised her eyes to Dr. Montgomery.
"Isn't that right? When Leah's *daed* needed tests last
year, it took some time to fit him into the schedule."

"The full battery of tests might happen before Christmas, but more likely afterwards." The doctor gave Linda
an apologetic smile. "I know it must be frustrating to
lose your memories, but having the tests won't guar-
antee their return. Time is the best healer. It's impor-

tant you don't bump your head until your brain has a chance to heal. Another trauma to your skull and your brain could be damaged worse."

"And keep my memories from coming back?"

"That's one possibility. Another possibility is that you'd suffer injuries leaving you unable to do physical things or talk."

Her eyes grew round with unabashed horror. "That could happen if I bump my head again?"

"I can't say what might happen or not happen. We know too little about the brain and how it handles an injury. If you feel dizzy, sit immediately. Don't take chances." She smiled sadly. "I don't want to scare you, but being careful is vital."

"We understand," Amos said when Linda didn't reply.

"I'd like to see Linda in my office after Christmas if she's still in pain. Can that be arranged?"

"Ja," said Amos.

"If she regains her memories—even bits of them— let me know. What she recalls may help determine what we do next."

"Danki, Dr. Montgomery," he added as he stepped aside to let *Mamm* walk the *doktorfraa* to the door. He guessed his *mamm* had other questions she wanted to ask without Linda overhearing.

If she got answers, Amos saw no sign of it when *Mamm* bustled into the living room and insisted Linda eat. Linda took the bowl of stew, setting it on the table in front of the sofa. She didn't touch it after his brother Ezra came inside when the barn chores were done. His other unmarried brothers returned home from work to eat their supper. The stew grew cold after Polly gave Linda a kiss good-night before Leah took her and Mandy upstairs to bed. *Mamm* refilled the bowl with warm stew before going through the connecting door to the *dawdi haus*, but Linda didn't taste it. When Leah and Ezra asked if she wanted help to go into the guest room beyond the kitchen, she thanked them and sat with her hands folded on her lap.

Amos said nothing as he sat in a chair near the couch and stared at the flames leaping in the gas fireplace. It, along with the old woodstove in the kitchen, kept the whole house warm except on the coldest days of the winter. He unlaced his work boots, then he toed off one and then the other.

"You know *Mamm* is going to be disappointed if you don't eat," he said as he glanced over at Linda, half-expecting her to be asleep.

"Moving makes me dizzy," she said in little more than a whisper.

"Do you want me to spoon it for you?"

He was so sure she'd say no he almost gasped aloud when she said, "*Ja.* I don't want to spill anything on the couch."

That she was thinking of others when she was suffering no longer surprised him. He'd seen how worried she was about Polly.

"Do you mind?" He pointed to the cushion beside her.

"Gently, if you don't mind."

He tried not to shift the cushion, but he must have because she closed her eyes and her breath caught. "Once you have something in your stomach, you should take some Tylenol."

"That's a *gut* idea."

He picked up the bowl and the napkin. He handed her the latter and couldn't help smiling when she tucked it into the top of her dress.

She smiled in return. "If I'm going to be fed like a *boppli*, I should dress like one, ain't so?"

Instead of answering, he lifted a spoonful of his *mamm*'s fragrant stew and held it out for her to eat. He couldn't think of Linda as a *boppli*. She was a grown woman, something he was too aware of when she gazed at him as the tip of her tongue chased a bit of gravy from the corner of her mouth. He looked at the bowl he held. He needed to keep his mind on his task and not on her lips.

When the last bit of stew was gone, she handed him the napkin and thanked him. He took the bowl to the kitchen. Leaving it in the sink, he got two tablets from the downstairs bathroom, and returned to the living room with them and a glass of water.

"If you want," he said as she swallowed Tylenol, "I can help you to the guest room."

"No," she replied, staring at the fire. "I shouldn't sleep. It's dangerous after a head injury."

"Did the *doktorfraa* mention that?"

"I remember someone saying that." She closed her eyes and sighed. "But not who. What do I do now?"

"Prayer always helps me. Turning my problems over to God."

She smiled sadly as she looked at him. "Trust me. I'm praying as hard as I know how."

"Then believe God sees everything."

"I wish He'd share a little bit of what He's seen lately with me."

He smiled in spite of himself. "*Mamm* always says a *gut* attitude helps in any situation."

"Even this one?"

"Why not give it a try? Maybe it'll work." *And then you can return to your life, and I can do the same.* He was contrite immediately, though he knew how Linda could mess up his well-organized life. He wasn't going to let a pretty woman do that again.

Chapter Three

Amos came down the stairs the next morning. He'd gone up to change into clean clothes because he didn't want to go to the store in what he'd worn all night. He'd stayed awake, making sure Linda did the same. It'd been tempting to close his eyes and drift to sleep, but he'd seen her fear when she asked him to help her to evade sleep.

He stifled a yawn as he walked into the kitchen, glad Leah had made the *kaffi* extra-strong this morning. His brothers and bleary-eyed Mandy were at the table, eating. With everyone having different schedules, they seldom ate together at breakfast. He listened as Micah and Daniel, the twins, debated some aspect of carpentry. They were working for an *Englischer* contractor to the east in Chester County.

Nodding to them and Jeremiah, who looked as exhausted as Amos felt, he went to the counter to pour himself a mug of *kaffi*. Ezra wasn't in from barn chores, and *Mamm* was helping Leah prepare breakfast as conversations swirled around the kitchen.

It became silent. He turned to see Linda walking in

from the guest room. She held Polly's hand, and she faltered when every eye turned in her direction. A hint of color in her face suggested she was feeling better in spite of a sleepless night. Her hair was covered by one of *Mamm*'s heart-shaped *kapps*.

The now familiar yearning to protect her surged through him, and he was on his feet before he realized he was moving. He strode across the room, giving her what he hoped was a bolstering grin. "Sit anywhere you'd like and grab what you can before my brothers eat everything in sight."

She smiled faintly while his brothers protested they'd left enough for her and the *kind*. When he put a steadying hand on her arm to make sure she didn't trip on the rag rugs scattered around the pale blue kitchen, she didn't pull away. He kept his steps short so she and Polly could match them.

Once Linda and the little girl were seated, Polly choosing a chair beside Mandy, he pointed to each of his brothers and told her their names. He sat across from her, and, after joining her and the *kind* in bowing their heads for grace, passed the steaming dishes of food. He frowned when Linda took a single spoonful of scrambled eggs and one slice of toast.

"Don't you want more?" asked *Mamm* as she sat.

"As unsteady as my stomach is," Linda said, "I'm not sure how much I can eat."

"Making haste slowly is always a *gut* choice."

Amos looked at the little girl beside Linda. Though her eyes were as heavy as Mandy's, Polly filled her plate to overflowing. When some fried potatoes fell onto the table, she scooped them up and put them on the plate with a giggle.

He assisted her with putting blackberry jam on her toast, explaining about the person who'd brought the berries into the store to sell the previous summer. Both girls listened, wide-eyed, while he spun a tale about the man noticing how the bushes were shaking. He'd assumed someone else was picking on the other side. The man discovered he was right when he looked over the bush to see a bear gorging itself on the juicy berries.

"What did he do?" Polly asked.

"The bear kept picking and eating."

"What about the man?" asked Mandy, just as excited.

Amos smiled. "He found another patch of blackberries to pick in."

The girls giggled. His brothers guffawed, though they'd heard the story before, and Linda gave him another feeble smile. Wondering if her head ached this morning, he motioned for his brothers to be quiet. They looked startled, but nodded, toning down their voices and their laughter.

When Linda had eaten what she'd taken, he offered her more. He was pleased when she took another spoonful of eggs.

As she continued to eat, his stomach growled. He looked at his plate and realized he hadn't taken more than a bite or two while he watched her and Polly. Digging his fork into the mound of fried potatoes, he took a bite before saying, "Linda, I was thinking—"

"You thinking?" asked Micah with a muted chuckle. "That's no surprise."

"He always thinks everything to death," his twin added with a wink at Linda.

The comment annoyed Amos more than his brothers' interruption. He didn't want them flirting with her.

He was the one who'd found her, and *he* had to make certain she was cared for until her memories returned. Startled by his reaction, because she wasn't a lost puppy anyone could claim, he kept his eyes on his plate as he continued, "I was thinking, Linda, you should come to the store today. We can retrace the steps you took yesterday to figure out what happened to you. I'm sure *Mamm* and Leah will be glad to entertain Polly."

Both women nodded before *Mamm* added, "Today is cookie-making day, and we could use help."

"Let me!" Polly bounced in her seat. "Can I help?"

"If Linda says it's okay." His *mamm* smiled at Mandy. "We won't make your favorite oatmeal raisin cookies until you get home from school."

"Linda?" The little girl looked at her as Mandy grinned in anticipation.

"*Ja.* You can stay and make cookies." She set her fork on her plate as the *kind* began to chatter with *Mamm* and Leah. To Amos, she added, "Are you sure she shouldn't come? She's sure to remember more than I do."

"I'm not sure how much value anything she remembers will be. It was growing dark by the time you reached the store."

Linda said nothing for a long minute, and he guessed she was considering his words. That was confirmed when she said, "You're right. Polly would try to help us, but expecting her to fill in the blanks is too much of a burden for a little girl. It'll be better for her to remain here."

Glad it was decided and trying not to notice how much he looked forward to spending the day with Linda, Amos began to eat with the same gusto as his brothers. He'd almost cleaned his plate when Mandy stood to leave the table.

After she'd dressed for the cold weather, his niece waved to everyone and went out the door, almost lost in her coat and scarf and hat. In her mittened hands, she carried a green lunch box.

"Where's she going?" Polly asked.

"To school," he and Linda said at the same time. He felt his face grow warm and wondered why he was flushing over such a silly thing. People frequently spoke at the same time. It didn't mean anything, did it?

The little girl ran to the window. "I want to go to school, too."

"When you're six," Linda replied.

"And I need you here to help me with cookies and helping me make up the extra beds in the *dawdi haus*," his *mamm* said.

"The *dawdi haus*?" Amos asked, astonished. "Are we having company for Christmas?"

"We already have company." She glanced at Linda. "Leah has enough to do taking care of you boys as well as her husband and Mandy. I thought it'd be nice for Linda and Polly to stay with me." *Mamm* smiled as Polly waved to Mandy, who was trudging along the farm lane in the snow. "From the looks of them, I doubt either girl slept much during the night."

"I heard them giggling several times," Leah said as she brought the *kaffi* pot over to refill everyone's cups, including her own. "Separating them is a *gut* idea."

Amos couldn't argue with that and neither did Linda. As soon as he finished his breakfast, he stood. He asked Linda if she was ready to leave. She went to get her coat, her steps growing surer. When he realized he was staring after her, he averted his eyes. His gaze was caught by *Mamm*'s, and she arched her eyebrows before beginning to clear the table.

Her message was clear: *take care*. He'd told himself that over and over, aware of how little he knew about Linda. But he couldn't deny he was aware of the way her eyes crinkled when her lips tilted, of how her expression softened while she spoke with Polly, of how her lashes curled when she closed her eyes.

When Linda returned with her coat buttoned, Polly ran to her and grabbed her hand. "Come back. Please!" the little girl cried. "Don't leave me again."

"Did I leave you before?" Her eyes were bleak with dismay.

"*Ja*. Don't you remember?"

"I don't," she whispered. Squaring her shoulders, she said a bit more loudly, "Tell me about it."

"You told me to sit at the bus station while you asked someone something." The *kind* shuddered hard. "You went away for a long time. You came back. You didn't say a word till we got off the bus."

"Nothing?"

"No. You touched your head." The little girl's eyes filled with tears, and her lower lip quivered. "Poor you. You've got a bad boo-boo."

"I'm feeling much better, *liebling*. You don't need to worry about me leaving you. I won't. Not ever." She glanced over the little girl's head toward him.

He was astonished when he realized Linda wanted *him* to believe her. He bit back his instinctive reply that he couldn't imagine her abandoning the *kind* unless she had an important reason. But he didn't know her. And he didn't know what had happened to them.

Quietly he said, "There's a Philadelphia bus that passes through Paradise Springs during the late afternoon."

"How do you know that?" Hope brightened Linda's face. The hope she might rediscover what she'd lost.

"I sell bus tickets, and I keep the schedule posted at the store. The new one arrived last week. I noticed one bus route changed quite a bit, but the bus still stops in Paradise Springs."

She reached for the door. "Let's go. I want to see where else the bus might have stopped. Maybe something will jog my memory."

"I pray so." He wondered if he'd ever meant words more.

"This is a comfortable buggy," Linda said to make conversation as Amos drove toward his store. A plow must have come through during the night because snow was in foot-high banks on either side of the road.

"My oldest brother, Joshua, built it," he replied, holding the reins easily. "He's built or rebuilt almost every vehicle around Paradise Springs." He paused, then went on as if he didn't want the silence to return, "Pretty morning, ain't so?"

"Ja." She gazed across the sparkling countryside. The snow clinging to the tree branches plopped on the ground, making dark crevices in the brilliant white. She swallowed another yawn.

Her fingers tightened in her lap when she saw the sign for the Stoltzfus Family Shops in the distance. Amos drove to the far end of the empty parking lot. She eased the grip when her knuckles hurt, but she couldn't help being impatient. Was it possible? Could her past be jogged from her mind by looking at a bus schedule? It was a long shot because she wasn't sure where their journey had begun. She'd asked Polly to describe the bus station, but what the little girl could tell them didn't help Amos or his family guess which one it was.

Her gaze flicked toward the man sitting beside her. She hadn't known him a full day, but he seemed to be a trustworthy man from a *gut* family. Could she be sure of her impressions of anyone? Her mind was scrambled, and she was unsure where to turn.

Help me, God, to find the answers.

Amos stopped the buggy at the back of the building. Beyond the open space behind it was what looked like a smithy. He got out and started around the buggy. She didn't wait, stepping down on her own. She stumbled, almost falling to her knees, but a tight grip on the door's frame kept her on her feet.

Amos's jaw worked, but he said only, "Let me unlock the door." He walked to the small back porch. He left a trail of prints in his wake.

She looked at her feet. About six inches of snow had fallen during the night, and her sneakers were growing damp. She stepped onto the covered concrete porch. Shaking one foot, then the other, she watched packed snow fall off her soles. She needed boots if she planned to go anywhere, but how was she going to buy them? Other than the single penny she'd found in her dress pocket, she had no money.

Amos inserted a key and opened the door. He went in, and she heard him snap on the electric lights. A dull rumble of a propane furnace came to life as he toggled another switch.

"Where's the bus schedule?" she asked, unable to wait a minute more.

"This way." He walked past the first aisle to where a cash register was set on a counter. Beside it a pole held a bulletin board. In one corner, he'd tacked the bus schedule. She ran a finger along one column, then another.

"The bus that stops in Paradise Springs is this one," he said, reaching past her to touch the sixth column from the left.

She recoiled from his outstretched arm, cowering like an abused dog. She saw his shock. She was stunned, too. Why was she cringing away from a man who'd been nothing but kind to her and Polly? Did her senses remember something appalling that her mind had forgotten?

"The bus to Philadelphia," Amos said, his voice strained, "has stops to the west in Lancaster, York, Gettysburg and Chambersburg." He listed off more towns. "Any sound familiar?"

"I recognize most of those towns, but I don't remember visiting them. How far away from here does the bus stop?"

"Down by Route 30." He hesitated, then asked, "Why don't we walk toward the bridge and see if you remember anything?"

"Don't you need to open the store?"

"Nobody's here, so we have time to go to the bridge and back."

"I'd like to, but…" She glanced at her sneakers, then put her fingers to her head. Any motion, and she wasn't sure which one or when, could send a lightning flash of pain across her skull.

She didn't realize she was wobbling until Amos put his hand under her arm and urged her to stand still until she was steady. A moan rose from inside her. Not from the pain, but at how he was being nice when she'd acted, moments ago, as if she feared he was going to hurt her.

The darkness nibbling at the edge of her vision faded, and she raised her head and whispered, *"Danki."*

"Would you like to sit?"

Linda wanted to say *ja*, but even more she longed to remember her past. "Let's go to the bridge."

"Come with me." He motioned for her to follow him along the aisle.

Not sure why he'd turned away from the front door, she trailed after him.

He paused in front of a large wooden crate and pulled out a pair of black rubber boots. "These look to be your size."

She didn't take them. "I appreciate your offer, but I don't have—"

"Stop right there." His mouth grew taut. "I know you don't have any money. I'm not asking for any. Not now or later."

"But those boots must have cost you something."

"Look." He pointed to the box.

She saw it was filled with boots and mittens and hats and umbrellas and a few coats.

"Folks around here," he said, "leave clothes they can't use any longer in this box in case someone gets caught in a storm. You might as well use these boots for as long as you're here."

"I hope it won't be long until I can remember who I am and where we were going."

"I know. Sit down while you're putting them on, or you may tumble on your cute nose." He gestured toward a nearby bench as she felt heat climbing her cheeks at his unexpected compliment. "I put this here for my older customers to use if they needed a rest during their shopping. On warm fall days, after the harvest was in, it's a gathering place for farmers to discuss the prices they hoped to get for their crops and for boys to pick apart every detail of the World Series."

Sitting, she drew off her sneakers and reached for the boots. The world tilted, and she gripped the bench.

"Steady there," Amos said as he knelt and helped her slide her feet into the boots. He laced them closed, then looked at her. "Maybe this is too much today, Linda. We can do this another day."

"I don't want whoever's missing Polly and me to wait an extra day to learn where we are."

She saw his doubt that they'd discover anything today while her head was still unstable. She couldn't allow herself to believe her memories wouldn't return. She had to hold on to hope.

Standing, he put his hand under her arm and brought her to her feet. She steeled her knees so they wouldn't betray her. Without a word, he led her to the front door.

"Wait here while I lock the back door." He was gone before she could reply.

She looked out the door. Clouds were building to the west and the sunshine growing thin. Another storm? It was early in the year for such heavy snow.

Amos edged around her and opened the front door. She appreciated his taking care not to move his arm close to her. What *had* happened to her? She resisted touching the painful spot behind her ear. Had someone snuck up behind her and struck her? But why hadn't anyone seen that? Perhaps it had happened while she was alone, but why had she left Polly on her own in the first place? Nothing made sense.

She was beginning to wonder if it ever would.

Chapter Four

Linda stood by the concrete abutment at the far end of the bridge. Looking along the road curving toward the village of Paradise Springs, she paid no attention to the snowflakes drifting around her. The wind cut through her black wool coat, but it was not as icy as the fear inside her.

"I still don't remember anything before we reached the bridge. It's as if my life started the moment we crossed it." She put her mittens to her bonnet and frowned. "Why can't I remember anything?"

"Don't force it," Amos said. "That's what Dr. Montgomery said."

"*Ja.* I remember that, but why can't I remember anything else?" Raising her head, she blinked back tears. "I want to know what the doctor charged for coming to see me. I'll repay you as soon as I can."

"I know you will. Why don't you concentrate on getting better and leave other worries until later?"

"I know I should, but it's not easy to think of the future when I don't have any past to build upon."

He gave her the kind smile that eased the iciness

around her frightened heart. "You've got this moment. That's all any of us have. This day, this moment the Lord has made for us. We can use it or waste it."

"That's a deep thought." She let her shoulders unstiffen as she gave in to the grin teasing her lips.

"I'm a deep thinking sort of man." He struck a pose worthy of a statue on a village green.

Her anxiety eased a bit as she laughed. She knew that was what he'd hoped she'd do because his dark brown eyes sparkled like sunshine. As more snow settled around them, muting the noise from cars out on the highway, she sent up a grateful prayer that Amos was the one who had found her and Polly. He and his family made her feel as if they were as invested in her recovering her memories as she was.

"I need to return to the store," he said as the snow continued to fall, harder with each passing second. "In case someone comes."

"All right." She didn't want to give in to failure, but standing in the storm wouldn't get her anything but a cold.

They walked toward the Stoltzfus Family Shops in silence. More than once she thought Amos was about to say something, but he didn't. She tried to think of something to say, but her head ached more with each step.

Another buggy was parked in front of Amos's store. It was a twin to the one she'd ridden in to the store, and Linda recalled what Amos had said about his brother building or rebuilding many buggies in the area.

A tall man with a bushy gray beard stood by the store's front door. When he turned to watch them approach, she saw the man had wild, untamed gray eyebrows to match his beard. He smiled, and his face altered from forbidding to friendly.

Amos called a greeting, and the gray-bearded man stepped aside to let Amos unlock the door. "I never thought I'd see the day when you open late, Amos."

"Reuben," he replied, glancing over his shoulder at her, "this is a guest at our house. Her name is Linda." He motioned for her to join them. When she did, he added, "Reuben Lapp is our bishop."

"Hello," she said, trying to hide the many new questions scurrying through her battered mind. What was the name of the bishop in her home district? Did he smile as compassionately as Reuben did? Was she a baptized member, or had she not made that step to commit her life to her faith?

And if she'd been baptized, did that mean she was walking out with a young man she planned to marry? Plain women didn't wear wedding bands, so there was no way to know if a husband was trying to find her.

"Christmas season is a *gut* time for family and friends to visit, isn't it?" Reuben asked with a broadening smile.

She was saved from having to answer when Amos gave his bishop a quick explanation of what had happened last night. As the older man's expression grew serious, she wondered how many more people were going to be dismayed by her situation before her memories returned. She held her breath, hoping when Amos asked if Reuben had heard of anyone looking for a young woman and a little girl that his response would provide the answers she sought.

Her heart collapsed when the bishop shook his head. "I wish I had better news for you, Linda. I haven't heard of anybody missing a woman with the name Linda or a *kind* named Polly." Genuine compassion filled his eyes. "I'm sorry. I'll contact my fellow bishops and make other inquiries. You belong somewhere with people who must be missing you and the *kind*. We'll do what we can to reunite you with those who miss you." His smile returned. "The Amish grapevine is always efficient. News like this will spread quickly from family to family."

"Danki," she said as she followed Amos and the bishop into the store. She wasn't sure what she was going to do. Should she return to the Stoltzfus house and help Wanda and Leah with the day's chores?

Normally it'd be an easy walk, but between the snow and her own unsteadiness, she didn't trust herself to get there on her own. She stood by the door while Reuben completed his purchase. She nodded when the bishop, as he left the store, told her he'd immediately let her know any news he heard.

Amos came around the counter. "Are you all right? You look as gray as the sky."

"I'm as *gut* as I can be now."

"Reuben will do everything in his power—and in prayer—to find the truth for you."

"I know." She rubbed her hands together. "But I despise the thought of people frightened and worried because they don't know where we are."

"Think of how joyous your reunion will be."

She raised her gaze to meet his eyes which were darker with his strong emotions. "I wish I had your optimism."

"It's not optimism. It's faith God has a plan for you and your family, and His plan is a *gut* one."

"What *gut* can there be in losing my memory?"

He shrugged. "You're asking the wrong guy. You need to ask God."

"I have been asking. Over and over."

"He'll answer. He always does." He gave her a grin. "Just not always on our schedule."

She returned his smile, feeling the weight on her shoulders ease. "*Danki* for the reminder." Her laugh surprised her as much as him when she added, "I need reminders about everything."

He shook his head. "No, you haven't needed a reminder about loving Polly. Though the situation looks bleak, think how much worse it would have been if you didn't recall anything about her."

"You *are* an optimist."

"Guess I'm guilty as charged. Or maybe it's this time of year. It's hard to be grim when we're surrounded by happiness. So many weddings and the Christmas holidays and the snow that's pretty when it blankets the ground and hushes the world." Looking past her toward the empty parking lot, he asked, "Would you consider coming to the store tomorrow?"

"Why?"

"Tomorrow is Saturday, and the store is always busy. Maybe one of my customers will recognize you." He laughed. "Maybe I should set up one of those games like *Englisch* shopkeepers do, but instead of guessing how many gumballs are in the jar, people can guess what your last name is." He shook his head with another chuckle. "Not that it'd be much of a challenge with so many Stoltzfuses, Millers, Yoders and Beilers around here."

She laughed along with him, ignoring the unending questions while she did. No matter what happened after she learned the truth of who she was, one thing wouldn't change. She'd forever be grateful to Amos Stoltzfus for lifting her out of her fears with the lilt of laughter.

The church Sunday service was being held about a mile away at the Chupp family's farm. Linda doubted Amos and his family would have hitched up their buggy horses except for the fact that she found it difficult to walk any distance.

Yesterday, her hopes had been dashed. Nobody who came into the store had recognized her, though Amos had asked every customer, plain and *Englisch*, if they did. Some had glanced at her and shrugged, but many had considered the question before they answered. Each time the answer was the same: they'd never seen her before. That meant she couldn't have been coming to Paradise Springs. Why had she and Polly gotten off the bus here?

"You stood and said it was time to go," Polly had told her when they went to bed in the cozy upstairs room in the *dawdi haus* last night. While she'd been at the store, Amos's brothers had moved two twin beds into the small space with its slanting ceilings and dormer window. "You didn't say anything else."

Maybe the bus tickets would point to where they were bound, but searching her pockets had revealed nothing. She asked Polly to check her own pockets. Nothing. If they'd had printed tickets, they'd been lost somewhere. Maybe she'd left them on the bus. Maybe they had slipped from her fingers on the walk to Amos's store. Finding them beneath the snow would be next to impossible.

And Linda was too exhausted for such a task. Nightmares had kept Polly awake through the night. What the little girl dreamed seemed to vanish as soon as Polly woke, crying in fright, but she knew someone bad was chasing them. Was it a memory, or was the little girl prone to night terrors? Yet another question with no answer.

When they reached the farm where the service would take place, Polly stayed close to Linda. The little girl's hand held on so tightly Linda's fingers began to cramp. She readjusted Polly's grip, but didn't let go of her hand.

"There are lots of *kinder* here," she said to reassure the little girl.

"Do you think they'll like me and play with me?"

"*Ja*, but not until after the worship service."

Polly gave her a disgusted glance. "I know, Linda. I'm not a *boppli*."

A lighthearted, resonating laugh startled Linda. She turned, knowing who stood behind them. Why hadn't Amos joined his brothers and the other men by the front porch where they were gathering before they were called inside for the worship service?

Her head spun, and she knew she'd moved too quickly. Her heart had propelled her around before her mind could warn her to be careful. She raised her eyes to meet his gaze, and he put his broad fingers on her arm. Warmth swirled through her, but oddly it didn't blur everything in front of her. Instead, she felt more grounded than she had since she woke on the sofa in his family's front room.

"If you feel too lousy to stay," he said in a whisper, "I can take you home at any time." He spoke quietly, she realized, because he worried that her headache had returned with a vengeance.

What a *gut* man he was! It would be so easy to listen to her heart that was pleading for her to risk it and tell him how much his kindness meant to her. She couldn't. Not when she had no idea if she was betrothed or married. "I'll be fine."

"I'm sure you will." His smile warmed her in spite of the icy wind. "You're a determined woman, and I suspect you can do whatever you put your mind to."

"How can you say that? You don't know me." She swallowed her gasp when he flinched as if she'd struck him. What had she said that upset him so much? Unsure, she kept going, hoping that her next words would bring back his smile. "*I* don't know me." She tried a laugh, but it was feeble and sounded fake even to her own ears.

When his name was called, Amos excused himself and went to join the men. She watched his easy lope through the snow. To look at him, nobody would guess he had anything on his mind other than what he wanted to discuss with his friends.

When the women entered the house, Linda wasn't surprised Polly clung to her hand and to Wanda's. Amos's *mamm* treated Polly as if she were one of her own *kins-kinder*. Her other grandchildren were giggling together behind them.

Linda sat with the rest of the *maedels* on a bench behind the married women. The *kinder* were scattered among the adults, some sitting with the women and a few of the boys with the men. Pushing aside any thoughts but of the moment, she joined in with the first hymn. She savored the slow pace of the music. Her heart drew in strength from the community of faith. When the congregation began the next song, *"Das Loblied,"* which was always sung as the second hymn, she let the opening words of the second verse sink into her:

Oh may thy servant be endowed
With wisdom from on high

She longed for wisdom to open the place where her memories were sealed away. Smiling at Polly, she raised her eyes and saw Amos watching her from across the room. He was a fine-looking man, standing a full head taller than the men on either side of him. When he looked away, his mouth hardening for a moment, she was startled. Why would he be upset she was staring at him when *he* had been studying her openly?

Linda sat as a minister moved to the center of the room to begin his sermon. He had the same height the Stoltzfus brothers possessed and resembled Amos, though his jaw was partially hidden beneath an uneven beard. Her guess was confirmed when Wanda whispered, "That's my third son, Isaiah."

Unsure if she'd met Isaiah the night she woke in the Stoltzfuses' living room and wondering which woman sitting among the married women was his wife, she listened as he began the longer sermon. She became enmeshed in the words as he spoke from the heart with an eloquence she wasn't surprised to hear from Amos's older brother.

Isaiah must be like Amos in more than the shape of his face. They both were deep thinkers. That was confirmed as he spoke on the subject of forgiveness.

"Even the most heinous act," Isaiah said with quiet dignity, "needs to be forgiven. We all know that, but we often forget that we must let that transgression be forgotten, as well."

She froze on the bench. Was she trying to forget something too horrible to remember? A shiver sliced down her spine.

What if what happened to her and Polly had been so appalling her mind had let go of everything in order to forget it?

Amos shifted on the church bench. His twin brothers glanced at him, and he halted. The last time he'd been antsy during church services was when he was not much older than Polly.

But it wasn't easy to sit still when, in the middle of his brother's sermon, he saw color wash from Linda's face. Was she in pain? She put her arm around Polly and slanted the *kind* against her. Her gaze flicked in his direction, sweeping away. Not before he saw the raw emotion in her eyes. Was it fear?

Maybe she'd remembered something. No, he didn't want to think of her recovered memories being so frightening, but he should be thankful she'd recalled something. She could return to her life...and he could stop thinking about her. Wouldn't that be for the best? He'd made an idiot of himself over one lovely woman, and Linda's recovery would keep him from doing so again. He'd noticed the glances his *mamm* had aimed at him while he was laughing with Linda. *Mamm* had worn a similar smile when his brothers grew serious about the women who became their wives.

But he wasn't walking out with Linda. He was trying to help her find the truth by regaining her memories. For all he knew, she was another man's wife. That thought hit him in the gut like an enraged billy goat. He didn't like thinking of her belonging with someone else.

He had to keep reminding himself how important it was to be certain. More and more with each passing day because Linda was becoming a part of his life. When he wasn't with her, thoughts of her filled his head. Unlike her, he couldn't forget anything: her kindness to Polly, her willingness to help at the store, the easy way she made him smile and laugh as he hadn't in far too long.

Amos scrambled to his feet when he realized others were standing. He'd lost track of the service, and Reuben was ending it with *"Da Herr sei mit du."*

He replied with the rest of the congregation, "And the Lord be with you, too."

His plan to ask Linda what was amiss went awry. He had to help rearrange some of the benches into tables for the communal meal, then his brothers insisted he join them to eat. Linda wasn't one of the women bringing the food from the kitchen. Wolfing down his sandwich and excusing himself, he went to find her.

Everywhere he looked she'd been moments ago. How could it be difficult to find her in the farmhouse? His search was interrupted by friends who wanted to draw him into conversations. He didn't want to be rude, but he needed to know why Linda's face had become ashen. Even after the women and *kinder* had finished their meals, he hadn't found her. Had she eaten in the kitchen? He'd check there again.

As he passed a living room window, he saw Linda standing in the front yard. He yanked his coat off the pile on the sofa. Grabbing a scarf and a hat and gloves, he didn't pay any attention if they were his. He didn't want to waste time looking for his own, because if he took his eyes off her, she might vanish.

The chilly breeze was gone, and the sunshine was melting snow from the roof and nearby trees. A clump of half-frozen snow found its way down his collar. When he yelped, Linda looked toward him. When he exaggerated shaking his coat to let the frigid remnants fall behind him, she gave him the smile he'd hoped for.

He ignored the warning crashing through his head. He shouldn't be so eager for her smiles. He was getting in too deep with a woman who might not be free to flirt with him. "Why are you out in the cold?"

"Keeping an eye on Polly." She pointed at where the *kinder* slid on a snowy hill in the pasture beyond the barn. "I don't know if she's gone sledding before."

"Why didn't you join her?"

Her smile faded. "You know why. I can't risk banging my head. Remember what the *doktorfraa* said? I could do greater damage, and I might never get my memories back."

He hadn't forgotten, but he doubted a tumble off a sled into the soft snow would do her any damage. Yet he understood her hesitation. She'd lost everything but Polly when she'd been hurt before. She couldn't risk injuring herself worse.

"Wait here," he said.

"But—"

"I wouldn't let you hurt yourself. Don't you know that?"

She paused for so long he wondered if she wanted to avoid an answer; then she said, "*Ja*, I trust you."

Her soft reply sent skyrockets soaring through him. Somehow managing a steady voice to tell her again to

wait where she was, he trotted toward the barn before
he had to say anything else. He wasn't sure he could
speak more without stumbling over his words like a
teenager asking a girl to walk out with him. Her confidence in him meant more than she could guess because
he'd had trouble trusting himself after Arlene made
such a public fool of him. How could he have guessed
she'd loudly list what she considered his shortcomings
in the midst of a taffy pull and in front of their friends?
His attempts to hush her and to take the argument outside away from everyone else only made her shriller.
He knew he wasn't perfect. No one was, but he'd been
shocked by her anger and indiscretion their last evening
as a couple. Only later did he discover that she had been
walking out with other men while letting him believe
he was the special one for her. He knew he was letting
bruised pride get in the way, but his efforts to move
past it had failed.

Until the simple words *I trust you* showed him the
way.

But he needed more. He needed the assurance he
knew Linda. Really knew her, instead of being beguiled
by her lovely face and gentle heart.

He shouldn't be thinking about that. He was simply taking her and Polly sledding. Grabbing what he
wanted from a shelf inside the door, he jogged to where
Linda waited.

He smiled as he handed her a black bicycle helmet.
When she looked at it, puzzled, he said, "The *kinder*
wear these when they ride their scooters. Steven Mc-
Murray, the local police chief, has been urging parents
to get them for their kids if they plan to ride along the
roads. With the dips and rises on these twisting roads,

a *kind* could come over the top of a hill and not be able to stop in time to make a corner." He chuckled. "I suspect Dr. Montgomery talked Chief McMurray into the whole idea, but it's a *gut* one."

She examined it from every angle. "Do you think it'll keep me safe?"

"I think it will protect your head. I can't claim it'll do anything else." He grinned. "But we'll stick to the gentler hills, and let the teenagers take the challenging slopes."

"How do I put it on?" She turned it around and around. "Both ends look pretty much the same, and I'm not sure which is the front and which is the back."

"Let me." He took the helmet from her. Turning it so the front faced him, he stepped closer. "Let me know if anything I do hurts you."

"I doubt that's possible," she murmured. She trusted him. He wished trust was as easy for him.

He shook the past from his head, knowing he shouldn't complain about troublesome memories. At least he had his memories. No matter how bad they might be, losing them as she had would be terrible. He settled the helmet over her bonnet. Taking the straps, he hooked them beneath her chin without crushing her head covering.

"Is that comfortable?" he asked.

"A little tight."

He reached to loosen the straps, but as soon as his fingers brushed her cheek, they refused to move. They lingered against her soft, cool skin. She kept her eyes lowered, and he wondered if she felt the same rush of delight he did. If so, she was acting smarter than he was.

He led the way through the pasture gate and toward

the hill. More than once, he considered taking her hand to help her through the snow, but didn't. If he enfolded her fingers in his, he wasn't sure he'd be able to let them go.

Polly ran up to them, jabbering about the rides she'd taken down the hill. Snow was ingrained in her wool coat, and her cheeks were a brilliant red. Her eyes glittered as brightly as the snow as she urged them to join her.

Amos borrowed a sled and positioned it at the top of the hill. It was long enough for Linda to sit in front of him with her arms around Polly. His heart danced in his chest like a runaway horse when he reached forward to grasp the ropes connected to the front. He'd have liked to slip his arm around Linda and draw her closer, but he needed to steer. There were trees flanking the hill. If the sled started heading for one side or the other, he needed to be able to pull it into the center of the hill. He couldn't let there be the slightest chance Linda was injured.

Polly shrieked with excitement as he pushed off before putting his feet against the steering bar at the front. His breath burst from him as Linda pressed back while the sled picked up speed. When they hit a bump and she rocked to one side, he clamped his arm around her waist as she did the same to the *kind*.

His eyes widened. They were going too fast. They weren't going to stop before the fence. He jammed his left boot against the bar, and the sled skidded to the side. Leaning, he shouted a warning as they toppled into the snow, skidding along with the empty sled.

As soon as he stopped, Amos clambered to his knees

and looked for Linda and Polly. He saw them sprawled in the snow.

"Are you okay?" he called.

His answer was a handful of snow thrust into his face. As he sputtered, he heard Linda laughing along with Polly. Not a strained laugh or a weak one. Her laughter was genuine and burst out of her, unrestrained.

"What did you do that for?" he asked, wiping away flakes.

She laughed. "You dumped us in the snow."

"To keep us from hitting the fence."

"I got snow in my face, so it's fair you did, too."

"Fair? I'm not sure what's fair about it." He pointed at the fence. "I saved you from hitting that."

"Maybe. Maybe not." She glanced at Polly who giggled. "Want to ride again?"

The little girl cheered, jumped up and ran to get the sled. As Linda stood, brushing herself off, her eyes were as bright as the *kind*'s. She helped Polly pull the sled up the hill.

Looking over her shoulder, Linda asked, "Coming?"

She didn't wait for his answer as he stood to follow.

Ja, he'd help them go fast down the hill. But he knew one thing. With Linda, he needed to take it slow. This time if he made a mistake, he could hurt her—and Polly—as much as he hurt himself.

Chapter Five

As soon as the school Christmas program on the first day of winter was over, Polly ran to hug Mandy and her cousin Debbie at the front of the schoolroom. Polly adored the two girls and followed them everywhere after school, and the two older girls always welcomed her.

Linda smiled as the girls showed Polly the display the scholars had made and hung on the blackboard. It was covered with pictures of the Nativity drawn on every possible shade of construction paper. *Joy to the World* was spelled in block letters on red and green sheets above the windows on one side of the room.

The school felt familiar. Desks were lined up five across for six rows. They faced the teacher's desk set by the blackboard. Everything looked exactly as she'd expected it to.

Linda was sure she must have attended a school like this, but was she also a teacher as Amos's younger sister Esther had been before her recent wedding? She tried to imagine herself teaching a class filled with *kinder* from six to fourteen years old. Glancing at the books stacked on the bookcase beneath one window, she knew their titles by the colors of the spines. Was it because she'd studied with similar books, or had she taught with them? If she was a teacher, that meant she wasn't married.

Her gaze went, before she could halt it, toward where Amos was talking with his *mamm*. He glanced at Linda and a slow, warm smile curved along his lips. The too-familiar quiver in her middle warned her to look away.

She couldn't. The buzz of conversations filling the room faded as he walked toward her. Would he brush his fingers against her cheek as he had on Sunday before they went sledding with Polly? Even four days later, her skin heated in anticipation of his gentle touch, though she knew he wouldn't be brash when his family and neighbors stood nearby.

"You look unsettled," he said quietly, though nobody was paying any attention as parents congratulated the scholars for remembering the lines they'd worked hard to memorize.

Linda sighed. "I am." She explained how she recognized the textbooks. "Why can I remember the name of the third grade reader, but I don't know my own last name?"

"Why are you unhappy you've recovered another memory? It may not be the one you hope for, but it's a memory, and it's yours."

"You're right. It's my memory. It's mine." She spoke those words like a prayer, then sent up a true prayer of gratitude to God for what she was able to recall.

And for Amos.

He was a steady rock in the storms swirling around her.

"I don't know if I could be as patient as you are," he said, leaning one hand on a nearby chair.

"What gave you the idea I'm patient?"

"You aren't stomping around displaying your frustration over the whole situation."

"I would if it'd help." She smiled at him. "Do you think it would?"

"If I say *ja*, will you stamp around?"

She appreciated his teasing that drew her out of her doldrums. If not for Amos, it'd be far too easy to give in to the grief tugging at her whenever she let her guard down.

Polly ran to them. "Mandy says she's going to teach me the songs they sang today, even the ones with *Englisch* words!"

"Isn't that *wunderbaar*?" Linda asked.

"Ja." The little girl dimpled. "I'm glad we're here. I miss *Grossmammi* and *Grossdawdi*, but Mandy is my bestest friend!"

Linda kept her smile in place, but it wasn't easy. She couldn't miss Polly's grandparents—whoever they might be—because she remembered nothing about them.

"And you're her friend," Amos said. "Hers and Debbie's."

"Debbie says I'm *gut* to practice on. Her little sister is a *boppli*."

"That she is." He stood straighter. "But she's growing fast."

Polly turned to her. "Linda, let's get a *boppli*, too."

Sure every ear in the room had heard Polly's question, Linda hoped her face was not as red as it felt. "A *boppli* needs a *mamm* and a *daed*."

"I know that." The little girl regarded her with an

expression that suggested Linda was the silly one. She looked at Amos. "You can be the *daed*."

Every word Linda had ever known fled from her mind, but Amos laughed and bent to look at the *kind*. "You've got everything planned, don't you?"

"*Ja!*"

"Can you keep a secret?" he asked in a conspiratorial tone.

Polly nodded eagerly.

"You won't tell anyone?"

"No."

"Not even Linda?"

The little girl hesitated, torn between needing to know what he had to say and knowing she'd want to share it with Linda.

Amos chuckled. "All right. You can tell Linda, but nobody else. Okay?"

She nodded and grinned. "What is it?"

Putting his hand next to his mouth, he bent to whisper in the little girl's ear. Linda couldn't hear what he said, but Polly's smile returned, growing wider with every passing second. Linda wondered what he was saying to the *kind* about her expectations.

Her naive expectations, Linda knew. But why was her own mind filled with images of her and Amos standing together and watching Polly participate in a Christmas program? Smaller *kinder*, their *kinder*, would be gathered around them, as eager as Polly was now.

Had she lost her mind as well as her memories? Mistaking Amos's kindness for anything else would be the worst thing she could do.

Amos drew back as Polly crowed, "Hooray! We're

going to have *snitz* pie tonight!" She put a finger to her lips. "Don't tell anyone. It's a secret."

"I won't," Linda said, astonished how easily Amos had turned the little girl's mind to other matters. She smiled over Polly's head and mouthed, *"Danki."*

He winked in response, and the motion sent another rush of warmth cascading through her. He cared as much about the little girl as she did.

She and Polly had spent a week at the Stoltzfus farm, and the odd situation of not knowing who she was and where she'd come from almost seemed normal. Depending on Amos to cheer her up when she felt blue was becoming a habit, too. She wished she could be sure if it were a *gut* one or not.

When Linda went with Polly to see Mandy's desk, Amos remained where he was. He couldn't tag after Linda like a puppy. That would cause more talk about the mysterious woman who'd appeared during a snowstorm. Nobody was unkind. Simply curious, and he couldn't fault them, because he wanted to know the truth about her, as well.

He pulled his gaze from where she stood by a desk with Mandy and Polly. *Mamm* was talking with Neva Fry, the new teacher. She'd done a *gut* job stepping in when she took over the responsibilities of the school and its scholars after his younger sister Esther married Nathaniel Zook two weeks ago. The newlyweds and the young boy who lived with them were visiting Nathaniel's family in Indiana for the holidays. Otherwise, Esther wouldn't have missed seeing the program.

It had been a splendid one. He listened to Polly join in each time a song was sung in *Deitsch*. The *kind* wouldn't learn to speak *Englisch* until she went to school, so when the carols were in *Englisch*, Linda whispered a translation into her ear. Though Linda had lost much, she hadn't forgotten her love for the *kind*.

He could admit to himself he was glad the *kind* had confirmed Linda wasn't her *mamm*. That was the one fact he was sure of. Watching Linda from the corner of his eye, he wondered—as he had many times before— why she'd been traveling with only a little girl. Surely if she had a husband, he would have come with them.

Amos knew he shouldn't let her become more a part of his life. He'd made a mistake over another woman, and he'd been certain he knew Arlene well. He couldn't say he knew Linda. She hid much of herself, more than what her lost memories could account for. Maybe she didn't want to make too many connections in Paradise Springs until she discovered where she belonged.

"Amos?" *Mamm*'s tone suggested she'd called to him more than once.

"Sorry. I was…thinking."

"I can see." She gave him an indulgent smile. "Could you bring Linda and Polly home in your buggy? Leah's is full."

"I hope you aren't trying to matchmake, *Mamm*."

"I leave that to the professional matchmakers."

He arched a brow, and she chuckled. "*Ja*, Linda and Polly can ride in my buggy."

"*Danki*, Amos. We'll see you there. Don't be late, or your brothers will devour your share of the *snitz* pie."

Laughing, he said, "I won't be late. Nobody wants to miss your famous *snitz* pie, *Mamm*."

"Hardly famous," she chided, but he could tell she was pleased at his compliment for her dried apple pie.

His *mamm* walked away to speak with a neighbor, and he headed toward Mandy's desk to let Linda know of the change in plans.

As he approached, he heard Polly saying, "I liked when you used to read stories to me, Linda."

"You did?"

"I like stories before I go to bed. You used to read to me every night. Until…" The light in the little girl's eyes became cloudy with distress.

Linda's face flushed, then went gray, but her voice gave no sign of her thoughts as she said, "I think we should have a story before bed tonight and every night. What do you think?"

"Ja!" She pressed her cheek against Linda and whispered, *"Ich liebe dich,* Linda.*"*

"I love you, too."

Something in Amos's chest loosened when he watched the two embrace. Was it his tight hold on his heart? He'd guarded it since Arlene had tossed it aside like last week's newspaper. Never had he imagined a pint-size *kind* would break the chokehold he'd kept in place for five years. No, not Polly, but Linda who couldn't hide her love for the little girl. He wondered what it'd be like to have her love him.

He stepped aside as several of the scholars' parents and grandparents paused to ask Linda how she was feeling. Her smile appeared to be genuine, but he noticed how her hands curled into fists before she concealed them behind her back. Their well-intentioned words were a reminder of how much she had lost.

If Linda's smile grew any more brittle, it was going to crack off her face. Amos wondered how much longer her composure could hold together. She looked exhausted, and he reminded himself it'd been only a little over a week since he'd found her, lost and in pain, in the parking lot.

He waited for a break in the conversation. "We need to leave," he said in his most casual tone when that pause came. "I've got to make a stop before we head home."

Linda nodded, but he could sense her relief as she said goodbye to the crowd. Taking Polly by the hand, she squatted to help the *kind* button her coat. She didn't notice the looks exchanged over her head, but he did.

He was glad she hadn't, because she would have been bothered by the sympathetic expressions. He bit back words he must not speak. The concern was meant kindly, but it made Linda uncomfortable. She hadn't given any quarter to the pain or her lost memories, and she didn't want to be seen as an object of pity.

Dusk was changing to dark on the shortest day of the year when Amos led the way to his buggy. Linda hadn't acted as if riding home with him was anything out of the ordinary. Because she didn't see him as someone she'd walk out with?

Polly chattered about what she'd seen, and Amos was grateful because he wasn't sure what to say to Linda when his thoughts were completely out of his control.

He broke the silence when they turned on the road leading through the middle of Paradise Springs. "I need to stop at the store, but I can take you to the farm first."

"I thought you were making an excuse at the school."

He shook his head as he glanced at the *Englisch* houses. Christmas lights twinkled on the eaves of many of them. "I need to stop at the store because of a late delivery, but like I said, I can take you home first."

"Nonsense. The store is on our way. Patch won't be happy to see his comfortable stable and then have to go out."

"How about me? You have sympathy for my horse, but none for me?"

"I assume if you don't want to go back out, you won't." She smiled, and he realized she was teasing him.

That pleased him. She was serious too often, and, when she jested with his family, he saw shadows of uncertainty and despair in her eyes. It was a constant reminder how her family must be anxious about where she and Polly were.

He kept the jesting going until he'd unlocked the front door and turned on the store's lights. Hearing a rumble on the road, he went to the window. The delivery truck from the warehouse that supplied his store was pulling into the parking lot.

"This won't take long," he said as he unwound his scarf and tossed it and his coat on the checkout counter. "I need to do a quick inventory to make sure everything matches the invoice."

"Can I help?" Linda asked.

He was about to tell her he could handle it himself as he always did, but he smiled. "Sure. It'll go more quickly with two of us working. I'm sure the driver will be glad, too."

While Polly raced up one aisle and down the other, pausing to look at any container that caught her eye, Linda followed him into the storage room. He opened the door, and the back-up beeps of the large truck became shrill. Taking his handcart from a dim corner, he pushed it onto the covered rear porch.

"Hello, Mac," he said to the truck driver. "Working late tonight?"

The older man, whose belly strained against his coat, grimaced. "These deliveries have to be made before Christmas, or the boss will get upset." He rolled his eyes. "And it's never a good idea to get the boss upset."

Amos took the invoices before the driver opened the truck and let down a ramp. Handing the pages to Linda, Amos asked her to put a check next to the line for each box as it came into the store.

"Do you have a highlighter?" she asked. "It'd be easier to see any missing items with one."

"That's a *gut* idea for next time."

She nodded and bent over the list as he helped unload the boxes and the bags of flour and sugar. He realized it was odd how he'd never invited Arlene to be part of his life at the store. Or maybe not odd because she'd never shown any interest. Most of their conversations had revolved around the intriguing gossip she adored.

On the other hand, it was too easy to imagine Linda working by his side again. He looked at where she made a neat check next to each item as he called it off. With her head bowed over the pages, a single strand of her white-blond hair fluttered against her cheek on the cold air blowing into the room. It took every bit of his strength not to push it behind her ear.

When everything was unloaded, Mac bid them a merry Christmas and shut the truck. Amos closed the door and locked it. As he turned, his gaze was caught by Linda's. Her face was blank, but many emotions swirled through her eyes. He felt dizzy. Or was the light-headedness because they stood close together in the otherwise—save for a four-year-old *kind*—deserted store?

Look away! The warning blared in his head, but he couldn't obey it. He took one step, then another toward her, closing the distance between them. He half expected her to turn and walk away. She remained where she was, her fingers clutching the invoice papers.

"Everything checked out," she said in an unsteady whisper. The strand of hair now curved along her face as he wished his fingers were.

"*Danki* for your help." He edged nearer.

"I'm glad to help. You and your family have done so much for Polly and me."

His hand rose of its own volition toward that enticing tress. Her name burst from him in a breathy whisper as he touched her cheek.

"Are you here, Amos?" came a deeper voice from the front of the store. "Is Linda here, too?"

Amos jerked his hand back as if he'd grabbed a lightning bolt. He avoided looking at Linda as he went to where his bishop stood by the front door. Reuben was listening as Polly tried to tell him every detail of the school program.

"Reuben, is there something in particular you're looking for?" Amos asked when the little girl was finished.

The bishop nodded. "I'm assuming Linda is here if Polly is."

"*Ja.*" Dozens of questions pounded his lips, but he didn't let a single one escape.

When the bishop looked past him, Amos peered over his shoulder at where Linda stood in the door to the back room. She walked to Amos and handed him the invoices as if she helped at the store every day.

"Guten owed, Reuben,*"* she said.

"Good evening to you, too." He drew in a deep breath and let it flow out in an extended sigh. "I hope I'm not going to ruin it by what I have to tell you."

"The truth may be harsh, but it's better when it's not half-hidden in niceties."

Reuben nodded, clearly pleased with her answer. Amos tried to ignore the pulse of pride bursting inside him. She was *wunderbaar,* a gutsy woman unwilling to buckle under the challenges she faced.

"Then," said the bishop, "I'll get right to the point and say the news isn't *gut.* I've contacted bishops between here and Lancaster. Each of them has asked members of their districts, and nobody reports knowing you and Polly."

She sank to the bench by the door and clasped her hands in her lap. "Oh…"

Amos looked at Reuben, and the bishop motioned for him to remain quiet. He understood needing to let Linda respond before he jumped in; yet, it was almost impossible not to offer her comfort. Not just words, but drawing her into his arms and holding her until he could find the right thing to say.

She raised her head, and he knew her courage had not wavered. Her eyes were bright with tears, but none streaked her face. When she spoke, her voice was more unwavering than his would have been if their situations were reversed.

"Danki for your efforts to help find Polly's and my family." She closed her eyes and sighed. "Or maybe I

should say families." Looking at him and Reuben, she added, "Either way, I appreciate your help."

"Don't give up," his bishop said in his kindest tone. "More people are being contacted. This search is spreading like ripples in a pond. We've assumed you took the bus from Lancaster, but there are connections at that station to many places. We won't give up until we know the truth, either by you regaining your memories or someone coming forward."

When she repeated her gratitude as Polly climbed into her lap and put her arms around Linda's neck, she hugged the *kind*.

Amos walked Reuben onto the porch and added his own thanks.

"It's difficult to be away from those we love during the Christmas season," Reuben said, "but at least we have our memories to comfort us. Linda has nothing."

"She has Polly, and she has her faith this will be set to rights. Somehow."

"And she has you, Amos."

"My whole family has pitched in."

"*Ja*, but you've set yourself up as her earthly protector." Reuben put a workworn hand on Amos's shoulder. "Be careful, son. Once her memories return, everything may be different."

"I think of that constantly."

Bidding Amos a good night, the bishop vanished into the night. The creak of springs and leather told Amos when Reuben had climbed into his buggy.

Amos went inside and paused to select a bag of lollipops. Opening it, he offered it to Polly. "You were such a *gut* girl at the program. Pick two or three to take home with you."

"And for Mandy?"

Touched by her generosity, he smiled. "Take two or three for her, too."

"And Debbie?"

"Maybe it'd be simpler if you take the whole bag. Go and get your coat, because we don't want my brothers to finish off the *snitz* pie before we get there. Lollipops are *gut*, but not as *gut* as *Mamm*'s pie."

With an excited shout, Polly ran to the far end of the store where she'd left her coat and mittens.

As soon as the *kind* was out of earshot, Amos asked, *"Bischt allrecht?"*

"*Ja*, I'm all right." Linda stood and smoothed her apron over her dress. "Nothing's changed, has it?"

He nodded, knowing it was true. No matter how much he wanted everything to change, for her to regain her memories and for him to be certain there was no other man in her heart, nothing had. He was beginning to wonder if it ever would and what they—what *he* would do if her memories never returned.

Chapter Six

The bedroom Linda shared with Polly in the *dawdi haus* had a view of the snow-covered pastures. Paw prints crisscrossed the field, showing where rabbits and a fox had traveled. Tinier marks pinpointed the landing spots of birds. Evergreens bent toward the ground with their burdens of snow, but bare branches were a lacy pattern against the bright blue sky.

It was a lovely, albeit chilly morning three days before Christmas, and, as she sat on her bed and stared out the window, Linda faced a troubling dilemma. Christmas was coming, and she had no gifts for the Stoltzfus family. She wanted to buy them gifts, but how could she? She didn't have any money.

"Was iss letz?" Polly asked, climbing onto the bed beside her.

"What makes you think something is wrong?" she asked the little girl.

"You look like a cloud on a stormy day."

In spite of her low spirits, Linda smiled. "Did you make that up yourself?"

Polly shook her head. "No. I heard *Mamm* say it a lot."

"What else did she say?" she asked. Polly hadn't said much about her parents, and the key to unlocking Linda's memories might be in one of Polly's recollections.

The little girl shrugged. "Lots of things."

"Tell me." She put her arm around Polly's small shoulders.

Polly screwed up her face in concentration. "She told me *gut* deeds have echoes, but I've never heard any."

"It means if you do something nice for someone, that person may be happy and do something *gut* for someone else."

"Like when I ask Mandy for some milk and we have cookies together?"

"*Ja*. Like that." She was delighted by Polly's perspective which always seemed to have something to do with Mandy and cookies. "Did Mandy tell you we'll be making sweets tomorrow for the cookie exchange on Christmas Eve?"

"Yummy." She grew serious as she asked, "Linda, can we get Mandy something special for Christmas?"

"You could make her—"

"No! I want to get her what she wants. A book about a little house and the woods."

Little House in the Big Woods, Linda translated. She'd heard Mandy mention the book more than once in the past few days.

"I'm sorry, Polly, I don't have any money to buy her a book."

"I've got money."

Linda stared at the *kind*. "You do?"

"*Ja*. Lots of it. Wait here." She jumped down from the bed and ran to pull her coat from a peg by the door. What was the *kind* doing?

Rooting around in one pocket and then the other, Polly drew out a cloth bag. She put her coat on a nearby chair before returning to Linda. "See?"

Linda took the bag, expecting to feel a few coins in it. Her eyes widened when she heard the crackle of paper. She undid the drawstring and peered in. She gasped. The bag was filled with money. Pulling it out, she counted in astonishment.

Why would anyone give a *kind* more than fifty dollars?

She didn't realize she'd asked the question aloud until Polly said, "You gave it to me, Linda. You asked me to take *gut* care of it."

She tried to remember doing what Polly had described. Nothing. The same gray cloud of nothingness filled her mind, standing between the woman she was now and the person she'd been before...before whatever had happened at the bus station.

Knowing that trying to recover a memory seemed to make it flee from her, she looked at the money in her hand. Instead of wondering why she'd given money to a young *kind*, she should be grateful she had it. She could buy gifts for Mandy and the rest of the Stoltzfus family.

"Put on your coat, Polly. We're going shopping."

"Yippee!" She ran to obey.

Linda found a sheet of paper and wrote a quick note to let Wanda know where they were going and why. She finished it with *We'll be back in a few hours.* Setting it on the table in the *dawdi haus*'s tiny living room, she put on her boots and, grabbing her own coat, flung it on as she walked to the door dividing the living room from the main house.

"Leah, can I use your buggy this morning?" she called into the kitchen.

"Of course. If you need help hitching the horse up, ask Ezra. He's in the barn." Her eyes crinkled in a smile. "He's working on a new type of cheese today, so I'm sure he'll be there to unhitch the horse when you get back. Nobody's going to budge him out of the cheese room today."

"Danki." Holding her hand out to Polly, she closed the connecting door. She was as excited as the little girl was to select gifts to thank the Stoltzfus family for their warm hospitality. She had ideas about what to get each one…except Amos.

How was she going to find him a gift that would express what he meant to her when she wasn't sure herself? No, that wasn't the truth. She *knew* she was falling in love with him, whether she should or not.

How long before he paced a path right through the floor? How many more looks could *Mamm* aim at him, each a silent reprimand that he was overreacting?

Amos didn't slow as he walked from the front door to the kitchen and back. Where were Linda and Polly? They'd taken Leah's buggy this morning and left a note saying they were going shopping, but he hadn't seen them at the store. When he'd come home and found they were missing, too many unsettling scenarios raced through his head.

Perhaps Linda had regained her memories and was heading to the place she and the *kind* had been going before she was hurt. Could she have gotten tired of waiting for those memories to return and decided to try to find her way to her original destination on her own? Or maybe she'd bumped her head and couldn't remember him.

The last bothered him most. To imagine her forgetting him when he knew he'd never be able to forget her was painful.

Suddenly Amos heard buggy wheels crunching through the frozen slush on the lane. He sped out of the house and across the yard. He recognized the dark brown buggy horse. The buggy's wheels had barely stopped turning before he grabbed the door handle and threw it open.

"Where have you been?" He reached into the buggy and grasped Linda by the shoulders.

Startled by his vehemence, she jerked away from him. "Amos, have you lost your mind?"

"Almost." He drew back his hands when he saw Polly's face was as pale as Linda's. Frightening the *kind* because he'd been fearful they'd left forever was foolish. "Where have you been?"

"I left a note for Wanda." She motioned for Polly to climb out, then looked at him pointedly.

He stepped aside to give her room to step down. "I know you did. I read it."

"Then why are you asking where we were? It said we were going—?"

"Shopping, but you weren't at the store. I know. I checked every inch when Leah came to tell me you and Polly hadn't come home for lunch."

"Yours isn't the only store in the world, Amos Stoltzfus."

Her words were like a slap to the face of a hysterical person. It shocked him out of his foolish fear.

"You're right," he said. "But I thought you'd lost your

purse along with your suitcase after you were injured at the bus station."

"I did, but Polly didn't lose the money I apparently gave her."

As she explained what the *kind* had told her, he waited for his heart to halt its frantic beat and return to its usual pace. He couldn't halt his fingers from curving around her shoulders, this time gently.

"Your note said you'd be back in a few hours," he said as he gazed into her amazing eyes shining in the light from the kitchen. "When you didn't return…"

"I wanted to surprise everyone with gifts on Christmas. I never guessed we'd be delayed by traffic and crowds."

"Where did you go?"

"To the Rockvale Outlet shops."

His hands tightened on her. He forced them to ease before he hurt her. "Did *you* lose your mind? Driving along that busy highway this close to Christmas?"

"When I saw the traffic whizzing by, I went to the post office. A man there told me how to go through Gordonville and toward Bird-in-Hand before heading south on the farm roads."

"At least you were sensible about that." He put up his hand before she could retort. "I'm sorry, Linda. I keep saying the wrong thing, but I've got a *gut* excuse. I was worried about you and Polly. I had the craziest thoughts about you forgetting us."

She shivered. "Don't even think that."

"I try not to."

"Maybe I should wear the bike helmet all the time." Her attempt at a smile sent a pulse of delight through him. She was trying to make *him* feel better.

"Maybe you should."

As she urged Polly to let *Mamm* know she and Linda were home, he unhitched the horse.

"Do you need help with your packages?" he asked as he led the horse toward the barn.

"So you can find out what I bought?" She wagged a finger at him as if he were no older than the little girl. "I'll handle them on my own."

"You're a stubborn woman."

"*Ja*, I am." She smiled while matching his steps. "And you're a caring man. *Danki* for worrying about us."

He wasn't sure how to reply to her comment, so he didn't. He enjoyed bantering with her as they walked into the barn. He didn't know how much time they'd have together, and he intended to enjoy every moment and try not to fret about the unknowns. He'd leave the future in God's hands where it belonged and be grateful for the time he had with her…however much there was.

Chapter Seven

Easing around half-frozen puddles of slush in the parking lot the next day, Linda was grateful for the boots Amos had lent her. The snow had started melting yesterday but hardened into ice in the evening. During the night, she'd heard a plow going along the road at the end of the farm lane. It'd scraped on the asphalt and spread sand to keep the road safe for *Englisch* vehicles.

And for her. More than once on the walk from the farm, her foot had skidded on black ice she hadn't noticed. Probably because her thoughts were on her conversation with Amos yesterday. So many things she'd wanted to say when they stood face-to-face. So much of the moment she wanted to enfold in her heart and treasure it forever. The powerful emotions in Amos's eyes and the strong but gentle way he'd gripped her arms as he revealed how worried he'd been for her. She savored the memory of the husky warmth in his relieved voice.

She was silly to think about such things. Pulling her knitted scarf closer to her mouth, she pushed it aside when the fabric swiftly became damp and cold from her breath. She ducked her head into the biting wind as she stepped into the parking lot of the Stoltzfus Family Shops. Several buggies were parked in front of the shop on the far end from Amos's store. It belonged to his older brother Joshua who worked on buggies.

A wisp of smoke tainted the air. It must have come from the smithy behind the shops.

Hurrying as the wind picked up, Linda's foot slid again. She grabbed a nearby buggy.

"Careful there," she heard from her right. "Are you okay?"

She saw a familiar face behind a clumpy, pale blond beard. "I am, Isaiah."

He nodded. "You've got a *gut* mem…" He flushed, making his uneven beard stand out more on his face.

"It's all right," she hurried to say. "Please don't watch your words around me. If everyone does, I'm going to feel more lost. Amos suggested if I make myself comfortable here, my memories might return."

"He may be right. Amos thinks deeply about things."

"I've noticed he doesn't talk just to have something to say."

"Which makes him a *gut* source of advice." He grinned. "Don't tell him I said that. It doesn't do for a little brother to be complimented by his older brother." He grew serious. "I don't know if anyone told you that I haven't been a minister very long. I'm still wet behind the ears, as *Mamm* would say. However, if you want to talk to me at any time, I'm willing to listen."

Linda thanked him. The Stoltzfus family members were eager to do whatever they could to help her live in this strange limbo.

"Reuben asked me," Isaiah said, "to let you know he's been contacting other plain communities, not just

Amish ones. Because you weren't wearing a *kapp*, we can't be certain you're Amish."

"I didn't consider that." Everything about the Amish life seemed right to her, but other groups in addition to Old Order Amish like the Stoltzfus family had the same customs and plain clothing and spoke *Deitsch*. Wanting to change the subject, she asked, "Will you be coming to your *mamm*'s house for Christmas Day or will you spend it with your wife's family?"

"My wife died earlier this year," he said, his voice wavering.

She wished she could take the question back. "Oh, I'm sorry. I didn't know."

"There's no need to apologize. Rose's family misses her as I do, and I worry any time I visit, it's another reminder to them of what should have been."

"I doubt they forget it, whether you visit or not." She put her gloved hands over her mouth, horrified she'd spoken so bluntly.

Instead of a scowl or a sharp retort—both of which she deserved—Isaiah gave her a sad smile. "I understand why you and Amos get along well. He cuts to the heart of the truth, and so do you."

"Forgive me. I shouldn't have said that."

"No, it's okay. I know her family grieves for her, and I fear them seeing my sorrow makes them feel worse." He turned away. "Be careful where you walk. The ice is treacherous." He didn't give her a chance to answer before he walked toward his smithy.

Linda sighed into her scarf. She needed to be more like Amos and think before she spoke. Bending her head into the wind, she walked toward his store.

Help me, Lord, to say the right thing to these kind

people who have taken me into their home. I don't want to burden them further.

She raised her head when a woman called a greeting to her. Linda waved, recognizing the woman she'd met on Sunday, but not sure of her name.

Going inside, Linda saw it was crowded with dozens of shoppers. Everyone waited as the person ahead of them in the aisle took what they needed off the shelf before they moved forward. Several women pushed shopping carts, but others carried plastic baskets.

She stepped forward when the door reopened and an elderly couple entered. Stretching, she picked up the last basket and handed it to them before slipping around the end of the aisle…and bumping into Amos. She was surprised he wasn't behind the counter taking care of his customers.

He juggled the cans he was carrying and managed not to drop any. Setting them in a cart behind her and nodding to the woman's thanks, he wiped his hands on the apron he wore over his light blue shirt and black trousers.

"Can I help you find something, Linda?" he asked as he smiled at two other customers who pushed between them.

"Busy day today, huh?"

He looked toward the cash register. "If Micah hadn't offered to help ring people up, it'd be even more chaotic. What do you need?"

She didn't give him the answer burning on her lips. That she needed his arms around her as she spilled the truth she wanted to give him her heart. "Two things. First, your *mamm* needs some Karo syrup. We're planning to make popcorn balls for the cookie exchange tomorrow."

His harried expression eased into a smile. "I hope you plan to keep a few at home for those of us with a sweet tooth."

"You'll have to wait and see. *Gut* things come to those who wait."

"I've told you before that I don't have a lot of patience."

"Then this is the perfect time to learn it."

He chuckled. "This way." He led her along the aisle. Plucking the plastic bottle from among other baking supplies, he handed it to her. "What's the other thing you're looking for?"

"Leah mentioned you sell fabric."

"*Ja.* My selection isn't big, but I try to keep a few bolts for those who don't want to drive to Intercourse."

"Would it be possible for me to work at the store in exchange for enough material to make a new dress for Polly? I'd like to work on it tonight and tomorrow night after she goes to bed, so she can have it Christmas morning."

He took her arm and steered her through the crowd gathered around the shelves. They went along another aisle leading toward the rear of the store. No other shoppers were there. He gestured toward a dozen bolts of cloth on the shelves behind the counter. "Take what you need."

"But I want to—"

"You don't have to work here. You're helping *Mamm* and Leah at home. That's payment enough for me."

"Amos—"

Again he interrupted her. "Haven't you heard it's

better to give than receive, Linda? Let me give you a couple of yards of fabric for Polly's dress."

"Danki," she said, putting her hand on his arm. "This will mean so much to Polly. She's tried not to complain."

"She has had a *gut* role model in not complaining."

"Who?"

"You." He tapped her nose and chuckled. "You have more right than anyone I know to complain, but you don't."

"I do. All the time."

"Really? I don't remember hearing you."

She smiled. "Well, maybe not aloud, but inside my head there's a lot of whining going on."

"It must be noisy in there."

"You've got no idea." She lowered her eyes. "Amos, I've done a terrible thing."

"You?"

"I asked Isaiah about spending the holiday with his wife's family. I didn't know she'd died. I feel…"

Amos waited for her to finish. He hated to see Linda miserable. Was that what she was going to say? She felt miserable? Embarrassed? Sad? Knowing his brother must have reassured her, he wasn't sure what he could say to comfort her. He'd been fighting the yearning to take her into his arms and hold her close since Reuben had given her the bad news yesterday. He wanted to keep her from being battered more.

"I feel ashamed," she whispered.

"Ashamed?" he repeated, astonished. He hadn't imagined her saying that.

"Ja. I've been feeling sorry for myself because I can't remember my past, but your brother has lost so much

more than memories. He's lost the woman he loves and his life with her." Tears she hadn't let fall before welled up in her eyes, teetered on her lashes, then tumbled down her cheeks. "How could I fail to see how blessed I've been that you and your family took us in? I may have lost my memories, but I've gained more with you."

What could he say? Any words he could think of seemed useless, but she was in pain.

He realized nobody else was in the back of the store. Knowing he was being bold, he splayed his fingers along her cheek and tipped her face so her gaze meshed with his. He could stand like this for the rest of his life.

No, he wanted more. He wanted to kiss her. When her eyes widened, he was certain her thoughts mirrored his. He started to bend toward her, but froze when he heard a guffaw behind him.

Larry Nissley grinned as he hefted his overstuffed shopping basket. It was filled with cheese. Despite his one-time crush on Leah, he didn't let Ezra winning her heart keep him from being a fan of Ezra's special cheeses.

"You've got a pretty assistant, Amos." Larry chuckled.

"I do." He winked at Linda who flushed.

"But you've always been one with an eye for a lovely lady, haven't you? Guess you didn't learn your lesson after Arlene dumped you. I'd heard you're courting another mysterious lady." He laughed as he turned to her. "What are you hiding from my buddy Amos? Hope it's not a boyfriend or two you've conveniently forgotten to mention."

Amos sensed rather than saw, because he was careful not to look in Linda's direction, her shock at what Larry said. She backed away and murmured something he couldn't discern before she rushed behind the counter. She grabbed a bolt of dark green cloth and fled with it.

"Did I say something wrong?" Larry asked.

"What do you think?" He left the man sputtering behind him as he went after Linda.

Why hadn't he guessed Larry could say something thoughtless? The man had a reputation for uttering the wrong thing at the worst time.

By the time Amos had made his way through the packed store, Linda was walking away along the road. Should he go after her? He never would have described his heart as careless, but he couldn't deny he'd been ignoring the truth. First, he'd fallen for Arlene Barkman's pretty face, not heeding his brothers' warnings she was playing him for a fool. He'd told himself everyone was due one mistake, and Arlene had been his.

But his heart did jumping jacks whenever Linda was near. For all he—and she—knew, she belonged to another man. He couldn't accuse her of leading him on, because she'd done nothing beyond the boundaries of friendship. Any betrayal was by his own thoughts as he wondered if her lips would be as sweet as her smile.

Should he let her go? No!

Amos called Linda's name and was relieved when she stopped. He caught up with her and said, "I owe you an apology."

"You don't owe me anything." She glanced at the cloth she carried. "I'd say the debt is mine."

"I should have told Larry to be quiet."

"You aren't to blame for what someone else says."

"But I'm to blame for knowing how he can be and not stopping him before he said something stupid."

She began walking again. "Don't worry about it, Amos. I know you need to get back to the store, and I want to hide this fabric so Polly doesn't guess what I'm doing. I'll see you at supper."

He couldn't let her walk away when Larry's words hung between them. "Linda, I need to be honest with you."

"Aren't you always?" She paused and faced him.

"*Ja*, except about one incident in my past."

"With Arlene?"

Amos nodded. "I should have told you before that Arlene Barkman and I walked out together for almost six months. Not many people knew, though my brothers suspected. Arlene wanted to keep our courting a big secret."

"Most couples keep quiet about walking out together."

"*Ja*, but they're seen leaving youth events together or caught flirting or talking to each other. Arlene insisted we be extra circumspect. She wouldn't let me take her home unless I left on my own and we met somewhere far from everyone else. She made it seem like a game, and it was, but not the one I thought we were playing. Fool that I was, I swallowed her unending excuses of why she couldn't take a ride with me some nights. I was like a trout on the line which she played with, but never reeled in."

"I don't understand. What game was she playing?"

"One I had no chance of winning." He met her eyes as he said, "I wasn't the only man who was hearing her excuses."

"She was being courted by another man at the same time?"

"Two others."

"Two?" she asked in disbelief. "She was walking out with three different men at the same time?"

"I believed her explanations while she strung me along. I couldn't imagine she wasn't being truthful. I even believed her when she publicly announced everything about me that she found fault with. At least, until her engagement to another man was published during a church Sunday service the morning after I'd taken her for a buggy ride."

Linda didn't speak for a long moment, and he wondered what she was thinking. That he was a besotted fool? That he couldn't be trusted to see the truth?

He'd misread her because, as she shifted the bolt in front of her to hold it with both arms, she asked, "How long ago did that happen?"

"Almost five years ago."

"And you haven't forgiven her?"

He laughed without humor. "Oh, I've forgiven her. It wasn't hard because I realized I didn't want a woman who'd lied from the beginning. I've had a harder time forgiving myself for such poor judgment."

"Each of us makes bad decisions sometimes, Amos." She put her hand on his arm. "I'm sure I've done stupid things. I wish I could remember them, so I could share them with you now."

"I wish you could, too. Not to make me feel better, but because you'd have your memories." He kicked a stone across the road. As it clattered on the asphalt, he said, "It's my turn to say I'm ashamed. No, let me finish," he added when she started to answer. "I've spent the past five years feeling sorry for myself. For so long I thought the best thing God could do was take away my memories of Arlene and my humiliation. I see how stupid that was because I'm watching you suffer from losing everything you knew. I'm ashamed I thought banishing memories was worth what it would cost me."

"It's okay." She put her gloved fingers on his arm, and he realized for the first time he'd left his coat in the store. He'd been determined to reach her and hadn't felt the cold.

Nor did he feel it now because from where her hand rested, a luscious warmth oozed through him, thawing the last of the ice clamped around his heart. But his breath froze in his chest when she spoke.

"When I remember what I've forgotten, Polly and I will have to leave. I don't want there to be any bad memories between us, Amos."

"You don't have to leave." The words escaped his lips before he could stop them; then he knew he didn't want to halt them.

"We must have at least one family waiting for us. Don't you think they've waited long enough for us to come to them?"

The words burned on the tip of his tongue. She could remain in Paradise Springs, and they could discover if the attraction between them could grow into love.

But as she turned and continued walking toward the farm, he didn't try to stop her. He couldn't, because he knew she was right. But knowing did nothing to relieve his sorrow at the thought of her leaving one day and never coming back.

Chapter Eight

❧

The snow fell all through the night. It piled up around the house, blocking doors and clinging to windows in icy patterns.

Linda glanced through her bedroom window while she dressed in the dark on Christmas morning, grateful she didn't have to go outside. The snow swirled, and the barns were barely visible. She saw movement. Amos's younger twin brothers. Last night, they'd announced their Christmas gift to Ezra was to do his chores this morning to allow him the rare chance to sleep later than 4:00 a.m.

Before leaving the room, she adjusted the quilt over Polly. The little girl had been awake late last night, complaining of a tummy ache. Linda suspected Polly had snuck extra cookies at the exchange yesterday.

The propane lamp in the kitchen was glowing when she emerged from the *dawdi haus*. She wasted no time going to the refrigerator and getting what she needed to make breakfast. Soon the aroma of *kaffi* wafted through the kitchen, and she was putting cinnamon rolls into the oven.

"Smells *gut*" came a voice from behind her, the voice that released a thousand butterflies in her stomach.

"Frelicher Grischtdaag, Amos." She closed the oven and straightened.

"Merry Christmas to you, too." He was barefoot as he entered the kitchen, and his hair was tousled as if he'd forgotten to comb it. She'd never seen him look so adorable. "I didn't expect to see you up this early."

"I overheard Micah and Daniel talking about their Christmas gift for Ezra, and I thought I'd offer the same to Leah." She began to break eggs into a bowl so she could scramble them. "She does a lot for us." She smiled. "I've offered to make breakfast every other day from now on."

"That's generous of you."

Her heart danced at his admiring tone, and she dared to believe the discomfort of yesterday at the store could be put behind them. She'd been surprised by his friend's words and saddened by how many years Amos had lived with the pain of betrayal.

But she didn't say that. If she chose the wrong words, she could make him feel worse, so instead she said, "You've been kind to Polly and me. Making breakfast is a small way to repay your kindness."

"Did you get Polly's gift finished?"

"Ja, except for the hem. I want to measure it on her. She's growing so fast."

"She's going to love it."

"I hope so." She poured milk in with the eggs and began to whip them.

"And what gift do you want most for Christmas?" he asked.

Linda put down the fork and faced him. "You know what I want most."

"To have your memories back?"

"Ja." She handed him a cup of *kaffi* before turning away. With her face averted, she said, "I can't stop thinking of the people wondering where Polly and I are. Her grandparents. The ones we were on our way to...for a visit? To stay? So many questions and too few answers."

"Have you noticed any change? Any faint glimpse of a memory?"

She shook her head.

"Nothing? Just emptiness?"

She stepped to the window. "Look at the storm."

"What am I supposed to see?"

"What do you see?"

"Snow blowing in every possible direction."

"And beyond the snow?"

He shrugged. "I know the barns and fences and trees are there, but I can't see them. Only snow."

"That's how it feels for me when I try to remember what my life was before I crossed the bridge. It's as if I stepped out of a blizzard in my mind. I know there are things on the other side of that bridge. Things that happened to me, experiences for more than two decades of my life. I know they're there. As you know the barns and fences and trees are there."

"But you can't see them." He sighed. "I think I'm beginning to understand for the first time all you've lost."

"I can't see my memories or hear them or feel them, but I know they're there." She turned to check the rolls in the oven. "Sit down, and I'll get your breakfast ready."

"No hurry. I'll wait until Micah and Daniel are back and *Mamm* is up."

Linda nodded. Christmas was meant to be spent with family. She thanked God that she had Polly and the Stoltzfus family with her to celebrate the day of Christ's birth.

As if she'd called the little girl, the door from the *dawdi haus* burst open, slamming against the wall. Polly ran in, sobbing so hard she teetered.

Linda went to her as Amos rose from the table. "*Liebling, was iss letz*? Are you hurt?"

Polly clung to her and wept. "I want my *grossmammi* and *grossdawdi*. You promised we'd see them on Christmas."

"I did?" She looked over the *kind*'s shuddering shoulders to Amos who regarded her sadly.

"*Ja*. You said we'd spend Christmas Day with them and *Grossmammi* would make chocolate pancakes."

She knelt by the little girl. Brushing damp hair from Polly's face, she said, "I'd give anything to keep that promise, Polly. I wish I could."

"You're mean! You don't want to share them with me."

Taken aback by the *kind*'s anger, she struggled for something to say. Amos stepped forward and held out his hand to Polly. The little girl put her much smaller one in his.

He sat at the table and lifted Polly to sit on one knee. "Do you believe Linda would lie to you?"

The little girl bowed her head, then shook it. "But she promised."

"And Linda always keeps her promises to you, doesn't she?"

Polly nodded.

"And Linda would keep this one if she could. Don't you think so?"

"Ja." The single word was reluctant. "But I want to see my *grossmammi* and my *grossdawdi.*"

"You will. *I* promise that as Linda did."

Looking at him, she whispered, "But she didn't keep her promise."

"She will as soon as she can, and I'm going to help her keep that promise to you."

"Really?"

He gave her a grin and a wink. *"Ja,* I promise." His smile broadened when Polly flung her arms around him and squeezed him. *"Ach!* Don't keep me from breathing." Bouncing her on his knee, he added to Linda, "When will those eggs be ready for a hungry little girl?"

"As soon as she wants them…unless she'd rather have French toast," she replied, more grateful to Amos than she could put into words. As Polly cheered about the special treat, Linda smiled at the man holding the *kind.*

He started to smile but glanced at the door as his brothers entered along with a blast of cold air. Soon everyone was saying *"Frelicher Grischtdaag"* as she cooked French toast. Serving the first piece to Polly, Linda hoped the rest of the day would get better.

An hour later, after gifts had been shared, Polly tugged on Linda's hand. "Let's go and play in the snow!"

"It's chilly."

"I want to use my new mittens." She grabbed the bright blue ones Wanda had knit for her. They were a smaller version of the red mittens Wanda had given Linda.

"I'll take her," Amos said, standing from his chair near the fireplace. "I want to check the sleigh to make sure it's ready to take us visiting tomorrow for Second Christmas." He smiled at Polly. "*Komm*. Let's go."

Linda was about to speak when she realized, though he offered the little girl his hand, his gaze was focused on Linda. What she saw in his eyes was warm enough to melt the snow. He arched his brows in a clear challenge.

Putting down Polly's dress that she'd started hemming, Linda stood. "I'll go, too, to keep an eye on her."

"Bundle up," Wanda said, "and don't stay out too long. This is the coldest Christmas I remember in a long time."

Linda did that and made sure Polly's coat was buttoned to her chin before wrapping a thick scarf around her neck and over her stocking hat. Pulling wool pants on beneath the *kind*'s dress, she tucked them into Polly's boots.

She followed the little girl and Amos outside. Polly danced around in the new snow, her despair from before breakfast set aside. Not forgotten, Linda knew, because every once in a while she saw tears bubbling into the little girl's eyes.

"She's going to be fine," Amos said as he walked beside Linda through the snow that reached the top of her boots.

"I've been praying for that."

He stopped and faced her. The mist from their breaths combined and hung in the air between them, an outward sign of the connection growing between them. That connection had allowed her when she was in his arms to toss aside her brave facade and release the tears that had been strangling her. With Amos, she didn't have to be stoic. He never jumped to conclusions when she spoke of fears and hopes. Instead, he thought long and hard about what she'd said.

"Praying is the best thing you can do." He smiled at her. "*Danki* again for the box of highlighters you got for me."

"I thought they'd make the perfect gift for the next time you have to check off an invoice."

"*Ja*, perfect. If you were there using them."

She looked away from the potent emotions in his eyes. He shouldn't be looking at her like that, but she couldn't deny how special she felt when he did.

He picked up one end of her scarf and tickled her nose. "*Komm*, before your nose is as red as the cherries in *Mamm*'s pie."

When he turned to walk away, Linda checked what Polly was up to. The little girl had made a snow angel and was rolling snow to make a snowman. Linda bent to scoop up a handful. It compacted into a ball. Without warning Amos, she let it fly. The snow exploded on his barn coat.

He turned and laughed. "Why couldn't you have forgotten how to make a snowball?"

"What fun would that be?" She gathered another handful of snow and shaped it before aiming it at him.

With a playful growl, he strode toward her. He caught her wrist and shook the snowball from her hand. He held up a snowball of his own.

She tried to knock it away, but the deep snow caught her legs. She couldn't keep from shrieking as they fell together. Flakes flew everywhere as Polly ran to them. The little girl threw herself on top of them.

It took longer than Linda had expected to get untangled because the snow made it difficult to move. When Amos picked up Polly and put her on her feet, she ran toward the snowman she was making.

"I don't know about you," he said, "but sitting in this snow is a cold business."

"Ja." Linda drew her feet beneath her to stand. When she got up, she looked down at him. "Are you going to stay there?"

"I may if you threaten to pelt me with snowballs again."

She laughed. "I'll take pity on you, Amos. No more snowballs."

"Gut." He stood and wiped snow off his wool trousers. "It's cold."

"It is." She turned toward the barn. "Shall we get warmed up?"

"I thought you'd never ask." His voice took on a gentle huskiness that made her look over her shoulder in surprise. Amusement had vanished from his face as his gloved hands framed her face and tilted it toward him.

For a moment, she relished the sweetness of his touch, then she yanked herself away. What was she doing? If she was married... She put her hands to her heated face.

"Linda..." He didn't continue.

She wished he would because she didn't know what to say either. She couldn't tell him she didn't want him to touch her or kiss her. That would be lying. But there were too many things about herself she didn't know. Things that might mean she shouldn't be standing face-to-face with him.

"Linda," he began again. *"Ich liebe dich."*

"How can you say you love me when you don't know

me?" She wrapped her arms around herself, wishing the arms were his.

"I know you, Linda."

"How can you know me when I don't know myself who I am? Who I *really* am?"

He put his hands on her arms, sliding them to cup her elbows. He didn't pull her closer as he bent so their eyes were level. "I know exactly who you are. You're a *wunderbaar* woman who cares about those around her."

"Am I? Am I *really*? What if I was different before and I can't remember?"

"What if you were?"

Her head jerked up at the question she hadn't expected him to ask. Maybe she should have, because Amos preferred the truth.

"Linda," he continued when she didn't answer, "you can always be the woman you are now, whether or not you regain your memories. God gave us free will to find ourselves and to choose whether we want to walk with Him or not. He loves us, no matter what we decide, though He must mourn when one of His *kinder* decides to turn away from Him. No matter what caused you to lose your memories, I believe it was part of His plan for your life. Not many of us get a chance to remake our lives. You have.

"How can you have been a horrible person?" He looked at where Polly was rolling a ball of snow as big as she was. "Every truth you need to know is in her eyes. Polly loves you with the simple trust of a *kind* who has never had a reason to question that trust. Think of what she's told you of the past you've shared. Of the stories you've read to her and the songs and games you've taught her. She hid money because you asked her to. She never questioned why you'd ask. She never questioned why you got off the bus in Paradise Springs that night. She trusts you. She *loves* you. Could she feel that way if you weren't a *gut* person?"

"Are you always wise?" She let her shoulders ease from the tension aching across them.

"Hardly. Otherwise, I would have been better prepared when you pelted me with snowballs."

She laughed, her dismay vanishing as if it'd never existed. The sound drifted away when his fingers brushed her cheek, sending music through her heart. As his mouth lowered toward hers, her eyes closed. He found her lips, and she leaned into his strength. As close as they stood, she was unsure if the shivers were hers or his or both. She slid her hands along the powerful muscles of his arms, and he enfolded her to him. His kiss offered everything she wanted. When he stroked her back, tingles raced along her spine.

He lifted his mouth far enough away to whisper, *"Ich liebe dich,* Linda.*"* His expression had become vulnerable and honest. "Do you love me, too?"

"Ja! Ich liebe dich." For a moment, joy soared through her, then she stepped away. Looking across the snow toward the barn, she said, "Falling in love with you should change everything, but it doesn't. Not when I don't know what life I had before I came here. I must know what my life was in the past before I can consider what my future should be. I shouldn't let you kiss me when I may be married."

"What if your memories never return?"

"I don't know." She doubted she'd ever spoken such hopeless words and she longed for him to say something to ease her desperation as he had before.

Instead he drew her into his arms and leaned her head against his chest. Hearing his heart thud beneath her ear, she knew the truth. For the first time, he didn't have an easy answer for her.

Or any answer at all.

When a knock came at the front door after Linda had excused herself to put Polly to bed, Amos frowned and looked at his brothers. Who was calling at such a late hour on Christmas? What visit couldn't wait until Second Christmas tomorrow?

To be honest, he wasn't in the mood to have company. He'd spent the day trying to pretend his dreams weren't being dashed into splinters again. But unlike when Arlene had dumped him, he had to see the pain on the face of the one he loved. Oh, Linda had done an excellent job of trying to hide her thoughts from everyone else, but his heart seemed linked to hers now, and he could sense her sorrow.

Amos was closest to the door, so he got up and went to open it. He didn't want to leave anyone standing out in the cold. Glancing out a window as he passed, he didn't see any lights in the yard, but *Englischers* often got lost on the country roads and stopped to ask for directions.

Lost… He understood that feeling. He'd believed if he ever found his way back to love, he'd have the certainty and reassurance he craved. Maybe he was a greater simpleton than he'd believed.

Opening the door, he stared. The people standing on the front porch weren't lost *Englischers* nor were they among the Stoltzfus family's neighbors. They were, however, plain in dress by what he could see beneath their dark wool coats. A man and a woman, at least a generation older than he was. Perhaps two.

"*Komm* in, *komm* in," he said when the old woman shivered.

Thanking him, they entered the house. He heard his brothers coming to their feet, as curious as he was.

"This is the Stoltzfus farm?" the old man asked as he unbuttoned his coat.

Amos nodded and glanced at Ezra who had come to stand beside him.

His older brother said, "I am Ezra Stoltzfus. This is my farm."

"I'm Norman Glick," the elderly man said. "This is my wife Yvonne."

"Take off your coats and get warm." Amos gestured toward the living room and the hearth.

As if Amos hadn't spoken, Norman went on, "I hope yours is the Stoltzfus farm we've been looking for. We're searching for our two missing *kins-kinder*. Our two granddaughters who were traveling from Millersburg, Ohio. They were supposed to arrive almost two weeks ago, but they never did. We and our son and his wife and family have been looking for them everywhere between here and Millersburg, but we ran into blank walls." He glanced at his wife, then hurried on. "That is, until we heard from our bishop that two girls had found their way to a Stoltzfus farm in this part of Lancaster County. We came as quickly as we could to discover if they were *our* girls."

Amos didn't hesitate. As shock paralyzed his brothers, he crossed the kitchen in a few long steps. The door to the *dawdi haus* was ajar. He yanked it aside and rushed inside. Hearing Linda's lyrical voice reading a story to Polly, he burst into the bedroom.

"Amos!" Shock brightened Linda's eyes. "Is everything okay?"

"Maybe better than okay." He grabbed her arm, plucked the storybook from her hand and pulled her to her feet. He motioned for Polly to follow as he tugged Linda from the room. "An older couple has just arrived. They're looking for their lost granddaughters. You and Polly!"

Linda tried to get her mind around what Amos was saying. Someone had come seeking her and Polly? She stared at him. "But I thought—"

"That you'd recover your memories and go looking for them?" He smiled as he lifted Polly and settled her on his shoulders. "What does it matter? *Komm!* They're waiting to see you."

How could she explain what she didn't understand? Since she'd stumbled into the parking lot at the shops, she'd believed her memories would return to her at any moment. Then *she'd* find the answers to the puzzles taunting her.

Now...

Forgive me, Lord, for questioning Your way. I should be grateful if these people know Polly and me. But You know my heart and how happiness and hope can live side by side with grief at the idea of leaving here.

Lifting her chin so nobody could guess the disparity between what she felt and what she should be experiencing, she went with Amos. A single glance at him told her, even if she could conceal the truth from others, he knew what was in her heart. She treasured that realization.

They went into the kitchen. In the front room, she could see Amos's brothers as well as Wanda and Leah.

Polly wiggled to get down. The moment Amos set her on the floor, she ran and threw herself into the old woman's outstretched arms. *"Grossmammi! Grossdawdi!"* The little girl sobbed with joy when the elderly man put his arms around her. Then Polly ran back to Linda and hugged her. "You kept your promise. Just as Amos said you would."

Everyone looked at Linda. On wooden feet that seemed to be trying to grow roots into the floor, she forced herself to move forward as the little girl ran back to her grandparents. Polly knew the couple, but Linda couldn't recall ever seeing them before. There was something about the shape of the old man's face that reminded her of Polly's, and the old woman had light blue eyes with navy edging them as Linda did.

The woman gasped, "It's you, Belinda! You're safe."

"My name is Belinda?" She'd hoped her name would feel comfortable on her lips and open her sealed memories so they could spill out, but the name was as unknown to her as the elderly couple.

"Ja." The old woman glanced from her to the others. "Why does she sound surprised at her own name?"

As Amos gave an abbreviated explanation, Linda learned the older couple's names. They were her grandparents, and Polly was her little sister. Their parents lived in Ohio, and she and Polly had come to Pennsylvania to spend the holidays with their grandparents who lived near Shippensburg, a long day's buggy ride to the west.

It made sense, and Polly knew the couple. It must be true, but...

"I'm sorry," Linda said as the Glicks looked at her with the hope she'd hug them as Polly had. "I don't know you. I can't—" Her voice broke as she thought of leaving the Stoltzfus family who had become *her* family and going with people who were strangers.

Yvonne smiled. "My dear *kind*, it doesn't matter if you don't remember us. We know you!"

When she held out her arms to her, Linda—she needed to think of herself as Belinda—embraced the old woman. Some sense having nothing to do with her brain but everything to do with heart recognized the hug's warmth.

"You're my *grossmammi*." It wasn't a question. It was a fact. As if someone flipped the pages of a book in her mind, her head was flooded with images. Not images, memories. Her memories! Not just the ones she'd made since she arrived in Paradise Springs, but an explosion of memories from her past. *Gut* ones of being with her family, including her little sister Polly...and her other five sisters and three brothers. Happy ones of friends and the other families in their district in Ohio. Sad ones of the passing of her other grandparents as well as the end of a relationship she'd started because she knew her family expected her to find a young man to marry. Because being with him had been wrong from the beginning, her heart had filled with guilt and sorrow for being less than honest with him.

And bad memories, including a very, very bad memory at a bus station on their way to Shippensburg. Pain thundered across her skull as it had when she'd been attacked and robbed when she went to find out about which bus she and Polly should take next. She'd left her little sister sitting in the waiting area, because she'd planned to go only as far as the ticket counter, which was right in plain sight. She hadn't even seen the ragged man approaching until he pressed his sharp knife against her side as he forced her around a corner. He stole her purse and struck her in the head with the knife's butt, leaving her forgetting even her own name.

Later, when Polly wasn't there to hear, she'd tell her family and Amos and his family the awful thing that had happened to her. For now, she silently thanked God for watching over her in that dark moment and guiding her to Amos.

Tears glistened in the eyes like her own. "*Ja,* I am your *grossmammi.* Thank the *gut* Lord that He restored your memories." Her *grossmammi* hugged her again before stepping back so she could be enfolded in her *grossdawdi*'s arms.

Dozens of questions were fired at her, too many for her to answer at once. She tried to explain, skirting what had happened at the bus station.

When she finished, from behind her, Amos cleared his throat. "May I ask you a question, Norman?"

"Ask anything, my boy," the old man said with a grin so wide it pushed his wrinkles to the edges of his cheeks. "You saved the lives of our *kins-kinder.* It's something we'll never forget."

"Is Linda—Belinda, I mean—married?"

She blushed at the smiles on his brothers' and *mamm*'s faces.

Norman replied, "No."

"Or walking out with anyone?" Amos asked.

The older couple glanced at each other and laughed

before Yvonne said, "The truth is, and Belinda didn't know anything about this, her parents sent her and Polly to us for the holiday in the hope she'd meet someone here who'd touch her heart as no one in Ohio had. From your grin, young man, I'd say their hopes have been fulfilled."

When Amos grasped her hand, Belinda let him tug her into the kitchen. In the front room, everyone else acted as if they were interested in the minuscule details of the Glicks' journey from Shippensburg. Their voices faded beneath her thundering heartbeat when Amos turned her to face him.

She gazed into his eyes, seeing the love that thrilled her heart. "My name is Belinda Glick. I know that is my real name. It is such a joy to know that."

"Then let me say this the right way. *Ich liebe dich*, Belinda." His fingers curved along her face, gentle, questing, joining their hearts together in the moment they'd longed for.

"I love you, too. My name may have changed, but my love for you hasn't."

He kissed her left cheek and murmured, "I can kiss you without guilt because I know you aren't walking out with anyone else." He brushed his lips on her right cheek. "And I can kiss you without remorse because you aren't married to someone else." Cupping her chin, he held her gaze. "There's one more way I want to kiss you. When you're my wife. Will you marry me?"

"*Ja*, I'll marry you."

His eyes twinkled as he pulled her against his broad chest. "I know a marriage proposal may not be as *wunderbaar* a gift as a box of highlighters, but—"

She laughed and wrapped her arms around his shoulders. "Being married to you'll be the highlight of my life."

Snorting, he teased, "Because until a few moments ago, you couldn't remember most of your life, I don't know if that's a compliment or an insult."

"But I have all my memories now, and I still say being married to you will be the highlight of my life." She stilled his laughter and hers as she kissed him. Life with Amos would never be serious or boring. They'd make many memories together in the years to come, but one she'd always hold dear. As dear as she did this beloved man. It was this Christmas that she'd never forget.

* * * * *

HER AMISH
CHRISTMAS SWEETHEART

Rebecca Kertz

For Linda C., a wonderful friend
who is generous in spirit and love.

Be completely humble and gentle;
be patient, bearing with one another in love.
—*Ephesians* 4:2

Chapter One

November, Lancaster County, Pennsylvania

The Adam Troyer barn was filled to capacity with Amish youth. Young people stood near or sat on benches on both sides of three long tables. Plates with leftovers, snacks and plastic cups with the remnants of iced tea or lemonade littered the tabletops. Meg Stoltzfus and her sister Ellie attended tonight's singing with their friends, including one man from another church district, Reuben Miller, whom Meg had set her eye on from the first moment she met him, over two years ago.

"Ellie," Meg whispered, "Reuben asked to take me home."

"Again?" Ellie teased with a grin.

"Ja." Meg glanced longingly at Reuben. She'd first met him when he and his sister attended a singing at her cousin Eli's invitation, and she hadn't seen him again until three weeks prior, when he'd sought her attention after an unexpected encounter in Whittier's Store.

"Go," Ellie urged, startling her from her thoughts. "You don't want to keep him waiting."

Meg nodded. "I'll be home soon." She turned with a smile, but her good humor vanished as she encountered Peter Zook. She had fallen for him when she was sixteen, and she'd thought they were friends. But she'd been wrong, and she'd found out the hard way after accidently eavesdropping on Peter and his brother. Peter had told Josiah that she was spoiled and in need of discipline. She'd been devastated. Every time she saw him now, she felt her hackles rise.

Determined not to allow him to get to her, Meg smiled politely. "Beautiful night, *ja*, Peter?"

"It's supposed to rain," he said.

She stiffened and turned. "Rain? Honestly, Peter? That's all you have to say?" She fought irritation and won. Her smile became genuine. "Rain or not, I hope you enjoy the rest of your evening." Then she walked to where Reuben waited for her near the door, settling her gaze on him.

"Ready?" Reuben's appreciative smile was a huge boost to her morale as she reached his side. The complete opposite of Peter Zook in looks, Reuben had blond hair and pale blue eyes. Peter, on the other hand, had dark hair and a gaze that was currently a stormy gray.

She froze, then berated herself. Why was she comparing the two men? Why think of Peter at all?

The night was balmy and pleasant as she and Reuben stepped outside. The stars were glistening points of light in a clear, dark sky. *Rain*, Meg thought. *Huh!*

Reuben helped her into his buggy, then climbed onto the seat next to her. She studied him as he picked up the leathers and steered the horse down the dirt lane and onto the main road.

She frowned. What was the matter with her? Reuben

was handsome, kind and good-humored. Yet her joyful mood had dimmed.

Because of Peter Zook. Peter had stolen the fun from her evening.

Meg released a calming breath as she studied the hands that held the reins. She'd felt the calluses on Reuben's fingers when he'd helped her onto the seat. He'd told her recently that he'd been working with a construction company. Strong, hardworking hands. Hands that could belong to a working husband.

Silence surrounded them as Reuben drove the buggy down the dark, deserted road. The only sounds were the clip-clop of horse hooves and the sound of carriage wheels on pavement.

Should she start a conversation? Meg wondered, uneasy with the silence.

"You're quiet," Reuben said softly.

"So are you," she replied with a light laugh.

He turned to regard her with curious eyes. "Did you enjoy the singing?"

"*Ja.* Did you?" She met his light blue eyes, then looked away from the intensity of the gaze.

"I did because you were there."

"That's kind of you to say."

"'Tis the truth." He smiled. She met his eyes again and managed to smile back. "Meg?"

"*Ja*, Reuben?"

"I hope one day soon you'll allow me to court you."

She caught her breath. "You want to court me?" It was what she'd longed for, wasn't it?

"*Ja.*" His lips curved. "I know it's been only a few weeks since we started seeing each other, but I care about you. I can see us having a family together."

She kept silent, unsure what to say. *This is what I wanted.* Yet despite his willingness to wait, she felt as if he was rushing her into a serious relationship. The image of Peter Zook entered her mind, and she fought to banish it.

"What do you think, Meg? Can you see me in your future? Can you see us marrying and having children together?" He steered his horse into a right turn off the main road.

"This isn't the way to my *haus*," she said, feeling vaguely uneasy.

"*Ja*, I know. I thought I'd take you home the long way." He regarded her warmly as he touched her cheek. "I'm not ready for tonight to end. I want to spend more time with you."

Meg struggled to breathe. "Reuben—"

"Don't worry. I won't pressure you."

She relaxed. "Why me? Why now?"

"I've been working to save money, Meg. I wasn't ready before for a wife and family." He flashed her a tender smile. "I am now. And when I saw you again, I remembered the one evening we spent together, and I just knew. I want you as my wife."

Meg hid her shock. She didn't know how to respond to him. He seemed determined to marry her. And hadn't she always wanted to marry and have children? To prove to her parents that she was strong and would make someone a good wife? And she'd been fixated on Reuben for a long time.

"I'm a patient man," he said softly. "I can wait until you're ready."

As if their wedding were a foregone conclusion. Meg looked out the window, watching the passing scenery.

Reuben's confidence bothered her when she should be flattered. She liked him. He was a nice man. But he wasn't what she'd expected.

This is all Peter's fault, she thought bitterly. She'd been trying to recover from her unrequited love for Peter. She'd been foolish enough to be convinced that Reuben was *the one*, despite the fact that she barely knew him. She'd been obsessed with finding him again. Now that he was in her life, she shouldn't be surprised that her feelings for him weren't exactly what she had expected—or hoped for. She should tell him. It wouldn't be right to allow him to hope in vain.

But how would she know that he wasn't the right man for her if she didn't give him a chance?

Clouds in the distance blanketed the sky, covering the stars. It started to drizzle. She scowled. Peter was right. But how could he have possibly known? Within minutes, the drizzle became a mist that coated the roadway and covered the buggy's windshield.

"Is something wrong?" Reuben asked.

She bit her lip. Should she explain how she was feeling? *Give him a chance.* "*Nay*, but I—" A car came around a corner too fast and sideswiped the buggy, forcing the horse off the road. "Reuben!" she screamed.

Meg anticipated her death as the animal reared up on its hind legs and then bolted, dragging the vehicle down an embankment. Pain reverberated in her head as it slammed against the carriage's sidewall. She felt a jerk, then the buggy tilted and rolled. Her body lurched painfully as it continued to tumble down the hill.

The pitching stopped suddenly with a splash. Searing agony and cold wetness enveloped her just before she blacked out.

* * *

Peter watched Meg leave with a sick heart. Even after all these years, he couldn't forget what she'd said to him after she'd overheard him talking with his brother about her. He'd been mortified to realize that she'd heard him speak of his feelings for her—and she'd been upset by it. He'd thought they were friends, and he'd hoped for more. Even if she hadn't returned his love, she could have let him down gently, he thought bitterly. Instead, she'd been angry and spoken scathingly to him.

"I overheard what you told your *bruder*, Peter Zook!" she'd snapped. "You have some nerve. I thought I knew you, but I was wrong. From now on, stay away from me! *Just leave me alone!*"

Yet despite her hurtful words, he'd been foolish enough to hope things between them would eventually change, so he'd been prepared to wait. After all, she'd been only sixteen. He'd hoped that with maturity they would come to an understanding, and he'd have a chance at winning her heart. But it would never happen now. Meg finally had the man she wanted—and it wasn't and would never be him. What was it about her that wouldn't let him move on and forget her?

Peter scowled. He knew she'd obsessed over Reuben, but he'd figured it was only a matter of time before Meg realized that she'd been infatuated with a memory. But now everything had changed, with Reuben's return to Meg's life. The man obviously reciprocated her affection.

His stomach clenched painfully. He couldn't stand seeing her with Reuben. He should have tried harder to become friends with her again, but he'd hoped that if he stood back, watched and waited, she'd eventually soften toward him.

I've been too patient. I've waited too long. Years before that awful day she'd spurned his love, he should have tried to woo her.

She wants nothing to do with me. He needed to forget about her and move on. He needed to wed soon. His father was getting too old to farm, and with Josiah married and living elsewhere, it was up to Peter to take over the family farmhouse. Once he married, his parents would move into the *dawdi haus* on the property where Grandfather and Grandmother Hershberger had lived before they'd passed on. His father had mentioned several times in the last month wanting to move. An accident years ago had left his *dat* with a severely broken leg, which still pained him on occasion.

Peter wanted his parents to be happy. He knew they were upset because his sister Barbara hadn't been home in over a year. Knowing his father would be delighted by the plan, Peter firmed his resolve to find a woman to marry before November of next year, the time for Amish weddings.

There were other girls within his community. Nice girls. Young women who seemed to like him. He would find a new love to marry. Someone like his good friend Agnes Beiler. Lately he'd glimpsed something in her gaze that hinted she was open to more than friendship with him.

Unfortunately, he would be working with Meg Stoltzfus in the coming weeks till Christmas, whether he wanted to or not. This morning his father had approached him and asked that he help with a surprise party for his mother. His *mam's* birthday was on Christmas Day—and so was Meg's father's. His *dat* and Meg's *mam* wanted the two of them to plan a joint surprise birthday party. He once would have looked forward to spending time with her, when he'd still had hopes of winning her heart. But not now. Planning a party with her was the last thing he wanted—or needed.

Perhaps he worried needlessly. Meg might refuse to work with him, and he'd be off the hook.

Yet how could he deny his mother a birthday party? His *mam's* father—his *grossdaddi*—had died several months ago, and *Grossmammi* had followed him to the grave less than a week later. It had been a terrible time for his *mam* and family. While his mother had a strong belief that her parents were with the Lord, *Mam* still felt the pain of her loss.

So he would work with Meg if it meant bringing a glimmer of happiness into his mother's life. *Mam* was a wonderful wife and mother, and Peter would not fail in the task his father had assigned him. Whether or not Meg wanted it, they would plan a party together that neither parent would forget.

Forcing Meg from his thoughts, he approached his friend. Agnes Beiler was a kind girl with an inherent sweetness. With the singing over, he decided to offer her a ride home. Although Agnes lived in the next church district, he figured he could manage the distance from the Troyer farm to the Beiler residence in a reasonable amount of time before heading home. Peter studied her, enjoying the view, anticipating taking their friendship to the next level. It just made solid sense to fall for a good friend. Friendship was a good basis for marriage.

He leaned close and softly asked, "Agnes, may I take you and your sister home?"

She beamed at him. "*Ja.* That would be *wunderbor,* Peter. Just let me tell Alice."

He watched her approach her sister, who briefly glanced in his direction and then nodded. He saw Agnes move to her younger brother, who had brought the girls. The sisters then headed in his direction, clearly delighted for him to take them home. A mental image of Meg intruded, but he banished it. Agnes was just the person to get her out of his thoughts—and his heart.

The young women reached him. He grinned. "All set?"

"*Ja.* Are you sure you don't mind?" Agnes had likely suspected his feelings for Meg, and her eyes were sympathetic as she gazed at him.

"*Nay,* I'm more than happy to take you." He regarded her with warmth, and was pleased to see Agnes's eyes light up and her lips curve with pleasure. He assisted the sisters into the open buggy and then steered the horse toward the Joshua Beiler farm. The ride went quickly. It started to drizzle as he helped the sisters from the vehicle.

"I'll see you again soon." Agnes hurried toward the house after her sister, then waved from the front stoop.

As he headed for home, Peter brightened at the possibility of a new, meaningful relationship with Agnes. There were no streetlights and the road was dark. Rain, which began as a mist, fell in earnest, and he had to watch carefully. The family buggy would have offered him some protection from the rain, but his parents had taken it to his sister Annie's for a light supper. Unfortunately, he'd forgotten to put back the umbrella usually stored under the wagon seat after Annie had returned it last week.

Water pooled on the brim of his Sunday best black felt hat and ran in rivulets down his back. A light wind gust tossed the rain into his face, and he used his sleeve to wipe his eyes. He would be soaked before he got home, but there was no getting around it. He caught sight of an Amish buggy's running lights directly ahead on his side of the road. The headlights of an oncoming car blinded him for a second and then veered. Peter watched with growing horror as the car took the turn too fast and struck the vehicle ahead of him. The horse reared up and ran off the road. His eyes widened as the carriage rolled, out of control, and the car raced past him.

Stunned, Peter spurred his horse into a canter. His heartbeat thundered in his chest when he spied the buggy upended on the far side of the creek. After braking, reining in and finally securing his horse to a tree, he tossed his hat on the ground and ran to the water's edge. Only to find Reuben Miller lying near the edge of the stream.

Peter ran to him. "Reuben! Are you *oll recht*?" He gently shook him. "Reuben!"

"Meg." His gaze unfocused, Reuben attempted to sit up, grimaced, then fell back and closed his eyes. The man had been thrown from the vehicle.

"Meg is with you?" Peter asked, overcome with sudden stark terror. This wasn't the road to the Arlin Stoltzfus farm!

Reuben groaned. "Meg."

"Meg!" The rain fell in earnest as Peter waded into the water toward the overturned buggy. By some miracle, the horse had broken free when the vehicle had overturned, and now stood several yards away, a piece of the damaged harness still attached to it. *"Meg!"*

The water was deeper than he'd thought. He held his breath and dived under. He panicked when he didn't see her. Gasping, he shot up for air, then, frantic to find her, went under again. Adrenaline rushed through him, allowing him to stay underwater longer. His lungs hurt, in need of oxygen, and he lunged up to the surface once more. And then he saw Meg, several feet away. Faceup, but submerged in water, her dark hair floating about her eerily, her legs wedged under the damaged vehicle. His throat tightened as he battled fear.

Meg! He drew a deep breath and swam underwater until he was by her side. He reached out a hand, grabbed her arm and gently tugged. His heart thundered with gratitude as he was able to pull her legs from under the buggy. *Please, Lord, let her be well.* He continued to silently pray for her.

Finally, he had her close, and he raised her head above the water as he swam with her to the shallows, where he could stand. Then he swung her up into his arms and cradled her against his chest as he carried her to land.

Emotion lurched within his chest as he tenderly brushed back wet strands of dark hair from her unusually pale face. He set her gently on the ground close to Reuben. *Please, Father, help me help her. I'll leave her alone. I'll move on with my life. Please just let her live!*

He knelt beside Meg. When he saw that she wasn't breathing, his blood ran cold. Peter turned her onto her belly, then pressed down on her back several times in a steady rhythm. When she didn't respond, he turned her over again, tilted her head back and bent to give her mouth-to-mouth. Her lips were soft but cold. As he drew breath, then blew air into her lungs, he felt his fear escalate, but he remained focused as he worked to save her life. He stopped the breaths to press his hands below her sternum a few times, then continued mouth-to-mouth. He prayed he was doing correctly what he'd learned from a first-aid course.

Meg sputtered and gagged. Dizzy with relief, Peter quickly turned her over yet again, and with his arm beneath her shoulders, held her up as she vomited water. Tears filled his eyes as she coughed, then took several rough, gasping breaths. He waited until she quieted, then eased her onto her back. When he saw that she was breathing normally again, he offered up a silent prayer of thanks. Then he moved to check on Reuben.

"Reuben, I'm going to get help. Meg is right here next to you."

The man groaned.

"Reuben, do you understand? Meg is *oll recht*." He hoped and prayed it was true.

When Reuben didn't answer, Peter raced up to the road. As a vehicle approached, he waved his arms and shouted, but the driver zipped by. This section of road was dark and lonely, and he feared he'd be unable to get Meg and Reuben the medical attention they needed. He caught sight of another car. This time he ran into the road to flag it down, and prayed the driver would stop in time to avoid hitting him.

The car slowed. Peter moved off the road as the vehicle pulled next to him, and someone rolled down the passenger window. It was a middle-aged couple, the man in the driver's seat.

"Do you need help?" the woman asked.

"Yes," he said. "Do you have a phone?" When she said she did, he asked, "Would you call for medical assistance? There's been an accident. My friends—they're down by the creek."

The man parked his car while the woman dialed emergency services. Peter paced, anxious to get Meg and Reuben the help they needed.

Meg's near drowning had flattened him. He'd managed to save her, but what if she'd been underwater too long? He wanted her to be all right. He loved her. He closed his eyes and sent up another prayer.

The woman stepped out of the car, drawing his attention. "An ambulance is on its way."

"Thank you," Peter said.

Within minutes, the ambulance arrived, and he watched helplessly as the paramedics rushed toward the creek. He saw them examine Reuben and Meg before carefully lifting Meg onto a stretcher. The EMTs carried her up the incline to the road. A second ambulance arrived on the scene, and the medics hurried toward Reuben.

Peter approached Meg's stretcher. "Is she all right?"

"We'll know more after the doctor examines her in the hospital." The EMT gazed at Peter through narrowed eyes. "You know her?"

"*Ja*, we belong to the same church," he said. After a brief hesitation, he added, "My sister is married to her cousin."

Peter stared with concern as they carried the stretcher toward the ambulance. To his shock, Meg's eyelids flickered without opening. "Reuben?" she said.

The technician met his gaze. Peter gestured toward

the stretcher currently being carried up from the water's edge. The man nodded with understanding.

"He's getting medical attention," the technician told her.

Meg didn't open her eyes. *"Oll recht?"*

Peter's heart thumped hard as he studied her. "She asked if he is all right," he told the EMT.

"He's awake and responding," the man said. "He'll be taken to the hospital for a complete checkup." He and his coworker hefted Meg's stretcher into the ambulance.

The other workers carried Reuben toward the second emergency vehicle. Peter approached it. "I'll get word to his family." The EMT nodded.

"Meg?" Reuben muttered.

"She's on her way to the hospital," he said. "She asked about you." He felt a pang when Reuben sighed and closed his eyes.

Peter stepped back and watched while the EMTs entered their vehicles and started their engines. He felt chilled as he stood in the heavy downpour as the ambulances left. *Lord, please help her.* He stared at the vehicles' bright, multicolored flashing lights as they dimmed with distance, then disappeared from sight. He retrieved Reuben's horse, tied it to the back of his buggy and headed toward the Miller farm to return the animal.

Chapter Two

Meg woke up in pain. Even with her eyes closed, she could tell by the familiar antiseptic smell that she was in the hospital. Her head hurt, but the heavy weight bearing down on her leg felt worse. She shifted and moaned as pain permeated every inch of her body. She opened her eyes and tried to sit up, then gasped at the searing agony in her left leg. She lay whimpering as she prayed for relief. *Make it stop. Please, Lord, make it stop!* Tears spilled down her cheeks as she continued to suffer.

"Meg?" a familiar voice said.

A face loomed in her line of vision as she opened her eyes. "Nell?"

"*Ja, schweschter.* How are you feeling?"

"Awful. I hurt everywhere, especially my leg." She turned her head to meet her sister's gaze and groaned. The simple movement had hurt.

"Hold on, Meg. I'll get help." Then Nell disappeared.

"Nell!" She felt alone and scared. How badly was she injured?

Her sister wasn't gone long. "Meg, I've brought a nurse. She'll give you something for the pain."

"What happened?"

Nell, who'd been watching the nurse insert a needle into Meg's IV, glanced at her with concern. "You don't remember?"

"Nay."

"You were in an accident last night. You and Reuben. He was driving you home when a car struck his buggy and forced it from the road."

It had been raining. She recalled the terror she'd felt as she saw the car's headlights, felt the horse rear and the buggy pick up speed as it upended and rolled. She'd felt a searing pain, heard the splash of cold water before it enveloped her—and then nothing. "I remember now." She felt drowsy all of a sudden, and her pain eased. "Is he *oll recht*?"

"Reuben?" Nell asked.

"Ja." She had a vague impression of hearing someone's voice after the accident. "How did I get here?"

"By ambulance. Reuben did, too. You have a concussion and some bruising." She hesitated. "Your left leg is broken."

Meg shifted and suddenly realized that the heavy weight on her leg was a cast. Her breath hitched. "How bad is Reuben hurt?"

"He fared better than you. He has some bumps and bruises, as well as a concussion, but no broken limbs."

"Is he here?" Meg asked drowsily.

"Ja, in a room down the hall. The nurse told me he'll be released today." Nell grew quiet. "You nearly drowned. Reuben pulled you out of the water. He saved your life."

A man she could rely on, she thought. Meg shivered.

"The water was so cold." She got chilled just thinking about it. "I'm so tired." She fought to keep her eyes open.

"'Tis the pain medication. Rest." Her sister covered her with another blanket.

The warmth and the weight made her sigh. "Where's *Dat* and *Mam*?"

"Downstairs eating breakfast. I sent our sisters home. Everyone has been here all night. They didn't want to leave, but I insisted."

"Gut," she murmured sleepily. *"Danki,* Nell." She managed to open one eye. "You're newly married. You shouldn't be here."

"Don't you worry. James isn't far. Sleep, Meg. We'll be here when you wake up."

Almost immediately, Meg drifted into sleep. When she next opened her eyes, she saw that she had slept for some time, for the light came through the window from a different angle. She tried to rise and cried out. Her leg throbbed as she fell back again.

Her father bolted up out of a chair near her bedside, drawing her attention. "Meg, *dochter,* you want to sit up?"

"Dat." She blinked back tears. "I want to, but it hurts too much when I try."

He reached toward the side of her bed. "I'm going to raise your head some. Tell me if it hurts."

Her bed rose slowly, and while Meg felt the movement, the shift didn't cause terrible pain. "That's *gut."* She managed a smile. *"Danki."*

He nodded and stepped back to examine her carefully. "I'm glad you're awake. We've been worried."

"I'm sorry, *Dat."* She could only imagine what her

family must have felt after receiving news of the accident.

"Not your fault," her father said with a slight smile. "All that matters is that you're alive and will recover."

"*Ja*, I'll be fine." She studied his tired features with concern. It looked as if he had aged several years in one night. The knowledge that it was her fault upset her. "You should go home and rest. Nell said you were here all night."

"You were in an accident. Where else would I be but by your side?"

"And now it's time for you to go home."

He waved her suggestion aside. "Not yet."

She worried that the accident would cause him to be more protective of her than he already was. Ever since her last hospital stay, he'd tried to shelter her from every little thing. Fortunately, during the past two years, she'd been able to stand up to him a bit, and he'd finally learned to relax. Now her new injuries would take away that freedom she'd fought so hard for.

"Nell said that Reuben is *oll recht*."

Dat nodded. "He'll be discharged today. He wants to stop in to see you before he leaves."

Her mother came into the room. "Meg!" She hurried toward the bed. "You're awake."

Meg managed to grin. *"Ja, Mam."*

Nell entered next, and then James, her husband of just over a week.

"Meg, it's good to see you awake and smiling," her brother-in-law said.

"I told you we wouldn't be far." Nell eyed her closely, her gaze sharp. "How are you feeling? Still in pain?"

"A little, but not it's not as bad as before," Meg assured her. "How long did I sleep?"

"Four hours," her father said.

Meg was alarmed. "Four hours!"

"You needed the rest," her mother murmured soothingly.

Her injuries had kept her family from their beds, and she felt guilty. "Please go home. I'll be fine. You all need to sleep." She captured her father's gaze. "Please, *Dat*?"

"We'll go, but we'll be back to visit this evening," her father said.

"Tomorrow is soon enough," Meg insisted. "You can't be traveling back and forth. 'Tis too much." She bit her lip then winced. "Is every part of me bruised?"

"Nay," Mam said too quickly.

Meg offered a lopsided smile. "I bet I have a black eye." She saw the truth in her father's gaze. Things could have been much worse, she realized. She recalled her last time in the hospital, when a ruptured appendix had nearly caused her death. Some bruises and a broken bone would heal.

"You don't look bad," Nell said.

Meg snorted. "It doesn't matter how awful I look when there is nothing I can do about it." She studied her family, recognizing the exhaustion caused by their night of worry and fear. "I love you all, but go home. I'll be fine." She held up the nurse-call button. "I have everything I need."

Reuben came into the room, but stopped abruptly when he saw her family.

Dat glanced at the young man. "We should leave."

"Please don't leave on my account," he said.

"They're leaving because of me," Meg explained, her lips curving. "I told them to go." She looked at her father. "They haven't slept."

Reuben approached the end of her bed. He froze when her father placed a hand on his shoulder. "*Danki* for saving her," *Dat* said.

To her amazement, Reuben blushed and looked slightly uncomfortable. "I…I'm sorry about the accident."

"It wasn't your fault." Her father met her gaze. "We'll see you again soon, *dochter*." He moved to leave, and her family followed.

"Be careful going home," she called out.

Each member of her family murmured quietly to Reuben as they passed him.

"Won't you sit a minute?" she asked softly, as she wondered what they'd said.

Reuben moved quickly then, as if eager to please, and took the seat her father had vacated. "You *oll recht*?"

"I'm fine. No serious injuries." She saw relief settle on his features. She studied him and immediately noted huge bruises on his left cheek and forehead. "Your face… Doesn't it hurt?"

His mouth curved crookedly. "A little. And yours?"

She shrugged, and winced with the simple movement. "I'm achy but I'll survive." She grinned to reassure him.

He studied her with concern. "Meg, I'm sorry—"

She saw regret flicker in his blue eyes. "*Nay! Dat's* right. It wasn't your fault. The car hit *us*."

He sighed. "I'm afraid I'm a little foggy about what happened."

Meg was concerned. "You don't remember anything?"

"I recall a blinding light."

"The car's headlights."

He nodded. "The car hit my buggy."

Meg regarded him with amusement. "*Ja*, it was traveling too fast around a curve and struck us. Your horse reared up and bolted off the road and then…"

"The buggy rolled," Reuben said hoarsely. "I remember that, but what happened afterward?"

"You must have whacked your head hard."

"Ja." He stood and gently took hold of her hand. "You must have, too." He studied her with troubled blue eyes. "Meg, I'd never do anything to hurt you intentionally."

The man was sweet, and she was grateful that he'd saved her life. She felt a wave of warm gratitude toward him. "I know."

He didn't move. He simply held her hand and gazed at her with affection that made her feel increasingly uncomfortable. He smiled and toyed with her fingers until Meg closed her eyes and silently prayed that he'd leave.

Peter couldn't get Meg out of his mind. Which was why he drove the two hours to the hospital to make sure she was all right. He parked his buggy near a hitching post, tied up his horse, then hurried inside to the information desk. "Can you tell me where to find Meg Stoltzfus? She's a patient."

The woman behind the counter searched the computer on her desk. "Room 202," she said. "The stairs are to the right. The elevator is farther down the hall."

"Thank you." Peter ran up the stairs to the second

floor and followed the signs that led him to Meg's room. His heart started to beat rapidly as he heard voices. He hesitated at the door, then peeked inside—and froze when he saw Reuben Miller at Meg's bedside. The man's face was bruised, but he was smiling affectionately at Meg as he held her hand.

Peter quietly backed away from the room and headed downstairs, his heart aching at the sight of them together. His first instinct was to go home, but then he thought better of it. He had come all this way to make sure Meg was all right. He refused to leave without talking with her. She wouldn't be glad to see him, but he couldn't care less. He needed to know if he'd caused her serious injury when he'd pulled her from the water.

It was well past noon, and he was hungry. He hadn't eaten since an early breakfast. He'd grab something from the hospital cafeteria before he returned to Meg's. If Reuben was still there, he'd go ahead and visit her, anyway. But he preferred to see Meg alone.

After lunch, he took the elevator back to her room. He paused before entering. Meg lay in bed, staring out the window as if lost in thought. She was alone. He stepped inside, and as if sensing him, she turned.

"Peter."

"*Hallo*, Meg." He approached, noting a myriad of expressions crossing her face. He sucked in his breath as he studied her. There were bruises on her forehead and left cheek, and around her left eye. Had he done that to her? "How are you feeling?"

Her lips twisted in a lopsided smile. "I've been better."

He nodded, taking in every inch of her features. Even

battered and bruised, she was still the prettiest girl he'd ever known. "I… How bad are your injuries?"

"Is your family here?"

"*Nay*, I came alone."

"What are you doing here?" she asked abruptly, and he tried not to flinch. Would it always be this way between them?

She released a sharp breath. "I'm sorry. I'm feeling out of sorts, but there is no need for me to be rude."

Peter cocked an eyebrow but didn't say anything. Meg flushed, and he softened his expression. "You're in pain. Do you want the nurse?"

Relief settled on her features. "*Nay*, I'm *oll recht*. My leg aches, but I'll live."

His gaze fell on the bedcovers, identifying the lump beneath them. "You broke your leg." Did she break it when he'd pulled her from under the buggy? His belly burned at the thought.

"*Ja*. That's what hurts the most."

"Is there anything I can do for you?"

She looked stunned by his concern. "I… Peter, I appreciate your concern but—"

"You don't want it."

To his shock, she shook her head. "I don't deserve it." She looked away. "I haven't exactly been nice to you."

He shrugged. "As I recall, you were very polite the night of the singing, before you left." He paused. "I was rude."

"You warned me about the rain." She shifted in bed, and he saw her wince at the slight movement. "I don't know how you knew."

"*Ja*, well, I have a confession to make," he said. Curiosity entered her blue eyes as she waited for him to finish. His lips twisted. "I didn't know it was going to rain when I said it. I was just…" He couldn't continue. The knowledge that he'd said it simply to ruin her night made him feel small and ashamed.

To his surprise, Meg laughed.

He stared at her, then found himself grinning. "I'm glad you think it's funny."

"I didn't then, but I do now. I guess the accident put things into perspective for me."

Peter stared at her, mesmerized by her bright azure eyes, one sporting a black bruise. Something kicked in his gut as he studied her. If only things could be different between them. But he reminded himself that she was in love with Reuben, and he had Agnes now. "I'm sorry you went through that."

Her eyelashes flickered. "You sound sincere."

"Have I been so terrible to you?" he asked quietly. When she opened her mouth and then promptly closed it, he said, "I see."

"Peter."

"'Tis fine, Meg. I understand." He shifted on his feet. "I'm sorry if what I said hurt you." He was referring to when she was sixteen and hadn't lived long in Happiness. "I'd hoped that after all this time, we could be friends." He couldn't read her demeanor. When she didn't respond, he sighed. "You need your rest. I should leave." He started toward the door, then stopped. "How is Reuben? Is he *oll recht*?" he asked, not wanting to give away that he'd seen the two of them together.

Meg's expression warmed. "He's well. He's been discharged." She studied her hands as if her fingers were fascinating. "Did you know that he rescued me? He pulled me out of the water." She rubbed the side of her face where another bruise had formed.

"I hadn't heard." Something jolted in Peter's chest, but he didn't refute her statement. It didn't matter that it was he and not Reuben who had rescued her. The only thing that mattered was that Meg was alive and well, and on the road to recovery. "He must be glad he was able to help you," he said carefully.

"I suppose." She frowned. "When I thanked him, he seemed uncomfortable, as if he didn't feel like a hero." She looked thoughtful. "He told me he doesn't remember what happened after the accident."

Peter nodded in understanding. Reuben obviously felt uncomfortable because he couldn't recall pulling Meg from the creek. "He hit his head?"

"*Ja*, he has a concussion." She closed her eyes for a moment before opening them again.

"Yet they are sending him home and keeping you here," he murmured.

"Just until tomorrow. Then I'll be released." She gestured toward her IV. "They're pumping me with antibiotics to prevent infection in my lungs."

"That makes sense." He saw her eyes drift shut and he stepped back. "I'll be heading home. Is there anything I can do for you before I go?"

Eyes closed, she shook her head.

"Get well, Meg," he said softly.

Her eyelashes flickered before she looked at him. "*Danki*, Peter," she murmured. "It was nice of you to come."

"Take care of yourself," Peter said, before he turned and left—and fought the urge to glance back. Seeing her again made it difficult to forget her…and how much he'd loved her.

As he climbed into his buggy minutes later, he had a sudden longing to see Agnes. He'd drive over to her family's farm before heading home. Because it was suddenly imperative that he see her today.

Chapter Three

"**A**re you ready to go?" Meg's *dat* asked as he entered her room.

Rick Martin, their English neighbor, was there to take them home. Grabbing her crutches, Meg rose on her one good foot. "I'm ready," she said softly. She glanced toward the door behind her father. "Where's *Mam*?"

"She's giving the nurses the apple pies she baked for them."

"How many?" Meg asked.

Her father shrugged. "Four."

She laughed, feeling warmth for her thoughtful mother. "I wish I could have seen the looks on their faces when she gave them the pies."

As she and her father left her room, Meg caught sight of her mother chatting with the women in the nurses' station.

"Mam," she said as she approached.

"Gut," Mam said. "We can finally get you home."

Nurse Nancy went for a wheelchair. When she returned, she helped Meg get seated and then gave her final instructions on the antibiotic medicine that she'd be taking for the next ten days at home, along with a slip of paper with appointment details for a follow-up with the doctor. Nancy rolled the wheelchair toward the elevator, which opened as they drew near. Meg was surprised to see her sister emerge.

"Look who I found downstairs!" Ellie exclaimed.

"It's the young man who came to see if you were all right yesterday," Nancy said.

Meg immediately thought of Peter, until Reuben stepped out of the elevator behind Ellie. Looking handsome despite the bruises on his cheek and forehead, he approached.

"I heard you were going home today." His blue eyes warmed as he studied her. "I wanted to see you before you left. I hope you don't mind."

"We're glad you came," *Mam* assured him, and Meg could hear warmth in her mother's voice.

Reuben chatted as he accompanied them to the ground floor and then to the car. Meg vaguely heard what he said. For some reason, all she could think about was Peter's visit to her hospital room yesterday. Had he really come because he was concerned? What had he heard that made him travel all this way just to see her?

Whatever his reason, she was surprised and a little pleased that he'd taken the time to visit her. Ellie had urged her to figure out a way for them to get along. From what he'd said, Peter wanted the same thing. If not for Reuben, she would have died from the accident. *Life is too short to hold a grudge.* Surely she could put the past where it belonged, and forgive and forget what he'd said.

After he walked them to Rick's car, Reuben left, after

promising to visit her later in the week. Once home, her father thanked Rick for driving them, then helped Meg into a chair in their great room and then grabbed a cushioned stool to rest her leg on.

"Danki." She sat back and closed her eyes…and soon drifted to sleep.

Meg woke sometime later. She didn't think she'd slept long, judging by the sunlight shining through the great room windows. Her leg hurt, and she shifted in the chair to find a better position just as her youngest sister, Charlie, entered the room.

"Meg!" she exclaimed. "You're awake. I've been wanting to talk with you. I'm sorry I didn't get back to the hospital before you came home."

Her sister's boundless energy was evident in her sparkling green eyes. Charlie pulled a chair close and studied Meg.

"Charlotte May," her mother said as she entered the room. "Did you wake up your sister?"

"Nay, Mam. She was already awake."

"She needs her rest. Run along and finish your chores." As Charlie left, *Mam* turned to her. "Do you think you'll feel well enough to come on visiting Sunday? We'll be going to Aunt Katie's."

Meg hesitated. Would she be able to manage a day's outing? Learning to use the crutches had exhausted her. She could find a chair and stay seated, she supposed. And she certainly wouldn't mind seeing her Lapp cousins and church community friends.

"Your *vadder* is borrowing a wheelchair for you to use while you recover," *Mam* said. "You might find it easier to move about."

Meg nodded. "That's thoughtful of him."

Her mother looked relieved. Meg realized her family would stay home if she wasn't up to visiting, and she became more determined than ever to show them that she was strong despite her recent hospital stay.

"There is something I need to discuss with you." *Mam* glanced briefly toward the kitchen once they were alone.

Meg eyed her with concern. "Are you *oll recht*?"

Her mother gazed at her with warmth. "I'm fine." She grabbed a wooden chair and set it to face her daughter's.

"Mam?"

"There is something I need you to do for me, Meg. You know that your *dat's* birthday will be here soon."

"Ja, on Christmas."

"Ja." She shifted her chair closer, indicating she wanted to speak in private. "I'd like to surprise him with a birthday party," she said quietly. "I've had a conversation with Horseshoe Joe. Did you know that Miriam's birthday is the same day as *Dat's*?"

"Nay, I didn't." Meg got a funny feeling inside.

"Joe wants to give Miriam a party, too. We've decided that we'd like you and Peter to plan one together."

Meg found it difficult to breathe. "You want me… and Peter to work together?"

"Ja, and before you say a word, Meg, I'd like to remind you that you have a broken leg and can't do chores. This celebration is important to me and to Horseshoe Joe. The best people for this task are you and Peter. You'll work with him, *ja*?"

Meg, in fact, had been ready to object to the arrangement, but she wisely kept silent. Her mother was right. She couldn't do chores while her leg was healing.

Working with Peter so her father and his mother could have a surprise birthday celebration was something she could do to be useful. "I'll be happy to work with Peter to plan the party."

"Wunderbor!" Mam rose and put her chair back where it belonged. "You mustn't tell a soul. Not even your sisters. Do you understand?"

Meg nodded.

"Gut." Her mother looked pleased. "Lunch will be ready in a minute. Do you need help getting to the kitchen?"

Meg shook her head. *"Nay.* I'll be there in a minute." Her mother left her alone with her thoughts. She sat a moment and contemplated working secretly with Peter Zook. How would she manage? How would he react to the news?

Yesterday she'd told Peter that the accident caused her to put things in perspective in her life. She sighed. She had to find a way to work with him without her painful past interfering with their working relationship.

She stood, grabbed her crutches and hobbled toward the kitchen. Did Peter already know of their parents' arrangement? Her stomach burned with anxiety. She'd see him tomorrow at her aunt and uncle's. Would he mention the party? Refuse to work with her?

Sunday morning, after a decent night's sleep provided by her pain medication, Meg rose from the bed in the first-floor sewing room. Her sisters, Leah, Ellie and Charlie, were working in the kitchen. Leah was at the stove, cooking eggs. Ellie was setting the table, and Charlie was putting out jars of jams and jellies. Meg had usually been up by six at the latest before the accident, and was shocked that she'd slept until eight thirty. "I'm sorry I slept so late."

"You needed the rest," Leah said with a smile. "Come and eat." She pulled out a chair and helped Meg get situated at the table. "Eggs and toast? Or muffins with jam?"

"A muffin will be fine. Without jam," Meg said, as she reached for a chocolate chip muffin. "Where's *Mam* and *Dat*?"

"*Dat's* outside getting the buggy ready. *Mam's* upstairs."

Meg broke open the muffin and took a bite. "Did *Dat* borrow a wheelchair?"

Ellie set down two cups of tea, one in front of Meg, before she sat across the table from her. "He did. He's already put it in our buggy."

Leah took the chair next to Meg and proceeded to fix her own cup of tea. "Does it bother you? The idea of being in a wheelchair again?"

Meg shook her head. "*Nay.* 'Tis not the same as before." She'd spent several weeks in a wheelchair after she'd been discharged from the hospital, when a ruptured appendix had nearly killed her. A broken leg and a few bruises would heal much faster than severe complications from appendicitis.

After breakfast, her family headed to the Samuel Lapp farm, where Meg saw people she knew gathered around as her father steered their horse into the barnyard. *Dat* parked next to the carriage belonging to her cousin Eli and his wife, Martha. She smiled and waved at them before she saw Horseshoe Joe and Miriam Zook, along with Peter, pull in on their other side. Meg locked gazes with Peter before he climbed out of the vehicle. Then she turned her attention to her father, who reached in to lift her from the back seat.

Meg stood on her good leg as her *dat* went for her wheelchair. She reached to grab the buggy as she teetered there, then struggled for a better handhold. An arm immediately slipped about her waist in support, and she sighed with relief, glad for her sister's help. But the clean, fresh scent of soap and man made her realize that the arm was masculine, strong, and most definitely belonged to Peter Zook. Her heart started to pound as she met his gaze.

"I'm steady now," she assured him, eager for him to move away. Her world tilted, but then righted itself as he released her and stepped back. He turned to leave.

"Peter." He halted and faced her. *"Danki,"* she said softly. Her throat constricted, and she felt her face heat.

Peter eyed her intently and nodded. Then he caught up with his mother and father as they approached the house. Meg watched him go with emotion akin to regret that he hadn't stayed to chat—because she'd chased him away.

Her father moved the wheelchair close to where she stood. "Hold on, and I'll help you."

She felt drained and weak, and was glad to sit. As *Dat* pushed her toward the farmhouse, she started to believe that coming today had been a mistake. She felt tired, shaky...and unsettled by the memory of the warmth and strength of Peter's arm as he'd steadied her.

Peter entered the Lapp house, his thoughts filled with Meg. He'd been fighting the emotion overwhelming him ever since he'd held her in his arms as he'd pulled her from the water.

He spied Agnes across the great room and immediately headed in her direction. His feelings about Meg would surely settle down if he spent time with his friend. "*Hallo*, you," he said, greeting her with a smile.

"*Hallo* back," she quipped with a crooked grin.

"I didn't expect to see you here." But he was glad she was, if only to take his mind off the sweet scent of Meg's hair and the warmth of her beneath his arm as he'd kept her from falling.

Agnes shrugged. "Katie invited us. She saw my *mudder* at the store."

The Joshua Beilers lived in another church district. Occasionally, they came to church service in the Zooks' community, but not often. Peter had met Agnes after a service last year and they'd become instant friends. Agnes was easy to talk with, and her obvious delight in the world was refreshing. She was the complete opposite of Meg, in looks as well as temperament.

Familiar voices in Katie Lapp's kitchen told him that the Stoltzfus family had entered through the back door of the house.

"Is that Meg?" Agnes asked. "I heard about the accident. How is she?"

He shrugged, pretending indifference. "Fine."

"Let's go see."

"Maybe we should let her get settled in first."

Agnes met his gaze. "I heard she broke her leg."

Peter inclined his head. "*Ja.* She's on crutches." He couldn't forget how she'd looked lying in her hospital bed, bruised, pale and vulnerable.

His brother came into the room, and Peter stared. "Josiah, you came! I haven't seen you in months."

Josiah grinned. He had married Nancy King of the

Amos Kings, who lived across the road from Samuel and Katie Lapp. The couple had moved after their marriage, and Peter rarely got to see the two of them. "We came in last night. We're staying with my in-laws. I wanted to surprise *Mam* and *Dat*."

"Have they seen you?"

His brother nodded. *"Ja."* He grinned, as if delighted by their parents' reaction. Josiah's gaze went to Agnes, who stood silently beside him.

"Sorry," Peter said to both of them. "Agnes, this is my older brother, Josiah. Josiah, meet Agnes Beiler."

The two greeted each other warmly. As Agnes turned to have a word with her twin sister, Josiah shot a pointed glance toward her before raising his eyebrows at Peter.

"We're friends," Peter said, before he could ask.

Josiah nodded. "I saw Meg Stoltzfus." He glanced toward the kitchen with concern. "She was in an accident."

"Ja, Reuben Miller was taking her home from last week's singing when a car hit his buggy and forced it from the road."

"Anything serious?" his brother inquired. "I didn't want to ask."

"Worst of it is a broken leg."

"You two getting along yet?"

"We're…polite." Peter had told his brother about Meg overhearing their conversation. His brother had understood and been sympathetic. "She's with Reuben Miller now."

"And you have Agnes?"

Peter shrugged. "If all goes well."

"There you are," a warm female voice said. His

brother smiled as his wife, Nancy, approached. "*Hallo*, Peter."

"*Hallo*, Nancy," he replied with a grin.

"You knew I wouldn't be far." Josiah regarded his wife with affection. "Weather's too chilly to be outside today."

His brother was lucky to have found a woman to spend his life with, Peter thought.

Elijah, Jedidiah and Jacob Lapp entered the room. "How about a game of baseball?" Elijah suggested. "'Tis cold out, but we'll be warm soon enough."

Martha overheard her husband. "You're going to play baseball outside?" Beside her, his sister Annie pushed Meg's wheelchair.

"They'd better not play inside," Annie retorted.

"Why not?" Jed said. "'Tis not raining."

Elijah's expression softened as he eyed his pregnant wife. "You'll stay inside, *ja*?"

"Why?"

Elijah opened his mouth as if to say something, but quickly shut it again.

"Why should any of us stay inside? We'll watch from the porch." Martha addressed Meg. "What do you say? Are you feeling up to watching your cousins smack a baseball around?"

It was clear that Eli didn't like his wife's decision. Martha was far along with child, and he was clearly concerned about her. "Martha…"

"I'll be fine, husband," she assured him. "Meg?"

"'Tis not like I can stand and watch them," she said with good humor.

Peter studied her with concern. Meg had only recently been released from the hospital. The doctor was treating her with antibiotics to help her lungs stay clear. Would the cold air be bad for her? Wouldn't it be better if she remained inside?

His brother-in-law, Jacob, frowned as he studied his cousin. "Meg, I'll get a blanket for you." He glanced at the other women. "I think you all should have blankets."

"*Gut* thinking." Annie beamed at her husband. "And I'll make us some hot tea."

"Peter?" Jedidiah smiled. "You playing?"

Peter glanced at Agnes, who returned his gaze. "I'll play for a while."

"I can't play long," Noah Lapp, another brother, said as he entered the room. "Food's almost ready."

The men avoided the kitchen entrance and left via the front door of the farmhouse. As they stepped outside, Peter caught sight of the younger Lapp brothers, Isaac, Daniel and Joseph, on the front lawn. Joseph held a ball and bat. Joshua and John King, neighboring boys from across the road, grinned as they all gathered on the dormant grass.

"Who wants to be a team captain?" Peter asked.

There was a good-natured debate as it was decided that Jedidiah and Noah would be captains with the privilege of choosing their teammates. Jedidiah chose Jacob, Peter, Daniel and Joshua. Noah's team was Elijah; Jacob's fraternal twin, Isaac; Joseph and John.

Playing in the outfield first, Peter saw the women emerge from the house and make themselves comfortable on the Lapps' covered front porch. Annie pushed Meg close to the rail, then took the chair next to her. Noah's wife, Rachel, along with Martha and Agnes, joined them, each settling in a rocking chair. Meg remained in her wheelchair with a blanket across her lap.

Peter noted that Agnes sat on the opposite side of the porch from them. She smiled and waved, and he nodded before he returned his attention to the game in time to catch a fly ball hit by Isaac. Jedidiah and his teammates cheered, as did Agnes and Annie.

The game continued. Jedidiah's team exchanged places with Peter, who went up to bat. As he waited for his turn at the plate, Peter glanced toward the porch and captured Meg's gaze. She stared at him without once looking away. His heart beat wildly as he refocused his attention on the game.

"Peter!" Jedidiah called from first base, where he'd landed safely. "You're up!"

He nodded, picked up the bat and slammed the ball across the yard, sending Jedidiah to second base and Jacob to third, before they both continued all the way home.

Katie Lapp stepped outside with her granddaughter Susanna on her hip and her grandson EJ standing next to her. "Food is ready!"

The game ended with a difference of opinion on which team had won, since the score was even, but Jedidiah's team didn't get to finish the inning. The men climbed the porch steps as the women turned to head inside. Martha and Elijah went in together. Agnes chatted with her sister Alice, who stood in the entryway and held the door open until Jedidiah grabbed hold of it. Everyone had entered the house except for Jacob, Annie, Meg and Peter.

"Peter," Annie said. "Will you push Meg's chair inside?"

"Ja." He and Meg gazed at each other. Her eyes wid-

ened slightly and her skin flushed red as he turned her chair toward the door.

"You don't have to help me," she said. "I can stand."

"Like you did when you arrived earlier?" he asked as he tipped up the front wheels of the chair and lifted it over the threshold. "Does it bother you to have me help you? You just got out of the hospital, Meg," he said, his voice gruff. "You shouldn't take chances."

Meg stiffened. It felt as if he was poking fun at her near fall earlier. "I don't need your help or a scolding, Peter Zook."

"Meg, I didn't mean—"

When they were inside the entryway, he came around the wheelchair to face her. She was offended by what he'd said. And she thought they could start over and work together on the party?

"*Danki*, Peter. I can manage from here," she said in a tight, dismissive voice. She grabbed hold of her chair's wheels and rolled forward, nearly hitting Peter, who instinctively jumped out of the way. He stared at her, and she flushed with guilt.

"Meg."

She stopped and waited for him to reach her.

Peter sighed. "Are you this difficult with everyone?" he asked. "Or just me?"

Meg refused to answer him. She alternately fumed and fought embarrassment as she wheeled herself into her aunt Katie's kitchen. She was aware that Peter Zook followed closely behind her. She bit her lip to keep herself from telling him to leave her alone. Perhaps she was overreacting. In fact, she probably was, but she was tired, in pain, and wanted nothing more than to go home.

As she rolled her chair into the bright kitchen, where food filled the table and countertops, she felt confused and ill. She shouldn't have come. She should have insisted that her family attend without her. It was too soon after her hospital stay for her to be out and about. She could have been napping or gazing silently out the window at home. Instead, she was aware of Peter behind her, a man who didn't like her. But he'd been thoughtful despite how he felt about her, she realized. Sometimes it seemed as if he could read her mind and gauge exactly how she was feeling.

She sighed. And she'd been rude to him. Again. She'd promised to be a better person. *Please, Lord, help me to be thoughtful and kind to everyone, especially to Peter Zook.*

"Meg." Her mother approached. "I'll fix you a plate."

"*Danki*, but *nay*. I can manage." She was determined to prove that she was fine. As soon as everyone left the room and couldn't watch her, she'd stand up and get some food. Her head and bruises hurt, and her leg throbbed. She looked around but saw no sign of her father or any of the older men. "Where's *Dat*?"

"In the barn," Mae King said. "Most everyone has moved out there."

Meg glanced at the older woman, who was a close friend and neighbor of her aunt's. "They've set up tables?"

"*Ja*," Mam said. "Samuel brought in a heater to take away the chill." She settled her gaze on someone behind Meg and smiled. "Peter, here's a plate."

"*Danki*, Missy," he said as he accepted it.

Meg rolled her chair into the corner, out of the way. Refusing to watch Peter while he selected food, she stared at her lap. The quilt that her cousin had gotten for her was done in pretty shades of green and yellow. She was glad it hid her heavy cast. Every time she saw it, she felt helpless and a little afraid.

"Peter." Agnes entered the room and swept past her. Meg watched as the young woman took his plate, then proceeded to fill it for him, with selections from every available cold meat platter, salad and dessert. "Do you want iced tea?"

Meg stared as Peter bent and murmured something in Agnes's ear. She heard her chuckle before Agnes turned toward Meg's aunt with an amused expression.

"Katie," she heard Agnes say, "got any Pepsi?"

"In the back room. Help yourself."

Meg watched as Agnes left. She couldn't keep her gaze from Peter, who had moved into her focus. He stared back, his dark gray eyes unreadable, and she quickly glanced away.

Agnes returned with the glass of cola. "Here you go."

"Missy," Mae King called, "come see what Katie has done to the quilt we've been making."

Her mother slipped from the room. Meg watched Peter and Agnes. The two were smiling, sometimes laughing, clearly enjoying each other's company. Meg blinked back tears. She didn't know why she had the sudden urge to cry. She realized that it had been a long time since she'd felt that free and joyful.

"Meg?"

Startled, she glanced up into Agnes's face. "*Hallo*, Agnes."

"How are you feeling?"

"Sore, but I'll live."

"I'm sorry you were hurt."

Agnes's sharp perusal made her squirm. She didn't want or need the girl's pity. "I'm fine." Meg glanced at Peter, who waited patiently next to Agnes. He eyed Meg intensely, as if he was debating whether or not to say something to her. She looked away.

"Do you need anything?" Agnes asked.

Meg managed a smile. "*Danki*, but *nay*. I appreciate the offer, though."

Her cousin Isaac opened the door and peeked into the room. "Peter, Agnes, are you coming out to the barn?"

"We'll be there soon," Agnes said airily. "Have everything you need, Peter?"

"Ja, danki," he told her warmly.

Agnes gave Meg a sympathetic look. "Take care of yourself."

"I will." Meg watched the couple leave the house. For a moment, she was alone, which was a relief. She should get up and fill a plate, but she wasn't really hungry. She leaned back and closed her eyes.

"Meg."

She gasped and opened her eyes to see a plate of food being thrust in her direction. *Peter.* He was eyeing her with concern. Something warmed inside her. She grew flustered as she realized he'd picked all her favorite foods. *"Danki,"* she whispered. Heart thundering in her chest, she wheeled herself closer to the table.

"Did you want to join us in the barn?"

"I… *Nay.* I think it will be better if I just stay here." She saw him nod, then watched the dark-haired, gray-eyed man depart to rejoin the others. Peter had been thoughtful enough to fill her a plate. The thought made her experience a strange myriad of emotions she couldn't understand. Her face felt warm as she stared at her food. She picked up a fried chicken drumstick and took a bite. It tasted delicious, and suddenly her appetite was back.

She thought of Peter's kindness as she ate every bite of her meal. The man confused and fascinated her. But did he still think as badly of her as he had years before? And if he did, why was he being so nice to her now?

Chapter Four

Peter sat with Agnes on a bench behind a table that Samuel Lapp had constructed using plywood on sawhorses. The girl beside him was chatting with her sister Alice and Meg's sisters Ellie and Charlie. He listened with half an ear, and only fully tuned in when picking up Meg's name during the conversation.

"She's *oll recht*?" Agnes asked, her expression filled with concern.

"Meg's tough," Ellie said. "She'll be fine in a week or so."

"She looks bad, though, doesn't she?" Meg's youngest sister, Charlie, added.

"*Ja*, poor dear."

Peter frowned, disturbed that Meg was the topic of conversation. Why weren't her sisters inside keeping her company? He felt a sharp kick to his innards. Why hadn't he stayed awhile to talk with her?

But he knew the answer—because he needed to get over her. Which had been harder for him to do since the day he'd found her floating in the water after the accident.

The girls switched to another subject, and the pain in his stomach eased. He turned his attention elsewhere. Directly across the table from him sat Eli and Jacob Lapp, with their wives, Martha and Annie. Annie held EJ in her lap, while Jacob had his arms filled with their daughter, Susanna. He studied them, glad his sister was happy with a man she loved and two beautiful children. He shifted his gaze from his little niece and found Annie eyeing him closely.

He arched his eyebrows. "What?"

His sister shrugged. "I guess you know what you're doing."

Peter stiffened. "What do you mean?"

"Not a *gut* time, *bruder*. Best if we talk later." Her impish look reminded him of all of the times during their childhood when she'd teased him.

"Annie…" Peter warned.

Jacob narrowed his gaze on Peter, then looked for an explanation from his wife. "Are you taunting Peter again?"

"With love, Jacob. Only with love," she murmured, her eyes soft as she regarded her husband, who tenderly shifted their young daughter on his lap, bringing her up to rest her sleepy head on his shoulder.

Peter felt restless. He turned to Agnes and touched her arm. "Want to go for a ride?"

Agnes faced him, her expression brightening. "We can if you'd like." She stood and pushed back her chair.

Peter hurried to help her. They were outside before she said, "I have an idea."

She headed toward the house, and he grinned with the thought of the desserts she'd pack for their buggy ride. But Agnes didn't head toward where the pies, cake and other goodies had been laid out. She went to Meg instead, seated in her wheelchair, finishing the last bite of her meal.

"Meg," Agnes said in greeting as he stood silently behind her. "We're going for a ride. Would you like to come?"

Meg appeared stunned by the invitation. Peter studied her, recognizing her surprise and confusion. She looked tired, as if the day had already been too much for her. The bruises on her face were more pronounced than they'd been when she was in the hospital. He should offer to drive her home, but he didn't think she'd appreciate it any more than she did Agnes's invitation. He'd known her long enough to read the subtle changes in her gaze that told him when she was overwhelmed and uncomfortable.

"*Danki*, Agnes," she said quietly. "It's kind of you to ask, but I'm not feeling my best, so it would be better if I just stayed here." Meg managed a smile. Peter couldn't help but feel relieved.

Agnes frowned. "I don't like seeing you sitting here alone."

Meg's expression made Peter ache. The last thing she wanted, he was sure, was for Agnes to try to change her mind while he watched. He touched Agnes's arm. "She's not feeling well, Agnes."

Agnes shot him a look. "I know." She turned a sympathetic gaze on Meg. "Rest now. I'm sorry I can't do anything to help."

"*Danki.*" Meg sounded suspiciously close to tears. Peter couldn't tear his eyes away from her. Despite her bruises, she looked beautiful. The royal blue dress she wore intensified the bright azure of her eyes. Her white prayer *kapp* was slightly askew, revealing shiny dark hair pulled back in the Amish way. Her gaze fell on him, and he had to glance away before he did something ridiculous like reach over, pick her up and carry her to his buggy to take her home.

Instead he followed Agnes from the room. Once outside, she faced him. "Let's not go for a ride. Why don't we go for a walk instead? I'll ask Alice to join us."

"The weather is nice enough," he agreed, as he followed her back toward the barn. Agnes went to talk with her sister. Unable to forget how tired Meg looked, Peter headed toward his sister Annie.

Meg was chatting with her mother and aunt when Jacob and Annie entered the kitchen from outside.

"Meg, we thought you might like to go home." Jacob smiled as he approached, carrying his daughter. "'Tis been a long day for you."

"We can take her," *Mam* immediately said.

"No need," Annie assured her. "Our little ones are ready to be home."

"Are you sure you don't mind?" Meg asked, delighted by Jacob's offer. She wanted nothing more than to rest.

"I don't think you should be alone," her mother murmured with concern.

"*Mam*, I'll be fine. I'll take a nap. Please stay here and enjoy yourself."

"We can stay with her for a while." Annie picked up EJ, who had been holding on to her hand.

Meg gazed at her cousin-in-law gratefully. "*Mam*, I'll be fine. I'm not seriously injured. I have a broken leg."

"I should check with your *vadder*."

"*Nay!*" Meg exclaimed. "You know how *Dat* is. He'll

want to bring me home. He's enjoying himself, *Mam*. I'll be fine for a couple of hours. Honestly. I'll just close my eyes and sleep."

"*Endie* Missy, Meg will be fine," Jacob assured her. "I'll make certain of it."

Her mother stood and retrieved Meg's coat. "*Oll recht*. I'll see you at home a little later."

Feeling sore and highly emotional, Meg rolled her chair closer to her mother. "I love you," she whispered with tears of gratitude.

Soon, she was riding in Jacob and Annie's buggy, with EJ seated next to her and Susanna on her mother's lap up front. Jacob had stowed her wheelchair behind Meg's seat.

She was never so glad to see her home as when Jacob pulled into the barnyard and parked close to the house. She watched him take out her wheelchair first. She expected him to open it for her, but he placed it near the porch instead, then came back to carry her up the steps and on inside. "*Danki*."

"You're *willkomm*," her cousin said with a grin. His good humor faded quickly, though. "I wish I'd thought to bring you home earlier. I should have suspected you weren't ready to be visiting."

Meg shook her head. "I didn't want *Dat* and *Mam* to stay home because of me. They would have refused to go if I'd admitted I wasn't feeling well."

"Poor Meg," Annie murmured with sympathy as she followed them into the great room.

Jacob placed Meg into a chair and went outside for her wheelchair.

"You look exhausted," Annie said as she sat on the

sofa not far from where Meg was seated. "Would you be more comfortable here?"

"*Nay*, I like it here," Meg assured her. "I can look out the window."

Jacob entered the room and set the wheelchair near the far wall. Meg smiled her thanks, then studied the children, who played on the floor near their mother. "I'll be *oll recht* by myself." She shifted her leg onto the stool her father recently had handmade for her. "I appreciate your help."

Annie smiled. "You gave us a *gut* excuse to get these little ones settled at home." She watched fondly as the two chatted quietly.

"EJ is a wonderful big *bruder.*"

The boy's mother laughed. "Most of the time, but not always."

Her husband agreed. "He's a *gut* boy, though."

"He looks like Elijah," Meg said without thinking.

Jacob's short bark of laughter startled her. "That's what Eli says. Blond hair and blue eyes. But my *bruder* is not the only one with those features." He fondly eyed his wife.

Meg couldn't help the small smile that came to her lips. "*Ja*, he does look like his *mam*, but he looks like his *dat*, too."

Her cousin beamed at her.

"Now, go home!" Meg ordered.

Jacob blinked at her vehemence. "I told your *mam* we'd stay for a while."

"And you did. Now, take your little ones home."

"Can we get you anything before we go?" Annie asked, her gaze sharp.

"I've had too much to eat and more than enough to drink today. I'll be fine."

Jacob picked up his son while Annie reached for their daughter.

"Thanks for noticing how tired I am," Meg said.

Her cousin shook his head. "Don't thank us. The credit goes to Peter. He's the one who suggested you might like to go home."

The young family left, leaving Meg with a lot to think about. It was as if Peter had read her mind again. The realization unsettled her.

Her parents and sisters came home an hour and a half later. Her father didn't look happy as he entered the great room.

"I'm well, *Dat*," she said, before he could speak. "Jacob and Annie made sure I was settled before they left."

"You should have told us you wanted to go." He looked upset. "I should have known it was too soon for you."

"I'm fine. Please don't worry about me."

Dat regarded her with what looked suspiciously like tears in his eyes.

"I could eat, though," she said teasingly, and she saw the worry leave his expression.

"Supper will be ready soon." He turned to leave.

"Dat." He faced her. *"Danki* for caring," she said.

His expression grew soft. "I'm your *vadder*."

The evening passed quietly after a simple meal of cold cuts and fresh bread, followed by apple pie. Meg hadn't actually slept after Jacob had brought her home, but she had rested. It didn't take long for her to fall asleep once she'd retired for the night.

She woke up to the sounds of birds outside her window the next morning. She relished the pleasant sensation of lying in bed, listening to birdsong, until it hit her. Peter. Alarmed, she sat up. She was going to be working with Peter for weeks, planning their parents' party.

She closed her eyes, recalling the way he had studied her when she'd last seen him. He'd been kind to her recently, and he'd convinced Jacob to take her home. She didn't know what to make of his thoughtfulness.

She stood, grabbed her crutches and tried not to think of him. But his face remained ever present in her thoughts.

Chapter Five

Monday afternoon Peter paused at the base of the stairs and stared up at the Stoltzfus farmhouse. The last thing he'd expected to be working on was planning a birthday party for his mother and Arlin Stoltzfus. He had learned about Missy Stoltzfus's and his father's arrangement to have him and Meg work together to plan the celebration the evening of the last singing, the night that Reuben Miller and Meg had had the accident. Peter had figured that because of the accident, their parents would have forgotten all about the arrangement. But apparently not. So here he stood, in front of Meg's house, after being told by his father this morning that Missy and Meg would be expecting him today.

He thought about Meg. How on earth was he going to work with her? Meg Stoltzfus could be difficult on a good day. Planning an event with her wasn't going to be easy.

He grinned as he realized that he was up for the challenge.

He thought of Agnes and the wonderful afternoon they'd shared on their walk with Alice. The three of them had chatted, laughed and had a nice time. It had been a stress-free afternoon. Still, he had thought of Meg during it. It felt as though something was missing when he spent time with Agnes.

Peter climbed the steps and knocked.

Meg's mother opened the door. "Peter!" She smiled as she stepped back to allow him entry. "Come in. Meg is in the great room."

"Is she feeling *oll recht*?" he asked, as he followed her through the kitchen.

"She's coming along," Missy said.

As he entered the room, he caught sight of Meg immediately, seated in a chair facing the window. She looked pensive as she gazed out into the yard.

"Meg, Peter's here."

She jerked as if burned, and met his gaze. "*Hallo*, Peter." She lifted her cast off a stool and tried to turn her chair.

He rushed forward to help, gently grabbing the back of her chair and swiveling it to face the room. He then retrieved the large stool she'd been resting her leg on and placed it directly in front of her.

Meg gave him an irritated look as she lifted both legs onto the stool. Clearly, she wasn't happy to accept his help. If this was the way their planning time would go, then it was going to be much more challenging than he'd envisioned.

He grabbed a wooden chair from the other side of the room and sat, facing her. She seemed much improved since yesterday. "You look better. You must have slept well."

She stared at him, then arched an eyebrow. "Why are you so concerned about my sleeping habits, Peter?"

He stiffened, no longer feeling sorry for her. "Who says that I am?"

"I don't like to be treated like an invalid."

He snorted. "Have I treated you that way?"

Meg sighed, and he watched as her anger deflated. "I apologize. I'm frustrated and feeling sorry for myself. You don't deserve the way I spoke to you." She reached to brush back a tiny strand of hair that had escaped from beneath her prayer *kapp*. She wore a bright purple dress, which looked lovely with her dark hair and blue eyes. Peter couldn't help admiring her as she reached for the quilt on a nearby table. She covered her legs, then met his gaze. "So, we're going to plan a party together."

"Ja," he said. "You up for the challenge?"

Her eyes widened before she choked out a laugh. "Direct," she said. "I like that." She gazed at him, and he stared back until she looked away.

"Your *vadder* is not home?"

Meg shook her head. "He's with *Onkel* Samuel. He'll be gone all day." She paused. "My sisters, too."

"Where do you think we should start?"

"How about a place to have the party?"

"We can have it at our *haus*," Peter suggested.

She wrinkled her nose. "Bad idea."

He frowned. "Why?"

"How will we keep it a surprise if it's at either of our houses? Your *mudder* and my *vadder* will figure out that something is going on." She fingered a bruise at her temple.

"Sore?" he asked, concerned despite himself.

She stiffened. "I'm fine."

"I didn't say you weren't, Meg," he said with patience. "I just wondered if that bruise is bothering you. I didn't mean to imply anything but concern."

"Sorry." Meg briefly closed her eyes. "Both," she admitted.

"Would you rather I come back another day?"

"Nay." She straightened her spine as if her pain had diminished, except he saw something in her eyes that said otherwise. "We need to get started on this. Christmas is next month. There isn't much time."

He inclined his head. "What about at your *endie* Katie's?" he suggested.

She shook her head. "Won't work. *Dat* is over there almost as much as he is here."

Peter stifled irritation. "Then where, Meg? Where would you like to have it?"

"I don't know!"

"Maybe we both should give it some thought," he said. "We'll need a location where neither one will suspect a party if our families decide to visit."

"Ja." Meg touched her prayer *kapp* as if wanting to straighten it. Her head covering looked fine to Peter, who wondered if something other than pain was causing her to shift uncomfortably in her seat. "I can't think of any place."

"Let's forget about a location for now," Peter suggested.

"But it's important!"

"Ja, I know, but we can put off talking about it until the next time we meet. *Oll recht?"*

"Ja."

Missy Stoltzfus entered the room and seemed pleased to see them working together. "Would either of you like anything to eat or drink?" she asked.

"I could use a cup of tea, *Mam*."

Peter's lips curved. "I'll have the same."

Her mother grinned. "Coming up. Cookies?"

"*Ja*, that would be nice," he replied, as Meg said the same thing. He met her glance, and he was startled but pleased when they shared a smile.

"What next?" Meg asked after a lengthy silence.

Peter gave it some thought. "Food? How about the cake? My *mudder* loves chocolate."

Meg frowned. "*Dat* prefers lemon."

"Another topic for our next meeting?" Peter suggested drily.

She glared at him. "We haven't agreed on anything."

"This is only the first time we've met, Meg. I'm sure we'll work it out." At least, he hoped so. He had the feeling she would disagree with all his suggestions just to be contrary.

"Here's your tea," Missy announced as she returned. She handed them each a steaming cup and set a plate of cookies on the table. "I put sugar and milk in it."

Meg smiled before she took a tentative sip. "That's *gut, Mam*."

Peter took a drink. "*Ja*, delicious, Missy." He gave her a lopsided smile. Finally, there was something he and Meg agreed on.

They drank their tea and ate chocolate chip cookies silently. Peter studied his planning partner, saw her normally bright eyes dim. Clearly, she'd had enough party planning for one day.

"I should go."

She gazed at him but didn't disagree, which told him just how exhausted she was. Or how quickly she wanted to be rid of him. "Wednesday?" she asked.

"Will your *dat* be home?"

"Mam!" she called.

Missy appeared in the doorway. *"Ja, dochter?"*

"Will *Dat* be home on Wednesday? Peter and I want to meet again."

Amused by Meg's choice of words, Peter hid a smile.

Her mother frowned. "I don't think so. Samuel's project is supposed to take a couple of days. I'll let you know if that changes." She eyed them both carefully. "Good start in planning? I guess you had enough for today."

"Ja, Missy. I need to get home." And Meg needed something for her headache, he thought. "I'll see you on Wednesday, Meg."

"See you then, Peter."

Missy walked him to the door. Peter paused with his hand on the doorknob. "She has a headache."

Her mother understood. "I'll get her pain medication."

Satisfied, he left, feeling as though he could breathe again. As he drove home, he went over every moment of their first planning meeting, brief as it had been. It was going to be hard for them to agree on anything, he realized. And while he'd asked whether or not Arlin would be home, he'd never given any thought to Meg's sisters. His father, Horseshoe Joe, had insisted that the party be a secret best kept to themselves. If others found out about it, then the surprise for their parents could be ruined.

This was going to be more complicated than he'd originally thought.

After Peter left, Meg leaned her head back and closed her eyes. She had a doozy of a headache, and every muscle in her body seemed to ache.

"Meg." Her *mam* came into the room. She handed Meg a glass of water and a white pill. "Peter said you have a headache."

It frightened her how Peter could read her so well. "*Mam*, I'll be fine. I don't need this."

"*Ja*, you do. You've barely taken anything since you've been home. Take it, Meg, so that you can rest and recover."

Meg sighed before she swallowed the pill with the water.

"Would you like to lie down?" *Mam* asked.

"I guess so."

With her mother's help, Meg crossed to the sewing room and lay on the bed.

"Sleep well, *dochter*. I'll call you when 'tis time to eat."

"I love you, *Mam*."

The next morning, Meg was in the kitchen, helping Leah and Ellie bake bread. Charlie had gone with their mother to visit Nell. Leah and Ellie assembled the dough, then Ellie dumped hers onto a wooden cutting board dusted with flour. Meg pulled it close and began to knead awkwardly. It wasn't easy while sitting down, but she wasn't going to complain. This simple chore was the least she could do when her sisters and mother were handling the rest of the housework.

"How are you making out with that, Meg?" Leah said.

"*Gut.*" Meg's lips curved upward. "I haven't been much help. I'm glad to do this."

"Meg," Ellie said softly, "you were in a terrible accident. We don't expect you to work."

"I like to help. I don't like feeling as if I'm not contributing."

"Ellie's right, Meg." Leah regarded her with a concerned gaze. "You shouldn't overdo it." Suddenly, she grinned. "There will be plenty of time for you to make it up to us later."

Meg laughed. "I'm sure."

A loud knock sounded on the back door that led outside from the kitchen.

Ellie went to open it. "Why, *hallo*! 'Tis nice of you to stop by!" She turned to Meg. "There's someone here to see you."

Meg looked up into Reuben's blue eyes. Relief that it wasn't Peter hit her full force and she beamed at him. "Reuben! Come in!"

Leah pulled a chair for him close to the worktable next to Meg.

Reuben wore a dark jacket over a royal blue shirt, with dark blue tri-blend denim pants held up by black suspenders. He had taken off his black-banded straw hat and held it in his right hand. He turned and hung the hat on a wooden peg near the door before he approached Meg and sat down. "You're looking better, Meg," he said, beaming.

"You are, too. Any lingering problems?"

"*Nay*, you?" His gaze dropped down to her cast beneath the table. "How is your leg?"

"I can't stand on it, but it doesn't hurt as much as it did."

"I'm glad."

"Reuben," Ellie said, "would you like a cup of coffee? There's some on the stove."

"That would be wonderful, Ellie."

Meg noted with interest that her sister blushed as she turned to get his coffee. "Did you get Eli to take a look at your buggy?"

His expression sobering, he nodded. "Hopeless, I'm afraid. I've commissioned him to make me a new one."

She blinked, surprised that he had the money for a new carriage.

"Your cousin has taken the old one for parts. He's giving me credit for them."

That was something Eli would do, she thought with affection.

"Since you're here, I'm guessing you're not back to work yet." Meg stated.

"Actually, I am, but I don't have to go until this afternoon."

"I see."

As they talked, she continued to knead the bread dough. Suddenly, he reached out to still her hands. At his touch, she froze and shot her sisters a glance. They were too busy washing bowls and utensils to notice.

"Meg."

Her breath stilled. *"Ja?"*

"I hope you've forgiven me," he said, too softly for her sisters to hear.

She eyed him with confusion. "For what?"

"The accident."

"Reuben, the accident wasn't your fault. There is nothing to forgive."

"Then you'll spend time with me again? Go for another ride after I get my new buggy?"

She nodded.

He appeared pleased. "*Gut.* I care about you, Meg." His mouth curved. "A lot."

The man had saved her life, she reminded herself. "You're a *gut* man, Reuben Miller," she said warmly.

"Here's your coffee," Ellie said, placing a cup in front of him. "I heated it up. If it's too strong, I'll make a fresh pot."

Reuben sipped from the cup. "'Tis *gut*, Ellie."

Her sister beamed. There was another rap on the back door just then and she went to answer it.

"Peter! Agnes! Nice to see you!"

"We've come to see how Meg's faring," Agnes said.

"Come in," Leah invited from across the room. "It seems to be a day for visitors."

Meg was startled by the couple's visit. She saw Agnes first. The girl's gaze brightened as it homed in on her. "Meg!" She hurried forward. "Oh, *hallo*, Reuben."

"*Hallo*, Agnes." Meg rolled the prepared bread dough and handed it to Ellie, who set it in the oven.

Reuben's expression was pleasant as he returned Agnes's greeting, but his features darkened when he looked at her companion. "Peter," he said.

"Reuben." Peter returned the greeting quietly. He met Meg's gaze. "Feeling better?"

"*Ja*, I'm doing well."

With an amused smile, he nodded before he approached her sisters. As she watched him speak with Leah and Ellie, Meg couldn't help but notice how good Peter looked in his black jacket with a green shirt and tri-blend pants. There was no sign of his hat, so she figured he'd left it in his vehicle or at home.

"It will be a fun outing," Agnes said, drawing Meg's attention. She realized that Agnes was talking with Reuben. "The four of us can go to lunch and then for a ride. That would be fun, *ja*?"

"Ja," Reuben agreed. "Meg? Are you up for lunch and a ride with Agnes and Peter one day this week?"

"I…I guess so." She glanced briefly at Peter. He looked about as enthused as she felt. "When?" She didn't want to go, but didn't wish to be rude, either, and Reuben appeared excited by the prospect. She wanted to make him happy because of everything he'd done for her.

"How about tomorrow at eleven?" Agnes suggested. "Reuben, will you be able to get off from work?"

"Ja. The crew is finishing up a job today. I should be free." His gaze warmed as it settled on Meg. "Meg?"

"I'm not busy these days." Her eyes widened a bit as she met Peter's gaze. They were supposed to meet again tomorrow. They couldn't on Thursday, since it was Thanksgiving. She caught his barely perceptible nod. "I don't think I have anything to do, but I'll need to make sure I don't have a doctor's appointment."

"Wunderbor!" Agnes exclaimed, as if the arrangements were settled. "We'll have a great time." She turned to Peter. "Won't we?"

"Great time," he echoed, but Meg could tell that he wasn't particularly excited.

Shortly afterward, Peter and Agnes got up to leave. While Agnes and Reuben chatted, Peter mouthed to Meg, "Eight?" Then she understood and dipped her head in agreement. He would come at eight for their meeting before he picked up Agnes later that morning.

"Lunch and a drive sounds like fun," Reuben said, when the others had left.

"Ja. Did you decide on a place to eat?"

He frowned, then his brow cleared as he laughed.

"We didn't talk about that. I'm sure Agnes has something in mind."

Meg inclined her head. "I'm sure she does."

Reuben glanced at his watch, then stood. "I've got to go, Meg. You'll be fine here."

"I'm at home, Reuben," she teased. "Why wouldn't I be?"

He went to the door and reached for his hat. "I'll see you tomorrow at ten thirty."

Was she destined to see Peter every day? Meg wondered, after Reuben had left. She closed her eyes. It was bad enough she and Peter had to work together. The last thing she needed on top of that was for her and Reuben to be spending leisure time with him and Agnes.

Chapter Six

❦

"I thought we could go to Honeysuckle and eat lunch at Margaret's Restaurant. Do you know it? Then afterward we can go for a drive before we take Meg and Reuben back to Meg's."

Peter listened to Agnes talk about the planned outing and felt his stomach burn. He didn't want to go anywhere with the other couple. It was bad enough that he had to spend time with Meg to plan the birthday party. The last thing he wanted to do was to go out socially with her and her new sweetheart.

"Honeysuckle is awfully far. We'd have to leave early in the morning, and we said we'd go at eleven. Besides, I'm not sure Meg is up to it yet. In fact, I'm not sure she is up for an outing at all. She's only been out of the hospital a week."

"*Ja*, but she's excited to go—and so is Reuben. Did you see the way his eyes lit up? Maybe Honeysuckle *is* too far. Where do you think we should go?"

He hadn't seen Meg's excitement. He'd glimpsed only wariness in her eyes until she'd recognized Reuben's delight. Then she'd relented and seemed willing to go. "I don't know, Agnes. I still have reservations."

Her silence told him that she wasn't happy with him. "Why? Is it Meg? You don't want to spend time with her? Or is it that you don't like seeing Meg with Reuben? Think about it, Peter. We can have fun. We won't go far. You have a point about Honeysuckle being a long drive, especially since you'll be the one taking us… You don't mind if we go in your buggy, do you?"

He turned to her. "I don't mind driving," he assured her with a smile. How could he not catch a glimmer of her infectious excitement?

She beamed at him. "We'll have a *gut* time. You'll see."

Peter continued to listen as he steered his horse and buggy down the road toward the Joshua Beiler home.

"What about the diner in Ephrata?" Agnes suggested.

"That would take about an hour and a half to get there. We're supposed to go for a drive afterward, *ja*?" He glanced over to see her nod. "Then we should go someplace closer."

"How about the Family Restaurant in New Holland?"

"I don't have a problem with that. It takes half the time to get to New Holland as it does to Ephrata."

"*Wunderbor!* Then it's all settled." She touched his arm. "*Danki*, Peter. I'm looking forward to this!"

Peter managed to grin at her, even though, despite her excitement, he was not looking forward to tomorrow's trip. But he wanted things to work between him and Agnes. He liked her. She'd been a good friend for almost a year. He would do this simply because it made her happy. Besides, he had to learn to accept the fact that Meg was with Reuben now and he would be seeing them together frequently.

He dropped Agnes at her house with the promise of picking her up at ten forty-five the next day, then headed home. He pulled onto the dirt lane that took him past Annie and Jacob's house on the left, then toward the main farmhouse, with his father's blacksmith shop in the barn next to it. He parked, took care of his horse, then on impulse headed toward Zook's Blacksmithy, hoping to get a private word with Jacob, who worked there. His brother-in-law was Horseshoe Joe's partner in the business.

He was in luck. Jacob was alone. His father had gone into the house, probably to eat his midday meal. Jacob had the fire in the furnace going, and Peter watched as he pulled a bright red piece of metal from the flame, then bent it into a horseshoe by striking it with a hammer on the heavy iron anvil.

Peter waited patiently as Jacob held the metal up to inspect it, before hammering it some more. He needed to talk with his brother-in-law, but didn't want to scare him. Because of his carelessness, he'd once gotten Jacob burned when he'd startled him while he was working with hot metal. He was more careful now. He had no intention of doing that again.

Jacob stopped hammering, held up the horseshoe once more, and then, apparently satisfied, set the bright glowing metal onto the anvil to cool. He stepped back, and Peter knew he was done.

"Jake?"

His brother-in-law turned to him with surprised delight in his brown gaze. "Peter! Come in."

"I didn't want to scare you."

"You didn't." Jacob removed his gloves and set them on a table under several wall shelves. "If you're looking for your *dat*, he's not here."

"*Nay.* I came to see you."

"I'm heading down to the house for lunch. Come with me. Your sister will be happy to see you."

Peter hesitated. "You know she'll be nosy, *ja*?"

Jacob laughed. "She's your *schweschter. Ja*, she'll be nosy."

They left the barn and started down the lane toward the small house that had been built about a hundred feet off the main road.

"Your sister loves you, Peter. She wouldn't intentionally hurt you."

He sighed. "*Ja*, I know. But I saw the way she looked at me and Agnes together the other day, and it's clear she has something she wants to say to me." He paused. "I'm not sure I want to hear it."

"Peter, are you afraid of my wife?"

"Sure am."

Jacob chuckled. "I don't think it's Annie you wanted to discuss with me. What is it?"

"Agnes," Peter said. "And Meg."

"Ah, the two women in your life."

"Meg isn't in my life."

His brother-in-law arched an eyebrow. "But Agnes is."

"They *are* both in my life, but not in the same way. Meg… She's with Reuben now. I've decided to move on. Agnes has been a *gut* friend for a long time. I like her. Why shouldn't we be more than friends?"

"No reason why you can't be more," Jacob reasoned.

"But is that what you really want? To forget about Meg and move on with Agnes?"

"I think it's a wise thing to do."

Her sister's husband nodded. "Then that's *gut*." He was quiet a moment. "Agnes is a nice girl."

"*Ja*, she is." But then he always felt that Meg could be a nice girl, too, if she wanted to be.

The gravel on the road crunched beneath their feet.

"I really cared for your cousin," Peter admitted after a lengthy silence.

"I know." Jacob eyed him with sympathy. "Women aren't easy to understand."

"How did you win Annie's heart?" He glanced toward the man, who he respected and admired.

"You want to know this to win Meg's? Or improve things with Agnes?"

"Agnes," he said quickly. Too quickly. It was just so difficult to forget about Meg when he'd liked her for so long. "You must know the secret to courting a woman. You managed to get my sister."

"And you think I simply courted her and she fell in love with me?" Jacob asked with disbelief. "Peter, I've loved your sister since I was eleven. She never looked twice at me, and even when she finally did, she refused to have anything to do with me. She was still suffering a broken heart from her previous relationship with my *bruder* Jed. And that only complicated matters. I nearly gave up on her. I don't know when it happened, but suddenly she was there, telling me she loved me. I almost didn't believe it. When it finally sunk in, I was the happiest man alive." His smile lit up his eyes. "I still am."

"I want that. I want what you and Annie have."

"Then be persistent, until you can't do any more.

If the Lord wants you and Agnes to be together, then you will be."

Agnes, Peter thought. They were talking about Agnes, but silently he was thinking of Meg, who was with someone else, but still owned a huge piece of his heart.

They reached the cottage, and Jacob went in through the back door, Peter following closely behind.

"Annie, I'm home!" Jacob called, when there was no sign of his wife in the kitchen.

"I'll be right there!"

"I've brought company for lunch."

"Who?" Annie asked, as she emerged, carrying her daughter on her hip and holding her son's hand.

"Peter." Jacob hurried to relieve her burden, pulling their daughter into his arms.

Annie's gaze speared her brother from across the room. "Peter's not company. He's family." Her expression was warm. "*Hallo, bruder.* Are you hungry?"

"I could eat." Peter was glad to see her, although he knew he'd change his mind within minutes if she started to grill him about his relationships with Agnes and Meg.

"Are your hands clean?" she asked.

Peter went to the kitchen sink and washed. He turned and showed her his palms. "They are now, *Mam.*" He grinned.

Annie laughed. "Sit down and I'll serve lunch. Jacob, would you please pull out a chair for EJ?"

"*Ja.*" He put EJ in a chair, then sat with Susanna on his lap, and the little girl appeared perfectly content.

Soon, they were all seated and eating lunch. The food was good. Annie had made Amish chicken potpie made with tasty, thick noodles, and the delicious aroma of the dish wafted through the kitchen, causing Peter's stomach to growl. When they were done eating, he thanked his sister and Jacob, excused himself as he rose from the table.

"So what's this I hear about you seeing Agnes?" Annie asked in her usual frank manner as he pushed in his chair.

Peter shifted uncomfortably. "She's a friend. You know that."

"Just a friend?" His sister raised an eyebrow. "And Meg?"

He glanced away. "Meg is Meg," he muttered.

Annie was silent a long moment. "Are you *oll recht*?"

He looked at her, surprised to see compassion in her blue eyes. *"Ja,"* he said.

"You know you can talk to me, and I won't judge." She gave him a crooked smile. "I may tease at times but not when something's bothering you." Her voice softened. "Not when 'tis important."

He swallowed against a sudden lump as he nodded.

"Go on!" she said. "Get out of here. I know you're eager to get away."

After a quick glance in Jacob's direction, he grabbed his hat on his way to the door. He halted and faced his sister. *"Danki*, Annie."

Early the next morning, Meg sat with her cast propped up on the chair on the other side of the kitchen table as she waited for Peter. She had a pencil and paper to take notes regarding decisions about the birthday party. Since their first meeting, she'd thought long and hard about a place for the party. It had come to her, as thoughts sometimes did, during the night. Bishop John

Fisher's house would be an ideal location. He was a widower with one small son and a house large enough for a good-sized crowd. That was, if they could convince him to host it. The bishop's wife had died this past summer, and the loss had been hard on him.

Meg wondered if Peter had come up with an idea for a location. She doubted he'd thought of one better than Bishop John's. Would he agree with her suggestion or give her a hard time? Sometimes she thought he was being difficult just to annoy her. She hoped she was wrong, but it certainly seemed that way.

The house was quiet. Her mother had found an excuse to send her father and sisters out of there early. The only one home was *Mam*, who'd said she would be busy upstairs all morning doing chores. Meg still felt bad that she couldn't be of more help in the house, but when she'd mentioned it, her mother had quickly waved away her concerns. "You're planning the party for me, Meg," she'd said. "It's a huge chore, and one I'm happy to leave in your and Peter's capable hands."

At precisely eight o'clock, she heard a knock on the back door. Meg felt a fluttering in her belly. Peter had arrived. She didn't get up. She was afraid she'd be clumsy and fall if she tried. "Come in!" she called loudly.

The doorknob turned before the door swung open and Peter stepped inside. The man looked way too handsome for her peace of mind in a blue tri-blend jacket and matching pants.

"Morning, Meg." He took off his hat and set it on the end of the table.

"*Hallo*, Peter," she said. She watched as he removed his coat. Meg's gaze went to his maroon shirt, which fit him well. The contrast in color emphasized the dark gray of his eyes.

"Ready to get started?" He skirted the table and pulled out the chair next to her. He hung his coat on its back before he sat down. "We don't have much time."

"Ja." She knew he referred to their eleven o'clock outing with Agnes and Reuben, but she didn't want to get into a discussion about it, in case it set a bad tone for their working together. "Everyone is gone but *Mam*, and she'll be busy upstairs for a while." She tried to act casual with him so near.

"What's that?" He shifted closer and gestured toward the paper before her.

Meg felt her neck tingle. He smelled like soap, outdoors and something uniquely Peter. She'd never been so aware of him as a man. "I thought I'd make note of our ideas and keep a record of our decisions."

"Gut idea." He glanced up, and she felt a jolt from the impact of his gray eyes. "What shall we discuss first? The location? I have an idea that you may like."

"I bet I have a better place," she challenged.

"And where is this *better* place?" he asked with a little smirk. "You haven't heard mine yet."

"Bishop John Fisher's *haus.*"

Peter laughed.

"What's so funny?" she asked, offended.

He sobered instantly. "We came up with the same idea."

Meg blinked. "Honestly?"

"Ja. I know he just lost his wife, but he has a large enough house, and I was thinking that at Christmas he might be feeling lonely. If we have the party there, he'll

be surrounded by family and friends, and it might make the holidays more bearable for him."

"My thoughts exactly," she said.

They looked at each other and grinned.

"Looks like we've found something we both actually agree on!" Meg was pleased. It seemed that this meeting would go smoother than the first one. "It may take some convincing."

Peter sighed. "*Ja*, that could prove difficult. We should pay him a visit." He appeared to give it some thought. "Can't tomorrow."

Meg nodded. Tomorrow was Thanksgiving. "Friday?"

"I'm free," he said.

"Would you mind bringing me?"

"Not at all. We should go together. We're planning partners, after all."

Meg hid a smile. She liked that he'd acknowledged they were in this together. Filled with good humor, she wrote down Bishop John's name followed by a question mark. When Peter raised his eyebrows, she said, "Until we can get him to agree."

"Makes sense." Peter stared at her list. "What next? The cake?"

"My *dat* still prefers lemon."

"And my *mudder* still loves chocolate." He thought for a moment. "Maybe a lemon cake with chocolate frosting?"

"*Ach, nay*, that sounds awful!"

Peter shrugged. "I suppose we could have two cakes, one for your *vadder* and another for my *mudder*."

"We'll need to know how many guests are coming

first," Meg said. "If it turns out to be a small party, we certainly won't need two cakes."

"We could always order a half lemon, half chocolate cake from Maggie Mast's bakery."

Meg stared at him. "That could work." She scribbled *cake with two halves* under *Bishop John* on her paper.

"What else do we need to discuss?"

"The invitation list," Meg said, then wrote that down.

"Food other than cake," Peter added.

Meg scribbled on. "Travel in the event of snow."

"*Gut* one!" Peter applauded, and Meg blushed, unused to his praise.

She felt strangely happy. She and Peter were getting along and coming up with ideas. The meeting so far had been a productive one. She was optimistic that the two of them could pull this off in a way that would surprise and please their parents.

"Would you like something to eat and drink?" Meg asked, relaxing now that things were going so well.

"*Nay*, but thanks." He shifted away from her, and Meg was stunned how the simple movement caused a chill in the room, where before there had been only warmth. "I was thinking we should wait until we visit Bishop John and get him to agree before we do anything else. What do you think?"

"That's probably the best idea," she agreed.

"What time on Friday?"

"Nine? Or is that too early?"

He shot her an annoyed look. "I came at eight this morning," he reminded her. "Do you actually think that I usually sleep past nine?"

"You don't?" she said, straight-faced.

"Nay." He narrowed his eyes as if debating whether or not she was teasing. Then he smiled. "Funny, Meg."

She laughed. Then a tender look entered his eyes that made her stop and catch her breath as he studied her. He was silent a long moment. Then he blinked, and his expression changed, his gaze becoming unreadable.

They talked for another half hour, trying to come up with any details they might have missed. Christmas decorations, for one.

Just before ten o'clock, Peter abruptly rose and grabbed his coat from the back of his chair. "I need to go. I have to pick up Agnes at ten forty-five."

Meg watched as he put a powerful arm into each sleeve. He pulled the edges of his coat closed and buttoned it before picking up his hat.

"We made a *gut* start today," he said softly.

"*Ja*, we did," she agreed.

He didn't move. "I'll see you in about an hour. Agnes and I will come for you and Reuben at eleven."

"Reuben said he'd be here by ten thirty."

"See you then," she heard him say, as put his hand on the doorknob. Then he left without looking back.

Chapter Seven

Reuben and Meg exited the Arlin Stoltzfus house and stepped onto the front porch as Peter pulled in to park his buggy close to the residence. His eyes focused on Meg, on crutches, as Reuben held the door open for her.

"Look! There they are!" Agnes exclaimed happily.

Peter tore his gaze from the couple to grin at the young woman beside him. She was a pretty girl, with blond hair and light blue eyes, which were focused on him. Her light blue dress with a white cape and apron emphasized the color of her eyes. "You're really excited about going today, aren't you?"

Agnes flashed him a smile. "*Ja!* We'll have a great time!" She opened her door and quickly climbed out of the vehicle. "I think they need help."

Exiting his side of the buggy slowly, Peter skirted the carriage, his jaw clenching as Reuben picked up Meg in his arms and carried her down the steps after handing her crutches to Agnes.

Meg laughed while she protested being carried. "Reuben! I can manage!"

"I don't want to take chances with you, Meg. Why

struggle with crutches when I can make the stairs a little easier for you?" He bent close and whispered, "You mean a lot to me. Let me help you."

Peter heard. His chest tightened as Meg rewarded Reuben with a wide smile. The other man eyed the buggy, and Peter saw his intention to lift Meg into the back seat. He fought the urge to rush to help, and stayed where he was—for a few seconds. Then he moved closer, ready to offer assistance if needed.

Reuben lifted Meg into the vehicle without incident, then went around to get in on the side. Peter followed, and as he waited to enter last, Reuben scowled at him.

After Reuben climbed in next to Meg, Peter got in and picked up the leathers. Agnes slid in next to him, and he steered the buggy toward the main road.

"Where are we going?" Meg asked, after they'd been riding for several minutes.

Agnes turned in her seat to face her. "I thought we'd eat lunch in New Holland and then enjoy a drive before we head back."

"That sounds good, Agnes," Reuben said warmly. "Family Restaurant?"

"*Ja*, the food is delicious there."

He nodded in agreement. "With a wide variety of things to eat." He smiled. "I've been there a time or two."

Peter remained silent, all too aware of Agnes beside him, and Meg, with her sweetheart, in the back. He felt tense and anxious until the others began to talk about their families and their plans for Thanksgiving the next day. Then he found himself relaxing as he listened to the pleasant conversation. He thought of Meg and their outing to see Bishop John on Friday.

"Peter?"

He jolted. *"Ja?"*

"You've been quiet," Agnes said.

"Just enjoying the ride."

"Oh, we're here!" she exclaimed. "See? Pull in over there." She gestured toward the restaurant parking lot. "There should be a hitching post around back."

Peter parked the buggy and tied up his horse. Reuben climbed out next, then reached inside to help Meg. As he turned, Peter watched Meg rise and try to maneuver on one foot. Her cast was bulky, and she had trouble moving toward the door. Reuben got back inside, gently clasped her arm and tried to extract her from the carriage. Peter hurried around the buggy and waited to see if he could assist them. Agnes had gotten out and was watching.

"Reuben," Peter began quietly, "let me help."

The other man shot him an angry look. Taken aback by his hostility, Peter raised his hands and backed off, then watched in silence. He became upset when Meg winced several times while Reuben attempted to help her. He kept bumping her cast against the back of the front seat each time he tried. Meg didn't say a word, but Peter could tell she was hurting. Finally, she was out of the vehicle. He met her gaze, and she looked away, as if embarrassed.

Peter tried to catch Reuben's attention to silently convey his dismay over his unwillingness to accept help, but the man refused to meet his gaze, choosing to focus on Meg instead.

"You *oll recht*?" Reuben asked softly as he handed Meg her crutches.

"Ja." She managed a smile, but Peter could see the

pain in her expression. He'd known Meg a lot longer than Reuben had, and knew how to read her.

"I'm sorry, Meg," Reuben murmured.

Her smile widened, becoming more genuine. "'Tis fine, Reuben. Let's go. I don't know about you, but I'm hungry."

Reuben grinned. "Me, too."

Peter was silent as they entered the building. He sensed Agnes's regard and flashed her a smile. "The place looks nice."

Agnes was slow to smile back. "The food is *gut*." She reached out to touch his arm as he turned away. "Peter."

He gazed at her silently.

"I'm sorry. I didn't think."

Peter frowned.

"She isn't ready to come out with us."

He released a sigh. "She could have said *nay*, Agnes," he told her softly, for her ears alone. "'Tis *oll recht*." But he wasn't about to allow Reuben to be stubborn and hurt Meg again. He had an idea of how things would go on the way home—whether Reuben liked it or not.

Soon, they were seated in the restaurant. Peter sat next to Agnes. Meg and Reuben on the opposite side of the table, with Peter directly across from Meg.

"What do you recommend?" Peter asked pleasantly. It was time to make the best of things.

"Their sandwiches are tasty," Agnes replied.

"Everything looks *gut*." He perused the menu and made his choice. The couples gave their orders to the waitress, then sat back to wait for their meals.

"It turned out to be a nice day," Meg said, as the server brought their drinks.

"*Ja*, we couldn't have asked for better November

weather," Peter agreed. He ignored Reuben's narrowed gaze and reached for the lemonade he'd ordered.

Meg felt self-conscious after the fiasco of Reuben assisting her from the buggy. She didn't understand the tension between him and Peter. She'd felt it as Peter had waited while Reuben struggled to help her. The strained air between the two men had remained as they'd entered the restaurant. It had seemed to ease, finally, after they'd given their food orders. Then they'd sat back with drinks and struck up a conversation.

Meg was conscious of Reuben beside her and Peter across from her. Agnes was animated as she actively tried to keep the conversation going. Eyeing the young woman, Meg couldn't help but like Agnes Beiler. She was thoughtful and kind, as proved when she'd asked after Meg's well-being on visiting Sunday, and later when she and Peter had stopped in to see her. Meg understood what Peter saw in her.

As she listened and occasionally added to the conversation about the holiday weekend, she became aware of the other restaurant patrons staring at her. Meg touched her face. Did she look that bad? Her bruises weren't as sore as they'd been right after the accident, and she'd nearly forgotten about them.

She sighed. She should have stayed home. She didn't like being the object of scrutiny, no matter how well intended. She stared down at her hands, suddenly feeling out of place.

"Meg."

She looked up and straight into Peter's gray eyes. "Headache?" he inquired gently.

She shook her head. "I'm fine."

"Of course you are," Reuben assured her with warmth.

Peter arched an eyebrow, as if he didn't believe her. She held his gaze, determined to prove that she was well.

"So my *eldre* decided we'd invite my cousins to Thanksgiving," Agnes was saying. "They live in New Wilmington. *Mam* sent a letter inviting them two weeks ago."

"How long has it been since you've seen them?" Meg asked, curious. She avoided looking at Peter, but sensed his regard.

"Over a year. It will be fun to see them again." She paused to eat a potato chip. "They should arrive sometime this evening."

Meg smiled. "It was wonderful when we moved to Happiness. It had been too long since we'd seen our Lapp cousins. I know my *dat* missed *Endie* Katie."

"So you don't mind living here," Peter said, drawing her attention.

She shook her head. "*Nay.* I like where we live. I enjoy our church community."

"And that's all you enjoy?" Reuben teased.

Meg grinned. "Maybe not all," she admitted. She felt Peter stiffen, but when she glanced at him, he seemed relaxed.

The waitress brought their food, and soon they were enjoying their meal. Reuben's attention made her feel special. He was a handsome man with a gentle and teasing nature. *Just the type of man I need in my life*, she told herself.

They finished their lunch with dessert. Meg glanced at the chocolate cake that the server set before Peter, then eyed the lemon dessert she'd ordered. Her lips twitched as she recalled their disagreement about the birthday cake flavor.

To her surprise, he was watching her, his masculine mouth curved upward. They shared a moment, until Reuben drew her attention with a touch on her arm.

"How's your pudding?" he inquired pleasantly.

"*Gut*. 'Tis been a long time since I've enjoyed lemon pudding." She paused. "'Tis my *dat's* favorite flavor." She heard a snort from across the table, but when she glanced over, Peter was smiling at Agnes as they discussed her dessert—rice pudding topped with cinnamon.

When it was time to leave, Reuben picked up Meg's crutches and held them for her as she pushed back from the table. She rose on her good foot, and he clasped her upper arm until she was balanced evenly on the crutches. "*Danki*, Reuben," she murmured, conscious of Peter and Agnes waiting patiently behind them.

As Meg drew close to the exit, Reuben rushed to open the door. She beamed at him as she hobbled past without mishap. Fortunately, there were no steps to the building. He stood close, ready to catch her if she fell, but she found her way to the buggy without incident.

She paused when she reached the vehicle. The thought of hurting her leg as she climbed into the back seat didn't sit well with her. She waited patiently as she contemplated what to do. She wished she could be up front with Peter, but Agnes was his sweetheart and had the right to sit next to him.

Reuben took her crutches and rested them against the buggy. When he spanned her waist with his hands, Meg blushed, embarrassed and overly self-conscious at the touch she was unaccustomed to. "Let me help," he murmured as he started to lift her.

Her leg struck the buggy's edge, and she winced. She heard Reuben's quick apology as he set her down. He picked her up again a moment later, and nearly had her in when the cast bumped against the vehicle again.

"Nay." Peter was suddenly close. "Reuben, Meg needs to sit up front. She'll be more comfortable there." He addressed Agnes softly. "Do you mind?"

"Of course not," she assured him.

Reuben looked as if he wanted to argue, but seemed to think better of it. He touched Meg's shoulder. "Is that *oll recht,* Meg?"

She nodded, relieved, and Reuben followed her around the vehicle until he realized that he couldn't help her, because he had to get into the back first. He glared at Peter, sighed, then climbed aboard.

Peter waited patiently, then held out his hand. Meg felt a fluttering in her belly as his warm fingers gripped hers firmly. He placed his other hand at the side of her waist. Without effort, he lifted her as if she weighed no more than a feather. She didn't bump her leg, and it took only seconds for him to get her settled on the front seat before he went around to climb in beside her.

Agnes was chatting with Reuben. Peter glanced at her as if to ensure that she was comfortable. After what seemed an eternity, he picked up the leathers and steered the buggy out of the parking lot and onto the main road. Meg was grateful to be in the front seat. Peter had understood what she needed and taken care of it for her. She felt something soften inside her.

The countryside was beautiful. Although she'd lived in Lancaster County for over four years, Meg still appreciated her surroundings. The farm fields had been harvested, but the sight of them still gave her a little thrill. She loved how the land looked when it was freshly tilled and seeded, then as the plants sprouted and grew tall. Spending so much time in the hospital when she'd been ill at fourteen had given her a healthy appreciation for everything that was alive outdoors. Peter remained silent, taking in the view, as well.

"Meg," Agnes said, "I'm sorry. I shouldn't have pushed for you to come."

"I'm fine," she answered. "I've enjoyed myself." And she realized that she had. Despite the bruises and dealing with her cast, she'd found the day more than pleasant.

She sensed Peter's look and met his gaze briefly. He appeared to be deciding whether or not she was telling the truth. Then something eased in his features.

"Look!" Agnes said. "There's a fox!"

"Where?" Meg glanced out the window, but saw nothing.

"In the field over there!"

"I see it," Reuben said, but Meg didn't.

"There, Meg." Peter gestured past her to an open field just ahead. "See?"

His voice was soft. She could detect the clean, masculine, pleasing scent of him. She swallowed hard. "*Ja,* I see it." She smiled and sent him a silent thank-you with her gaze.

Peter steered the buggy on a leisurely tour of the countryside before turning to head for home. Meg was exhausted by the time he drove onto the lane to her family farmhouse. He pulled close to the porch, got out and came around to help her.

But Reuben jumped out of the vehicle and rushed around the carriage, so he could reach her first. "*Danki*, Peter," he said pleasantly, "I'll help her."

Peter stepped back. Agnes climbed out and stood beside him. "It was fun," she said. "Let's do it again sometime."

Meg looked from Peter to Reuben. She couldn't read Peter's expression, but Reuben looked happy at the prospect of another outing. "It was a nice afternoon," Reuben said.

"I'm glad you had fun." Agnes shifted closer to Peter. "Rest well, Meg," she said, before she climbed back into his buggy.

"Peter," Meg murmured. "I'll see you Sunday."

Something flickered in his gray eyes. "*Ja*, Meg. Have a *gut* night." He turned toward Reuben. "You, too, Reuben." He extended his hand. The man hesitated before he finally shook it.

Meg stood by Reuben as Peter and Agnes left. "I'll be heading home. I know you must be tired." Reuben paused, and warmth entered his expression. "I'm glad we got to spend time together today."

She managed a smile. "*Ja*. Lunch was *gut*." She wrinkled her nose impishly. "The company wasn't bad, either."

"I'm sorry about your leg." He paused. "And that you had to sit up front."

Meg frowned. "It was fine, Reuben. This cast is bulky. It was easier to sit there."

"I'd have liked it if you were next to me in the back."

His words made her uncomfortable, but she let them go. "I should get inside."

"Will you be up for the next youth singing?" he asked.

"I won't know how I'll be feeling until closer to the time."

He opened his mouth as if to say something else, but then shut it. He reached for her hand and gave it a squeeze instead. "Enjoy your evening, Meg Stoltzfus."

"You, too, Reuben."

He insisted on carrying her up to the front porch before he left. She stood at the railing and waved to him as he drove away—and then her thoughts turned toward Peter and the outing to see Bishop John Fisher in two days. She wondered if Peter would comment on today's outing, or mention any of the awkwardness.

She turned and, using her crutches, went inside the house.

Chapter Eight

❧

"Are you ready to go?" Peter asked.

Meg gasped and looked up. "I didn't know you were here."

Her mother entered the great room from behind him. "I told him to come right in." She eyed the two of them. "What are your plans for today?"

"We've figured out a location for the party." Meg explained about their idea to hold the celebration at Bishop John's.

Mam's gaze flickered. "'Tis a *gut* idea if you can convince him. He's had a tough time since Catherine passed."

"*Ja*, I know," Meg said.

"We thought it might be *gut* for him to have company at Christmas," Peter added. "To be surrounded by our community and people who care about him."

"That's true." Her mother looked thoughtful. "How long will you be gone?"

"Not long, I imagine." Peter approached Meg and reached for her crutches. "Is anyone expected back soon?"

"*Nay*, Arlin and my *dechter* are gone for the morning. If you're back by noon, you should be fine." *Mam* watched as Peter extended a hand to help Meg rise. "Since you're going to see John anyway, would you bring him a cake I baked for him this morning? I was going to ask Leah to drop it off after she got home, but you can do it instead."

Peter grinned. "I've got bread for him in the buggy from *Mam*. She baked extra before Thanksgiving."

"Everyone wants to help," Meg said, as her mother left to get the cake. Peter had released her hand, but she still felt the tingling of his touch on her fingers. "Do you think we'll be able to convince him?"

He handed her the crutches, and she slipped one under each arm. "*Ja*. It may be hard at first, but I think he'll agree in the end. It must be lonely for him in that house with just his son for company."

Mam entered the room with the cake. "We feel terrible about what John's going through." She watched approvingly as Meg maneuvered toward the door with her crutches. "Remember, your *vadder* will be back by noon."

"We'll be back before then," Peter assured her as he held the door open, first for *Mam* to precede them, then for Meg to hobble through. "I've got to work in the shop today. *Dat* and Jacob received some last-minute orders. With winter coming, everyone wants to make sure they're ready."

"We could have postponed the visit," Meg said with a frown. She felt bad for taking him from his work.

Peter flashed her a smile that made her heart race. "Why? You think I'd rather be working in the shop? *Dat* doesn't need me until later. I think we should get the place for the party settled before doing anything else."

Meg nodded. That was what they'd discussed, and it made good sense.

"I'll have lunch ready for when you return," *Mam* promised as she reached the bottom of the steps. She headed toward the buggy with the cake.

"That's kind of you, Missy." Peter didn't rush to carry Meg as Reuben had, but waited patiently for her to manage the porch stairs on her own. She appreciated how he treated her. She found his way much less stressful than Reuben's hovering, take-charge methods.

She felt a moment's unease over Reuben. She shouldn't think poorly of him for it. Reuben, no doubt, felt responsible for her injuries, since the accident had happened while he was taking her home.

Meg paused to watch as her mother put the cake into the back of the buggy. Then she started carefully down the porch steps, with Peter close behind her. She wavered and nearly lost her footing, but his quick grip on her arm steadied her. *"Danki,"* she murmured, overly aware of his strength.

"You want me to carry you like Reuben does?" he teased.

She felt her face heat. *"Nay!"*

He was silent a long moment. "I didn't think so." His tone was dry.

Feeling foolish, Meg negotiated the rest of the way to his buggy. Without asking, Peter grabbed her crutches and set them in the vehicle. He then caught her about the waist and lifted her easily onto the front seat, before going around to slide in next to her. They waved to her mother as they left.

Bishop John Fisher's house wasn't far, less than ten minutes at a canter. Peter kept his gaze fixed on the road as he steered the vehicle. His continued silence after several minutes made Meg antsy. They'd gotten along so well during their last meeting. Had something changed? Was it because of Wednesday's outing?

She heard him sigh. "I hope John agrees to the party. If not, I don't know what we'll do."

"We'll have to find a way to convince him," Meg said.

He flashed her a smile. "You're determined. I like that. Will you do the talking, or should I?"

She responded to his good humor with a smile. "We both will."

"Who should go first?" he teased.

Her lips twitched. "You can." Meg relaxed as the tension between them dissipated.

Peter flipped on the battery-operated blinker and made a right turn. "When do you go get your cast off?" His tone was conversational.

"After four weeks. The doctor said it normally takes six weeks for a broken leg to heal. I don't think mine will take longer."

"Four weeks… That would be the week of the party."

"Ja." She sighed, annoyed by the weight of her cast.

"Do you know what the doctor will do?" Peter steered the horse onto the bishop's road.

"He'll want to do X-rays to see how my leg is healing."

Peter was quiet as he parked near Bishop John's barn. "I can take you to the doctor's if you want." He hesitated. "And to physical therapy when you need it."

She got a funny feeling in her stomach. *"Danki,*

Peter. That's kind of you. If I need you to take me, I'll let you know." She felt her cheeks warm.

Peter jumped out of the buggy and came around to help her.

"I wonder who's here," Meg murmured as she spied two other vehicles in the barnyard. "I hope we don't have to postpone our conversation with him."

"We'll stop in to visit, and if we can't talk, we'll give him the baked goods, then come back another time."

Peter assisted her from the buggy, then waited for her to precede him around the vehicle toward the house. Meg exchanged glances with him as he joined her. He rapped on the wooden door. When no one answered, he tried again. This time the door opened, revealing a familiar young woman with Bishop John's baby son, Nicholas, on her hip.

"Peter!" she cried.

"Sally," he answered warmly. "I'm surprised to see you here."

His cousin shrugged. "It was my turn to come." She pushed the door open and stepped back to allow them to enter. "*Hallo*, Meg." She eyed her and Peter carefully.

"*Hallo*, Sally." Meg shot Peter a look. Sally Hershberger was not only Peter's cousin; she was the daughter of Alta Hershberger, the busybody of their church community. Could they trust Sally with their party plans? His aunt Alta had never been able to keep a secret.

"I'm surprised to see the two of you."

"We're not together," Meg said quickly. Too quickly, she realized, when she felt Peter stiffen beside her.

"*Nay*," he agreed. "We've got something we'd like to discuss with John."

At his tight tone, Meg shot him a glance, but his expression was unreadable as he explained the reason for their visit. She tensed as she stood with him in the hallway. She felt as if she'd offended him, and that hadn't been her intention.

"John's in the back room," Sally told them as she moved down the hall. "I'll tell him you're here."

Meg felt the air between her and Peter turn chilly as they waited. "I'm sorry. Peter, I didn't mean—"

"It was nothing, Meg. You told the truth. We're not together." His words shocked her and made her feel awful. She could only hope they could get back to their friendly working relationship.

"Sally's not like her *mam*, is she? She won't tell anyone why we've come?"

She heard him sigh. *"Nay,* she's not like Alta. She's suffered because of her mother's tendency to natter. She'll not say a word."

After a long moment of silence, Meg said, *"Gut."* She felt awkward. She was pretty sure their easy working relationship had been tested by her earlier comment. And she should have kept her mouth shut about his cousin, she realized with regret.

Sally returned within moments. "Come on back." Her voice grew soft, but her eyes held sadness. "I think he's searching for a reason to be thankful." She bit her lip. "He spent Thanksgiving alone—him and Nicholas." She opened her mouth. "I wanted to come and cook for him, but he didn't want to keep me from my family. I would have invited him to the *haus*, but *Mam*…"

Meg felt a rush of sympathy. "How was your Thanksgiving?"

"It was fine." Sally smiled shyly, and Meg stared, stunned by the beauty in her expression. Meg thought that the young woman looked like a natural mother, with the bishop's baby son clearly happy in her arms. But she knew that Sally had never married, and as far as she knew, there wasn't any sweetheart in the picture.

They followed Sally to a small room off the main living area. John sat at a table, his attention on the piece of paper before him as he scribbled on it with a pencil.

"John," Sally said softly.

The bishop looked up. "Peter. Meg." He rose from his chair and moved into the larger room. Meg and Peter joined him, each taking a seat across from him.

Meg wondered if he felt more encumbered by his position in the church now that his wife was dead. Catherine Fisher had been ill and frail since the birth of their son. On the day his wife had collapsed and died, John had learned that she'd developed a serious heart problem. He'd been chosen by the church elders. He would be the bishop in charge of their church district until the day he died. It was both a blessing and a curse to be selected as bishop. Most community men didn't want the position. But John had taken it and done a good job. Still, Meg could see the tired lines around his soft brown eyes and the deep sadness there. She could only imagine what it felt like to lose someone you loved, someone who meant the world to you.

"Sally said you wanted to talk with me."

Meg hesitated and flashed Peter a glance.

"We have a favor to ask of you, John," Peter began. He explained that his father and her mother wanted to give their spouses a special surprise birthday celebration, and that Arlin and Miriam both had Christmas birthdays.

"And you need me for?"

Meg bit her lip. "We were hoping you'd allow us to hold the party here."

John looked surprised—and understandably leery. "I don't know." He appeared lost, like a young boy unsure of facing the world after a terrible disappointment.

"I know it's a huge imposition, but we'd handle everything." She softened her expression as she took in his hesitation. John had grown thinner since Catherine had died, and she hated to see him that way. She wondered why the Lord provided someone to love and spend the rest of his life with, only to take her home, leaving a grief-stricken man to raise his child alone. As people of God, their Amish community took comfort in the fact that their deceased loved ones were at home with the Lord, but that didn't necessarily make it easier for those who still grieved.

The bishop rubbed a hand across his forehead. "I don't—"

"John," Peter said, his voice soft and filled with compassion, "wouldn't it be better to spend the holiday with us, surrounded by our church community, people who care about you, than to spend it alone in this house all by yourself with only Nicholas for company?"

"The decision is yours." Meg rose, warmed by the gentle way Peter spoke to him. Still, she knew the man needed time to mull over their request. "Will you please think about it? We'll come back another time. We don't want to pressure you."

Peter stood on cue. "If there is anything you need me to do, will you call on me?" He paused. "Are your horses ready for the winter? I heard there is a possibility of snow in the next few days."

John looked surprised, as if he hadn't considered

that he might need to do anything for his horses before the worst of the winter weather rolled in. "I think they're *oll recht.*"

"I can check them if you'd like, before we leave," Peter offered.

The bishop nodded. "I'd appreciate that. *Danki.*"

Sally showed them out. "I think it's a wonderful idea—having your parents' party here," Peter's cousin said.

"He has the space, and we figured it would help him, too."

Sally nodded as she led the way through the kitchen. "He needs all the help he can get." Without conscious thought, it seemed, she ran her fingers lovingly through Nicholas's soft, baby-fine hair. "This poor boy needs his *dat.* John manages to take care of him at night, but during the day he seems too lost to pay much attention to him." She frowned. "I don't mean he's not a *gut vadder,* because he is. He's just grieving so."

"The churchwomen will be pushing for him to marry soon," Meg said.

"*Ja,*" the other woman said. "Nicholas needs a *mudder.*" She gazed at the baby with longing. Then she blushed, as if embarrassed. She quickly shuttered her expression and her lips curved. "So you will be back to get his answer?"

"*Ja,*" Peter said. "You'll not tell your *mam?*"

"You have to ask?" Her laughter was harsh. "It wouldn't be a surprise party if I told her. You don't have to worry about me telling my *mudder* anything." She scowled. "*Mam* is pushing me to wed, and she's decided on John. It seems she thinks I'll make a *gut* second wife for him."

"I'm sorry," Peter said, eyeing his cousin with concern.

Studying her, Meg suspected that Sally would love to be John's wife and a mother to his son, but she was afraid that with her *mam's* interference, she'd lose her chance at happiness. Meg didn't doubt that Alta's methods would hurt rather than help Sally's future with the kind bishop.

"*Ach, nay,* I nearly forgot," Peter said, as his gaze settled on Nicholas's wooden high chair, which was pushed close to the kitchen table. "The food." He glanced at Meg. "Wait here," he said. "I'll be right back."

Meg nodded. Her gaze went to Sally. "That little boy thinks the world of you," she murmured.

Sally beamed. "He's a sweet baby. I just wish…"

"*Ja?*" Meg waited a heartbeat before finishing her sentence. "That he could be more to you?"

"I wish he could be, but the likelihood of that is close to zero chance."

"Why do you say that?" Meg readjusted the crutches under her arms.

"I'm sorry," the woman said. "Please sit down. Your leg must be bothering you."

"It's getting better." She stared down at her cast as she eased into a kitchen chair. "I can't wait to get it off, but it will be a while yet." She returned her gaze to Sally. "You like him. The bishop."

"And he still loves his wife."

"She's gone," Meg reminded her.

"But he can't get past her memory. And for me to have a chance? With my *mam*, there's not much of one." Sally sighed. "I love my *mudder*. I know how devastated she was after my *vadder* passed. She's been a *gut mam* despite her tendency to…"

"Talk?" Meg suggested.

Sally agreed, her lips turning up in a smile. "I'd love to be here for John and Nicholas. I'm trying to be here for them, but when there are many women who want to see their daughters wed to a man as kind and caring as John is, it's hard to have hope."

"How often do you come here to help out?"

"As often as I can." She shifted the little boy in her arms. "And we have a *gut* time together, don't we, Nicholas?" The baby patted her cheek as if he understood.

"Do the other daughters come?" Meg couldn't think of which women had the other daughters.

Sally shrugged. "Some, but not many and not often. 'Tis been the older women who have been taking a turn, but since I don't have a family of my own, they usually accept the fact that I can be here more often than they can." She was quiet a moment. "I guess they don't believe I have a chance with him."

Meg studied Sally, who was lovely, with soft brown hair and light blue eyes. "I hope you get it all, Sally. I'll pray for it."

Delight spread on the girl's face. "*Danki*, Meg. I heard that Reuben Miller wants to court you. I hope he makes you happy."

Her words made Meg feel awful for what she'd said earlier—jumping to deny the fact that she and Peter were a couple. Rejecting him. "About earlier. Peter and I are…"

"Working together as friends."

Meg nodded. "*Ja*, we've found a way to be friends."

Sally nodded. *"Gut."* She appeared to search for words. "He liked you for a long time."

"He did?" She didn't believe her. She'd cared for him

once, too, until she'd overheard what he'd said, and she'd confronted him later that same day.

"*Ja*, but I understand that you want Reuben. And I'm glad you've found a way for you and Peter to get along."

Peter came into the house with the cake and two loaves of bread. He grinned as he set them on the kitchen table. "From my *mudder* and Meg's."

"*Danki*," Sally said. "That will save me from baking today and tomorrow."

Peter raised his eyebrows. Meg, hoping to spare Sally any discomfort, quickly suggested they leave. "You did say you had to work in the shop today," she reminded him.

Peter politely held the door open for her as Meg hobbled outside, down one step toward the carriage. She paused as something occurred to her, then halted and faced him. "Did your *mam* know why you were coming to see the bishop?"

"She baked for him. She's the one who wanted me to come." His grin was noticeably absent. "She knows nothing about our plans."

Meg felt something inside tighten and clench. She'd hurt him again, and she hadn't meant to.

He was courteous as he helped her into his buggy, but then was quiet on the ride back, until he pulled up close to the house. He got out and came around to the left side of the vehicle.

"I guess we'll give John a few days before we check back about the party."

She nodded, fighting tears.

He held out his hand and helped her down. "Take care, Meg," he said, his voice overly polite.

"Bye, Peter." And despite the fact that she knew

she'd see him again regarding the party, Meg felt as if it was really a goodbye to the camaraderie bordering on friendship they'd discovered since their first planning meeting.

After Peter left, Meg moved through the house toward the kitchen.

"*Gut*, you're back!" *Mam* said as she turned from the stove. "I've got lunch almost ready." She looked behind her and frowned. "Where's Peter?"

"He had to get to the shop." Meg felt worse than ever. She and Peter had been getting along and now she'd offended him. Again. When the only thing she wanted was for him to like her. She should have kept her mouth closed after seeing Sally's surprise at seeing her and Peter together. Why hadn't she? Because she didn't want to be courted by Reuben Miller, she realized.

She wanted Peter Zook.

Chapter Nine

Peter decided to stop at Agnes's before he headed to his father's blacksmith shop. Meg's quick denial to Sally's comment about them being together bothered him. He felt raw, and he needed to see his friend, to be soothed by her friendship and kind humor. She and her sister were outside hanging clothes on the line when he pulled up to their house.

He parked, got out and approached without their knowledge. They were too far out in the yard to have heard his buggy. He felt his lips curve as he jogged across the grass. "Agnes!"

She turned. Her eyes widened as she grinned. "Peter!" She met him halfway. "What are you doing here?"

"Came to see you, since I didn't get to stop by on Thanksgiving."

Agnes didn't look the least bit upset. "It was a busy day, what with my cousins' arrival late the night before." She waved to the other young woman who watched them from near the clothesline. "Lydia!" she called. "Come meet Peter."

The girl who Peter had thought was Alice advanced. As she drew near, he saw that she was much younger than Alice. While she was blonde like Agnes and her twin sister, she had dark brown eyes instead of light blue ones.

Agnes grabbed his hand as she made introductions. Lydia smiled shyly as she regarded him curiously. She wore a lavender dress with a black coat. She was pretty, but Peter thought Agnes and Meg were prettier. He frowned. The last person he should be thinking about was Meg Stoltzfus.

"Will you eat with us?" Agnes asked a few moments later.

"Sorry, but I can't. I have to work in the shop today." He couldn't keep from smiling at both girls. Agnes's good mood was a soothing balm to his battered defenses. It had been easy to become fast friends with her when she'd come with her sister and brother to the youth singing in his church community, where they'd met. Now he was determined that they become more.

"Are you coming to our church service on Sunday?" he asked.

Agnes shook her head. "Not this Sunday. *Mam* wants us to attend church service in our own community, with our family in from out of town."

Peter nodded. "Lydia, how many siblings do you have?"

"Five older brothers and a younger sister."

When his eyes widened, the girl laughed. "*Ja*, five older brothers. You would be kind to a *schweschter, ja*?"

"*Ja*. I've got two sisters and I'm kind to them. Annie is married. Barbara isn't." He frowned as he thought of Barbara. She'd been staying with relatives in New Wilmington for over a year. At one time, he'd thought that Barbara and Preacher Levi would marry, but something had happened between them. And then Barbara had left. It had been too long since his family had seen her.

"Do you want to come to our Sunday services?" Agnes asked, drawing his attention.

Peter thought about it, then quickly rejected the idea. It would be nice to spend time with Agnes without tension or concerns, but he still had a party to plan with Meg. And he had to find a way to work with her again. "I can't this week." He smiled to show that he would have liked to go.

"Are you going to the singing?"

Peter nodded. "You want me to come get you?" he offered. He couldn't take all of Agnes's cousins, but he could take Agnes, Alice and Lydia.

Agnes beamed at him. "That would be *wunderbor*."

"I need to get to the shop." He made arrangements to pick up the twins and Lydia Sunday evening before the youth singing. Agnes seemed fine with attending the one in his community despite the fact that there would be one in hers, as well.

"We'll see you on Sunday, Peter," Lydia said quietly.

He nodded, then left, hurrying as he realized the time—he should have been hard at work in his father's blacksmith shop by now.

Reuben surprised Meg with a visit later that afternoon, after Peter had dropped her off and she'd eaten lunch with her family.

"Reuben!" she exclaimed, when Ellie ushered him into the room. "I didn't expect to see you today."

"I hope it's *oll recht* that I've come. 'Tis been a while since I've seen you."

"I'm glad you came," Meg said sincerely. After the way Peter had left her abruptly, it felt good to have someone genuinely happy to see her. *Peter*, she thought. *Why is it always so difficult to deal with Peter?*

"Sit down, Reuben," her mother said warmly. "Would you like a piece of apple pie?"

He smiled. "*Ja*, that would be nice, Missy." He chose the seat across from Meg, who regarded him with affection. "'Tis *gut* to see you, Meg."

"You've been working hard, I hear," she said. The crew he worked with was apparently trying to get a commercial building done before winter rolled in full force.

The good humor left his face as he regarded her with concern. "Meg, I won't be able to make Sunday's youth singing. My *eldre* wants us to visit my *grossmudder* in Millersburg."

Meg knew of the Amish community. "I didn't know your *grossmammi* lived in Ohio."

"Ja." He seemed to relax. "I have an aunt, an uncle and lots of cousins there."

"That will be nice for you to see them." She was pleased for him. Family was important. Her father had taught her that.

"Ja." He seemed to study her, as if trying to gauge her reaction about his absence.

"Reuben, you're not worried I'm upset that you're leaving?"

He waited a heartbeat. "I am. I care about you, Meg. I don't want you to think differently."

"I know, Reuben. And I believe you." She wished

she could feel more excited about his serious interest in her. Her lips curved. "When do you go?"

"In two hours."

"It was nice of you to stop by and let me know."

He reached for her hand across the table. Fortunately, there was no one in the room besides them. She should have withdrawn her fingers, but Reuben was clearly upset to be leaving her.

Yet, she wasn't. And why was that? She didn't want to think about it too closely.

"Meg, I'll come see you when I get back." His touch was warm, but it didn't make her tingle like…Peter's.

"Will you be gone a week?"

"Three days," he told her. "*Dat* has hired a driver to take us."

She understood why. The distance was too far to travel by buggy.

"Will you miss me?"

"Of course." *As a friend and nothing more*, she thought. Reuben was a kind, thoughtful man, but she'd been unsure about her feelings for him since they'd started to see each other. Since he'd saved her from drowning the night of the accident, she'd made a silent promise to give their relationship a chance.

She had a mental vision of Peter and quickly fought to banish it.

Reuben grinned, then stood. Her mother entered the room. "Don't you want your pie?" she asked him.

"May I take it with me? We're leaving for Ohio in a couple hours."

Mam wrapped up Reuben's pie, and the man left shortly afterward. "That was nice of him to stop by before he left."

"*Ja*, it was." Meg knew Reuben was a kind and thoughtful man. She just had to decide whether or not he was the right man for her.

Sunday arrived quickly, and the family left for church services at the William Mast farm. As they neared the property, Meg saw several buggies ahead of theirs and knew them to belong to other church community members.

As she climbed the steps to the door leading to Josie Mast's kitchen, Meg saw Josie's daughter Ellen talking with Annie Lapp, Peter's sister. On the other side of the room, her aunt Katie stood with Meg's friend Martha, who was her cousin Eli's wife. Meg carefully negotiated the three steps onto the porch. Catching sight of her, Ellen rushed forward to open the door.

"Meg!" she said in greeting. "You're looking so much better."

Meg smiled. "I feel better." She glanced around the room, noting other familiar female faces within her community. "*Mam's* outside. We've brought cheesecake and German potato salad."

The other woman's eyes gleamed. "I love German potato salad."

"Where's my cousin?" Meg teased.

"Which one?" But Ellen blushed, so Meg knew she understood that she meant Isaac, Ellen's sweetheart. "He's outside in the barn."

"I like him for you," Meg said, and the young woman beamed at her. "Can I do anything?"

Have you seen Peter? she wanted to ask, but didn't. She couldn't allow others to know they were working together, but since Peter had left without their making any plans to meet again, she'd have to find a way to talk with him without anyone guessing.

"There you are, Meg," Annie said as she approached. She held her daughter, Susanna, on her hip. Her four-year-old son was absent, no doubt with his father, Meg thought. "Did you happen to see Peter outside?"

Meg shook her head. "*Nay.* I didn't see anyone out in the yard except those of us who just arrived." Which included Alta and Sally Hershberger and the Abram Peachys. *Peter is here*, she thought. Suddenly, she felt nervous. Could she find some way to smooth things over between them so they could continue to work together? She hoped so.

She wondered if he'd be going to the singing tonight. If he did, he would go with Agnes. Reuben wasn't here, so she should probably stay home. But did she want to?

She didn't see Peter until church service began. Furniture had been removed from the Masts' great room. Since it was November, the service would be inside the house rather than the barn, where there was more space. She spied him seated next to her cousin Jacob. Peter held EJ in the men's section. The smaller children often sat with their mother, but EJ had become a well-behaved little boy who clearly enjoyed his uncle's attention.

Meg was unable to look away from them. She had arrived before the men and was seated between Martha and Leah. As if sensing her regard, Peter met her gaze. She tried to smile, but found she couldn't. He didn't look happy with her, and could she blame him? *Nay, I can't.*

The service proceeded as usual—with over two hours of singing, preaching and more hymns. Soon, Preacher Levi Stoltzfus—who was no relation to Meg—

finished speaking, and everyone started to leave the room. The men headed outside, while the women started to get the midday meal ready to be served indoors.

Meg rose on her crutches and headed toward the kitchen. Then she stopped and sighed. There wasn't anything she could do to help. She couldn't carry food and walk with crutches at the same time.

The kitchen was filled with happy chatter and women pulling covers off cold food items. Meg sat down in a chair, leaned the crutches against the wall, then reached across the table to uncover her sister's German potato salad.

"I'll take that," Annie said, as she pulled the uncovered bowl toward the edge of the table. She handed Meg her two-year-old daughter. "Will you hold her?"

Meg smiled. "I'll be happy to." She settled Susanna on her lap across her uninjured leg. "*Hallo*, little one. Are you hungry?"

The child nodded vigorously.

"Anything special you hope to eat?"

"Pie."

She arched her eyebrow. "Pie? No cake or cookies? Just pie?"

"Cho-co-lit," Susanna said, nodding. "And appa-sauce."

"That's a fine idea. I like applesauce and chocolate."

The toddler grinned, and Meg felt her heart melt. There was something so sweet about a child's smile. When Susanna looked at her with approval, she felt as if her whole world brightened with the sun. Holding the little girl in her arms, smelling her clean baby scent made Meg long to have a baby of her own. She tried to envision her child. She was unable to picture one with blond hair and blue eyes. Meg drew a sharp breath. She could see her daughter with dark hair and gray eyes...

Nay! She wouldn't allow herself to fall for him again. She'd done it once, and it hadn't worked out well. Thankfully, Peter hadn't had a clue that she'd had a crush on him.

Peter. She had to finish planning this party with him. In order to do so, they would have to meet again—and soon. Christmas was only four weeks away, and they had yet to get Bishop John's answer on whether or not they could use his house for the celebration.

Meg sat, enjoying the little girl as the other women of the community unwrapped and set out all the food in the other room. The men would eat first, so she stayed where she was while Josie Mast went to let the men know that their meal was ready.

She heard them come in through the main door. The sound of deep young male tones, intermingled with older, more mature and masculine voices, filtered into the kitchen from the main room.

"Would you like me to take her?" Annie asked, stepping back to see how Meg was faring with her daughter.

"We're fine, aren't we, Susanna?"

The child nodded. "*Gut, Mam.* Meg's going to have cho-co-lit pie, too. And appa-sauce."

Annie laughed as she and Meg exchanged amused glances. "She is, is she?"

"*Ja.*" Susanna frowned. "Where's EJ?"

"He's with *Dat,*" her mother said.

The child's lip quivered. "I want to be with *Dat.*"

"'Tis the men's turn to eat, *dochter.* You'll have to eat with me." She paused. "And Meg."

Meg nodded. "*Ja*, we'll get to eat applesauce and pie together. And other things, as well."

"Lots of pie?" Susanna asked.

"Plenty for a little girl just your size," Meg assured her, and was pleased when Annie shot her a grateful look.

The men finished their meal and, despite the cold, moved outside to the barn, where they often had discussions about their farms, the weather and other topics that interested them. Annie came for her daughter and Meg rose, grabbed her crutches and followed the two into the next room more slowly. There was plenty of food left on tables against the two walls. Meg saw Annie get Susanna situated before fixing her a plate of food. Smiling, Meg hobbled toward the seat next to the child, until she saw Peter crouched down beside his niece. His expression was warm and loving as he spoke with her. Susanna clearly loved her uncle, if her beaming expression was any indication.

Her heart beating wildly, Meg froze. Peter looked up, saw her and abruptly stood. He bent to say something to Susanna that made her laugh. Suddenly anxious, Meg felt her face heat. *Did he say something about me?* She swallowed hard and continued her awkward approach.

"Mee!" Susanna cried, warming her heart. "Seat!"

Continuing forward, praying she didn't trip and fall, Meg moved toward the little girl and her now-silent uncle.

"*Hallo*, Peter," she said, as she tried to maneuver into the chair that Annie and her daughter had saved for her.

"Meg." He pulled it out and helped her to sit.

She blushed, wondering why she was embarrassed by his thoughtfulness now, when he'd helped her before without her feeling awkward. She thanked him quietly and he started to move away. "Peter," she called softly. He halted and glanced back. "Will we..." she began.

He nodded.

"Monday?" she suggested.

He remained silent too long.

"Monday what?" Annie asked, as she walked up.

"Tomorrow is Monday," Peter said. "And it may snow."

Annie frowned.

Meg thought quickly. "I was hoping that Peter would come early to check on our horses. You know, with winter coming..."

His sister's brow cleared. "*Ja*, you and Jacob have been busy," she said.

"If you're too busy..." Meg said.

"'Tis no problem. We're nearly caught up."

"*Ja*, Meg, he'll be happy to come." Annie turned her daughter's plate so that the applesauce was directly in front of her. "Better than waiting until after the first snowfall."

"I heard it will snow this week." Meg avoided Peter's gaze.

"I'll be over tomorrow," he promised.

She looked at him then, saw nothing in his expression that suggested he was still angry with her.

"I'll let you eat your meal," he said, then left.

"Look!" Susanna said. "I've eaten all my appasauce." She pouted. "You don't have any food yet."

Leah came up to the table and set a plate before Meg. "Let me know if there's anything else you'd like," she said.

"Appa-sauce," Susanna exclaimed. "And cho-co-lit

pie." She grinned up at Meg's sister. "We're supposed to eat it together."

Amusement entered Leah's expression. "I'd better get her some of both then," she declared.

As she regarded Susanna, smiling in turn, Meg suddenly felt as if she was being watched. She glanced up and saw Peter in the doorway, staring at her. She blinked and wondered what he was thinking. Tomorrow they'd talk, and she would apologize. Except, did she have anything to apologize for? As he'd said, she and Peter weren't together—not as a couple, but they were as a party-planning team.

She gave him a smile, and something shifted in his expression before he turned abruptly and left the house.

"Here you go," Leah said, putting another smaller plate before her.

"Danki," she murmured. But as she picked up her spoon to try her applesauce, she found that she was too tense to eat—until Susanna started to chat nonstop. Then Meg found herself relaxing and purposely put the child's uncle from her thoughts.

Tomorrow would be soon enough to deal with Peter Zook.

Chapter Ten

The next day Peter was on his way to see Meg when he spied a puppy on the side of the road. The little dog was injured, and while he knew he had to get to Meg's, he pulled his buggy over and parked. The animal was a tiny thing, with lots of fur. He approached carefully and it moved, lifting its little head to gaze up at him with sad eyes.

He felt something shift inside him. He couldn't leave the dog there. The animal needed medical care. He'd have to take it to James Pierce, Meg's brother-in-law and a veterinarian.

He removed the quilt his family kept under the front seat of the buggy, spread it on the ground close to the dog and carefully reached for the animal, silently praying it didn't bite or snap at him. He eased his hands closer, then slipped them under its body. The dog whimpered but didn't strike out. He picked it up and eased it gently onto the quilt. Then he wrapped up the dog loosely, like swaddling a baby, with only its head visible above the fabric. Peter placed the animal on the floor in front, then grabbed the leathers and began the journey to Meg's.

His first thought had been to take the dog directly to the veterinarian, then to send word to Meg why he didn't show. But that would only make things more difficult between them, so he drove on to her place so he could explain the situation and she could see the dog for herself.

It didn't take long to reach the Arlin Stoltzfus residence. Peter left the dog in the buggy while he hurried up the steps and knocked on the door. No one answered, so he tried again. After what seemed like a long time, the door opened, revealing Meg on her crutches.

"Peter, glad you could make it," she said hesitantly.

"I can't stay," he said. He saw her face fall. "Meg, I've got an injured dog in my buggy. I found him on the side of the road."

Her brow cleared. "May I see him?"

He held the door open for her as she came out onto the porch.

"What happened to him? Do you know?"

He stayed right behind Meg as she moved down the steps. She was using the crutches much better now, as if she'd become used to them as an extension of her.

"*Nay*, but I'd guess that he was hit by a car." The dog wasn't bloody, but Peter wondered if that was a good or bad thing. If it had been hit by a car, the little dog could be suffering internal injuries. The only thing that gave him hope was that the animal had opened its eyes once and looked at him.

They reached the buggy at the same time. Peter opened the door.

"Aww," Meg breathed. "Poor thing."

He was stunned by the softness in her expression. This was a totally different side of Meg. Not that he hadn't seen her smile—with someone else—or heard her laugh. He recalled with startling clarity the day they'd each announced their choice of party location. The fact that they'd agreed had shocked them both. The feeling he'd experienced that day had buoyed his spirits and given him hope that he and Meg could work well together.

"I thought I'd take him to James."

Meg met his gaze, her blue eyes shining. "*Ja*, that is a *gut* plan." She bit her lip, as if she'd had an idea but was afraid to suggest it.

"But?" he asked gently, encouragingly.

"What if you put him in our barn? We can have James come here. Now that Nell is married, the stall where she kept Jonas and Naomi is empty. It's a nice space, and he'll be safe there."

Peter looked at the dog, then returned his attention to Meg. "That's a fine plan."

She seemed relieved. "I wish I could hold him."

He softened his expression as he eyed her thoughtfully. "He's a little thing. I'm sure I can manage to carry him on my own."

"Oh, I didn't mean—"

"Meg," he said quickly, "I'm teasing you."

She stared at him a moment, then he saw her relax. "I'm sorry, but I seem to be on tenterhooks here."

"Meg, 'tis *oll recht*." He reached inside and picked up the quilt-wrapped dog. "He's so small. I hope there's nothing seriously wrong." He cradled the animal against his body.

"I hope so, too." Meg was eyeing the dog with obvious sorrow and longing. "Come, I'll show you where to put him."

She started toward the barn, then flashed him a smile over her shoulder that made him inhale sharply. "It's a boy?"

His lips curved slightly. "Not sure. I didn't pay much attention to anything but that he's hurt and I want to help."

She paused at the barn door. "You're a *gut* man, Peter Zook."

Her words stunned him into silence.

Despite her crutches, Meg managed to open the door and lead the way. She walked down the aisle to a stall, unlatched the door and gestured inside. "I know it might not seem like much." She bit her lip, and he found himself fascinated by the nervous gesture. "But Jonas and Naomi were happy here. I think this little one will be, too, once Nell and James are here to help him."

Peter entered the stall and hunkered down to set the dog on a bed of straw. "This is a *gut* space, Meg. Sheltered and with straw to keep him warm. He'll do well here. Now we just have to get Nell and James to come." He stroked the dog's back for a minute, then rose to his feet.

"Ellie is due home any minute. She has a cell phone. We can use it to call James." Meg looked as if she wanted to pet and hold the puppy. "We wouldn't have been able to stay here to make plans."

He arched his eyebrow. "I see."

She blushed. "*Nay*, Peter, you don't. I didn't know that she'd be back. I just found the note she left my *mudder*. *Mam's* not home, either. 'Tis just me today."

Concern laced her voice. "I didn't have a way to let you know."

He softened his expression. "'Tis fine. Everything worked out for the best, *ja*?"

He heard her release a heavy sigh. "I suppose so." She turned her attention back to the dog. "Should we give him water?"

"Sure. We don't know if he'll drink it, but he may be thirsty. I don't know how long he was lying there."

Meg smiled. "I'll get him some." She moved from the stall and hobbled down the length of the barn.

Peter hurried after her. "Meg, wait!"

She stopped and turned. *"Ja?"*

He was reluctant to continue. "May I carry it for you?" His gaze fell to her crutches.

Meg scowled. *"Ja*, that would be *gut*. Can't do much with these things." She was obviously frustrated.

He reached her side. "'Tis *oll recht*, Meg. You'll soon heal and be able to do all the things you did before." He fought the urge to caress her cheek.

She nodded, then pointed toward the bowls on a workbench against the wall directly in front of them. "The blue one is Jonas's bowl—we keep it here for when we watch Jonas and Naomi. The little one can use it."

Peter reached for the bowl and went outside to the pump to fill it. When he returned, he found Meg still standing there, staring into space. "What's wrong?" he asked.

She gasped. "I didn't see you come in." Her lips twisted. "I don't like being helpless."

"I'd hardly call you helpless, Meg. And we're planning a party together, which is work."

Her chuckle rang false. "Haven't gotten much done."

"We will," he assured her. "Today might have been a waste, but it will all come together."

Meg started back to the little dog's stall. "We need to check back with the bishop."

"Would you like me to do it on my way home?"

She was silent a long moment. "*Ja*, we have to know." She hesitated before continuing. "When can we get together again?"

"When is a *gut* time for you?" He went inside the stall and set the water within the dog's easy reach. He gently unwrapped the quilt, giving the animal room to move. The dog opened its eyes and stretched its head toward the water bowl. Peter carefully picked him up so he could drink.

"Wednesday?"

He nodded as he gently lowered the animal to the quilt. He had things to do tomorrow. Wednesday would be a better day.

"What if my sisters are home?" Meg asked.

Satisfied that the dog was set for now, Peter stood and joined her outside the stall, making sure to close the door after him. "Then we'll find someplace else to work."

Meg appeared satisfied. "Wednesday then."

They made their way out of the barn. A buggy pulled into the barnyard and stopped as they exited the building. Ellie stepped out.

"Ellie!" Meg called.

Her sister turned to her. "*Hallo*, Meg." Her gaze widened as it settled on Peter as she approached. "*Hallo*, Peter."

"Ellie, do you have your cell phone with you?" Meg asked.

Her sister frowned. "*Ja*, why?"

"Would you please call James? Peter found an injured dog. He's in our barn."

"*Ja*, I'll call him." Ellie walked away from them to place the call. She talked animatedly as she spoke with either Nell or James, then returned a few minutes later. "They are on their way."

"*Danki*, Ellie," Peter said.

"May I see him?"

"*Ja*, I've put him in Jonas and Naomi's old space."

Ellie accompanied them to the barn. Peter watched Meg's sister as she entered the confined area and crouched beside the dog. "Did you say it was a he?" She regarded them with twinkling eyes. "Looks more like a she."

Peter laughed. "She it is. I didn't look too closely." He and Meg locked gazes. He regarded her with amusement, and to his surprise, she flashed him a grin. Her good humor made his stomach flutter.

Nell and James arrived minutes later. "We were in the area," Nell explained, as she and her husband stepped into the barn.

"He's in Jonas's old stall."

Nell smiled. "*Gut* place to put him." She spied the little dog on the quilt and her expression went soft. "Oh, look at him, James!"

James gazed at his wife with affection. "*Ja*, she's a pretty girl."

"Peter thought it was a he," Ellie teased.

Peter snorted. "I didn't care to look too closely."

James went into the stall and hunkered down beside his wife, who was stroking the little dog's head. "Shih Tzu," he said. When Nell met his gaze, he explained,

"Her breed. Full grown." As he spoke, he tenderly maneuvered the little dog to examine her. "I don't see any external injuries."

"Could she have been hit by a car?" Peter asked.

"You say you found her by the side of the road?"

"Ja," he said. "When I went to get her, she looked up at me with big sad eyes. I had to help her."

Nell regarded Peter with approval. "You did the right thing." She rubbed the animal's neck as her husband listened to the dog's belly with a stethoscope. "'Tis a good thing we were close by. If you'd brought her to the clinic, we would have missed you."

Peter gazed at Meg. "I'm glad I brought her here, too," he said quietly. Something flickered in Meg's expression before she averted her gaze. He felt a rush of warmth.

"I'm going to have to bring her home with us," James said. "I'll stop by the clinic first and ask Drew to x-ray her for me. We need to know if she has internal injuries."

Standing beside Meg and Ellie, Peter watched as Nell and James carefully picked up the little dog and carried her to their buggy. "You can come and see her later today if you'd like," Nell said. "I'll call Ellie and let her know how the little one's doing."

"She has no collar. Do you think we can come up with a name for her?" Meg eyed the dog longingly.

"What do you suggest?" Peter asked.

Meg was silent for a long moment. "How about Honey?" She blushed. "She looks like she's been sprinkled with wild honey."

"Honey," Nell murmured. "I like it."

"Me, too," James said, as he turned to study each of

them. "We'll take *gut* care of Honey." Then he and Nell climbed into the buggy and left.

Ellie headed for the house. "I appreciate you calling them," Peter said to her.

"I'm glad I have a phone and could do it. Glad, too, that the church elders have given Nell and James permission to have one, too."

The elders of their church community allowed mobile phones under certain circumstances, such as for those who were in business. Ellie cleaned houses for the English, so she was granted one. James, the resident Amish veterinarian who treated farm animals and pets, was given another.

Ellie disappeared inside the farmhouse, leaving Peter and Meg alone.

They were quiet for several seconds. "I'll see you on Wednesday?" she asked tentatively.

Peter caught and held her gaze. "*Ja.* Will ten thirty be too late?"

"*Nay*, that will be fine." She teetered a bit on her crutches.

"You must be tired," he said with compassion. "'Tis a long time to stand on crutches, I imagine."

Meg sighed. "*Ja*, I am. I'll go in and lie down for a while after lunch." She studied the ground at her feet, and Peter had the impression that she was nervous for some reason. "Would you like to stay for lunch?"

"*Danki*, Meg, but I should get home." He smiled as she looked at him. "Remember, I want to stop at Bishop John's on the way. If he agrees, then we can continue with our plans. If not, I guess we'll be searching for another place to hold the party."

He headed toward his buggy, with Meg following. "I'll see you in the morning, Peter," she said.

He nodded, climbed into his buggy and steered the vehicle toward the road. She hadn't moved, but stood watching him, giving Peter a funny feeling inside his chest. He raised his hand to wave. She shifted her arm from her crutch and managed to wave back.

Tomorrow, they would sit down together like they had before. But for now Peter's head was filled with images of today: Meg's smile, her look of compassion for Honey, her nervous shifting.

He inhaled sharply and released the breath. "*Nay*, I must be imagining things. There is no reason for Meg to be nervous with me." She was seeing Reuben, and he was spending time with Agnes.

He readjusted his straw hat. "Meg Stoltzfus, we'll get the job done. Only four weeks to go. Surely, I can manage to spend a few hours in your company planning this party for your *vadder* and my *mudder*."

It shouldn't be too difficult. He hoped.

Meg watched Peter's departure before she returned to the house. Her heart fluttered as she recalled the way he'd been with Honey. He didn't seem to mind her name for the little dog. He no longer seemed upset with her, either, and she was glad. It meant they could work together again.

Would Bishop John agree to let them use his house? She didn't have a chance to ask on Sunday. John hadn't stayed after the service—which likely meant he was still unhappy and grieving.

Could Peter change his mind if John initially refused? She hoped so. She should try to think of another place just in case. But where? Where could they take their parents without them becoming suspicious?

She hobbled into the kitchen, where Ellie was pulling plates and glasses out for their midday meal. "May I help?"

Ellie turned. "*Ja*, if you'd like."

Meg grinned. "You're not going to insist I sit and rest?"

Her sister chuckled. "Would it make a difference if I did?"

"*Nay*." She set one crutch against the wall, then hobbled with the other toward the counter, where she picked up the plates. "*Gut* thing 'tis only you and me."

She set the table while Ellie took the fixings for sandwiches out of the refrigerator and pantry. They made their lunch, and Ellie poured them each a glass of milk.

"So," Ellie began, "Peter brought the dog to you."

Meg felt her face heat. "*Ja*. He found her just up the road, so he brought her here. He wanted to make sure it'd be *oll recht* to bring her to James."

"Hmm."

Meg narrowed her eyes. "What's that supposed to mean?"

"Only that he didn't continue on to Nell and James's *haus*."

"Because I knew you'd be home soon, and I thought it would be better for Honey if she stayed in the barn until Nell and James got here." She gazed at her sister, daring her to argue with her logic. "As it turns out, it's a *gut* thing you called them, since Peter would have wasted a trip with Honey to their place."

"True," Ellie agreed. She took a bite of her sandwich and swallowed. "Have you seen Reuben?"

"He's away. I expect him back in a day or two. Then he'll have to work, so I may not see him until the end of the week."

"Are you sure you like Reuben better than Peter?"

"Ellie!"

"'Tis a *gut* question, *ja*?" She took a sip of milk. "You can tell me. I won't tell a soul."

"Ellie...Peter is with Agnes now."

Ellie arched an eyebrow. "That's not what I asked."

"Reuben is a thoughtful, kind man. He'll make a *gut* husband."

"But is he the one you want?" her sister pressed.

Now that she was working with Peter, spending extra time with him, Meg felt pulled in two directions. She sighed, then said in a little voice, "I don't know."

Chapter Eleven

Meg sat on the exam table with her legs extended before her. Her mother waited in a chair. The doctor would be in soon with the results of her X-rays.

"I hope it's healing well," Meg murmured. "I can't wait to get this cast off. I want to be able to sleep upstairs again."

"You can sleep upstairs if you want. You've learned to use the crutches. It may be slow going up the steps, but I'm sure you'll manage."

"*Ja*, I suppose I could." But the thought of trying to maneuver up the stairs on crutches didn't sit well with her. She could hop on one foot all the way to the top landing, but what if she fell? Then she would be in worse shape than she was now.

The doorknob rattled, and the orthopedist the hospital had recommended entered the room. He was nice enough, but Meg didn't want to see him. She wanted to get over her leg injury and get back to her chores and her life.

"Well, Meg, I have your films," Dr. Reckling said. The man was middle-aged and wore a white lab coat over a white shirt and dark slacks. He slipped the X-ray films into the clip on the light. He flipped a switch, then gestured toward an area on her X-ray. "This is where you fractured the bone. It was a simple stress fracture, which is good. Do you see this?" He used his finger to outline a certain section. "It looks good. You're healing well, and because of this, I'm going to take off the cast and give you a brace instead." He turned to regard her with serious brown eyes. "You'll be able to take off the brace to shower, or to put up your leg for a short time, but, Meg, it's important that you wear it as much as possible. Do you understand?"

Meg was elated. She was getting the cast off! The fact that she'd have to wear a brace didn't bother her in the least. If she could shower without it, she was happy. "I understand," she said. "Will I be able to climb stairs in it?"

"You can if you're careful. You'll find the brace easier to get around on than this cast with crutches." His smile reached his eyes. "I'm sure you're sick and tired of those, aren't you?"

Meg nodded. "I'm eager to get rid of them."

"Let's do it now then." He reached into a cabinet and withdrew a small circular saw. Meg's eyes widened, and he laughed. "It won't hurt you. See?" He turned on the saw, then held it to his hand. "It vibrates and will cut the blue cast, but not the gauze underneath or your skin." He switched off the blade. "Are you ready?"

"I'm ready."

Less than half an hour later Meg and her mother were heading home. "How does it feel?" *Mam* asked.

"Different." In a way the boot seemed more cumbersome than the cast, but Meg figured it was just because she had to get used to it.

"Your *vadder* will be anxious to see you. He wanted to be the one to bring you, but he couldn't come. He'd promised to go with your *onkel* Samuel to see the bishop."

Meg blinked. Her father had gone to see the bishop? "Why?" She hoped John didn't say anything about their visit the other day. In the man's constant state of grief, what if he let it slip that she and Peter had stopped by?

"A repair to his house. Apparently, the glass is cracked in a back window, and with the colder weather here, it's been difficult to keep the house warm."

Forcing herself to relax, Meg asked, "Can they fix it in one day?"

"Ja," Mam said. "Samuel ordered a new piece of glass. They're going to replace the pane, not the window."

Praise be to God, Meg thought. It could be awkward if the bishop agreed to the party and she and Peter stopped over for planning purposes, and her father and her uncle were working on the premises.

"I'm glad *Dat* could help. I know *Onkel* Samuel's been busy lately. I heard Daniel has been working for the construction company that frequently employs Jed whenever he wants extra work."

"Ja, Isaac helps out there, too."

Meg liked living close to her father's family. But what of her mother? Did she regret moving so far from her parents and siblings? *"Mam?"*

Her mother put on the blinker and steered the buggy onto the road on the right. "Do you miss seeing your parents?" Meg asked.

"Sometimes, but not too often, because I have your *vadder*, you girls and Katie and her family." She was silent for a moment. "My *eldre* never approved of my choice to become Amish."

"Why?" Meg suspected she knew, but she wanted to hear her mother's side of things.

"They thought I should have the material things they enjoyed. I am happy with the life I've chosen, but I couldn't make them understand that."

"I'm sorry."

Mam smiled. "I'm not. There is nothing to be sorry for. I love you and your sisters. And if I had to relive my life, I'd marry your father again in an instant."

"I love you, *Mam*."

Her mother flashed a warm smile. "Love you, too, *dochter*. We're home!" She turned onto their dirt drive to park near the house, then ran around to help Meg.

"I can manage, *Mam. Danki*." And she realized she could. Her foot and leg felt strange inside the boot rather than a cast, but she was able to get out of the buggy unaided. She grinned at her mother. "Looks like I'll be able to sleep upstairs in my own room tonight."

"I'll move my sewing things back downstairs."

As she started up the porch steps, the front door opened. To her surprise, in addition to her father stepping outside to greet her, Reuben was there as well, watching her with a bright light in his pale blue eyes.

"Why, *hallo*!" Meg greeted them. She raised her hand to halt Reuben after he started toward her. "I can manage." She saw his crestfallen look, and smiled to take the sting from her rejection.

Her father watched with approval as he waited for her

to precede them indoors. "You're doing well, *dochter*," he murmured and she rewarded him with a grin.

"Let's eat. I don't know about you, but I'm hungry." Meg glanced back at Reuben. "You staying for lunch?" It was kind of him to visit, and she was happy to spend time with him.

"*Ja*, I'd like that." He looked pleased by her invitation.

"*Gut*," her mother said. "It won't take me long to put food on the table."

"It won't take *us* long," Meg corrected as she headed toward the kitchen, where she planned to use her broader range of movement to help prepare lunch.

Peter parked near Meg's house and ran up the steps to the front door. There were no buggies in the yard, which meant there was a good chance she would be alone, except perhaps for her mother. He felt a flash of excitement as he knocked on the door.

"Come in!" someone called.

He opened the door, walked in and froze. Meg stood a few feet from him without crutches. He looked down, saw her medical boot and smiled. "You got your cast off."

She nodded but didn't return his smile.

"What's wrong?"

"Reuben is here."

Peter stiffened. "I didn't see his buggy."

She sent him an apologetic look. "His sister dropped him off. She'll be back for him soon, but…"

"I see." Peter felt his jaw tighten. "I'll go." He turned to leave.

"Peter," she said beseechingly, "you'll come back?"

He sighed and faced her. "In about an hour?"

She looked relieved. "*Ja*, that would be *gut*."

He nodded and hurried out the door before Reuben could see him and wonder why he was here. It bugged him that Reuben's visit took precedence over their planning meeting, but he couldn't find fault with Meg. Or could he? He told himself that he was over her and had moved on, but it still bothered him that she spent time with Reuben, the man she'd wanted for what seemed like forever, while he…

He ran around his buggy, climbed in and picked up the leathers. He had Agnes, he thought as he drove onto the road and made a right-hand turn. He might as well spend a little time with his nephew and niece, since he was over this way. He was sure Annie would be about ready for a break from her children right now.

Peter was able to push aside his bad humor as he thought about seeing EJ and Susanna, who meant a lot to him. The way they had taken to him from the first made him feel better. He pulled up alongside Annie and Jacob's house, got out, tied up his mare, then went to the back door.

"Honey, I'm home!" he called teasingly as he pushed the door slightly open.

Annie turned from the kitchen counter with Susanna perched on her hip. EJ was on the floor near her feet, playing with her pots and pans, making a racket as he beat on the bottom of a metal stockpot with a wooden spoon.

"Peter!"

He grinned. He was right. Annie was ready to be free of her beautiful children for just a few moments, until she could catch her breath. He rushed forward and took Susanna out of her arms. "Thought I'd stop over to spend time with my favorite *kinner*. *Hallo* there, Susie May."

"Pee-ter," she gushed, with an adorable baby-faced smile.

"*Onkel* Peter," her mother corrected.

"Her name is Susanna," EJ insisted. "Not Susie May."

"Her middle name is May," Peter pointed out.

"*Ja*, it is, EJ," Annie said. "Your *onkel* can call her anything he likes."

Peter gazed into the little girl's dark eyes, so like Jacob's. "Where is Jake? He's not at the shop, is he? I thought we got caught up yesterday."

"You did," Annie said, "until Aaron Troyer brought his four horses this morning. You know, the ones he uses for his buggy-ride business?"

"I didn't know." He frowned. How could he not know about the extra business? He'd talked with his father before heading over to Meg's. Then he realized that *Dat* must have thought it more important for him to meet with Meg than to work in the shop today. "I should go up to help."

"*Nay!* Please hang around until I get lunch prepared. It's been a bit of a difficult morning. Susanna is more clingy than usual, and EJ is feeling out of sorts. I'm afraid he's coming down with something."

Peter frowned. "EJ, come up here." He patted his right knee. Susanna was seated on his left one.

EJ didn't move. He pretended he hadn't heard his uncle, until Peter stared at him and said, "EJ, come sit on my lap." His second request was louder and more authoritative. Annie flashed him a look of approval. "*EJ.*"

The little boy turned over the pot and dropped the wooden spoon inside with a clunk. He rose and approached Peter, who was instantly concerned when he saw his flushed cheeks. "Come up, buddy."

EJ climbed onto Peter's lap next to his sister. Peter reached around to feel the boy's forehead. "You're right, Annie. He feels feverish to me."

"I'm fine," the boy insisted.

"No, you're not. You have a fever." He rose with a child in each arm. "Do you have anything I can give him? Like aspirin? Maybe he should go to bed for a while."

"I don't need a nap," EJ complained.

"Not for a nap," Peter said. "For a story." He glanced at the kitchen wall clock and noted the time. He had forty-five minutes left before he had to return to Meg.

EJ perked up, clearly excited at the prospect of his uncle reading to him. "*Mam*, can I lie in bed for a story?"

Annie threw a casserole into the oven, then rose and faced her son. "You may."

Peter watched as his sister withdrew a small plastic bottle from a cabinet. Their grandmother's remedy for a fever had been to rub apple cider vinegar on the soles of their feet and on their palms. He hadn't known whether or not the vinegar helped. He only knew that he'd suffered through the awful smell because *Grossmammi* had insisted.

His other grandmother had used a different cure. She'd beaten the white of an egg with a spoon until it was foamy, then added a little sugar and some hot water, which she'd insisted he drink. He was glad that Annie used the more modern method for reducing a fever.

Annie gave her son two acetaminophen tablets, then Peter carried both children into the boy's bedroom. EJ stretched out on his quilt-covered bed, while his little sister cuddled against Peter's side.

"What story would you like to hear?" Peter hoped it was a quick one.

"*Dat* brought home a new book the other day," EJ announced as he adjusted the pillow under his head. "Will you read it? 'Tis called *May I Please Have a Cookie?*"

Peter found the book and began to read. He hid his delight in the way the children's author taught about using good manners through her story. When he finished reading, he saw that EJ had fallen asleep. Susanna, he realized, was also dozing in his arms. He stood with her and went into the living room, where he placed the sleeping child in a crib Annie kept there.

"They're both napping," he told his sister as he entered the kitchen.

She shot him a grateful smile. "Want some coffee?"

"*Nay*, I have errands to run. I just wanted to stop and visit."

Annie handed him a cookie. "You don't know how much it means to me that you love spending time with my children."

Peter shrugged. "They're my niece and nephew." He picked up his hat from where he'd set it on the table when he'd entered. "EJ is in his room, and Susie May is in her crib in the living room."

Annie's expression was soft as she watched him eat the cookie. "Again, *danki*."

He regarded her fondly. "My pleasure."

He left and headed back toward the Arlin Stoltzfus

residence. What would he do if he got there and her father and sisters had returned?

He hesitated and considered going home, but he'd told Meg he'd be back in an hour, and he wouldn't break his word. The mental image of her floating in the water after the accident suddenly overwhelmed him. He felt his heart race and his stomach clench. Would he ever get that awful night out of his mind? He'd been able to control that memory for the most part, shoving it aside as if it hadn't made an impact on him. Had it returned when he'd learned that Reuben was in Meg's house? Reuben, who'd been driving, who had been injured along with Meg?

Agnes, he thought. He needed to see Agnes to remind himself that she was his future, and Meg was best left in his past. Which would be difficult, as long as he and Meg had to work together. But that was only for a few weeks more. The party date was fast approaching, which reminded Peter that they still had a lot to do. He shook away the horrible thoughts of the accident and used the rest of the drive to Meg's to focus on the party.

He smiled. As promised the day he'd found the dog, he'd stopped on his way home to check back with the bishop, and it looked as if John was going to allow them to use his house. Peter and Meg would visit him again to make sure. Sally hadn't been there when he had dropped by, but hopefully she'd be at John's today, and they could enlist her help if needed.

As he approached Meg's family's farmhouse, he saw a buggy parked next it. Reuben and his sister were outside, talking with Meg. The three were laughing, clearly enjoying themselves. Peter clenched his fingers around the reins and continued on. The sight of her looking so comfortable with Reuben and Rebekkah bothered him. It was as if she belonged in Reuben's world but not his. He and Meg were like oil and water at times. They didn't mix for long after being stirred.

He went to Whittier's Store and meandered about the aisles. He picked up a few things he knew his mother needed, and treats for EJ and Susanna. After paying for the items, he turned back toward Meg's. If Reuben was still there, he'd call it a day and go home.

It was half past twelve, and he was feeling hungry and out of sorts. He reached into his bag of purchases and withdrew a peanut butter candy bar. He quickly unwrapped it and took a bite, and the chocolate and peanut combination immediately made him feel better.

Until he thought of Reuben at Meg's house, and he scowled, the sweet treat now tasting bitter in his mouth.

Chapter Twelve

Meg looked pleased to see Peter as she opened the door and invited him in. "I wasn't sure you were coming back."

He tensed, then forced himself to relax. "I said I would." He paused. "Reuben get away *oll recht*?"

She appeared uncomfortable. "*Ja*, he left about fifteen minutes ago." She turned abruptly and walked into their living area, then gestured for him to sit. She sat some distance away, and it irritated him. "Did you see Bishop John?"

Peter nodded and forced himself to concentrate. "*Ja*, he's leaning toward allowing us to host the party there, but…"

"*Ja?* There's a but?"

"He didn't come right out and give his consent. I think we should visit him today and try again." He studied her concerned face and was drawn in by the deep blue of her eyes. His breath caught. "I think you can convince him. I'm willing to bet you can, in fact."

She seemed surprised by his comment. "You want to go now?"

"Is that a problem?"

"Nay," she assured him. "I'll let my mother know. She just stepped across the yard to see Mrs. Morgan, our neighbor."

Her *mam* had been home when Reuben was visiting. Something eased inside of Peter. He'd thought he'd heard her voice earlier, but he hadn't been sure.

"Would you like me to tell her for you?" he asked.

She beamed at him. "You don't mind?"

"Nay. I'll be happy to go. Just point me in the right direction."

After Meg explained that it was just next door, he hurried across the property to the house of the Englisher who lived there. He tapped on the door, and a woman immediately answered. "I'm sorry to bother you, but is—"

"Peter!" Missy was right behind her, as if she'd been preparing to leave.

"I came to let you know that Meg and I are heading over to Bishop John's."

Missy smiled. "I appreciate your telling me."

As Peter turned to run back, he heard Meg's mother say something to Mrs. Morgan, but he couldn't hear the words. He raced across the yard to Meg, who stood next to his buggy, waiting for him. Emotion rose up inside him at the sight of her. If only things were different between them...

He silently scolded himself as he slowed his approach, and calmed himself enough to smile at her as he reached the vehicle.

"Ready to go?" he asked.

She nodded. He stood close as she opened the door, grabbed hold of the side and placed her good foot inside the buggy. She attempted to heft herself up, but struggled and eventually stepped back.

"May I help?" He kept his voice soft. He knew she wanted to manage on her own.

She turned to give him a frustrated look.

"Wait! I have an idea." He ran to the barn and found a wooden crate he knew the Stoltzfus girls used for picking apples. When he returned, he saw Meg's eyes widen with delight. Peter placed it close to the carriage so that she had an extra step to make it easier for her to climb inside.

"*Danki*, Peter," she said quietly, her blue eyes warm.

He nodded and watched with satisfaction as she grasped the side of the buggy, then stepped onto the crate with her good foot. Peter remained close in the event that she wobbled and fell. But when Meg climbed into the buggy without incident, warmth and happiness flooded through him. He picked up the crate and set it on the floor in the back before getting into the front next to Meg.

"Today we'll convince Bishop John to host the party," he said with determination, "then we can continue with our plans."

Meg chuckled. "One way or another."

Meg was grateful for Peter's quick thinking in using a crate as a step for the buggy. It was as if he sensed that she wouldn't appreciate being lifted into the buggy like an invalid. If Reuben had tried to lift her, she would have been upset, but she wouldn't have said anything. After all, Reuben had saved her from drowning. She couldn't be rude to him. She owed him her life. But Peter? When he'd offered to help, she'd expected him to assist her into the buggy as he'd done when they had gone on their lunch outing with Reuben and Agnes.

She shot him a secretive glance, but looked away before he could catch her staring. For some reason, the idea of Peter lifting her into the carriage didn't bother her the way it did with Reuben. Which made no sense, since up until recently, she and Peter hadn't gotten along.

When they arrived at Bishop John's house, Peter got out and retrieved the crate from the back of the vehicle. He gazed at her across the front seat. She smiled as he gave it to her, almost reluctantly. Meg pushed open the door and dropped the crate on the ground as Peter went around the front of the buggy to wait for her. She twisted in her seat and extended her good foot toward the crate.

"Meg," he warned, "it's not on solid ground. Hold on a second." He readjusted the wooden box so that it wouldn't shift and was closer to the buggy.

She reached down with her foot, then hesitated. If she lost her balance, she could do some serious harm to the leg while it was healing. As if sensing her thoughts, Peter held out his hand, and she accepted his help happily as she stepped off onto the ground. He released her fingers as soon as she could stand without help. Meg stifled the longing to grab his hand again as she met his gaze. *"Danki."*

He nodded then turned toward the house. "I hope he's home."

"He is," Meg said with certainty. When Peter frowned, she gestured toward the buggy parked next to the barn.

He smiled. "Sally's here."

Meg blinked. "You recognize her buggy?"

"Ja." But there was a look in his gaze that said he wasn't telling her something. He knocked and the door immediately swung open. *"Hallo*, Sally. We've come to talk with him again."

"Come in." She stepped aside. "I just put Nicholas down for a nap."

Peter entered and then reached back for Meg's hand. She placed her fingers in his grasp, and he tugged gently to help her up the last step. Meg smiled and turned to follow his cousin. She took two steps into the house before she realized that John was sitting at the kitchen table.

"John," Peter greeted the man.

The bishop looked up. Meg thought he didn't look as tired as he'd seemed during their last visit. "You've come about the party."

Meg moved carefully as she approached. "It would mean a lot to us and our *eldre* if we could use your *haus*. You won't have to do anything. Just come." She glanced at Sally for help.

"It might be a *gut* thing," the young woman said quietly, drawing John's attention.

Was she imagining it, Meg wondered, or did John's expression soften slightly when he looked at Sally?

"It will be Christmas," Meg added. "Actually, Christmas is on church service day." She glanced toward Peter. "It would be better to have it on Second Christmas."

To her relief, Peter nodded. Second Christmas was the Amish holiday, the day after Christmas, when community members visited each other.

"John? What do you think?" she pressed. "Will you allow us to use your *haus* on Second Christmas?"

"John?" Peter said encouragingly.

John sought guidance from Sally with a look. Meg saw her nod. *"Ja,* that will be fine," the bishop replied. "You can have your birthday party here."

Meg felt a rush of warmth and relief. *"Danki."*

The man inclined his head.

"You know this is to be a surprise?" Peter said. "We want to keep my mother and Meg's father in the dark until they step inside and see everyone."

"I understand," John said, while Sally murmured in agreement.

"We should go and leave you to your day." Meg glanced about the kitchen space, gauging where the food would go.

"John, Sally," Peter said as he turned with Meg toward the door. "We appreciate it. Sally, I'll see you on Sunday."

She smiled and followed them out, watched as Meg and Peter got into the buggy, then waved.

As she glanced back, Meg saw the bishop join Sally at the door, and witnessed her quick smile for him when she realized he was there. Meg smiled in turn. She hoped that Sally and the bishop would find a new life together. They were both good people who deserved every happiness.

Meg kept her thoughts to herself as Peter drove her home. She wondered what it would be like to marry the man she loved. She frowned as she thought of Reuben Miller. She would have to make a decision about him soon, for although she was falling again for Peter Zook, and Peter was with Agnes now, it wouldn't be fair for Meg to encourage Reuben when she didn't love him.

She liked him, but didn't think her feelings would ever turn into love.

Her heart fluttered as she sat next to Peter. If only she had a chance with him. She recalled the day his conversation with Josiah had revealed how he thought of her. After all these years, did he still believe her spoiled and in need of discipline? She swallowed hard. She would have to confront him and find out, though she groaned at the thought.

"Are you *oll recht*?" Peter asked with concern, and she realized he'd heard her groan.

She managed to smile, although she was feeling regret over lost time. "I'm fine," she assured him. *At least, I will be fine...eventually.*

Peter was concerned about Meg. She'd been unusually quiet since they'd left John Fisher's house, when she should be excited. They'd confirmed the party location, which was reason to celebrate. But something was clearly bothering her, and he couldn't guess what.

"Meg, we have a place to have the party," he said with a smile.

The upward curve of her lips seemed forced. He found himself wanting to grab hold of her hand, give her fingers a squeeze and ask her to tell him what was the matter. Except he had no right. She was Reuben Miller's sweetheart.

His teeth snapped together. She was Reuben's, and although he'd been trying hard to forget her and think of Agnes instead, he was having trouble getting Meg out of his mind—and out of his heart. Still, he would continue to pursue things with Agnes, because he had no choice.

Meg's house loomed ahead, and Peter took the turn. He saw another buggy in the barnyard and froze. "Meg, is that your *dat's*?" he asked, gesturing toward the other vehicle.

Meg frowned. "*Nay*, that's not ours."

Peter parked in front of the buggy. When he'd opened his door and come around to Meg's side with the wooden crate, he stiffened, seeing Reuben Miller climb out of the other vehicle.

"Reuben." Meg smiled as she carefully climbed out of the buggy without Peter's help. "I didn't expect you again today."

Peter could see the tension in Reuben's expression as he greeted the other man. "Reuben."

"Peter," he snapped in return.

"Reuben!" Meg exclaimed, clearly taken aback by his tone.

"Where have you been, Meg?"

"We had to run an errand for my father," Peter answered, before Meg could reply.

"And Meg had to ride with you?" the other man asked accusingly. "Why?"

"Because he needed my help," Meg said.

"Meg—"

"Reuben, if you're going to be rude, perhaps you should go home."

"Meg, I'm sorry."

Her face softened. "We've done nothing wrong, and I don't like that you inferred otherwise."

Peter watched the silent exchange that followed. Reuben clearly cared a great deal for Meg. Could Peter blame the man for feeling jealous? If Meg was his sweetheart, he'd have little understanding if she had come home with Reuben or any other man who wasn't family.

"I'm going to go." Peter paused and looked at Meg. "*Danki* for your help today."

She met his gaze. "You're *willkomm*, Peter." She hesitated as if she wanted to say more. "Give your *mudder* and *vadder* my best."

"I will." He turned to Reuben. "Have a nice evening, Reuben."

"Peter," the other man said, then promptly returned his attention to Meg.

As he walked around the carriage and got in, Peter couldn't help but overhear their conversation.

"Meg, I didn't mean to suggest—"

"I'm tired, Reuben. It was nice that you stopped by to see me, but I'm going upstairs to my room to take a nap. I'll see you later."

Reuben sighed. "May I come see you tomorrow?"

"I don't think so." She hesitated. "Perhaps on Friday?"

"On Friday."

Peter could hear the warmth in Reuben's voice.

Unable to stand any more of this, Peter grabbed the reins and turned his buggy toward the road. Before he pulled onto it, he turned to see that Meg and Reuben were still talking. He closed his eyes for a brief second, feeling a wave of pain. *Agnes*, he thought and turned his vehicle in the direction of the Beiler residence.

He couldn't wait for the party planning to be over. He didn't like feeling this way, caring for Meg when he knew there was no chance of having her as his sweetheart.

She might have been upset with Reuben, but Peter

understood it was because of Reuben's insinuation that she'd ignored their relationship simply to spend time with him. Which Reuben would find ridiculous if he'd known the truth. But Meg couldn't tell him what was going on. She'd promised her mother, and he'd promised his father. The party would remain a secret.

As he drove toward Agnes's house, he felt the beginning of a headache. When the throbbing behind his eyes worsened, Peter decided to forget about the visit to Agnes, and he headed home instead.

As soon as the party is over, I can get on with my life...without Meg.

And that had become the most important thing—finishing and moving on without having to see Meg day in and day out, when she didn't belong to him.

Peter felt better after a good night's sleep. As he thought about his meeting with Meg, he decided that they'd spend all day together if they had to. Second Christmas was only three weeks away. The sooner they finished their plans, the better.

Meg was waiting for him by the road as he approached. She wore a black cloak over a pink dress and a matching black traveling bonnet over her prayer *kapp*. The day was chilly, and he had chosen to wear a long-sleeved shirt under his tri-blend jacket. He pulled to the side of the road and waited for her to walk the remaining few feet.

"My *vadder* and sisters are home," she gasped, out of breath.

He felt bad. Walking from her house to the street, and then to his carriage must have winded her. "What do you want to do?"

"Can we still meet? I have an idea where."

He slid over and opened the passenger-side door. He pulled out a wooden crate that he now kept in the back just for her, climbed out on her side and set it on the ground close to the buggy. He held out his hand, and she stared at it a moment before accepting his help. Peter tried not to be offended by her hesitation, but failed. Once she was settled, he ran around, stored the crate behind his seat, then climbed into the driver's seat. "Where to?" He picked up the reins and faced her.

"My *onkel* Samuel's. There is an old building in the back of the property. He doesn't use it anymore. You can access it from the road behind his farm." She stopped for a breath. "No one will know we're there."

Peter knew which road ran behind Samuel Lapp's property. He headed that direction, aware of the sudden tense silence between him and Meg as he drove.

It didn't take them long to reach the back of the property. Peter spotted the building Meg referred to, and pulled off the road to park next to it, and also behind a tree to keep the vehicle hidden.

He climbed out and eyed the old, dilapidated structure. Would they have enough light inside to see? "Meg…"

She came up next to him. "I know it's not ideal, but we can make it work. We'll find a better place next time."

Peter reached for the door, which squeaked as he swung it open. He glanced inside, saw that it was cleaner than he'd expected, and went in first to make sure it was safe for Meg. "I think this will do fine," he said, feeling better than he had upon first seeing the building.

Meg hesitated, but then ventured in. There was a scurrying sound in the corner. She gasped and backed up into him. He grabbed hold of her shoulders to keep her from falling. The scent of her shampoo and soap rose to tantalize his nose. He immediately released her. "What's wrong?"

"I heard something," she declared. "A mouse, maybe."

He bent to check every corner. "I don't see anything."

"Are you sure?" she asked, sounding nervous.

He laughed. "I'm sure. Relax, Meg. I doubt any mouse would want to stay here for long." He studied the room for something to sit on, and not finding anything, headed toward the door.

"Peter?" Meg's voice was soft, scared.

"I'll be right back," he said. "I need to get something from the buggy. Don't worry. You're safe." He saw her relax at his words. He gazed at her a long moment, admiring the blue of her eyes and the bright pink of her lips. Then he left the shed to retrieve the wooden crate. "Your chair," he said with a bow when he returned.

Meg saw the crate, and her expression warmed. "What will you sit on?"

He experienced a strange rush of pleasure that she cared. "I can sit on the ground. I'll be fine."

"Don't be silly, Peter," she objected. "We can share the crate."

He stared at the wooden box and wondered how he would be able to concentrate on the party with her sitting so close to him. He shrugged. "I'll sit when I'm tired of standing."

She gazed at him a long moment, her features unreadable, before giving a nod.

"What should we discuss first?" he asked, as she made herself comfortable on the cold wood. Peter eyed the small amount of space that she purposely left open as a seat for him. "The weather?" he said, then turned his back on her briefly as he drew a deep, silent breath. He faced her again with a smile.

"Can I talk with you about something else first?" she asked shyly.

"Certainly. What do you want to talk about?"

"I…" She briefly closed her eyes. "This is awkward."

"Go ahead. What is it?"

"Peter, do you still feel the same way about me? The way you did when I overheard you that day?"

He froze. "Meg."

"I know you considered me spoiled and in need of discipline, but do you still think that about me?"

Peter gaped at her. "Where are on earth did you get that idea?"

"I heard you, remember?"

He gazed at, his eyes widening. "I never said that about you."

"But I heard it!" she said heatedly.

He stopped, frowned and suddenly realized what she'd overheard. Then he burst out laughing. "You thought I was talking about you?" He shook his head. "I was talking about Molly! My sister's dog? Annie hadn't had her that long. She was an uncontrollable puppy when we first got her. She's a fine dog now, and my *dat* is happy to have her in the house."

Meg paled. "You were talking about a dog, and not me?"

Watching her closely, Peter gave a nod. "Not you." He sighed. "Is that what you thought?" He closed his eyes as he paced about the old wooden shed. "I never thought that about you, Meg," he said softly.

"*Ach, nay,*" she breathed. "I..." Her voice trailed off. She seemed confused, then grew thoughtful. "Then why did you look guilty when I confronted you?"

Peter looked away.

"You had been talking about me! What did you say? What did you tell Josiah?"

He scowled. "It doesn't matter. 'Tis too late, anyway."

"Peter," she murmured, "did you like me?"

He released a sharp breath. "*Ja,*" he admitted. "I did back then."

"I'm sorry," was her only reply, which told him it wouldn't have made a difference if she had known how he felt about her.

Suddenly he'd had enough talking about the past. "Can we get back to our party planning?" he asked brusquely. "'Tis why we're here."

He saw her flinch, but couldn't do anything about it. The reminder of the day she'd yelled at him was still painful, even after all this time.

"What about if it snows?"

And just like that, they were back to business.

Chapter Thirteen

"What do you think we should do?" Meg asked hesitantly. "Have a snow date?"

Peter continued to stand. He was unwilling to sit close to her. The last thing he needed was for her to guess that he still harbored strong feelings for her. "I was thinking we could talk with your cousin Eli," he said, his voice pleasant as he tried to smooth things over. "He has a sleigh, and I know he's made one or two for other members of our community."

"That's a great idea." She seemed relaxed now that she understood what she'd heard that day, and his heart thumped hard. "We can arrange for those with sleighs to pick up those without them." She suddenly frowned. "I forgot my pencil and notes."

"I think we'll remember this. Don't you?"

"Ja." She shivered and hugged herself.

"Are you cold?" A breeze had filtered in through a crack in the wall, and he felt chilled, as well.

Meg inclined her head. "It's freezing in here."

Peter searched the room and thought about making a fire, but then quickly nixed that idea. If he tried, he was liable to burn down the old structure. He gazed at Meg, saw the look on her face and suddenly forgot his misgivings. He wanted—needed—to ensure her comfort. He moved closer, and as if understanding his intention, Meg shifted to allow him room on the stool. He sat beside her, hoping the close proximity would warm her. "I don't think it's safe to build a fire."

"Nay," she agreed, as he shifted closer to block the cold air. But he could feel her shivering. He could see their breath in the air. Her cloak wasn't keeping her warm enough.

Despite the warning his heart issued, he slipped his arm around her shoulders. He tried to ignore the fact that she felt good against him. He was there to warm her. Anyone would assist another in need, he reasoned.

"Does this help?" he asked softly. His voice sounded gravelly to his ears.

He saw her swallow. "It does. *Danki.*"

He shouldn't sit near her for long. He'd cared for her for years and was having difficulty putting aside his lingering feelings. She'd heard him talk about Molly. She hadn't heard him tell Josiah how much he loved her. Now that she knew about the dog, he didn't want her to suspect how deep his feelings for her had been—and still were. Peter knew he took a terrible risk by sitting next to her now.

"What else do we have to discuss?" He knew he should remove his arm. Instead, he kept it where it was, but shifted away slightly. He stifled a groan when Meg followed him as he moved; she clearly enjoyed the warmth he provided.

"We'll have to ask my *mam* and your *dat* about who to invite. If we're going to keep it a surprise, we'll have to be careful to ensure the gathering stays relatively small. Otherwise word will get out." She placed her hands in her lap.

She seemed to be feeling warmer, he thought with a sense of satisfaction. "I agree. Can you think of anything else?" He needed to put distance between them. This situation wasn't easy for him. He conjured up thoughts of Agnes—her blond hair…her bright expression…her smile—but Meg's image kept superimposing itself over Agnes's features. He scowled and shifted farther away.

A long moment of silence ensued. Peter caught her staring at him. Awareness sprang up between them, shocking him with its intensity. She looked startled, so he knew she felt it, too. With a sound of regret, he stood. "We should leave." He walked away, desperate to escape her.

He knew the exact moment she stood. He stiffened as he heard her approach from behind. "Peter," she murmured. There was an odd little catch in her voice.

He felt off balance when she touched his shoulder. He spun out of instinct. A tremor of feeling overwhelmed and angered him. "What are you doing, Meg?" he growled. "I'm with Agnes." And he didn't have to add, "And you're with Reuben."

She retreated as if stung. Her mouth worked, like she wanted to say something but didn't know how to respond. To his dismay, he watched as tears filled her blue eyes. He felt a tightening in his belly. Regret overwhelmed him, but he kept silent.

"I think you should take me home," she whispered brokenly.

Unable to look away, he held her hurt-filled gaze.

He felt the urge to hold and comfort her, but fought to ignore it. Instead he nodded and picked up the crate. She hurried outside, seemingly unmindful of her leg brace. Peter followed quickly, and when Meg stumbled, he reached out to steady her. She immediately jerked away, then continued slowly to the passenger side of the buggy, as though taking extra care to ensure she wouldn't have to endure his touch again. When she reached the vehicle, she eyed the step and froze. He knew she was upset that she couldn't climb in without help.

Without a word, Peter set the crate down for her, then stepped back. He had wounded her, and it hadn't been his intention. When she hurt, he did, too. But he could take only so much while trying to get over his feelings for a woman who confused and confounded him.

It took two tries before Meg was successfully situated in the front seat. Without a word, he picked up the crate, went around to his side and set it behind him before he slid in next to her. He swiveled in his seat to face her, but she stared ahead, unwilling to meet his gaze.

"Meg." She stiffened. "Are we going to be able to work together?"

She faced him briefly, her eyes bright, her expression cold, before she averted her gaze. *"Ja."*

He picked up the leathers and focused on the road ahead. He'd known it had been a mistake to sit next to her. It had been a terrible error on his part to think that he could be alone with her in an abandoned building. What were they going to do the next time they needed a private place to plan the party?

He drove in silence. Meg didn't say a word until he

pulled into her yard and came around the vehicle with the crate.

She stepped down. "Bye, Peter." And with that, she promptly started toward the house.

"Meg!"

Her shoulders tensed as she halted, then turned. *"Ja?"*

He was filled with regret, gazing at her. "I'm sorry," he said. "I didn't mean to upset you." His anger was actually directed at himself. "I feel as though we've become friends. Are you still willing to work with me? We have a lot to do."

It seemed, for a moment, that she would refuse. "We can talk about it on Sunday."

Visiting Sunday was just days away. He released a pent-up breath as Meg entered the house. Considering their past history, there would be some explaining to do if anyone other than her mother discovered that he and Meg had spent time together.

Meg blinked back tears as she watched from inside the house as Peter left. What had happened to set him off? Their morning had started out well. He'd been kind, and it seemed as if today they would accomplish a lot. Then he'd thought of her comfort when she'd been chilled by the cold breeze in the shed. He'd sat close to warm her, and it had felt right. Especially after she'd confronted him and finally learned the truth about the past—that he and Josiah had been discussing Molly, the dog, not her. And when she realized that they had discussed her as well, she'd wanted to know what they'd said. The strange look on his face had simply made her wonder, and so she'd asked. To learn that he had liked her was both a vindication and a curse, because it was too late to do anything about it now that Peter had Agnes in his life.

After they'd talked a bit about the party, the next thing she knew Peter was suddenly bolting out of his seat, clearly upset for some reason—over what, she had no idea. She'd gotten up to comfort him, to see if she could help. And he'd turned on her.

He'd become angry. Why? He'd all but accused her of stealing him away from Agnes! She wouldn't do that. *As if I could.* She cared for Peter. That he had the power to hurt her told her just how much. And because she did, she wanted him to be happy. Even if his happiness hinged on being with Agnes Beiler.

Meg headed toward the back of the house. *"Mam?"* There was no answer. She tried again. She prayed that no one other than her mother was at home. The last thing she needed was for any of her sisters to realize she'd been with Peter.

She heard footsteps on the stairs. She turned back as Ellie descended from the second floor.

"Meg?" Ellie looked concerned at first, then relieved at seeing her. "Where have you been?"

"I had an errand to run and got a ride."

Her sister narrowed her gaze but didn't pursue the conversation, and for that Meg was grateful.

"What are you doing home?" Meg asked. "I thought you had a house to clean."

Ellie made a face. "I did, but on my way over, my client called and canceled on me."

"I'm sorry," she said, and started toward the kitchen.

"Meg, are you crying?"

She shook her head.

"But you were," Ellie pressed.

"I'm fine. It's cold out." She glanced back and smiled to ease her sibling's concern. "Just hungry."

Ellie grinned. "Let's eat then. What would you like? I'll cook."

"I think *Mam* already made lunch." Meg frowned. "Where is she? She was next door earlier. She can't still be there."

"She's meeting *Dat* in town." Ellie smirked. "They're eating out."

Meg felt a jolt of surprise. "That's nice."

Her heart gave a lurch as she thought of Peter. He was constantly in her thoughts.

She helped Ellie by setting the table while her sister pulled out the pot of soup her mother had made earlier that morning. When they finally sat down together, Meg looked at Ellie. "Do you know where we're going for visiting day?"

"I believe the Zooks have invited us for this Sunday."

Meg suddenly lost her appetite. They'd be going to Peter's house. She knew she'd have to talk with him, to decide when they would meet next, for she knew that she wouldn't be able to stop working with him. Despite the fact that he apparently liked Agnes enough to have her as his sweetheart, Meg realized that she still wanted—needed—to spend time with him. Planning the party would be the only time she'd have with him. Once the party was over, they'd go their separate ways. She'd still see him at church services and occasionally on visiting day, but it wouldn't be the same. They'd say *hallo*, then spend the rest of their time apart.

She experienced a burning in her chest. He'd hurt her, made her feel as if she'd done something wrong, but except for this morning, she couldn't regret her time with him. If only she hadn't overheard him that day years ago. If only she hadn't yelled at him.

And Reuben. She needed to have a conversation with Reuben. She couldn't go on allowing him to think she was serious about him when she wasn't. Maybe someday she'd find a man to love and marry, but it wouldn't be anytime soon. Not while her heart still longed for Peter.

The next morning Meg helped her mother and sisters make food to bring to the Joseph Zook homestead. Then on Sunday morning, she got into the buggy with her parents and her sisters Leah, Ellie and Charlie, who still lived at home. She had almost asked to stay back, but then realized that would only upset her family.

Meg closed her eyes and prayed that today would go better than the last day she'd spent time with Peter Zook.

When they arrived, Peter was outside with her cousin Jacob. He glanced her way as she got out of the buggy with her father's help. She thought she saw his lips curve in a half smile as her *dat* released her arm.

The last thing she expected was for Peter to break away from Jacob and approach her.

"Arlin," he said in greeting. "Missy. May I have a quick word with Meg?"

Her father looked surprised, but nodded. "We'll be inside, *dochter*," he said.

Meg swallowed as she watched her parents leave her. Ellie lingered until Meg shot her a warning glance. Leah waved for Charlie and Ellie to follow. Meg felt her tension grow as her family disappeared into the house, leaving her alone with Peter.

"Meg."

She met his gaze. "Peter."

"I'm sorry." There was genuine sorrow in his expression, and it moved her. "I can't explain, but please know that it wasn't my intention to hurt you."

She couldn't look away. His gray eyes had darkened to almost black. There was an earnestness in them that touched her heart and encouraged her to forgive him. And it was easy to forgive him, she realized. She loved him, although she'd make sure that he never knew.

She became lost in his focused attention. "Apology accepted."

Relief softened his features. "So you'll still work with me on the party?"

She nodded. "When—and where—would you like to meet?"

He appeared to give it some thought. "Tuesday? I have to handle some business for my *vadder* tomorrow."

"Tuesday will be fine. Where?"

A flicker of relief moved across his face. "I can come get you, and we'll go to Ephrata for lunch. No one will see us there."

"But where should I say I'm going?"

"I'm sure your *mudder* will help with that. Just explain to her that it will be difficult to keep the party a surprise if any of our family members see us together."

Peter observed the changing expressions on Meg's face. Going all the way to Ephrata was the best plan, but before he went with Meg, he needed to pay a visit to Agnes. It had been days since he'd seen her, and while previously she'd been distracted by her cousins' visit, he suspected that her relatives had been long gone. He had working in the shop as an excuse for some of that time. But some of it he'd spent with Meg. And if she found out, Agnes would never understand.

"You don't have to pick me up. We can meet at Whittier's Store if it will help?"

"*Nay*, everyone we know and his *bruder* shops at that store. We're bound to see someone if we meet there. I don't think that's wise." Peter thought a minute. "When do you go back to the doctor? Maybe I can take you."

Her eyes brightened. "That would work." Her expression dimmed. "But I'm not due to see the doctor for another two weeks."

Peter grinned. "But do your sisters and father know that?"

"I'm not sure. I doubt it." A slow smile settled on her pink mouth. "I'll see what *Mam* says." She glanced toward the house. "We should go or they will think something is up."

"And it is," he said. "But you're right." He paused. "Tell your *mam* your appointment should be at eleven." When she looked at him in question, he explained, "We'll eat lunch while we plan."

She agreed. "What should I say if anyone asks why you wanted to speak with me?"

"Tell them I was concerned about your leg and wanted to know how you were managing."

She eyed him carefully. "And are you concerned? About my leg?" she added, after a brief hesitation.

"*Ja*, I'm concerned about your leg." *I'm concerned about you.* Which was why he stayed close, ready to help her in case she fell. And why he'd used the crate to help her get into his buggy.

A softness entered her blue eyes, warming him, making him wish for things that could never be. She blinked, and he pulled himself together. He headed toward the house with her by his side, and the rightness of the moment hit him hard.

He sighed. It was just an illusion—he and Meg together.

To his surprise, she allowed him to assist her into the house. People were scattered throughout his home, some in the living room, others in the kitchen. To his relief, no one looked at him strangely when he and Meg entered together. Except Meg's sister Ellie. Peter smiled at her and gestured toward Meg's leg brace. As if she understood, Ellie nodded and returned his smile before she continued her conversation with Annie.

Meg took off her coat, then went in one direction while he left for the opposite side of the room. But as he joined his father and the group of men who decided they should head to the barn this fine blustery cold day, Peter found his thoughts still with Meg, who stayed inside with the women.

Suddenly, despite himself, he discovered he was looking forward to their next party-planning meeting on Tuesday in Ephrata.

Chapter Fourteen

It was freezing in the barn. Peter stood by his father and listened as he talked about spring crops and their horses in the stable. Peter thought they'd be better off in the forge, where they could light a fire and stay warm, but the others—Samuel Lapp and five of his seven sons, Abram Peachy and his three sons, and Arlin Stoltzfus— didn't seem affected by the cold. Peter wore a long-sleeved shirt under his black woolen jacket, but still he shivered.

As he wrapped his arms around himself, he thought of Meg and how cold she'd been in Samuel Lapp's old outbuilding—and the way he'd tried to warm her. Those few moments seated close to her had felt wonderful and right, until he'd realized the direction of his thoughts and known he'd have to keep fighting the way he felt about her. Before he did something he couldn't take back. Like profess his love for her. Which would be an awful mistake, since Reuben was her sweetheart now. Except for their recent working relationship, Meg had never given him any attention, except when forced and then she'd seemed annoyed.

His ears were like ice. He readjusted his woolen hat. It was ridiculous to stand out here when there was perfectly good heat in the house.

"I'm considering planting potatoes this spring," his father said.

"Potatoes?" Peter stared at him with disbelief. "I like potatoes, *Dat*, but we may need to look into it first." He shifted uncomfortably when the men turned their gazes on him. "You plan to sell them?"

Horseshoe Joe shrugged. "Just thinking about it. Not sure if it will be potatoes or corn." Was his *dat* angered or pleased by Peter's concern?

"You can't feed potatoes to your livestock, Joe," Noah Lapp pointed out.

"True." He eyed Peter with a strange look.

Tension followed in the ensuing silence. Peter decided it was a signal for him to leave. He and his father could talk about potatoes later, after everyone had gone home. "I'm going back to the house. I could use a cup of hot coffee." He headed for the barn door.

"Me, too," Noah Lapp said. His wife, Rachel, was inside with their two children, Katherine and four-month-old Luke.

Peter paused to wait for Meg's cousin, then the two of them hurried out of the barn and toward the house.

"I don't know what it is about our *vadders*," Noah said. "I'm a *dat* now, and I can't see the sense in standing in the cold, freezing my toes off."

He laughed. "Yet there we were, following them as if we had to." Peter regarded him with a grin. "But we came to our senses."

"*Ja*, praise the Lord."

A buggy pulled onto the lane, drawing Peter's attention. "I wonder who that is."

Noah narrowed his eyes. "Can't tell, but it looks like there are two women inside."

"Agnes," Peter decided, as he took a closer look. And Alice.

"Who's Agnes?" Noah asked. Peter hadn't realized he'd spoken aloud.

"A friend."

Meg's cousin arched one eyebrow. "A close one?"

"Not yet."

"Given up on Meg, have you?"

Peter sighed as he met the other man's gaze. "Trying to."

"I see." Noah's warm eyes held understanding.

The buggy pulled off onto the grass and stopped. Agnes hopped out on the driver's side while her sister got out of the vehicle more slowly. After a quick glance at Noah, Peter veered toward the girls.

"Surprise!" Agnes exclaimed with a grin.

Peter smiled. He couldn't help himself. How could he with Agnes beaming at him? He realized that Noah had approached, too. Apparently, the man was willing to brave the cold long enough to satisfy his curiosity.

"A nice surprise," Peter said. "*Hallo*, Agnes. Alice." The girls' gazes settled on Noah.

"This is Noah Lapp." He saw something flicker in Agnes's gaze. "Noah, meet Agnes and her sister Alice."

"Twins," Noah murmured. "And identical. I have twin brothers, but they look nothing alike." His lips curved upward. "We were just headed inside. It must be zero degrees out here."

"There's a thermometer on the porch," Peter said. He addressed the sisters. "Want to get warm?"

Agnes nodded and fell into step with him. "I know I took a chance coming here without being invited."

"You don't need an invitation, Agnes." He waited for her to precede him up the steps. Behind them, Alice chatted with Noah.

"I wasn't sure." Agnes met his gaze. "I haven't seen you for a while."

Peter felt his stomach muscles clench. "*Ja*, you had company and I had to help my *dat* in the shop."

"You could have come over while my cousins were still here."

"I know," he admitted, "and I'm sorry."

She accepted his apology with warmth. "'Tis *oll recht*." Her gaze roamed over him, making him uneasy.

As he held the door open for Agnes and Alice, with Noah following them into the house, Peter thought of Meg. How would she react to seeing Agnes again? Especially after the way he'd brought up her name in the shed. Perhaps a bigger question was how *he* was reacting to seeing Agnes, after he'd given in to his feelings for Meg, the ones he'd been forever struggling to forget?

Meg came out of the kitchen as he and Agnes headed that way. "Agnes," she said with a smile. "I didn't know you were here."

He caught an odd look in Agnes's eyes as she smiled back. "Meg, you're looking well." She took in Meg's leg brace. "You've gotten your cast off." She seemed genuinely pleased for her.

"*Ja*, thanks be to *Gott*. The cast was cumbersome. With this, I can walk without crutches."

Peter met Meg's gaze over the top of Agnes's head.

Their eyes held, and he felt something transpire between them before he averted his glance. Agnes stepped back to allow him to move up from behind her.

"We've come in to warm up. Any coffee or tea on?" he asked.

Something altered in Meg's expression, but it was gone so fast, he thought he'd imagined it. "*Ja*, both." She smiled again. "I've come to visit with Rachel. I haven't had a chance to hold Luke yet."

"Luke is Noah's infant son," Peter explained.

Their attention shifted to where Noah stood beside his wife, smiling down at her. As he watched, Peter saw Noah reach out to run a finger gently over his son's baby-soft skin. The sight filled Peter with yearning. He'd like to have children of his own. He turned back— and locked gazes with Meg.

"I'd better move, before Rachel decides to put Luke down for a nap upstairs and I lose this opportunity." Meg walked carefully to the couple and their children. Katherine sat at her mother's feet, playing with a doll. As with all their children's dolls, Katherine's had no face, but she wore a black bonnet and blue dress with a black apron.

"Noah seems happy," Agnes commented, drawing Peter's gaze.

He smiled. "He is. I've not seen a happier man since he fell in love and married Rachel."

Agnes peered up at him with an intensity that made the hairs at the back of his neck rise. "How did they meet?" She reined back her look, and he relaxed.

"Rachel is Amos King's niece. She came to Happiness to be our new schoolteacher." He studied Noah's wife with warmth that turned to concern as he thought of everything Rachel had suffered in the past. "She was in a terrible buggy accident several months before she came here. Happiness was a new start for her. But she wasn't our schoolteacher for long. Noah swept her off her feet and they wed. It doesn't appear she regrets her choice of husband."

"Nay," Agnes agreed softly.

Something in her tone troubled him, but he still managed to grin. "Ready for something hot to drink?" She nodded. "Coffee or tea?"

"Either one is fine." She followed him into the kitchen. "Unless you have the fixings for hot chocolate."

Peter faced her. "I believe I do." He greeted his mother and introduced Agnes to the women who hadn't met her previously. *"Mam,* I'm going to make us some hot cocoa."

Miriam Zook smiled. "Help yourself."

While he heated milk in a saucepan, Peter listened as Agnes chatted with his mother and his aunt Alta Hershberger. Alta, his cousin Sally's mother, would natter about Agnes and him the first opportunity she got. Unfortunately for her, many of their friends were here and had already seen them together, which would bother his dear aunt to no end, to have no fresh gossip.

"Anyone else want a cup of hot chocolate?" Peter asked, as the milk heated and started to steam.

"Nay," his mother said, echoed by the other women.

He added cocoa powder to the hot milk, then sweetened it with sugar and a touch of vanilla. "Would you like to sit here? Or in the other room?" Peter asked, a cup of hot chocolate in each hand.

"Alice is in the other room," Agnes said.

"Other room it is." He flashed the women a grin. "If you see another one like her, it's her twin sister, Alice."

"We've seen them both before," Alta informed him with a sniff. "They came to church services and once to visiting Sunday in the past."

Peter nodded. "*Ja*, they did," he said patiently. He turned to Agnes. "We can sit at that table."

He set the mugs on the table near the window and pulled up a wooden chair for Agnes. Alice was on the other side of the room talking with Isaac, Daniel and Joseph Lapp. She caught Agnes's glance and waved with a smile, but didn't approach.

"How is it?" Peter asked, as Agnes picked up her mug and took a sip.

"Delicious."

"I'm a man of many talents."

She arched an eyebrow. "Are you? What else can you do?"

"I can shoe a horse and farm a field, and I can make a pot of coffee when I want to."

Agnes's gaze intensified. "You are talented indeed. I don't know of a single man who would do more than those first two things. But you can make hot cocoa and a pot of coffee. Impressive."

"'Tis nothing," he murmured. Laughter drew his gaze. It was Meg, seated in the chair that Rachel had vacated, with little Luke in her lap. She was nose to nose with him. When the baby cooed, Meg's pleasure rippled out with a joyful chuckle.

"He's adorable, Rachel," Meg said with a grin.

"We think so," Noah agreed. "Takes after his father."

Rachel snorted. "Does he now?"

Noah gazed at his wife with adoration. "You know

he does. You told me yourself only this morning." He glanced down at his son. "When he was sleeping like the sweet boy he is."

Peter saw Rachel put her hand on Noah's arm. Most husbands and wives in their world didn't display their affection around others, but Peter could see the love Rachel and Noah had for each other in a simple touch, a quick smile.

"I'd like one of those," Agnes commented softly.

"Those?" He met her gaze.

"A baby." Her face filled with longing as she studied the child from across the room. When her attention returned to him, Agnes looked hopeful.

Peter suffered a momentary discomfort. He'd felt the pressure to marry because of his parents. And Agnes would make a good wife. He wanted a future with her, didn't he? Then why couldn't he see himself married to Agnes, or visualize the child they might have? The only images in his mind that seemed real were of a little girl with dark hair and blue eyes—and of Meg as his bride and his child's mother.

He experienced a tight feeling in his chest. Lord help him. He was still desperately in love with Meg Stoltzfus.

Meg could feel Peter's gaze on her as she played with little Luke. She didn't look in his direction. He had studied her earlier, with an odd glimmer in his eyes. She hadn't known what to make of it at the time.

She cooed to the baby, and Luke cooed back. She laughed and looked up to see a smile on Rachel's face, and an expression of happiness on Noah's. She met the boy's gaze again and could tell that Luke was getting tired. "Rachel? I have a feeling your son is about to become upset." As if on cue, the baby scrunched up his little features and let out a whimper, then a wail.

Meg handed the child to his mother and rose awkwardly to her feet. Her brace made getting up and down a little difficult, but it was much better than the cast she'd worn previously. "And this is my cue to leave." She murmured to Noah, "*Ja*, Noah, you're right." When he frowned, she teased, "He takes after his father."

She caught his grin before she turned. Her gaze collided with Peter's. She felt the impact of meeting his eyes in the tingle at her nape and the hot flush of her cheeks. Eager to escape, she started toward the kitchen.

"Meg." Agnes appeared at her elbow. The young woman held a mug and walked with her. "How's Reuben?"

Meg sensed Peter's presence as he approached from behind. The air went still. She hadn't seen Reuben for a while, but she didn't want Agnes—or Peter—to know that. After a heartbeat, she said, "He's fine. He's completely healed after the accident. Like me, the bruises on his face have disappeared."

"But you still wear a brace," Agnes commiserated.

She didn't know why, but something in the girl's tone got her back up. She reined in her impatience and smiled. "The doctor said the bone's healing nicely. I may get rid of this thing early."

"How nice."

Meg couldn't tell if Agnes's smile was genuine. She wanted to leave. She didn't feel like having idle chitchat with Peter's sweetheart. "I think I'll head outside for a breath of air." She moved toward the front of the house, grabbed her coat from a hook near the door, slipped it on, then ventured outside.

The air was frigid, and Meg saw her breath wisp out as visible steam. Her heart beat hard within her chest. She closed her eyes and tried to forget the sight of Peter and Agnes seated side by side, drinking hot chocolate as if they'd done it together many times.

The fact that she hadn't seen Reuben should bother her, but it didn't. And that alone told her it was past time for her to break it off with him. *The next time I see him, I will.*

The door behind her opened, and she stiffened. Surely Agnes hadn't decided to join her outside. She turned and saw with relief that it was her sister Charlie. "Hey."

Charlie joined her at the porch railing. "'Tis quiet out here. Too crowded in there," she said.

Meg shrugged. "I didn't think so." Until Agnes and her sister had shown up. Then the house had seemed too full with their presence—and Agnes's role in Peter's life.

"I wish we could go home."

Something in her little sister's tone alerted her. Meg faced her and touched her arm. "What's wrong, Charlotte?"

Charlie twisted her lips at being addressed by her given name. She'd always used her nickname since they'd moved to Happiness, especially since Abram Peachy's wife was also named Charlotte. "I didn't know the Peachys would be here," her sister complained.

"They're *gut* people. Why are you upset?"

"Nathaniel Peachy." Charlie's features contorted with disgust. "I don't like him."

"Nate," Meg mused. "He giving you a hard time, little *schweschter*?" Her sister nodded. "Want me to go and take him down a peg or two? Give him a severe talking-to for treating you poorly?"

Charlie appeared horrified by Meg's offer. "*Nay*, don't you dare!" She hugged herself tightly. "You'll give him a swollen head, making him think he has the power to annoy me. Better to ignore him."

Meg nodded with approval. "You're learning, *maydel*." She grinned. "You've made me happy to be your big sister."

The door behind them opened again, and the object of her sister's frustration exited the house. Meg watched as Charlie studied the man, who swept by them with a murmur, hurrying toward his family's buggy. The sound of the door opening again had Meg turning. She'd expected to see the rest of the Peachy family, but it was Peter and the Beiler twins. Peter's gaze glanced off her as he accompanied the sisters toward their parked vehicle.

"Have a nice day, Meg," Agnes said, as she continued past. Her arm brushed against Peter's, she hovered so close. "Take care of that leg."

"I will, Agnes." Meg felt her teeth snap together as she watched Agnes deliberately bump against Peter several times. "I wonder if *Dat* and *Mam* are ready to leave yet," she said to her sister when they were out of earshot.

Charlie sighed. "I doubt it. We haven't eaten yet."

Meg knew she was right. They would have to stay for the midday meal, but as soon as she could, she would suggest they head home. She'd plead exhaustion if she had to, for she was tired from having to endure the sight of Peter with Agnes.

Her sister turned back to the house and Meg followed. She wasn't hungry. Her appetite had vanished the instant Agnes had walked in.

A man she didn't love wanted her, while she yearned for someone who didn't care for her, a man she didn't have a hope of having for her own. Meg sighed. She wanted nothing more than to go home, crawl into bed and sleep to forget the heartache she was destined to suffer in the weeks ahead. For things in her life would certainly change between now and the party. She'd no longer have Reuben in her life, and would no longer get to work with the man she loved—a man who wanted another.

Chapter Fifteen

As she came out of the house, Meg looked perturbed, Peter noted. He was waiting for her at the bottom of the steps for their day in Ephrata.

"What's wrong?" he asked with a frown.

"Remember that great idea we had that my *mam* could tell my family you'd be taking me to the doctor? We thought it a *gut* excuse for us to be in each other's company."

"Ja." Peter studied her with concern. Her expression was sheepish. "How bad can it be? Just tell me."

"Mam made sure she'd be telling the truth when she told my *dat* and sisters." She paused, looking upset. "I have a doctor's appointment today at eleven." She met his gaze as if begging for understanding. "In thirty minutes."

"Is that all?" he asked. Peter was relieved. He thought something terrible had happened. "That's not a problem. I'll take you to your doctor's appointment, then we can go to Ephrata for lunch when you're done."

Meg blinked. "Are you sure? You knew nothing about this—"

"Meg, I did offer to take you to your doctor's and physical therapy appointments."

Her face cleared. "*Ja*, you did."

"Then let's go, shall we?" He offered her his arm, because it felt like the right thing to do.

She didn't hesitate this time, but grabbed hold and allowed him to help her down the few steps and then into the carriage. "I don't know why she made this appointment. I didn't think I was due for one until another week at least."

"Did your *mudder* talk with the doctor the last time you were there?"

"*Ja*." Meg sighed. "Maybe he told her something he didn't tell me?"

"Could be. Maybe he thinks you're healing well enough that you can start physical therapy sooner than expected, and he didn't want to get your hopes up until he could x-ray your leg and know for sure."

Her blue eyes brightened as she turned in her seat to meet his gaze while he climbed into the buggy. "Do you think so?"

"I guess we'll find out." There was a nip in the air, but Peter barely noticed it. He was feeling warm inside with Meg beside him. He was glad they'd mended their working relationship. Now that she knew the truth about what she'd overheard, Meg seemed more willing to be friends. They hadn't yet reached the depth of friendship that he shared with Agnes, but it meant a lot to him. Considering how he'd felt about her for so long, it was a big deal to him.

They made it to the doctor's office and had Meg checked in within twenty minutes of leaving her house. As he sat beside her in the waiting room after hanging

up their coats, Peter studied her leg brace and hoped
he was right, and she was ready for physical therapy.
She looked pretty in a purple dress that did wonderful
things to her dark hair and blue eyes.

"Did you bring your invitation list?" Meg asked,
drawing his attention from her leg to her face.

He nodded. "When I asked, *Dat* had a list ready. As
if he was expecting me to ask."

"My *mam* did, too."

A nurse called Meg's name. Peter helped her to rise,
then watched as she made her way across the room to
the door where the woman waited. "Sir," the nurse said,
"you may come in with your wife."

Peter experienced a jolt. "I…"

Meg met his gaze, and to his surprise, he saw her
lips curve with amusement. "That's all right. My husband is a bit squeamish. He can wait here."

The nurse nodded as if she understood, and Meg
disappeared into a back room.

The minutes went by, and it seemed as if Meg was
gone a long time. Peter began to worry. Was she all
right? Had the doctor discovered a problem with her
leg? Maybe it hadn't healed as well as he'd first thought.

The door to the back area opened. "Peter?" the nurse
called. "Meg would like you to come on back."

Peter rose as the shock of Meg's request had his heart
thumping hard, ready to burst out of his chest. If only
he were Meg's husband, with the right to be there for
her as he'd longed for since he'd first set eyes on her
and fallen in love. His legs trembled as he approached,
until reason gave him pause and the strength to continue on. Meg wanted him in the exam room with her.
Either she had received terrible news and needed his

support, or she had learned something *gut* enough to want to share the moment.

"Here you are. She's in room two, waiting for you."

Peter swallowed hard before he entered. The doctor was typing into a computer on a tiny table that extended from a countertop. Meg sat in a chair close to the exam table, and immediately locked gazes with Peter. Concern filled him. He wanted to comfort her if the news was bad, and hug her if the news was good. Her expression unreadable, she stared at him a long moment, then gestured toward the next seat.

The doctor finished typing, then looked up. "*Hallo.* You must be Peter." He turned to Meg. "I looked at the X-rays from your last visit, Meg, and compared them to those." He indicated the light on the wall that lit up a set of films. "I have to say that I'm surprised by the change."

Peter felt Meg shift. "Is it a good change or bad?" she asked, as she reached to grab Peter's hand.

The physician smiled. "Good change. Meg, your leg is healed. I can't believe it myself. You must have amazing recuperative powers because your leg is healed enough for you to begin physical therapy. Normally it takes six to eight weeks for a broken bone to mend. Sometimes longer, but you… Your leg has repaired itself in just under five weeks from your accident."

Peter flashed her a smile as he squeezed her fingers gently. He expected her to pull her hand away, but she didn't. Instead, she held on and squeezed back.

"I didn't always have amazing healing ability," Meg murmured.

"*Ja*, you have, Meg," Peter assured her. She had come

through a serious illness where her life could have been cut short at age fourteen.

She held his gaze, seemed to glean his thoughts. She faced the doctor. "I can start physical therapy?"

"Yes," the doctor said. "But you need to continue to wear the brace as much as possible. You may take it off for short periods, though. That'll be a nice change, won't it?"

Meg grinned. "Yes."

"Where should she go for therapy?" Peter asked, as if he were her husband and had the right to know.

Dr. Reckling mentioned a facility that was close enough to make it easy for both Meg and him as the driver.

As they left the office shortly afterward, Meg stood on the sidewalk and drew in a deep breath. "That was worth the trip," she said quietly.

Peter's lips curved upward. "*Ja*, it was." He had the urge to hug her. They gazed at each other a long moment, and he gave in to the feeling. He moved close, reached out and pulled her into his arms for a hug. He made it quick so it didn't feel awkward for either of them, but he felt a rush of satisfaction that he had the chance to hold her in his arms, however briefly.

Meg's face was red as he stepped back. He pretended not to notice. "Let's go eat," he said. "We've got a party to finish planning."

They ate lunch in a diner nearby and looked over each other's invitation lists. "They're the same," Meg said with raised eyebrows.

Peter chuckled. "As if our parents created it together."

"They probably did, when they decided they wanted the birthday party."

"Well, that simplifies things," Peter said as he pulled out cash for the check. When Meg opened her mouth as if she would object, he held up his hand. "I asked you to lunch, Meg."

Her lips firmed, but she didn't say another word, as if she knew she couldn't win the argument.

As they drove back to Happiness, they talked about the party food, knowing that the women who were to be invited would want to contribute.

Meg convinced him to allow others to fix food. "I'd want to bring my share if I was invited to a party or gathering."

The list included family of the birthday pair and a number of their closest friends. Not too many, though, that they couldn't invite them personally, starting the next day.

At her house, Peter came around the buggy to help her up her porch steps. "Don't want to do anything to postpone your physical therapy," he said with a little smirk.

The door opened as they reached the landing. Missy Stoltzfus stood in the opening, as if waiting for them.

"Mam," Meg cried with excitement. "My leg's healed. Dr. Reckling wants me to wear the brace for a while longer, but I can start physical therapy, and I don't have to wear it all the time."

Her mother was delighted. "Peter," she said, *"danki* for taking her."

"I was happy to help." He hesitated. "I'd be glad to take Meg to her physical therapy appointments if you don't mind." He kept his eyes focused on Meg's mother.

Missy nodded. "That would be wonderful. She'll

have to go often, and while her father or I can take her to some of them, we'd really appreciate your help."

"Gut," Peter said. "Then it's all set. Her first therapy session is on Monday. I'll take her then." He met Missy's gaze. "We can talk about last-minute party arrangements."

"An excellent idea. In fact, you can take her to all her appointments next week if you have the time."

"I should," he said. "If for some reason I can't, I'll let you know." He turned to Meg. "I'll come by for you tomorrow."

She nodded. When she caught her mother's questioning look, Meg said, "We thought we'd invite those on your list personally."

Her *mam* eyed them with approval. "If someone asks why you're here again, Peter, I'll explain that you're taking Meg to see where she'll be having her therapy before she starts next week."

"We'll find the office," Peter said. His gaze settled gently on Meg. "We got a lot done today. Just over two weeks, and the party will have come and gone." And the thought, he realized, saddened him. "I should get home and check in with *Dat* and Jacob in the shop. I'll see you tomorrow, Meg. Missy."

He left, thinking of Meg and how happy she was about her leg. He was glad he'd be the one taking her to PT some of the time, if not all. Peter suddenly thought of Reuben Miller, and the joy in his day with Meg dissipated. He had to stay committed to Agnes. In fact, he'd stop in briefly to see her before he headed home.

He made a turn that took him onto the road that led to the Joshua Beiler farm and Agnes. He attempted to see the bright side. Agnes's disposition could brighten anyone's day. If anyone could help him fight his feelings for Meg, it would be Agnes.

Then why couldn't he forget the way Meg had held on to his hand in the doctor's office?

Agnes, he thought. *Think of Agnes*. And so he did... until he reached her house and learned that she wasn't there. He went home then, his thoughts veering from Meg to Agnes, then back to Meg. *Nay!*

But Meg's smiling face haunted him. No matter how hard he tried, he couldn't get her out of his mind.

Meg rose early with a grin on her face. She was ready for her day. Peter would be coming for her at ten. She sat up, swung her legs off the bed and reached for her brace. It took a moment's struggle, but she was able to slip it on. She rose carefully, stood a moment until her body settled and she felt stable.

When she was ready, she went downstairs to breakfast. She had reached the bottom of the steps when she heard her mother call out to her.

"Ja, Mam?"

"Come into the kitchen. You have a visitor!"

Peter. Her heart thumped. "Coming!" The man turned as she entered the kitchen. "Reuben!" She experienced a vague disappointment. "You're here."

He smiled. "I had to work a lot these last two weeks, Meg. Sorry I couldn't stop by before now."

She moved to sit in her chair. "I was just going to have something to eat. Want to join me?"

Reuben shook his head. He had taken off his hat, and his blond hair was thick and shiny. The sun pouring through the window glistened on the golden strands.

"I can't stay, Meg. I wanted to see you before I went to the construction site."

"You still have to work?" She was actually glad he'd be gone before Peter's arrival. It would have been awkward for the two of them to meet up again, given the fact that there was something about Peter that Reuben didn't like. And vice versa.

"I'm sorry, Meg." His blue eyes shone with regret.

"I understand," she assured him. "Maybe you can stop by again, tomorrow after work? I'd like to talk with you. Will you come?" She paused. "If you don't have to work too late."

Reuben smiled. "*Ja,* I'll come tomorrow after work." He stood, picked up his hat. "You look well, Meg. Missy told me that your leg has healed nicely and you'll be starting physical therapy next week."

"*Ja.*" She eyed him carefully. "Your bruises are gone, and you are back to work, so I imagine you're feeling your former self."

"The only soreness I feel now is from a full day's work." He started for the door, where he paused. "I'll see you tomorrow."

He left, and Meg reached across the table for the plate of muffins. "It was nice of Reuben to visit," she commented to her mother.

"You didn't expect him to come?"

Meg took a bite of a chocolate muffin and shook her head. "*Nay,* it's been a while since I saw him last." She met her mother's gaze. "He was out of town, visiting family, and then he had to work," she explained.

"Would you like me to invite him to supper tomorrow night?" her mother asked.

Shaking her head, Meg said, "*Nay*, I don't know that he'll want to stay after I talk with him."

Mam widened her eyes. "Ah, so that's the way of it then."

"*Ja*, I'm afraid so."

"Better now than later."

Meg hoped that Reuben felt the same after she broke up with him, although the truth was she'd never consented to his courtship of her in the first place.

"*Hallo!* Anybody home? Meg?"

Meg heard Peter's voice before he entered the kitchen. "Your *vadder* told me to come right in. I hope that's *oll recht*."

"Why wouldn't it be?" Missy asked. She watched as Meg took a second bite of muffin. "Sit, Peter. Have a muffin, and I'll get you both a cup of tea."

Peter sat, and Meg shoved the plate in his direction. "Chocolate?" he asked, as he looked at what was left of her muffin.

"I love chocolate," she admitted with a smirk.

"I thought you preferred lemon," he said, reminding her of their banter over what kind of birthday cake they would order for the party.

She laughed. "I love chocolate *and* lemon."

"That makes it easier then, doesn't it? As I do, too."

"*Ja*, we'll have to order two cakes, one in each flavor. Can't have either parent feeling deprived," Meg said. Her mother set cups of tea before each of them. Meg thanked her, then gazed at Peter, who had taken the seat across the table from her. "You're here early."

"Am I?" he queried. "I don't remember arranging a time."

Meg frowned. "Ten. We said ten." She bit her lip. "'Tis only nine fifteen."

His lips twitched. "You want me to go and come back later?"

"*Nay*, I'm ready, or I will be after I've enjoyed another muffin and this cup of tea."

"Well, then *gut*." He ate his chocolate muffin and drank his tea.

When they were done eating and drinking, Meg grabbed her coat and followed Peter through the front door. He waited outside, ready to assist if necessary. It wasn't.

"Meg!" Her father crossed the yard. "Reuben left, then. That's *gut*. Peter, you'll show my *dochter* where she'll be going on Monday?"

"I will."

Arlin nodded with approval. "You'll be back afterward?"

"I thought I'd ask Peter to take me to the store while we're out and about." She hesitated, feeling sheepish. "Peter?"

"I'll bring her back after she shops, apparently."

Her father laughed. "Better you than me, Peter."

Peter was unusually quiet as he stood by while Meg climbed into the carriage, and then as he got in beside her. He steered his horse away from the house and onto the road in the direction of the physical therapy clinic. There was an edge of tension between them, and Meg tried to recall the moment it had crept in.

"Peter?"

He glanced at her.

"Is something wrong?"

"Nay." He sighed. "I'm just full. I ate too many of your *mudder's* muffins."

Meg stared at him and forced a smile. She didn't believe for one moment that having eaten too much was the reason for his silence. Their banter had been light as they'd enjoyed breakfast together. She thought about it and froze. It was after her father had mentioned Reuben's visit that Peter had grown especially quiet. She studied him unobtrusively. Why? Because he didn't care for Reuben as much as Reuben didn't care for him? Or was there another reason?

A tiny seed of hope blossomed in her heart. *Is it possible that Peter is jealous?*

Chapter Sixteen

It had been a good day. Peter had brought her home a half hour ago, and Meg was pleased with how many invitations they'd gotten done. They'd gone from house to house, personally inviting family and friends, starting with her aunt Katie, then moving on to visit each of Katie's married sons. It had been great to visit her cousins' homes. Every one of them was excited to be included in the party surprise, and as she'd thought, each of their spouses wanted to help with the food. After the Lapps, Peter had driven to the Amos Kings and the Abram Peachys. Both families were close friends of her *dat* and Peter's *mam*.

Tomorrow they planned to invite Peter's cousin Mary and her husband, Ethan. The Bontragers were newlyweds, having married the same week as Nell and James. They lived in New Holland, and Meg looked forward to the drive there. Mary was Sally's sister and the eldest daughter of Alta Hershberger. As their plan for tomorrow, Peter had assured her that Mary, like Sally, would have no trouble keeping news of the party from their mother. They would tell her a few days prior, not before, when it was too late for Alta to unleash the secret and ruin the surprise.

During their journey back, Peter had asked, "Are you going to invite Reuben?"

"Nay," she'd replied. There was no indication that the thought made him jealous. "If I did, I'd have to invite his family, and they don't know my *dat* or your *mam*. I think 'tis best to keep things simple. Don't you?" She'd heard him agree, then had dared to casually ask, "Will you be inviting Agnes?"

"Nay," he'd said, "for the same reason." And Meg had been relieved.

As she waited for Reuben's arrival, she realized that she looked forward to sharing with Peter the results of their hard work.

It was three o'clock. Reuben got off work at three thirty, he'd said, and he'd be coming here right afterward. Meg wandered into the kitchen, looking for her mother. Her *mam* stood by the stove, stirring a simmering pot. Whatever she was making for dinner smelled delicious. "Is that chicken and dumplings?"

"Ja." Her mother gave one last stir before she set down her spoon.

Meg moved closer for a peek. "My favorite." She closed her eyes as she sniffed.

Missy put on the teakettle. "How was your day?"

"Gut." She told her mother about the people Peter and she had invited, and their plans for the next day.

Her mother looked pleased. "'Tis coming together."

"Ja." Meg stood by the stove, enjoying the warmth of the kitchen and her mother's company. "Reuben will be here soon."

"You need a place to talk?"

Meg bobbed her head. "Where is everyone?"

"Ellie is out cleaning a house, and Charlie went with Leah to visit Nell." Missy took cups and saucers out of the cabinet, taking for granted that Meg wanted tea. "You can talk in the great room. 'Tis too cold outside for a walk."

"And I'm still wearing this brace, so I wouldn't want to go far," Meg added.

Forty-five minutes later, Reuben knocked on the back door. Meg rose to let him in.

"*Hallo*, Meg." His grin pierced her heart as she returned the greeting. She knew his happiness at seeing her wouldn't last for long.

He really was an attractive man, and right now she smelled the outdoors on him. He wore a navy knit hat, which he tugged off as he entered. As he removed his coat, she noticed he wore a long-sleeved blue shirt tucked into blue tri-blend denim pants held up by black suspenders. On his feet, he wore work boots. His blond hair was partly matted, while other strands were tousled from his cap. His cheeks, nose and ears were red, a good look on the man, who was not only kind, but thoughtful, too. Meg wondered why she couldn't love him as she should. Her thoughts raced to Peter. She knew why, but it didn't make her feel any less guilty for what she was about to say to Reuben.

"You're cold. Let me fix us tea, and we can take it into the other room." Her mother had gone outside to the barn to feed the animals. Meg longed for the day when she could take over the chore again.

She felt Reuben's gaze on her as she brewed two cups of tea, and he accepted one. He followed her into the great room and sat down. "You're looking well, Meg. Really *gut*. I'm so glad you're healing."

Meg experienced a rush of excitement as she told him about her leg. "I start physical therapy next week."

Reuben beamed. "Thanks be to *Gott*. You don't know how happy I am that you're *oll recht*." He reached across the distance between their chairs to grasp her hand.

Meg stifled the urge to jerk away. She waited a heartbeat before using the excuse of her tea to slowly withdraw, as if she needed both hands to hold her cup. "Reuben."

"Meg," he responded playfully.

Setting down her teacup, Meg sighed. "Reuben, I…I don't think we belong together. I like you, but it doesn't feel right."

He stiffened, and stared at her. "You're breaking up with me."

Meg saw disappointment in his blue eyes. "We weren't actually a couple, were we? You said you wanted to court me, but did I agree? *Nay*, I didn't."

"Meg—"

"I'm sorry, Reuben. I didn't want to hurt you." She regarded him with sadness, because she was causing him pain. *Better now than later*, her mother had said. Meg straightened in her chair. "I owe you a lot. You saved my life, and I thought to give us a chance because of it, but I just can't."

Reuben leaned back in his seat. "You don't owe me anything."

"But I do," she insisted. "You pulled me from the water. You saved me."

He was shaking his head. "I know the paramedics and EMTs said I saved you, but I didn't. I couldn't have."

His lips firmed, and embarrassment flickered in his blue eyes. "I couldn't have saved you. I'm afraid of water. I can't swim."

Meg stared at him as his words registered. "You didn't save me?"

"Nay." He lifted a hand to run his fingers through his unruly hair.

"Then who did?"

"I didn't recall at first, but recently it came back to me. That night." He laughed. "Peter. It was Peter Zook. I remember seeing him. I heard his voice, asking if I was *oll recht*, telling me that you were right beside me and he was going to get us help." He glanced away. "Peter is the reason you don't want me."

"Reuben—" But she broke off as it hit her. Peter had saved her?

"Don't deny it, Meg. I've seen the way you look at him."

"He's with Agnes," she whispered, stunned by his certainty.

Reuben raised his eyebrows. "Are you sure?"

Meg nodded. *"Ja.* I know this."

"Maybe you should do something about that. Tell him how you feel. Meg, one thing I've learned since our accident is that life can be cut short in an instant." He studied her with affection. "'Tis fine, Meg. I'll be fine."

"I'm sorry."

"I can't know this for certain, but Peter—he sounded broken up when he spoke of you at the accident scene. He might care for you as you do him."

"Nay."

"You sound so sure."

"Ja." She gazed up at Reuben as he stood.

"I should go. I wish you all the best." He looked regretful. "I'm sorry I wasn't the one who kept you from drowning, Meg. I'm sorry I couldn't be the hero you wanted me to be."

Meg pushed herself upright. "You're a *gut* man, Reuben Miller. There is a woman out there for you. Not me, but someone else. Someone who'll love you as you deserve to be loved."

The tiny upward curve of his mouth only made his good looks better. "Take care of yourself, Meg."

She followed him to the door. "I won't forget how *gut* you were to me, Reuben. I know we probably can't be friends right now, but know that I'm here if you feel differently someday."

With a heart that ached for him, she watched him leave. As Reuben's buggy disappeared from sight, Meg tried to wrap her head around the fact that Peter had been the one to save her. He'd rescued her, but had never said a word.

Tears filled her eyes. "He didn't want me to think anything of it. He didn't want my gratitude. *He doesn't want me.*"

She had to work with him for only a little longer. After the party, she'd make sure he wasn't held to his offer of taking her to physical therapy. He had simply used the excuse so they could continue with the party planning.

Dare she tell Peter what she'd learned? What Reuben had told her?

"Nay," she whispered, as she slowly climbed the stairs to her room. If he'd wanted her to know, Peter would have told her himself. Yet her heart hurt, not for Reuben, but for herself.

It made sense now why Peter had come to visit her in the hospital. He'd said he wanted to see how she was faring. And she'd been startlingly polite as she tried to mend fences with a man who hadn't liked her. Then she'd learned that he actually *had* liked her, years ago… and she'd felt better, until she remembered Agnes's role in Peter's life.

He'd wanted a friendly working relationship. What he didn't know was that he'd stolen Meg's heart.

Peter would be back for her tomorrow. Between now and then, she had to find the strength to pretend that she didn't know he'd been the one to rescue her. He would never learn about her feelings for him, and he'd never find out that she'd broken things off with Reuben.

But for now, Meg lay on her bed and had herself a good cry.

Meg was unusually quiet when Peter came for her the next day. Since they'd left her house, she'd given one-word replies whenever he'd asked her anything. "Think we can finish the invitations today?" he'd asked.

"Ja," she'd replied.

And the conversation had continued that way for the first mile, then two, until he'd become quiet himself. The silence was painful.

Peter frowned as they reached the Ethan Bontrager home. Would she act withdrawn while they spoke with his cousins?

He had his answer moments later. Meg came alive as she greeted Mary and Ethan and entered their house. He felt a painful tightening in his chest as he observed her. Apparently, she was silent and unhappy only with him. Why? Had he done something to upset her? She'd been fine yesterday, pleasant and smiling.

As they left the house with the Bontragers' promise to attend and continued to the next family on their list— the Adam Troyers—Peter opened his mouth to demand to know what was wrong. But then he shut it, realizing he didn't want to make matters between them worse.

After the Troyers, they visited Nell and James. Peter listened while Meg explained about the party to her eldest sister and her husband. Satisfied when they agreed to attend, she seemed less tense as they left.

"Meg?"

Her eyes dimmed as she met his gaze. *"Ja?"*

His heart tripped painfully. "Nothing." She frowned, and he said the first thing that came to mind. "Anyone else on our list?"

"Just the William Masts."

He inclined his head and drove in that direction. After a quick visit to the Masts, during which Meg again came alive and did all the talking, Peter took her home.

"I guess we've done all we can until we get closer to the party," he said.

"Ja." She studied her house as if eager to get inside.

Forlorn, he started to turn away, then paused. "Meg? What about Christmas decorations? Shouldn't we cut pine boughs and holly?"

She glanced at him, her expression hooded. *"Ja,* you're right. When?"

"Tomorrow?" he asked, hopeful that the tension between them would ease by then.

She nodded.

"I'll be by tomorrow morning at ten. We'll go over to the tree farm." He paused. "Will that be okay?"

She looked for a moment as if she would argue, but nodded instead. Then without another word, she went into the house, while he got into his buggy and departed.

The next day turned out to be a good one to cut Christmas greenery. They knew the owner of the farm, and he was willing to allow them their cuttings for a small fee. As they walked through the grounds, Peter prayed to see more enthusiasm from Meg. Again, she was too quiet, and he nearly demanded that she talk with him. So he prayed that whatever it was that bothered her, she'd be able to set it aside so they could continue to work together. He wanted his mother to have an enjoyable birthday party, a little bit of celebration to cheer her up after a rough year.

And he wanted him and Meg to be friends. Or maybe more.

"Are you sure we're not cutting too early?" Meg asked, after Peter had snipped off a few pine limbs.

"If they don't make it, we can always return for more," he said with a grin.

But she didn't smile back, so he made quick work of the cuttings, then took her home.

"I'll come for you on Monday to take you to physical therapy," he said, after he'd helped her from the carriage.

"Peter..."

"'Tis no trouble."

She nodded, then turned toward the house.

"Meg?"

He saw her stiffen before she faced him. *"Ja?"*

"Have a nice day."

He didn't know what to make of her weak, "You, too" in response.

Scolding himself for being all kinds of a fool, he drove to Agnes's house and invited her for a drive Monday afternoon. Meg's physical therapy was in the morning. He could make it to the Beiler home by two o'clock.

But Peter regretted the invitation he'd made to Agnes right after she'd accepted, because his thoughts remained with Meg.

Visiting Sunday rolled around, but Peter didn't go. He felt ill. He urged his parents to attend, said he knew how to reach them if he needed them. They'd be at the Abram Peachys, and he knew Meg would be there. He wasn't ready to see her. And he was sick—sick at heart, wondering what he should do about his feelings for Meg and his commitment to Agnes, which he was struggling with.

When his parents returned at the end of the day, Peter was at the kitchen table, trying to choke down a cup of tea. "Peter," his mother said. "Still not feeling well?"

"I'm getting there. Figured I should try to eat something with a cup of tea." He gestured toward the cracker box on the countertop across the room. He'd munched on a few saltines and felt better for doing so.

"Well, you don't have to worry about taking Meg to her physical therapy appointment tomorrow morning," his *dat* said. "Arlin wants to take her."

Peter knew he should feel relieved, not disappointed. But this was the last week before the party, and he and Meg had a lot to do. It would have been better to see her alone, on his own terms, to smooth things over so that they could work well together these next few days. "I can take her," he said, sincerely wanting to. "I'm feeling better already."

But Horseshoe Joe shook his head. "Arlin wants to see what Meg has to do. He's determined that she get the best care, and he said he needs to meet her physical therapist."

"Oh." Peter hid his disappointment.

"But he said you can take her on Tuesday."

He brightened. "*Gut* to know."

The next afternoon Peter went to get Agnes. It was a typical prewinter day, with temperatures in the low thirties. He'd brought an extra quilt and a thermos of the hot chocolate he knew Agnes liked.

She came out of the house as soon as he steered his horse into the yard.

"*Hallo!*" he called.

Her lips tilted, but the good humor didn't reach her eyes. Peter frowned. Was she feeling poorly?

He reached under his seat for the extra quilt and handed it to her. "It's chilly. Thought you'd like to stay warm." He gestured toward the back seat. "A thermos of hot chocolate, especially for you."

Her smile seemed more genuine as she covered her legs with the quilt. "That's kind of you, Peter, but I'm not thirsty right now."

"No Alice today?" he said conversationally, after a lengthy silence.

She stiffened. "Do you want to go back and get her?"

He glanced at her with surprise. "*Nay*, I wanted this time with you. Not your sister." He returned his attention to the road. "It's just that you usually like her to come with us."

He heard her sigh. "*Ja,* I usually do."

She was quiet, reflective, and he could tell something was wrong. "Agnes, what's bothering you?" he asked with a quick look in her direction. He saw her bite the inside of her cheek. The sound of her breath struck him as labored. "Agnes?"

"'Tis not working out between us, Peter. I liked that we were friends and I'd hoped for more, but it's not to be."

He saw a clearing on the side of the road near an old Amish cemetery. He pulled off the road and then turned to her. "What exactly are you saying, Agnes? That you don't want to be my friend? My sweetheart? What?"

Her eyes filled with tears. "You don't love me, Peter, and I don't love you. This will never work between us. We shouldn't deny our hearts and try to make something more from a simple friendship."

"Agnes—"

But she held up her hand. "Let me say what I have to say," she whispered. He nodded for her to go ahead. "Meg," she said. "You've cared for her, *loved* her, for a long time."

"Our families are friends—"

"There is someone else, Peter. I found someone that I might make a life with. I know where your heart lies and it's not with me. It's with Meg Stoltzfus." Her smile was sad. "You should tell her how you feel. She may have no idea. I watched her with Reuben. Doesn't look like she cares for him. I think she's trying to, but I don't think she's succeeding."

Peter stared at her, realizing the truth. "You've been a *gut* friend to me, Agnes. You deserve better than what I could have offered you. I hope whoever you've set your heart on is worthy of your love."

She reached for his hand. "I'll always have happy memories of our friendship, Peter, but I don't think we should see each other again. 'Tis easy enough when you're in one church district while I'm in another."

He agreed. "I'll take you home." As he turned the buggy and headed back, Peter listened to Agnes's happy chatter. It was as if, now unburdened, she'd returned to her old self. Yet he knew a moment's sadness. He would miss Agnes's bright smile and high spirits. She had always been able to put a grin on his face. But that was done. There would be only one way for him to feel happy, and that was if someday, somehow, Meg became a permanent part of his life, first as his sweetheart and then as his wife.

Do you care for Reuben, Meg? Or was Agnes right about her having feelings for him?

Do I have a chance of winning your heart if I confess how much I love you?

Chapter Seventeen

It was two days before Christmas. Meg was in Bishop John's house overseeing her sisters and three other community women, including Sally Hershberger and her sister, Mary Bontrager, as they cleaned to get ready for the Christmas holiday and the party the day after.

She hadn't seen Peter in over a week. He hadn't come to visiting day at the Peachys' and she'd sent word to him that she no longer needed for him to take her to her physical therapy appointments. Her father had taken her to her first appointment, and after that, the duty was passed from Leah to Nell, then finally to her mother. She was both glad and disappointed that she hadn't talked with him. Their last-minute plans were in the works. Meg had sent a message about the house-cleaning, and Peter had replied through Annie that he'd ordered the two birthday cakes from Maggie Mast's bakery.

The party was in three days, and then it would be over. She felt an underlying sadness that she and Peter would no longer have any reason to spend time together. Despite the hurt she'd felt upon learning that he'd kept his rescue of her a secret, she'd enjoyed the time they'd spent together as they planned their parents' party.

She wasn't wearing her brace today. Her physical therapy sessions had apparently already made a big difference in strengthening her calf muscles and foot. The party would be the first time that Peter would see her without the leg brace. Would he even care? She doubted it. Why should he care at all about her? He had Agnes.

"We've finished, Meg," Leah said, as she and Ellie came down the stairs.

"Me, too." She conveyed her thanks to all the women who'd helped today. Meg studied her surroundings. The great room looked festive, with holly branches and pine boughs set out to give the place a splash of Christmas cheer. The cuttings that she and Peter had gathered hadn't made it. So she'd told Eli to ask him to cut more, which he had.

Sally entered from the kitchen area. "I've put the food for tomorrow and Christmas in the bishop's pantry. He should have plenty to eat before we all descend on him for the party."

As if he heard his name, John Fisher came into the house from outside. "You've been busy," he said, as he noted the holly and pine.

"We hope you don't mind, but we did a little decorating," Meg said. Her Amish community didn't put up Christmas trees, but they did enjoy the greenery with bright red berries.

"Looks *gut*," he said gruffly.

Meg noticed that he'd lost some of the sadness in his eyes. When his gaze swept briefly toward Sally, she had an inkling the man felt a little something for the one woman who'd been there to help him whenever he'd needed her. "We should go and leave you in peace."

"Where's Nicholas?" Mary asked. "I haven't seen him since he was an infant."

"I'll check on him," Sally offered, and disappeared up the stairs.

No one moved. Sally returned downstairs moments later, carrying the bishop's adorable son.

"Ah, he's sweet," Mary cooed, and the women who were still there echoed her sentiments. "I want one like him." Mary's eyes warmed. "I'd like a lot of children."

Nicholas rested his head on Sally's shoulder, clearly at ease with the woman who held him, as if she were his mother. John gazed at Sally with his son, and Meg saw emotion shift in his expression. Longing. Warmth. Affection.

Meg experienced a longing of her own. She wanted children as well, but there'd be none if she couldn't have them with the man she loved. Peter.

She encouraged the others to leave. Only Sally lingered, to fix lunch for little Nicholas and his father.

Reuben had encouraged Meg to tell Peter she loved him. Could she do it? She didn't know. She could try to tell him at the party.

She had spent the last few weeks making Christmas gifts for her family, and birthday gifts for her father and Peter's mother. She had made a special thank-you present for Peter for helping her to plan the party. She would give it to him that night. She would act breezy, as if it was no big deal, but she had put a lot of love and hard work into the scarf she'd knitted for him.

She blinked back tears. It would be the last time she'd see him but for Sundays. Rarely would their paths cross during the week. "Foolish girl," she murmured. "Why did I have to fall in love with him again?" Or had she ever been out of love with him?

Her family spent Christmas together, just her parents, her sisters and Nell's husband, James. They exchanged gifts, and Meg was happy that everyone seemed to like the little presents she'd made for each of them. She knew how to sew. She and Martha—Eli's wife and a widow before her cousin had married her—had made craft items for the local fire company's mud sales. She'd attended a lot of them in past years, hoping to see Reuben, who sometimes worked as auctioneer. The sales auctioned off donations from Amish families, including quilts, furniture, farm equipment and small items like the pot holders, aprons and numerous other kitchen and household crafts that she and Martha had made and donated.

The family enjoyed a turkey dinner with all the fixings, including stuffing, cranberry sauce, green beans, mashed potatoes with gravy, dried corn casserole and apple pie with ice cream. They'd celebrated her father's birthday as they usually did, with a pan of lemon squares she'd made especially for him.

When her sisters decided to walk off the food outside, Meg followed. It had snowed during the night, a dusting that caused no travel issues and simply looked beautiful.

She loved walking without the restriction of the brace. She felt stronger every day. She'd been sleeping well at night, and her spirits had risen with the knowledge that the birthday party was tomorrow, and she would see Peter.

On the morning of Second Christmas, Meg and her sister Leah drove to Bishop John's for one last assessment of what else needed to be done. They had a lot of food in the back of their buggy. She and her mother and sisters had cooked and baked up a storm. Her aunt had brought her food contribution by as well—three vegetable dishes and a huge pan of chocolate fudge.

As she helped to carry everything inside, Meg couldn't help grinning as she thought of the fudge and Peter. He liked chocolate, and he said his mother preferred it over lemon, as well. Did that mean he would like the fudge more than the second pan of lemon squares she'd baked early that morning?

Everything was ready. She was doing a last check of the house when she heard a male voice in the kitchen. Meg headed that way, then froze on the threshold. Peter Zook had come with the two birthday cakes. He glanced up and saw her, and his eyes brightened. Suddenly, Meg was overwhelmed with joy. Tomorrow, things might be different, but tonight was for his mother and her father, and everyone would enjoy the evening because of the work they'd done together.

After placing the cakes out of sight in the bishop's pantry, Peter approached her. *"Hallo*, Meg." His expression was warm, and she felt a tingle from the top of her head to the bottom of her feet. "Looks like we're ready to go."

"Ja," she breathed. "Everything looks *gut*. I see you picked up the cakes from Maggie's."

"Smelled delicious in there. It was nice of her to keep them in her bakery until we needed them. Nicer still that she opened up early so I could get them."

"I should get home before my *vadder* wonders where

I am." She waved to Leah, who motioned that she'd be right there. Meg met Peter's gray eyes again. "I'll see you later."

"You will." He said it like a promise, and her heart thrilled at his tone.

The party guests arrived an hour before Meg and Peter's families. The Zooks and Stoltzfuses met up outside—prearranged by Peter and Meg—and walked up to the bishop's house together.

"I'm glad John is having guests. It must be lonely for him now that Catherine is gone," Miriam Zook said.

"But he must be coming around, if he's willing to have us all here, *ja*?" Meg raised her hand and knocked. She was overly aware of Peter's presence behind her, but didn't look back.

"*Ja*, that is encouraging. The man should marry again, if only to have a mother for that sweet little boy of his," Alta Hershberger said. She had come with the Zooks. Miriam, Peter's mother, was sister to Alta's late husband, John, the love of Alta's life. She made a sound of annoyance. "I don't know why Sally had to go with Mary and Ethan. She could have come with us."

Meg knocked again, and the door opened, revealing a smiling Sally, who held Nicholas in her arms. Alta blinked. "Sally—"

"Come in, *Mam*. Mary and Ethan are waiting inside. A few others are here to visit, as well." Sally blushed. "John has something important to tell everyone."

The families entered the house, hung up their coats and followed Sally to the great room. "You go first, *Dat*," Meg said.

At the same time, Peter urged, "*Mam*, you lead the way."

Miriam Zook and Arlin Stoltzfus entered the room just as everyone shouted, "Surprise! Happy birthday!"

Meg saw the stunned look on her father's face. She glanced at Miriam and witnessed her equally shocked expression.

"What's this?" she heard Alta exclaim. "Why didn't I know about this?"

Her daughters laughed. "Because we wanted to surprise them, *Mam*. If you'd known, then so would everyone else!" Mary said.

Alta looked momentarily offended, until Sally thrust little Nicholas into her arms. "Hold him, *Mam*. He's a sweetheart. Look how much he likes you."

Peter's aunt's face softened with joy. "What a precious *bubbel*!"

Meg exchanged happy glances with Peter. They had done well working together. They'd had their rough spots, she thought, but they'd gotten the job done.

Peter moved away to mingle with the guests. Meg stood by her father and mother, along with Horseshoe Joe and Miriam Zook.

"How did you do this?" Arlin asked his wife.

"Meg did it." Meg's *mam* eyed him with affection. "With Peter."

When her father regarded her with awe, Meg shrugged. "I had to do something while I was recuperating."

Alta approached, still holding Nicholas. "What a nice party," she said. Her daughters came up behind her. "Such a sweet boy." Alta rubbed her hand lovingly over the child's head. She flashed Mary a look. "When are you and Ethan going to give me a grandchild?"

Mary smirked. "In about seven months."

Alta gaped. "Did you say seven months?"

Ethan strolled up to place an arm around his wife. "*Ja.* You'll be a grandmother by next July."

To Meg's shock, tears filled the woman's eyes. "I…" She drew a sharp breath. *"Danki,"* she whispered.

Bishop John approached. "Sally," he said.

Sally inclined her head. *"Mam?* That precious little boy—he's to be your *kinskindt,* too. John has asked me to marry him."

Alta looked stunned. "You'll be marrying the bishop and Nicholas will be ours?"

John appeared amused. *"Ja,* but we'll be marrying soon. I want Sally in my life as soon as possible." His voice lowered as he eyed his bride-to-be with affection. "I never thought I'd feel this way again."

Meg placed a hand on Sally's arm. "I'm happy for you." She had guessed from the start about Sally's love for Bishop John. To know that John returned her feelings gave her hope that with the Lord's help, sometimes life turned out the way people wanted.

She loved Peter. She wanted to tell him. She had to tell him. If she didn't, she'd never know whether or not she could have had a life with him.

Moving away from the group, Meg went to look for him. She spied him in the other room, smiling, talking with…Agnes. Meg felt her stomach bottom out. He'd told her that he wouldn't invite her, but there she was, laughing with him. Agnes looked bright, happy. And Peter seemed pleased that she was there.

He suddenly caught sight of her, and his mouth

started to curve. Meg spun, unable to bear the sight of the man she loved with the woman he wanted instead of her. She grabbed her coat and rushed outside. She needed to escape. Pain threatened to overwhelm her, to the point that she wanted to curl into a little ball and cry.

Meg stood outside, thinking hard. Was this the way to get over him? Would she allow Peter to take away any chances of her happiness? She stomped back inside, hung up her coat and sought out the attention of another man. She saw Nate Peachy in the corner, gazing about the room as he sipped a soda. She approached. "Nate."

He saw her and grinned. "Meg. Nice party."

She gave him a half smile. "I'm glad you could come."

Nate shrugged, his eyes perking up at the sight of Meg's sister Charlie as she crossed the room to talk with a group of young people. "I remember the time your sister climbed into my father's pigpen. Charlie wanted to pet the pigs, but all she got was her dress covered in mud and a hard nudge from our sow."

Meg laughed, imagining the scene. "She's fearless."

He grinned. "She is."

Charlie left the others to grab food from a table across the room. Nate was quiet as he watched her. Realizing that she'd lost his attention, Meg eased away, observing as he moved in Charlie's direction. Her sister lifted her head and met his gaze. She stiffened and quickly escaped, with Nate following.

Meg felt deep heartache as she watched them. Would she ever have someone who loved her enough to want to marry her?

With tears threatening, she found her coat again and hurried back outside. She'd couldn't bear watching Nate and Charlie. She couldn't stand watching Peter and Agnes.

The blast of cold air caught her by surprise. It was as if the wind had picked up in the moments since she'd been inside. Now it taunted her, made her shiver, and she once more wanted to cry. She leaned against the front porch railing and stared at the night sky. Would she ever get over Peter? Would the pain ever go away, or would she be destined to hurt like this forever?

"You came with Daniel," Peter said. He studied Alice Beiler, noted her pleasure in the company she was keeping.

"Ja," she said. "I like him. We only met recently, and we got along from the start. When he asked me to come, I couldn't say *nay.*"

Peter understood. He listened while Alice told him how she and Daniel had met, all the while searching the room for Meg. He'd caught her glance earlier. He'd been happy to see her gazing at him, until she'd turned abruptly and left the room.

"Alice, there's something I have to do," he said after their conversation had continued for a bit. "Will you excuse me?"

Alice merely smiled. Daniel had come to stand beside her, and her focus was on him.

Eager to find her, Peter went looking for Meg. The memory of Agnes's words rang in his ears. *You should tell her how you feel.*

He had to talk with her, tell her how much he loved her. He smiled. Give her the Christmas gift he'd arranged for her with the help of her family—Honey, the little dog they'd rescued.

Peter caught sight of her parents in the kitchen with his. "Have you seen Meg?"

Arlin frowned. "*Nay.* She's not in the other room?"

"Maybe she escaped outside for a breath of fresh air," his mother suggested.

Peter thanked her and said he'd check. He moved to where the coats were hung in the front of the house. He donned his woolen jacket and went outside. He didn't have to go far. He immediately saw her by the porch railing, bathed in moonlight. The sight of her stole his breath. Warmth and love rushed through him as he moved to her side.

"Meg." He heard her gasp, saw her shoulders stiffen. "It's just me," he told her. "Peter."

She turned slowly, and he saw tears shimmering in her eyes.

"What's wrong?" He shifted closer and slipped his arm around her. "Talk to me. Why are you crying?"

"'Tis nothing."

He scowled. "Doesn't seem like nothing." He hesitated. "Meg, I need to talk with you. I know we're done with the party planning, but there is no reason we can't stop seeing each other. I can take you to your physical therapy sessions. We can go out to lunch—"

"*Nay.*" Refusing to meet his gaze, she stared out into the yard. "I don't think that would be wise, do you?" She paused. "Agnes is *gut* for you. We'll see each other at church gatherings, but otherwise, it would be best if someone else took me for my physical therapy."

"Meg…" he objected.

"Go back into the house, Peter. Please leave me alone. I don't want to see you right now."

He inhaled sharply as pain squeezed his heart. He

went blindly inside. She didn't want him. He'd hoped, but now he knew she didn't care for him at all. He stumbled into the great room, caught Reuben's and Meg's names mentioned in the conversation between her sisters and his cousins. He hung back and shamelessly eavesdropped.

"Meg broke it off with Reuben," Ellie was saying. "No surprise there, when she's loved Peter for as long as she's known him. But will she tell him? *Nay*. Sometimes I think I'd like to knock some sense into her."

Peter's heart started to thrum. Meg loved him? And she'd broken off her relationship with Reuben? Then why had she chased him away?

She'd mentioned Agnes. He should have spoken up and told her that they were no longer seeing each other.

He froze. *Alice*. She must have thought he'd been talking with Agnes, had invited her to the party when he'd told her he wouldn't.

His pulse started to race with hope. He turned, rushed to grab his coat, and slipped it on before he opened the door to confront Meg on the front porch. "Meg."

But the space was empty. There was no sign of her anywhere. Calling her name, he ran out into the yard. "Meg! *Meg!* Where are you? Please, Lord, tell me where she went."

The wind picked up, a gust chilling him to the bone. She'd need to get warm. He stared at the bishop's barn and prayed that she'd headed in that direction. He sprinted to the outbuilding, slid open the barn door and slipped inside. "Meg!"

There was no answer. But he knew if she was upset

with him, there was every likelihood that she'd pretend she wasn't there.

And then he heard it. A soft, heartfelt sob, one Peter would know anywhere. Meg was crying somewhere in the building. He saw a faint glow of light, hurried in that direction and found her in an empty stall. She was huddled in the straw with a flashlight to keep the dark at bay, shivering, crying.

"Oh, Meg," he murmured, as he slipped inside the stable to be with her. He hunkered down beside her. She gasped, startled, when he reached out, placed a finger beneath her chin and lifted her face to meet his gaze. "How can I help you?"

She inhaled sharply and stared. "What are you doing here, Peter?"

"I love you, Meg Stoltzfus. You—not Agnes. Agnes and I broke up. She knew—has always known—that my feelings for you would never go away."

"But you invited Agnes." Still, there was a glimmer of hope in her gaze.

"*Nay*, I didn't. You saw me talking with Alice, her twin sister. She came with your cousin Daniel. He invited her to the party."

Meg blinked, and he enjoyed the way her thick dark eyelashes swept down, then rose as she peered up at him. Using his finger, Peter caressed her cheek. "Meg, will you be my sweetheart? Will you allow me to court you? I want to court, then marry you. Will you give me a chance? I've loved you for so long. Please, Meg. Be my girl."

Meg started to cry harder.

Concerned, Peter could only stare at her. "I'm sorry," he muttered. "I thought—"

"You rescued me," she said, as her tears continued to fall. "And you didn't tell me." She sniffed. "Why didn't you tell me?"

"You were with Reuben. You wanted him. It didn't matter who rescued you, only that you were saved." He tenderly cupped her face, then wiped away her tears with his thumbs.

"You love me?" When he nodded, she quieted and straightened away from the barn wall. As she studied him, Peter saw her blue eyes fill with longing and love...and joy. She lifted a hand to cover his fingers and cradled them against her cheek. "I wanted you to be happy, even if it was with Agnes."

"I never loved her as I do you." He kissed her forehead. "Will you be my girl?"

In the flashlight's golden glow, her face lit up like sunshine. "*Ja*, I'd like that." She bit her lip. "Peter, I love you."

His heart sang out with joy as he stood and gently eased her up to stand beside him. "I never thought I'd have you. You're all I've wanted for so long."

"I am?"

He gave her a smile. "*Ja*. I fell for you from the first moment I laid eyes on you. I couldn't stop looking at you. I couldn't stop staring."

Her breath came out in a shaky laugh. "I thought you stared because you found something lacking in me, especially after what I overheard."

"*Nay*, sweetheart. *Nay!* Never that."

She shot him a look of loving affection. "Thank you, Lord," she murmured.

Peter pulled her into his arms. "Amen." After a hug,

he released her and reached for her hand. "'Tis cold here. Let's go inside and get warm."

Meg beamed at him as they walked together toward the house.

Epilogue

The weather was unseasonably warm for November. The crops were harvested, and it was the time for weddings. Dressed in her new light blue dress, Meg sat next to Peter in the front row of the congregation in her aunt and uncle's great room. She glanced over at her bridegroom with a ready smile. Her heart tripped. Peter wore his black Sunday best, and she'd never known a more handsome and loving man.

As if sensing her regard, he met her gaze, his gray eyes dark and filled with emotion. They had waited eleven long months for this day, and both of them were eager for this moment when they would start their lives as man and wife. He loved her, and Meg had never been happier.

Meg's day had begun at four o'clock this morning, when the family had taken care of their daily chores. Later, at six thirty, women from the community had arrived to help prepare the house and ready the wedding feast. The wedding ceremony would be held at her aunt Katie's before everyone came to enjoy the celebration.

At the start of the three-hour service, while the

church community members had sang hymns, Meg and Peter were drawn aside by Preacher Levi, who counseled them in another room. Then the bride and groom returned to the service in time for a prayer, scriptures and a long sermon.

As she paid attention to the preacher's words, she felt Peter's fingers entwine with hers. He gave them a squeeze, and when she looked at him, she saw a small smile curve his lips as he continued to gaze ahead.

Their wedding party sat nearby—Nell and James, Annie and Meg's cousin Jacob, Josiah with his wife, Nancy, and her other Lapp married cousins, Eli, Noah and Jedidiah, with their wives.

Preacher Levi called Peter and Meg to the front of the gathering room. He asked them to tell them what their marriage was to be, then he blessed them. Bishop John Fisher and Deacon Abram Peachy joined them, along with other church members, to give testimony about their marriage.

To everyone's delighted surprise, Meg's mother and Horseshoe Joe stood and told everyone that they'd known about their children's love for each other for years and had shared a hand in giving them a little push. Meg gazed at Peter in shock. His lips twitched as he contained his laughter. She grinned back.

A final prayer concluded the ceremony, and the newly wedded couple climbed into a waiting buggy, driven by Josiah. Soon they were back at the Arlin Stoltzfus house for the wedding feast. As Peter and Meg took their seats in the *Eck*, the honored place in the corner of the room for the bride and groom and their wedding party, invited guests sat at tables set up as a U shape in the room. Settling at Peter's left, Meg thought of all the wonderful things her husband had done and continued to do for her. He was always showering her with kindness and affection. She smiled. He did the same for her dog, Honey, whom he cared for as much as she did.

"How are you feeling, wife?" Peter whispered as he leaned close. His breath was a soft puff of air in her ear.

"I'm feeling happy, husband." Her gaze lingered on Peter's handsome face, her heart filled with all the love she felt for him. They would be living in the main Zook farmhouse. His father and mother already had moved into the *dawdi haus* on the property, the house where Peter's grandparents once had lived.

"You're not sorry to be married to me, are you?"

Startled, she could only stare, her pulse fluttering. "*Nay*, are you?"

"Never." His smile warmed her like the rays of a summer sun. He caressed her cheek, then leaned in to kiss her properly, on the lips. "Wife," he murmured. "I love you, Meg Zook."

She sighed dreamily. Peter was her Christmas blessing, one that had continued throughout the past year and would forever. "As I love you, Peter Zook, forever and for always until death do us part—" she paused and reached under the table for his hand "—and into the next life."

* * * * *

WE HOPE YOU
ENJOYED THIS

LOVE
INSPIRED®

BOOK.

If you were **inspired** by this

uplifting, **heartwarming** romance,

be sure to look for all six Love

Inspired® books every month.

Love Inspired®

Love Inspired®

Save $1.00

on the purchase of ANY Love Inspired® book.

Available wherever books are sold, including most bookstores, supermarkets, drugstores and discount stores.

Save $1.00

on the purchase of ANY Love Inspired® book.

Coupon valid until February 28, 2019.
Redeemable at participating retail outlets in the U.S. and Canada only.
Limit one coupon per customer.

52616121

5 65373 00076 2 (8100)0 12399

Canadian Retailers: Harlequin Enterprises Limited will pay the face value of this coupon plus 10.25¢ if submitted by customer for this product only. Any other use constitutes fraud. Coupon is nonassignable. Void if taxed, prohibited or restricted by law. Consumer must pay any government taxes. Void if copied. Inmar Promotional Services ("IPS") customers submit coupons and proof of sales to Harlequin Enterprises Limited, P.O. Box 31000, Scarborough, ON M1R 0E7, Canada. Non-IPS retailer—for reimbursement submit coupons and proof of sales directly to Harlequin Enterprises Limited, Retail Marketing Department, 22 Adelaide St. West, 40th Floor, Toronto, Ontario M5H 4E3, Canada.

U.S. Retailers: Harlequin Enterprises Limited will pay the face value of this coupon plus 8¢ if submitted by customer for this product only. Any other use constitutes fraud. Coupon is nonassignable. Void if taxed, prohibited or restricted by law. Consumer must pay any government taxes. Void if copied. For reimbursement submit coupons and proof of sales directly to Harlequin Enterprises, Ltd 482, NCH Marketing Services, P.O. Box 880001, El Paso, TX 88588-0001, U.S.A. Cash value 1/100 cents.

® and ™ are trademarks owned and used by the trademark owner and/or its licensee.

© 2018 Harlequin Enterprises Limited

LICOUP94823

"What's your name?"

The woman's eyes widened and her hand shook so that she could barely hold the mug of tea without spilling it. She set it carefully on the coffee table. "I don't—I don't know my name."

"How can you not know your own name?" Caleb asked. "Do you know where you live?"

"Nein."

"What were you doing out there?"

"Out where?"

"Where was your coat and your *kapp*?"

"Caleb, now's not the time to interrogate the poor girl." His *mamm* stood and moved beside her on the couch. She picked up the small book of poetry. "You were carrying this, when Caleb found you. Do you remember it?"

"I don't. This was mine?"

"Found it in the snow," Caleb said. "Right beside where you collapsed."

"So it must be mine."

Caleb noticed that the woman's hands trembled as she opened the cover and stared down at the first page. With one finger, she traced the handwriting there.

"Rachel. I think my name is Rachel."

Rachel let her fingers brush over the word again and again. Rachel. Yes, that was her name. She was sure of it. She remembered writing it in the front of the book—she'd used a pen that her *mamm* had given her. She could almost picture herself, somewhere else. She could almost see her mother.

"My *mamm* gave me the pen and the book…for my birthday, I think. I wrote my name—wrote it right here."

"Your *mamm*. So you remember her?"

"Praise be to *Gotte*," Caleb's *dat* said, a smile spreading across his face.

"Is there someone we can call? If you remember the name of your bishop…" Caleb had sat down in the rocker his mother had vacated and was staring at her intensely.

They all were.

She closed her eyes, hoping to feel the memory again. She tried to see the room or the house or the people, but the memory had receded as quickly as it had come, leaving her with a pulsing headache.

She struggled to keep the feelings of panic at bay. Her heart was hammering, and her hands were shaking, and she could barely make sense of the questions they were pelting at her.

Who were these people?

Where was she?

Who was she?

She needed to remember what had happened.

She needed to go home.

Don't miss
Amish Christmas Memories *by Vannetta Chapman,*
available December 2018 wherever
Love Inspired® books and ebooks are sold.

www.LoveInspired.com

Inspirational Romance to Warm Your Heart and Soul

Join our social communities to connect with other readers who share your love!

Sign up for the Love Inspired newsletter at **www.LoveInspired.com** to be the first to find out about upcoming titles, special promotions and exclusive content.

CONNECT WITH US AT:

Facebook.com/groups/HarlequinConnection

 Facebook.com/LoveInspiredBooks

 Twitter.com/LoveInspiredBks

LISOCIAL2018